The Gathering Dark

ALSO BY CHRISTINE JOHNSON

Claire de Lune

Nocturne

The Gathering Dark

CHRISTINE JOHNSON

SIMON PULSE

NEW YORK LONDON TORONTO SYDNEY NEW DELHI

SIMON PULSE

An imprint of Simon & Schuster Children's Publishing Division

1230 Avenue of the Americas, New York, NY 10020

First Simon Pulse hardcover edition February 2013

Copyright © 2013 by Christine Johnson

All rights reserved, including the right of reproduction in whole or in part in any form.

SIMON PULSE and colophon are registered trademarks of Simon & Schuster, Inc.

For information about special discounts for bulk purchases, please contact Simon & Schuster Special Sales at 1-866-506-1949 or business@simonandschuster.com.

The Simon & Schuster Speakers Bureau can bring authors to your live event. For more information or to book an event contact the Simon & Schuster Speakers Bureau at 1-866-248-3049 or visit our website at www.simonspeakers.com.

Designed by Hilary Zarycky

The text of this book was set in Adobe Caslon Pro.

Manufactured in the United States of America

2 4 6 8 10 9 7 5 3 1

Library of Congress Cataloging-in-Publication Data

Johnson, Christine, 1978–

The gathering dark / Christine Johnson. — 1st Simon Pulse hardcover ed.

p. cm.

Summary: A gifted pianist discovers that she and the mysterious boy she's falling for are part of an alternate world made from dark matter, and in a race of love against fear, she must somehow save her life without losing herself.

ISBN 978-1-4424-3903-0

[1. Fantasy. 2. Musicians—Fiction. 3. Love—Fiction.] I. Title.

PZ7.J63092Gat 2013

[Fic]—dc23   2012008121

ISBN 978-1-4424-3905-4 (eBook)

For Asher and Lucy,
with all my love, always

The Gathering Dark

Chapter One

NORMALLY, KEIRA DIDN'T NOTICE the shoppers that trickled through the department store. She just sat, head down, playing the obnoxious, white-lacquered baby grand. But this time was different. The oily-smooth voice cracked her focus like an egg smashing against a windowpane.

"Keeeeira. Still doing the piano thing, huh?"

Keira's fingers hesitated above the keys, breaking the rhythm of the unobtrusive music that Mr. Seever, the store manager, insisted she play. Live music was never going to make the mall in Sherwin, Maine, a classy place, but Keira didn't care. She was making money with her music. Good money. Even if the music was horrible, it was still a chance to flex her fingers. To work on her concentration.

Concert pianists have to be able to focus, no matter what else is happening. Come on, Keira. Pay attention.

Two guys, both sporting gelled hair and over-applied body spray, sidled up next to the piano. They weren't just a couple of popular guys—they were practically famous in Sherwin. People fawned over Jeremy Reynolds and his friends, teachers and girlfriends and high school peons alike. Except Keira. She didn't care about their parties or their clothes. They used to treat her like a freak, until one guy in Jeremy's inner circle, Tommy Hutchinson, started dating Keira's best friend, Susan Kim.

Jeremy's endless attempts to flirt with her were worse than his snide comments. She ended up fending him off whenever he and Tommy came to the store to visit Susan.

Keira had to shut him down every single time she saw him. It was exhausting. And distracting.

"You're way too hot to play such boring music." Jeremy leaned an elbow on the piano. "You should play something that has more *feeling*."

Lamest come-on of the week. She watched her right hand stretch, her pinkie reaching for the F-sharp key. Something tickled Keira's nose, breaking through the cloud of Jeremy's cologne.

Cigarette smoke.

Startled, she glanced up. Sure enough, a lit cigarette dangled from Jeremy's fingers. The smoke curled away from it like a gray ribbon.

"There's a party Friday night. You should come with me. I'll even take you to dinner or something first."

Keira didn't date.

Especially not a smoker.

Extra-especially not a smoker who was also a jerk.

Sometimes when Keira looked at him, she still saw a seventh-grader, standing as far from her as he could at the bus stop. She'd watched him claw his way to the top rung of Sherwin High, in spite of the fact that he came from the wrong side of town.

Keira's side of town.

Jeremy'd lived one street behind and three doors south of Keira's house his whole life. He wasn't rich, but now he was powerful. He knew the right people. Screw silver spoons—the rest of Jeremy's friends had been born with sets of Mustang keys in their mouths.

Keira glanced around for Tommy, who had headed over to the nearby perfume counter to say hi to Susan. He caught her watching him and held her gaze, his face breaking into an encouraging smile when he saw Jeremy leaning in close.

Keira frowned back at Tommy, but Tommy's gaze had drifted over to Jeremy.

She watched Jeremy put the cigarette to his lips and take a deliberate drag. Jeremy exhaled a halo of smoke so foul and thick that Keira choked on it, coughing hard enough that she instinctively jerked her fingers off the keyboard and covered her mouth.

With the smell of cigarettes permeating the cosmetics section and the sudden pause in the music, Keira knew Mr. Seever was bound to appear any second. Her fear of losing her job swelled, eclipsing her fear of pissing everyone off.

"You can't smoke in here! You'll get me fired!" she growled. She was already on thin ice after a fur-jacketed old woman demanded Keira play some Johnny Mercer, then complained to the manager when Keira had said she didn't know any of his songs. *Don't make me regret hiring you,* Mr. Seever'd warned.

Behind the perfume counter, she could see Susan watching with a worried frown. Susan was the one who'd gotten her the job in the first place. It was supposed to be fun, working right next to each other.

Because this is such a super good time we're having. Right.

Jeremy clutched his cigarette protectively. "Don't be like that. We're just playing around, right?" He fake pouted. It was distinctly un-sexy.

"Jeremy!" Susan said, exasperated. She turned to Tommy. "Can you . . . please?"

Tommy rubbed a hand across his head, messing up his hair. He looked so torn that Keira could practically hear him ripping at the seams. "Come on, Keira," he wheedled. "Lighten up, okay? There's no one around, or anything."

Susan crossed her arms and made an irritated noise. Tommy's cheeks went blotchy.

"Please," Keira said to Jeremy, trying not to beg. "I'll get in trouble."

Tommy stepped closer. "Maybe we should get out of here, Jer. I need to get some food, anyway."

"I think we should stay. It's not like I'm gonna set the scarves on fire or anything."

The guys leaned in on either side of Keira. She felt trapped.

"Seriously, man, I gotta get something to eat or I'm gonna starve." Tommy reached over Keira and pushed Jeremy's shoulder playfully.

"Watch the jacket, man!" Jeremy grabbed Tommy's wrist, looking genuinely angry.

Keira stood up, completely abandoning the piano. All she wanted was to get away from the two guys. Before she could get around them, Tommy stepped to the side to slip out of Jeremy's grip and tripped over the legs of the piano bench. His fall pulled Jeremy into Keira, knocking her against the piano. The glowing cherry of his cigarette pressed against the arm of her shirt.

By the time he'd righted himself and pulled the cigarette away, it had burned through her cotton shirt. With her heart tapping out a panicked staccato, Keira looked at the skin beneath it. There was a small, circular indentation in her arm, where the smoldering tobacco had pressed against her skin, but there was no burn. No blister. Nothing.

How can that be?

The guys backed away from the piano.

"You pushed me into her!"

"What? You were the one holding on to me!"

"You grabbed me first! And anyway, she's not hurt!" Jeremy looked at Keira. "You're not hurt, right? I mean, you're not crying or anything."

"I'm fine. Could you leave now?" The words were sharp as pins, and Jeremy's eyes narrowed.

"Keira! Are you okay?" Susan shouldered her way between the two guys. "Just get out of here!" She spat the words at Jeremy as she brushed past.

"Sorry, Keira. I'll make it up to you, okay?" Jeremy glanced over his shoulder apologetically as he and Tommy scrambled for the exit.

"Did he burn you?" Susan tugged at Keira's arm, her dark eyes widening when she saw the ruined sleeve. "Oh, my God."

"No, it's okay. It just got . . ." She was going to say, *It just got my shirt*, but that wasn't true. That cigarette had ground against her like an overeager sophomore. Only, it hadn't burned her. Thinking about it made her hands shake. "I'm fine, I guess."

"Jesus. You are so lucky. I wish Tommy would quit hanging out with Jeremy. He's such an—" Susan's gaze snapped to the side.

Keira heard the squeak of leather shoes against the tile floor. With his comb-over flapping like an errant wing, Mr. Seever scurried up to them.

"What happened? Do you know those boys who just ran out of my store?" he demanded.

Keira crossed her arms to hide the hole in her shirt, then leaned against the piano for support. The white lacquer might be ugly, but it still made her feel better to be touching it.

"No. I mean . . . yes, we go to school together, but—"

Mr. Seever interrupted her. "I told you when you were hired that it would be unacceptable for your friends to come and 'hang out' with you while you were working."

"They're not my friends!" Keira protested. Out of the corner of her eye, she could see Susan shifting nervously. She looked like she couldn't decide if she was supposed to say something or shut up.

Keira shook her head at Susan. There was no reason for her to get in trouble too.

Apparently, Susan disagreed.

"They're my friends, Mr. Seever."

Mr. Seever turned and arched an eyebrow at Susan. "There's no need to try to cover for Keira, Miss Kim. I saw those boys by the piano. I heard the music stop."

He pursed his lips. "And all this after we had that unfortunate incident with the customer's request last week. Having you here is taking up far too much of my attention. Clearly, I should have hired a *professional* musician for this job."

Keira's insides felt too light beneath her skin. She lifted her chin. "Are you firing me?"

Mr. Seever sighed. "I'm sorry, but it's just proving too disruptive to the shoppers."

"But it wasn't her fault!" Susan insisted.

"Ms. Kim. I appreciate your loyalty to your *friend* here, but I think you'll find that—in this situation—it is misplaced. I would hate to have to fire both of you."

Keira swallowed her retort—that he had a lot of nerve talking about loyalty after he'd just fired someone who hadn't done anything wrong. But it wouldn't do her any good to say it, and she was *not* going to get Susan fired. Keira bit the inside of her cheek and waited silently until he was finished.

"Your check for this week is in the office." Mr. Seever cleared his throat. "It'll be your last one." He turned to Susan. "Don't you have displays to dust?"

Susan started to say something, then snapped her mouth shut.

"I'll call you later," Keira said to Susan, who scrambled back behind the perfume counter. When she looked back, Mr. Seever had already disappeared into the racks of belts and purses.

"Sorry, Keira," Susan whispered.

Keira shrugged. "No, I'm sorry. You're the one who's stuck working for the asshole. And hey, there are other jobs, right?" She forced herself to smile. "In the meantime, I'll have more time to practice. That's always a good thing."

Susan gave her a knowing look. As in—she knew how badly Keira needed the money.

Keira's hands trembled as she waved good-bye and headed for the office. She pulled on her jacket and stuffed the check in her bag, with the twenty-three dollars in cash that represented her current life-savings.

With a last glance around the office, Keira headed for the parking lot, praying that her car would start.

Chapter Two

KEIRA DROVE TOWARD HER house, past the run-down strip malls and fast-food restaurants. She wanted to get back to her piano, but in the deepening gloom of the afternoon the lights of Take Note—the independent music store where she spent most of her money—glowed temptingly as she waited at the last stoplight on her drive.

It was like seeing a cup of hot chocolate on a snowy day. She couldn't resist, especially not with her paycheck tucked into the front pocket of her book bag.

Thank God for my college fund, she thought. Without the money her uncle Pike had left her when he died, she'd be worried about paying for college and not thinking of buying new music.

Her car practically drove itself into the parking lot.

A fine mist sifted down from the sky as Keira hurried into the store. The droplets tangled in her eyelashes, giving the dusty store a diamond shimmer as she blinked the moisture away.

The musty warmth of the store pulled her in, as familiar as an old friend. The cash register sat untended, and the sound of boxes being shuffled around drifted from the store's tiny back room.

Keira strode over to the bins of sheet music and began to flip through the scores. She wanted something that would suit her uneasy mood. She flicked past one book after another, but all the music she found was either too easy or she already owned it. Finally, she found a Beethoven piano sonata that she'd never played, "The Tempest." Scanning the music, she could tell that it would be emotional and intense—and also hard as hell.

Which will totally take my mind off this screwed-up afternoon. Perfect.

Besides, she wasn't really happy with the Brahms piece she'd been working on for her Juilliard audition, and a Beethoven sonata would fulfill the same requirement. She set the music off to one side, reaching for the reject pile of scores she'd left on the edge of the bin.

"Are you looking for something special?" The rich baritone voice made her jump, and she whirled around, knocking the stack of music to the floor. With a shushing sound, it fanned into a hopeless mess. She only had a moment to register the long, lanky body and shock of dark hair before a streak of embarrassment burned through her.

Keira bent to grab the music. The guy at her side reached for the scores at the same time and their heads cracked together, Keira's red hair tangling momentarily in his crow-black corkscrew curls.

"Ow!" She backed away as he straightened, rubbing his forehead, his eyes squeezed shut.

"Sorry," he apologized. "I guess that's what happens when I try to be polite." He had an accent that Keira couldn't quite place. One of those English-Australian-South African accents that guaranteed a wrong guess.

With a final wince, he let go of his head and looked at her. His iron-colored eyes widened. "Oh. Hi."

All of Keira's carefully hardened edges began to melt. Thick lashes fringed his eyes, and the cleft in his chin drew her attention straight to his full lips. He was gorgeous. And she was staring. It was like he'd sucked all the light out of the store and the only thing she could still see was him.

"Hi. I was just . . ." The words faltered in her mouth.

He quirked an eyebrow at her, and Keira felt herself flush. Her coat was suddenly too warm, her leggings suddenly too revealing. "I was just browsing. But thanks." She turned to stack the music back in the bin.

"Here." He reached out. "I'll do that. I might as well earn my money for once, right?"

Keira's lips parted, surprised. "Wait—you *work* here?"

"Just started." His smile was like a bolt of lightning—sudden and glowing. "I'm Walker, by the way. It doesn't seem fair for me to give you a concussion without at least introducing myself." He paused, his gaze flicking up to the ceiling. "There are lots of good ways I can think of to meet a beautiful girl, but knocking her nearly unconscious is not on the list." He brought his gaze back down to Keira. His eyes were mesmerizing—like watching the gray sheets of rain working their way in from the Atlantic.

God, he was cute.

Guys are nothing but a distraction, she reminded herself sternly. *There will be hot guys at Juilliard who love music.*

"Um, this would be the part where you tell me your name," he prompted, giving Keira an amused grin.

"I'm Keira," she said, turning back to the music in her hands. No amount of cute was worth blowing her chances at a scholarship and getting stuck in Sherwin forever. "You don't go to Lawrence High," she said. "And you sound like you're from away."

"Nope, not a native Mainer," he agreed. She waited for him to say where he'd come from, exactly, but he didn't elaborate. "I got my GED last fall," he offered. "I'm—I wasn't really cut out for school."

Keira thought of her unfinished history project, all the classes she'd spent tapping her fingers against the edge of her desk, practicing on an invisible piano instead of taking notes.

Her own grades hovered barely above the cutoff for the good conservatory college programs. "I'm not exactly going out for the Academic Decathlon," she admitted.

Working carefully, Walker piled the scores back into the bins. He handled them like they were some sort of rare, valuable books, and Keira's opinion of him rose a few inches. He glanced around and reached for the Beethoven sonata. Keira's hand shot out, her fingers curling protectively around the spine. "That one's mine."

Walker started to pull his hand away, then hesitated. He gave her an appraising look.

"Can I see?" he asked. The curiosity that flared on his face warmed her. No one ever cared about what she played—well, that, or they *only* cared about what she played. If she showed Walker her music, it would tell him something about her, and from the look on his face, he knew it would too. She was surprised to realize that part of her wanted to show him what she'd picked. Still, it felt private. Letting him see the music—it was like letting him read her diary.

Not that she kept one.

But still.

Holding on to her thin veneer of aloof-and-sarcastic, she shrugged. "I guess—I mean, it's not like it belongs to me. Yet."

He reached again for the score. His hands were broad and sure, with battered leather cuffs circling his wrists. A black mark snaked from underneath one of them like a whip of licorice.

Intrigued, she wondered what the rest of his tattoo looked

like. As she stared, the edges of the mark went blurry, fading from sight. Just before it disappeared, it gave a last twitch, like the flick of a serpentine tongue. Then there was nothing left but smooth olive skin. No mark. Not even a shadow.

I—did I really imagine *that?*

Keira stared at his arm. Walker cleared his throat, jolting her out of her confusion.

"Everything okay?" There was a thread of suspicion in his voice—like he wasn't sure she was totally with it. Like maybe the piano she played was in a padded room in a locked ward somewhere.

"F-fine," she stammered. She hated being rattled and it had been a bone-shaking afternoon. "I was—I like your wrist cuffs."

Something dark and hot shone in his eyes. It made her *want*, and she immediately regretted the compliment.

"Thanks. Most people don't even notice them." He shook his head, flipping through the sonata. "This looks really hard." His accent pulled and stretched the words like saltwater taffy.

Keira slid back into her familiar defensiveness. "I *like* hard pieces," she said confidently. "They're more interesting."

Walker looked down at her. He was considerably taller than she was. "More interesting how?"

"It's complicated." She fiddled with a collection of Burt Bacharach songs, scraping absentmindedly at the price tag with her short fingernail. "It takes more to play them. More focus. More time. More talent. All of that goes into the music.

And when I hear those pieces, I hear all of that stuff too. It makes me want someone else to hear all of those things when I play." She cleared her throat, shoving the book of pathetic ballads back into the correct spot.

"I know exactly what you mean," Walker said quietly.

"You play?" she asked.

"No," he said simply, his gaze skittering over her hair, her eyes, her fingers. "I can't read music." Something hard and magnetic crossed his face, sending her pulse scrambling. "I just understand."

Keira searched his expression. "Really?"

"You're not the only one who likes a challenge." An I-dare-you-to-contradict-me smile spread across his face.

I am not going to flirt with him. I haven't gone this long without a boyfriend just to blow it when I'm so close to getting out of here for good. Juilliard slid through her mind—the pictures she'd seen online of the practice rooms looked like her own personal heaven. She wasn't going to miss out on that for some guy she wouldn't even remember in five years.

"Good to know." Keira glanced at the price tag on the Beethoven score that was still in his hands. The music was nearly fifteen dollars—almost all the cash she had, and there wouldn't be any more paychecks coming. The music sang to her, sweet and low. Begging her to give in.

She could scrape by. "How about you face the challenge of ringing this up for me?" She hadn't meant to be quite so snarky, but he didn't seem to mind. In fact, Walker looked pleased.

"Sure."

He strolled around the counter to the old-fashioned register. "Right. Um, it's sixteen fifty-seven, including tax." He slid the thin book into a brown paper bag and Keira dug her crumpled twenty out of her backpack.

"Thanks," she said.

He handed her the bag and her change. "So, do you think you'll see me again?" he said casually.

"Um, you mean, like in the store?" she drawled.

"That's one possibility," he said finally, like he'd thought the words would mean something different to her. He rested his arms on the counter between them.

The sight of his leather wrist cuffs reminded her of the inky tentacle she'd seen disappear from Walker's arm. Maybe he'd been right to sound suspicious. Maybe she was losing it. "Yeah, well, I'm sure I'll need more music sometime," she said. "But thanks. It's been . . . interesting." More shaken and uncertain than she was after the incident with Jeremy and the cigarette, Keira headed for her car.

It doesn't matter what *he thinks,* she reminded herself. *He's only a guy.* She was the one who'd made the no-dating rule, getting rid of all the distractions. She had to focus on what was really important—her piano. Which she was going home to play before the memory of Walker's tempting smile really did make her lose her mind.

Chapter Three

WHEN KEIRA GOT HOME, her house was empty and dark. The smell of chicken simmering in cream-of-mushroom soup drifted out of the Crock-Pot on the kitchen counter. A note was propped against it:

Have a late meeting. Please turn this down to warm when you get home. Help yourself whenever you're hungry. Salad in the fridge.

Love,

Mom

Keira flipped the switch on the slow-cooker and tossed the note in the trash. Having dinner waiting wasn't the same thing as having her parents home to eat with her. The answering machine flashed at her. As her dad's voice, tinny and distorted, slipped out of the speaker, she wished—again—that he would call her cell like a normal person. It was one of the few luxuries her parents paid for. It would be nice if they'd use it.

"Hey." Her dad cleared his throat, sending a static-y burst through the kitchen. "Um, something came up and I'm going to be kind of late tonight. You two go ahead and eat without me."

Keira hit the delete button with more force than was necessary. If her parents would admit they didn't want to see each other, then they wouldn't both avoid the house and at least one of them could be home once in a while. Both of them assuming the other would be around just left Keira alone.

Again.

She walked into the dark living room, where her piano crouched like a tiger in a too-small cage. The baby grand had been the other big gift from her uncle Pike. Pike hadn't been her mom's actual brother, but they'd been close enough that Keira still thought of him as part of the family.

Some of Keira's earliest memories were of Pike. Like him pushing her on the swings at the playground. She could see the shoes on her feet. They were purple, with sparkles on the sides. Had he bought them for her? She couldn't remember.

What she remembered was the *way* he'd pushed her. Pike was the only one she wanted to do it. Her father never came to the park, and her mother would only give her tentative nudges, not even enough to make the chains creak in her hands.

But when Pike pushed her, she sailed so high that the rest of the world fell away, until all she could hear was Pike's delighted laughter. Then her mother's worrying voice would interrupt, begging them to be careful, and the swing would slow so abruptly that it brought her stomach crashing down with it.

Not long after that, Pike had died and left them her college fund and the piano. The piano had arrived in a flurry of sweating, cursing men. She'd slept under it that night, rolling her purple sleeping bag out beneath the gleaming mahogany, staring at her five-year-old reflection in the polished brass that tipped the legs. The next day, she'd begged her mother to let her take piano lessons, but it was her father who finally relented.

"If it's going to take up half our living room, at least one of us should know what to do with it," he pointed out.

"Fine," her mother snapped. "But if you start complaining every time you see me writing a check for those lessons, then so help me God—" And off they'd gone.

Again.

That time, Keira hadn't even bothered with the sleeping bag. She'd just curled up on the worn carpet beneath the piano and put her hands over her ears. She'd fallen asleep to the sound of her parents arguing, as she huddled beneath the protective bulk of the piano.

Of course, once she'd actually started the lessons—once her

parents realized that the white keys were practically extensions of her own fingers—no one had complained about the piano at all.

Talent, she heard them whispering, long after she was supposed to have gone to sleep. *Scholarship.* And then, eventually, *career.*

Shaking off the memory, Keira sat down on the bench. The edge of the wood cut into her thighs in a familiar way. There was a fingerprint on the music stand. Keira pulled the cuff of her shirt down over her hand, rubbing at it until the wood shone.

Keira cracked the spine of her new music so that it would stay open, and clicked on the ugly brass floor lamp beside her. The unfamiliar spatter of black notes on the page stared at her. With a quick squint at the first line, she positioned her hands and began to play.

It was every bit as challenging as she'd been expecting. The music crashed over her like a froth-tipped wave, surrounding her. Driving her. She worked the first movement over and over, not even allowing herself to touch the Largo until she could run through the Allegro without stopping. Finally, the fingering started to take shape, her hands moving with the music rather than against it.

The creak of the front door interrupted her concentration.

"Keira? Honey? Why is it so dark in here?" Her mother's voice drooped with fatigue. It sounded discordant and alien after the rich notes of the piano.

Keira turned to face her mother, her back popping in protest as she twisted. Her eyes swept past the clock that hung over the TV stand. It was nine o'clock.

"I was practicing," Keira said, her tongue thick in her mouth, her mind still chasing the last trill.

"Did you stop to eat, at least?" Her mother sounded exasperated. The thought of food made Keira's stomach growl.

She'd *meant* to eat.

"I thought I'd wait until someone else got home," she said. Her mother's face collapsed beneath the guilt-trip. A tiny landscape of wrinkles formed around her eyes and mouth.

"Your father isn't here?"

Keira shook her head. "He left a message—he'll be late again."

"Well"—her mother shrugged out of her coat and kicked off her scuffed pumps—"we might as well have dinner together. Will you set the table while I change?"

Keira glanced back at the music. The last page of the movement beckoned. It dared her to play what came next.

Instead, she forced herself to stand up.

Twenty minutes to eat, and a half hour on the stupid history project. Then I'll come back. There'd be a little time left before her mother would go to bed—before she started to complain that the music was keeping her awake. With a last, promising touch to the keys, Keira headed into the kitchen.

• • •

She forced down the gummy chicken while her mother pretended she wasn't scanning the driveway, ready to bolt at the first sign of her dad's car.

"You know," her mom said. "I don't think I ever missed a meal when I was training."

The chicken caught in Keira's throat. Her mom almost never talked about her singing days. She'd sung opera. Well enough to get an offer to train with the Lyric Opera in Chicago. But after a month away from Sherwin, Keira's dad had lured her back with an engagement ring.

There was no opera in Sherwin. The best Keira's mom had been able to do was to join the local church choir. That's where Pike had found her mother—singing solos on Sunday and the "Ave Maria" at weddings. He'd encouraged her to get serious about her music. But then Keira had come along, and her mother stalled her plans to care for Keira. When Keira was little, her mother had sung arias. She and Keira would meet Pike in the empty church, and Keira would sit on the scratched piano bench and listen while her mother's voice bounced off the walls around her, stretching the Italian words.

She remembered Uncle Pike nudging her with a friendly elbow. "Do you think you'll be a singer too?" he asked.

Keira had shaken her head.

Her uncle hadn't looked disappointed exactly, but he had frowned the littlest bit. Pike never frowned. "But you would like to be a musician, wouldn't you?"

Even though she couldn't have been more than four, Keira knew that the answer was yes.

"So, what will you play? Guitar? Flute?"

Keira had looked around the church, her eyes drawn—as they always were—to the scuffed baby grand that squatted next to the dais. She'd pointed at it, the keys smiling back at her with their chipped-tooth grin.

"That's a wonderful choice," he said, giving her ponytail a gentle tug. "You'll make a remarkable pianist."

"But we don't have a piano, Uncle Pike." As young as she was, she knew that she couldn't play something she didn't have.

"You will, baby girl," he'd promised her. "When the time comes, you will."

And then not even a year later, Pike had died.

Afterward, her mother barely sang "Happy Birthday," much less Italian arias. She'd given up church choir for extra hours doing medical transcription.

The only music left in the Brannon house came from Keira. She couldn't imagine giving up her music for some crappy job and crappy house in Sherwin. Sometimes, she wasn't sure her mother could really imagine it either.

Keira watched her, toying with the remains of her dinner. "You really never even skipped a lunch because you were practicing?"

Her mother pushed away her plate. "My stomach would get sour and twisty if I did. It made my voice funny." She cleared her throat. "So. Do you have homework, or are you going to practice?"

"Homework," Keira admitted.

Her mother stacked their dishes. "Well, get to it. I know you want to get back to the piano tonight."

That was the best thing about her mom: She understood how badly Keira needed music. She didn't push Keira. Keira pushed herself. Her mom got out of the way and let Keira play.

Keira escaped to her room. Folding herself up on her bed, she glanced down at her sleeve—the hole stared at her like an accusing eye. She stripped off her shirt, and then hesitated, the wad of fabric dangling from her fist. It was her favorite. And there wasn't exactly money lying around to run out and buy another one. But every time she looked at it, she knew she'd see Mr. Seever's disappointed face and feel Jeremy and his cigarette pressed up against her.

With a sigh, she dropped it into the trash and pulled on an old sweatshirt before getting out her history textbook.

She'd only flipped through a couple of pages when the phone rang, and Keira leaned over to answer it, grateful for an excuse to put off her homework.

"Hey," Susan said. "Are you busy?"

"I was going to start on the misery of that history project, but I just—"

"Don't care?" Susan finished.

"Exactly." Keira shoved the book away and rolled over onto her back.

"So, how was the rest of your afternoon? Did you get home okay? I was kind of worried. It's not every day you get branded by Jeremy Reynolds and fired in the same afternoon."

"Thanks for reminding me. I'm fine."

The sound of Mrs. Kim harping at Susan crackled across the phone line. Even though Keira couldn't understand a word of Korean, irritation and suspicion had the same timbre in any language.

"Yeah, Mom. I'm getting to it," Susan huffed.

Keira heard Susan's bedroom door snap shut.

"Sorry," Susan sighed. "Did you know they immigrated here to give me a chance at a better life and I'm *wasting* it on the phone while she *works her fingers to the bone*?" Her voice was soaked with sarcasm.

"Actually, I think I *have* heard that somewhere before." It was pretty much the way Mrs. Kim started every conversation she had with Susan.

"Well, at least it was *you* I was talking to. If it'd been Tommy, she would have hung up the phone herself."

Susan had been dating Tommy for almost two months and her parents were still suspicious of the whole thing. Susan spent as much time worrying about how to get around her parents' dating rules as she did actually *dating* Tommy. Keira couldn't imagine spending that much time on a guy.

Walker leapt to mind. Keira rubbed a hand across her eyes as if she could erase his image and then sat up suddenly.

"Hey, you buy your music at Take Note sometimes, right?"

"Sure, why?"

"Have you ever seen anyone—I mean, besides Mr. Palmer—working there?"

"Someone like who?" Susan sounded confused.

"A guy. Like, a guy our age. Curly hair, leather wrist cuffs, accent?" She hesitated.

"Cute?" Susan asked.

Keira closed her eyes, picturing Walker, his dark eyebrows drawn together in concentration as he stared at the ancient cash register. The curve of his shoulder beneath his flannel shirt. The gray of his eyes. "Yeah," she admitted. "Cute."

"No, I haven't," Susan said, "but I'd sure as hell love to see a guy that even *you* will admit is cute. Maybe we should stop by. My flute teacher's after me to find something with 'wow-factor' for state—like that's somehow going to help me." She snorted. "You wanna go with me tomorrow afternoon? Is he cute enough to go to a movie with?"

"You know I don't date." Keira's voice was harder than she'd meant it to be.

"I know," Susan sighed. "But can you blame me for wishing you did? God, that's one of so many reasons Jeremy should act normal for once. Then we could go on a double date together and my mother might not follow me to the theater and sit in the back, making sure I act like a 'good girl.'"

The Movie Theater Incident was what had made Susan so

determined to date Tommy in spite of her parents' old-fashioned rules. Keira tried to picture Susan and Tommy sitting in a dark theater, holding hands, while she and Jeremy shared a bucket of popcorn.

Only it wasn't Jeremy she imagined herself with. It was Walker.

It should have seemed ridiculous. Instead, it sent a tingle through her.

And what? You'd miss three hours of piano practice while pretending you didn't see Tommy and Susan slobbering all over each other? Come on, Keira.

She sucked in a breath and shook out her hands. "After he put his cigarette out on me, there's no way I'd even *speak* to Jeremy, much less go on a date with him. I'll absolutely go with you to Take Note, though. I got some new music today, and I know we can find something there that—" She started to say, *That you can play*, but there was no reason to rub it in. "That'll impress the judges."

"As long as it's not too hard," Susan hedged.

"Yeah, yeah, I know. Hey, I should probably go—if I don't get started on this poster for history, I won't be able to practice any more tonight."

"I'll see you tomorrow?"

"Yep," Keira said. She stared at the textbook in front of her and wished she were looking at her new music instead. "Tomorrow."

She hung up and stretched out on the bed. The remembered sounds of the sonata rang in her ears, and while she listened, she saw Walker's gray eyes staring back at her from her thoughts. She tried to see the notes instead, but no matter how much she worked at it, his eyes were still there, watching her from behind the music.

Chapter Four

WHEN SHE WOKE UP, the clock on her nightstand said that it was three in the morning. Groggy, Keira sat up and looked at the textbook still splayed open on her bed. Crap. How could she have fallen asleep without doing any of her homework? She couldn't let her grades slip any lower.

Cursing, she slid off the bed and stumbled down the hall toward the kitchen in search of a snack. She needed something that would keep her awake long enough to write a limerick about 1930s politics that Mrs. Eddiston would deem worthy of a passing grade.

The bluish glow of the streetlight filtered in through the

window, giving her barely enough light to see. On the counter next to the sink sat a single, lonely piece of fruit. A puddle of shadow surrounded it, like a spotlight in reverse. It looked like a banana, except the skin was as red and shiny as an apple's.

Great. Dad's shopping at the fancy grocery store again.

Her mother would have a fit—she was always griping about Keira's dad's "champagne tastes." Exotic food wasn't in the budget.

Keira reached for the fruit, but her fingers wouldn't close around its smooth skin. They curled in on themselves, as though she'd grabbed at empty air. She blinked hard, clearing the last of the sleep-fog from her eyes. There was definitely something on the counter. She could see the stem, the bruised spot along one side. She reached for it again, her fingers slipping through the pool of inky shadow.

Her heart twisted in her chest. Something was wrong. Really wrong.

She grabbed for the fruit one more time, hoping it was all a dream. An optical illusion. A mistake.

The overhead light flicked on, flooding the kitchen with its glare, and Keira barely managed to bite down on a shriek before it escaped her mouth.

"Keira? What are you doing up? It's the middle of the night." Her father stood squinting in the doorway between the kitchen and the living room. His face was marked with ridges from the throw pillows. He was sleeping on the couch. Again.

"I fell asleep before I finished my homework," she said. "I needed a snack to wake up enough to do it."

She gestured at the counter, which was empty and worn and scratched. There was no weird fruit. No weird shadows, either. It had all disappeared.

Her father scratched at his stubbly chin. "Well, hurry. I don't want you exhausted tomorrow. You don't get enough sleep as it is. It makes me worry, you know." He shuffled back into the living room, not even bothering with any pretext of going back into the bedroom.

Her empty stomach forgotten, Keira walked over to the light switch. She flipped off the light and stared at the counter while her eyes adjusted to the dark. The shadow was gone. The fruit was gone.

It was never there in the first place, she reasoned. *A trick, like some sort of eyestrain. Or migraine. Maybe I was sleepwalking or something.*

She clung to all of the rational explanations, ignoring the sense-memory in her fingers of the cool, liquid dark of the shadow.

It. Was. Just. A. Fluke.

Limericks. That's what I need to be thinking about.

Keira walked back to her safe, normal, lamp-lit room. On the bed, her history book waited. When she reached for the cover, it was smooth and hard beneath her hand. Solid. Normal.

It was the only time Keira could ever remember feeling relieved to open a textbook. With a sigh, she settled down and started to read.

"He might not be working today," Keira warned Susan. In front of them, Take Note's glass door shone in the almost-warm March sun. "It's not like he told me his schedule or anything."

"I know. But if he *is* here, I can force you to flirt with him. And if he isn't, I can still tell my flute teacher that I looked for some music. It's win-win, really."

Susan opened the door and Keira stepped in behind her, scanning the shop for Walker. Her shoulders fell when she saw Mr. Palmer sitting behind the counter, a catalog open in front of him and listening to the classical station on the bent-antennaed radio.

You will not *be disappointed that some random guy isn't here.* Keira gave herself a mental slap. She shouldn't have come. She shouldn't even have told Susan about Walker. She *should* be home practicing, like the rest of the people who were applying to Juilliard.

Mr. Palmer's wrinkled face, all jowls and disapproval, softened when he caught sight of Keira. "Oh, hi," he said. "You need help?"

"No thanks—just looking today."

Susan headed to the far corner of the store, disappearing behind a stand of instrument cases and special cleaners for brass and ivory.

Mr. Palmer made a gruff noise somewhere between a grunt and a cough. "Well, don't be getting things out of order," he warned her.

"We won't," Keira promised, following Susan.

Susan stood in front of a wobbly bookcase stuffed with bound music. Her lower lip was pushed out into a pout. "I'm never going to find anything in here," she complained.

"You will," Keira promised. "Because I'm going to help you. Come on." She lowered herself to the floor and grabbed a stack of music. "Let's get started."

The two of them flipped through the pages, laughing quietly over some of the stranger pieces—the idea of "Flight of the Bumblebee" on the saxophone was beyond ridiculous.

"Hey, this might be something." Keira leaned over to show Susan the plain white cover with the name "Syrinx" and a flute on it. "Listen." She flipped the book open and began to whistle the melody. It was simple and haunting.

"Do you really think I can play that?" Susan wrinkled her nose. "It sounds . . . hard."

Keira gave her a pointed look. "You can play it, you'll just have to practice. It's not that you're not good enough, Suz, it's just that you want the flute to get better all by itself."

Once upon a time, Susan had matched Keira's practicing minute for minute. But then Susan had discovered French club. And guys. And all sorts of other things that took up her time while Keira still logged hour after hour on the piano.

Before, they'd talked about going to Juilliard together. Now Susan talked about going to a school near Juilliard, so they could visit each other. Seeing how fast Susan's dream had evaporated only made Keira cling more tightly to her own, afraid that all her hard work would vaporize if she so much as looked away from it.

Susan tugged at the end of her braid. "I know I don't practice enough. You're right. Sometimes I wish I could give up music—focus on my grades and French club and hope that'd be enough to get me into a decent college. I'm not ever going to be a pro. Not like you will be." She took the book out of Keira's hands. "But you know my parents would kill me if I ended up at a state school, and I need the extracurriculars." She looked down at the music. "At least this one sounds pretty. I'd better go pay before Mr. Palmer accuses me of illegally memorizing music or something."

"I'll put the rest of it back," Keira said. "That way, if I misshelve something, he won't blame you."

"He'd still blame me," Susan said, ducking her head as she slung her messenger bag over her shoulder. "You can't do any wrong according to him."

Keira turned back to the bookshelf, listening to Mr. Palmer's grumpy exclamations as he put aside his crossword to ring up Susan's music. The grumbling increased when Susan pulled out a credit card instead of cash.

"Hey." Walker knelt down next to her.

Keira stared at him. His unexpected presence made the world feel suddenly unsteady, like she'd stepped onto a boat without realizing it.

"Where did you come from?"

"Well." He cleared his throat. "It all started when my great-great-great-great-grandfather became dissatisfied with the options available to him and decided to go make a new life for himself." His accent made the words dance.

"Smart-ass."

His eyebrow arched, pleased, and he leaned across her to pick up a score. A row of inky dots circled his bicep, right below the sleeve of his T-shirt. The sight of them made Keira shiver in warning. They looked like the mark she'd seen on his wrist the day before—unusual, somehow. Like they were *under* his skin. Like they'd come from inside him, instead of being tattooed on.

Walker stacked the scores, tapping them against the floor and snapping Keira out of her uneasy reverie. She was suddenly all too aware that she'd been staring.

"Do you come in here just to mess up the music, or what?" he asked.

His arm brushed against hers and the hair on the back of Keira's neck stood up. "I'm pretty sure I know the filing system at least as well as you do," she countered. Behind them, she could hear Susan arguing with Mr. Palmer about whether or not she had to sign two copies of the receipt.

Walker smirked at her. "Maybe. Wanna bet?"

Keira stared back at him, her competitive streak glowing inside her. "Sure."

"Fine. Loser buys coffee," he said.

Oh, hell. Is this just some way to ask me out?

There was a gleam in his eye that dared her to refuse.

"I don't date," she said, reaching for her bag. Even as the words came out of her mouth, she hated them. It sounded so final, but she'd never had trouble saying it to anyone else who'd asked her out.

"It's not a date," he said firmly. His full lips twitched like he was trying not to smile. "It's a bet. But I'm flattered that you think of me that way. Unless you're actually worried you might lose?"

His confidence made her want to stomp her foot like a frustrated kid.

"Fine. Movie scores—how are they filed?" she practically spat the question at him.

"Alphabetically," he said.

Triumph spread through her, sweet and forbidden.

"Ha! Wrong. They're—"

"By composer," he interrupted. "Alphabetically by composer. Since the music's the most important part of the movie, the composer's more important than the title."

"Mr. Palmer's cinematic hierarchy." Keira grimaced. Walker was right. "It's your turn, then."

"Raffi." He said simply.

She wrinkled her nose. "Like—the children's music guy?"

"Yep." Walker leaned his head back against the shelves, eyeing her. Waiting.

It had to be a trick. Did he have a secret last name or something? Unless Walker assumed she'd leap to that sort of conclusion—that she was the sort of person who automatically overcomplicated everything.

Still, her only guess was the obvious. "Alphabetical. With the R's."

"Nope. It's not here at all." He smiled at her, victorious. "Didn't you know? Mr. Palmer—"

"Hates kids," she finished with a groan, thinking of the NO UNATTENDED CHILDREN ALLOWED! sign posted on the front door.

"Keira?" Susan called from the front of the store. "Are you ready?"

Mr. Palmer shushed her from his perch behind the counter.

"Uh, almost," Keira called as quietly as she could.

"Miss Brannon!" Mr. Palmer protested. "Really! I'm surprised at you. This isn't some sort of student union. Please keep it down."

"Fine," Susan huffed. "I'll wait for you outside, Keira."

Susan was the one who'd been dying to meet Walker, but she'd never see him back here behind the instrument-case display. Now Keira'd gotten herself roped into having coffee with him, and Susan had missed the whole thing.

I should have known this wouldn't go well. I should have just gone home to practice. Damn!

Walker stared at her intently. His eyes met hers and the last of his teasing bravado slipped off his face. He stood up, his body a few inches too close to hers, but Keira didn't back away. She had to tilt her head up to see his face. It made her want to buy a pair of high heels, so they'd be even again.

"I expect you to make good on our wager, Keira Brannon." His gaze was dangerous and delicious at the same time. "Did you realize that your eyes are exactly the color of espresso?" he asked slowly, reaching out a careful finger to trace the hollow curve below her eye.

There didn't seem to be any air left for her to breathe. "I don't drink coffee," she managed to choke out. "And I don't go out with guys whose last names I don't even know."

"Andover." His hand lingered by her face. "It's Walker Andover. And I don't mind that you don't like coffee. There must be *something* you want?" The curve of his lips said that he intended every bit of the double meaning in his words.

"Tea," she whispered. "And that's all."

"Tea. I'll remember that." He leaned in close. The smell of him, peat smoke and flint, wrapped around her, invisible and as heady as ether. She couldn't think.

Walker watched her. His eyelashes were black as coal and close enough to count. "Friday? Three thirty? There's a diner around the corner from here—I'm pretty sure they have tea. I'll meet you."

"Okay—fine," she stammered, struggling to regain the

self-control she was always so proud of. She wrapped her arms around her middle protectively. "But only because I owe you, and I don't like owing people."

"Good enough for me." He smiled a lazy smile. A *waiting* smile. "For now, at least."

The front door clanged. "Keira? Are you coming or what?" Susan sounded distinctly irritated.

"Yeah." Keira ducked under Walker's arm. "I'm coming."

"See you Friday," he said, turning back to work like nothing had happened.

With a disgruntled snort, Keira turned on her heel and headed for the door, barely pausing to say good-bye to Mr. Palmer, who gave her a grudging wave in response.

Chapter Five

"It's about time!" Susan stormed off in the direction of the parking lot. "You'd think it was the freaking Smithsonian in there, the way that old man acts! I don't know why you shop there at all. And what took you so long?"

"I was talking to Walker," Keira said, hating the way her lips tingled when she said his name. Two days in a row, he'd managed to set her internal compass spinning like a merry-go-round. She kicked a loose chunk of blacktop in frustration.

"You—there was no one else in there!" Susan protested.

Keira jammed her key into the driver's-side door, unlocking it. "There was," she said. "He appeared out of freaking nowhere when you went up to pay for your music. And then he baited me into meeting him for coffee. His ego is the size of Montana."

Susan flopped into the passenger seat, clutching her bag like a shocked old lady. "You have a *date* with him?" Susan turned and looked through the rear window.

"What are you doing?"

"Checking for the four horsemen of the apocalypse."

Keira jammed the gearshift into drive and the transmission whined in response. "It's not a date. I have a score to settle. He made me a bet that he knew Take Note better than I do, and I lost. You know how I feel about owing someone." What she didn't mention were all the other feelings Walker stirred up in her.

Susan let out a long, slow whistle. "So, when are you going to go out? Because what I really want to know is when we can all go out *together*. You'll be my *chaperone*. Jeremy's going to be supergluing his little heart back together but hey, any date without my parents is a good date, right?"

"Yes! That's it! I'm not going to see him alone. You'll come with me. And Tommy, too! You can have a momless date, and Walker'll get the coffee I owe him and that'll be all. It's perfect. Friday afternoon, okay?"

"Friday? I can't. I have my flute lesson. And besides, I think you need to see him alone first. Otherwise, what if he thinks the coffee is just a *friends* thing? He might, if all four of us are there."

"That would be fine with me," Keira said.

"God. If I'd known you were up for something like that, I would've forced you to say yes to Trevor when he asked you to go to the Valentine's dance last month."

Keira opened her mouth, but she couldn't find the words to explain that nice guys—like Trevor Benson, who asked her out every couple of months, even though she rejected him each time—made her even more desperate to get away from Sherwin for good. Nice guys made it easy not to date, but though she hated to admit it, Walker was making it really, really difficult.

It's not a date, she reminded herself. *It was a bet.*

"When I'm a famous pianist, then I'll think about finding a boyfriend," Keira finally said. "But I'm not doing anything to ruin my chances at getting out of here, and dating's just—"

"A distraction," Susan finished for her. "You sound exactly like my mother when you say that. If I was half as driven with my schoolwork as you are with your piano, I'd be valedictorian by now."

"You don't need to be valedictorian. You're going to get into a good school and make your parents happy, and then go to law school and be a massive success," Keira insisted.

"Damn, do I hope you're right." Susan slumped down in the seat next to her. Keira had enough determination for both of them. Neither of them were going to spend their lives in this decaying town.

She didn't care what she had to give up.

Over the next two days, Keira practiced even more than usual. She ignored the memory of Walker's smile, playing until her legs went numb from sitting at the piano for so long—until her mind was nothing but a wash of notes and tempos, her only emotions dictated by the mood of the music.

By the time she'd gotten herself back under control, Keira was exhausted. Friday morning, she overslept. Both of her parents left the house early on Fridays, and neither of them had bothered to wake her.

She leapt out of bed and yanked on the jeans and gray sweatshirt that were slung over her desk chair, pulled her hair up into a sloppy ponytail, and raced down the hall. She grabbed her bag and a granola bar, and hoped like hell the car would start. On the third try, after she'd smacked the dashboard in frustration and sworn at the engine, it did.

The halls were silent as she tore down them, praying that her English teacher would understand, just this once. Keira took a deep breath, trying to slow her galloping pulse before she eased open the door.

Her eyes were drawn to the thin shadow that ran underneath the door. Nothing else had a shadow in the fluorescent light. Especially not a midnight-colored one. The shadow on the counter the other night leapt into her head. This cool, dark slash of nothingness looked exactly the same. A horrible, nagging voice inside wondered if she was imagining this, too.

Keira bent down, her long fingers shaking as they closed in on the black patch. Right before her fingertips crossed the edge of the shadow, she felt a sudden jerk on her wrist, like something was tugging her into the blackness. The sensation sent her stomach plummeting.

Keira yanked her arm back as the door swung open, and she barely managed to keep herself from tumbling headlong into the classroom. Without the cover of the door, the shadow that had seemed so solid evaporated into nubby, district-issue carpet beneath her knees.

"Nice of you to join us, Miss Brannon." Mrs. Garcia towered over her, a piece of chalk clutched in her hand. "Perhaps you'd like to take a seat instead of listening at the door?"

Keira slipped into her seat, ignoring the snickers around her.

"Okay, let's start with Arthur Miller." Mrs. Garcia scanned the room.

Keira started tapping out the sweeping opening notes of the Allegretto movement she'd been working on. She was too jittery after her dash to school to focus on a boring lecture about "the changing face of theatre." She'd catch up later.

Maybe.

After class, she ducked into the bathroom to see how disastrous her hair really was and wash her face. The rough brown paper towels left her cheeks pink. Keira smoothed back her ponytail with damp fingers, hoping that it would pass as "artfully messy."

Susan bounded into the bathroom and stopped short when she saw Keira.

"Well, *there* you . . . whoa. You look—are you okay?"

Keira looked in the mirror and saw the black circles that ringed her eyes and the way her water-spattered shirt hung shapelessly from her shoulders.

"Yeah, I just overslept," she said. "I've been working on this new piece of music and—"

"Are you still meeting Walker this afternoon?" Susan interrupted.

Keira closed her eyes. In the hurry of the morning, she'd finally done what she'd been trying to do all week: She'd forgotten about Walker.

"Uh, yeah, I guess I am." she said. She mentally counted the money in her backpack, wondering whether she had enough to pay for his coffee. Buying the new music had used up most of her cash. She'd have to see if she could scrounge some change from between the seats of her car or something.

"You don't sound very excited." A note of disappointment rang in Susan's voice.

Keira leaned back against the cool, hard porcelain of the sink. "I know. I'm not. Listen, once I've paid my debt to him, I really, really don't have any plans to see him again."

Susan's face fell. "One double date wouldn't kill you."

"You're right. The thing is, I don't want to spend three weeks convincing him that I'm too busy to see him again, afterward. I'm sorry, Susan." The first bell rang. "You're going to be late, you know."

Susan shot a last glance at the clock. "Who cares?" Her voice was glum, but her steps were still quick as she swept past two sophomores, who came rushing in amid a flutter of giggles. With a last, hopeless glance in the mirror, Keira pushed her way out the door.

And crashed smack into Jeremy Reynolds's shoulder.

Jeremy grunted in surprise and his eyes flashed sparks. But when he realized who had run into him, the sparks turned into a flame-lit smile.

"Keira." He looked at her hair. "Are you doing the bed-head thing on purpose, or did you oversleep?" He leaned in as he laughed and Keira automatically stepped back, maintaining the distance between them. Something about the way he smiled at her was a shade too sweet.

"Just overslept, actually. Sorry—I've gotta get to class, Jeremy. If I'm late, I'll get detention."

The second bell rang, as though time itself was trying to get her out of the conversation.

"I'd hate to think of you wasting your time in the holding cell they call detention. I can think of way better things for you to do."

Keira couldn't hide her shock fast enough.

Jeremy blushed. "Like your piano, I mean. It would be stupid for you to miss that for detention."

Something about his sudden attention and concern made her want to tell him that she had a date after school thankyou-verymuch. If Susan hadn't already. Which she probably had.

And anyway, it's not a date. I'm paying a debt. That's all.

"Yeah. Thanks. I've really gotta go," she said again, trying to skirt Jeremy. He caught the strap of her bag as she passed, and her neck snapped around painfully as she jerked to a stop.

"Ow! Jeremy, what the—?!"

"Oh. Sorry. I wanted you to know that I'm going over to Tommy's after school. I think Susan's coming by after her flute lesson. You should come too. It would be fun." He was looking at her like she was a carnival prize and he had a pocket full of quarters.

What was his *deal?*

"That's sweet." She peeled his fingers off the strap of her bag.

"Awesome! I'll be there about three—"

She interrupted him. "It's really nice of you to offer, but I have plans. The three of you have fun, okay?"

Before he could grab her again, Keira darted down the hall. She'd never been so relieved to get to math class. On top of everything else, it looked like she was going to spend the after-noon dodging awkward invitations from Jeremy.

One more reason to wish that the day would hurry up and end.

When it finally did, though, she kind of wished it hadn't.

Chapter Six

KEIRA STOOD IN FRONT of the diner at exactly three thirty, with seven dollars and twenty-three cents in her pocket. The angle of the sun kept her from seeing who was inside. Even though she didn't have the slightest idea what sort of car Walker might drive, it didn't stop her from scanning the tiny parking lot, looking for something that fit him.

You're stalling, she chided herself. *Get in there and get it over with.*

The inside of the diner was dim and it reeked of maple syrup and hot grease. Walker was stretched across one side of a booth near the back of the restaurant, looking oddly at home.

In spite of the fact that it was March, he was wearing a T-shirt that showed off his arms. He raised a languid hand in her direction, but his eyes were bright.

Admit it, he's gorgeous.

But that doesn't make any difference, I still can't date him, she argued with herself.

Keira marched the length of the restaurant and slid stiffly into the vinyl booth. A cup of tea was already waiting for her, steam curling off its surface. Walker had a mug of coffee at his elbow, pale with milk and a third empty.

"You came," Walker observed, not bothering to hide the pleasure in his low voice. It rumbled through Keira like an earthquake, sending all of her resolve tumbling to the ground. Everything around them had gone into soft-focus, as though they were the only solid things in the restaurant.

"I said I would, didn't I?" She'd meant the question to be tart, but all the sting had leaked out of her voice. She drummed her fingers on the edge of the table, trying to regain her balance.

"So you keep your word," Walker said quietly. "I like that." He slid a hand across the table and put his fingers on top of hers, stopping her virtual playing midchord. "What are you—oh, I get it." He smiled. It was like the sun on water—a million diamond reflections. Blinding. Wonderful. "You're playing piano."

She nodded and slid her hands out from underneath his. Immediately, she wanted to put them back—to feel the touch of his fingertips again. "Nervous habit. Sorry," she said. "It drives my mom crazy. And most of my teachers, too."

"What were you playing?" He was watching her—listening to her—like she was the only person in the room.

"Uh, just an étude." Clearing her throat, she reached for her mug, desperate for something to do with her hands. "This is for me?"

"I hope you don't mind," Walker said. "But you might want to—"

She downed a huge gulp, then winced.

"Sorry." He made a sympathetic face.

"I'm the one who didn't put in any sugar," she said, reaching for the canister.

Walker frowned. "You didn't—it wasn't too hot? It should be scalding."

Keira looked down into the mug. "No. It's bitter. Why?" The memory of Jeremy's cigarette pressed against her skin crawled through her memory, and she slapped it away. It was just a coincidence. She'd gotten lucky, that's all.

Walker reached out a fingertip to touch the side of her mug, lifting his eyes to study her. "You're different," he said slowly.

Keira wrinkled her nose, stirring a mountain of sugar into her tea. "You mean I'm weird."

Walker laughed. "No. Well, yeah, a little I guess."

She started to cross her arms but he reached across the table and twined his fingers through hers. His touch coursed through her like a drug.

"I like weird," he murmured, holding her steady with his gaze. She didn't even try to push him away.

She wanted him, and there was nothing she could do about it. The fact of it sat in her middle. With a twist of her wrist, she slid her hand away.

Surprise shimmered across his features, but he didn't seem hurt. "Too soon, huh?" he said lightly, lifting his mug and taking a long drink. Under the table, his feet shifted so that their knees touched briefly. It seemed like an accident, but Keira tucked her legs close to her side of the table.

"Holding hands? Yeah." Before she could tell him that it would *always* be too soon, he jumped in.

"Maybe on the next date." The corner of his mouth quirked up, all confidence and promise. The almost-smile sent a tingle through her, and Keira let herself enjoy it. It wasn't like she couldn't ever notice a guy. She was human, after all.

Look but don't touch, she reminded herself.

"I'm here because I owe you coffee," she said.

"But you're *here.*"

She tilted her chin up. "Just because you're cute doesn't mean this is a date." The words tumbled out.

"But you think I'm cute."

Keira tugged at the end of her ponytail, finally lost in the rising tide of her embarrassment. She felt him lean toward her, his lips close to her ear.

"I'm glad," he whispered. "Because I think you're the most

gorgeous thing I've seen in as long as I can remember."

If she'd turned her head, they would have kissed. Without meaning to, she imagined what his mouth would feel like against hers.

Music, she told herself strictly. *Career. That's what I need. Not a kiss.*

"You barely know me." She fought to sound firm. His lips brushed against her ear as he settled back into his side of the booth. He sipped his coffee patiently. "Let's fix that. I already know the most important thing about you," he said. "But you tell me what I'm missing. Deep dark secrets? Divorced parents? Still sleep with your teddy bear?"

"Not telling you, no, and none of your business," she shot back. "What about you?"

He gave her the studying look again, but the gray of his eyes looked more June-warm than February-bleak. "Plenty of deep dark secrets. My parents are . . ." He hesitated. "Well, I guess they're probably dead. No one's heard from them since I was little."

"Oh—I'm sorry," Keira said sincerely. She couldn't imagine how awful that must be. Her own parents might be too caught up in their own falling-apart lives to notice much of hers, but at least they were *there.*

Walker shrugged. "It was years ago. It's gotten easier. Not easy, but easier." The playful twinkle returned to his eyes. "And no, I don't sleep with a teddy bear. And no to the pajamas, too, in case that was your next question."

Keira felt herself flush but tried to hide it by taking another drink of her very sweet tea.

"So you won't tell me about your stuffed animals—how about whatever it is that's hanging over you? What makes you so driven? Why so much piano? Why no dating? It's like you're already somewhere else." His words were leaden with meaning.

"Exactly," Keira said fiercely. "I don't want to get trapped here. I don't *belong* here. I've felt that way ever since I was a little kid. I only feel like things are right when I'm playing the piano. I don't want to screw it up—end up married and working as a bank teller or something miserable like that." She glanced up at him. "I know that sounds snotty and horrible. I don't mean it that way. But I'll go crazy if I stay in Sherwin."

"And music's your ticket out?" he guessed.

"I hope so," she said fervently. "It depends on what Juilliard thinks of my audition recordings."

"I never planned to stay here long myself. . . ." He ran a hand through his hair, the curls snaking around his fingers. "But it's already been two years. I finally broke down and got a job."

"I noticed," Keira said playfully. "Better to work at Take Note than the credit union, though, right? Speaking of which," Keira said, "I should probably go. I haven't practiced yet today and it's getting late."

Keira slid out of the booth, ignoring Walker's disappointed expression. She was anxious to get in front of the piano.

"Sure," he said. "You go ahead. I'll take care of this."

"No way!" She dug in her pocket for her cash, but Walker put a hand on her hip, stopping her.

"I want to see you again. It doesn't have to be a date. You can 'owe' me the coffee then."

She took his hand off her hip, the wanting that swirled inside her braiding itself into frustration. She tossed her money on the table and one of the pennies rolled off, bouncing against the tile floor.

"I don't welch on a debt. *Ever.*"

"Gorgeous and proud," he said, letting go of her. "I like it. Give me your number and we'll call it even."

If he thought that he could use her pride against her like that, he was totally and completely wrong. "I don't think so. Maybe I'll see you at the music store sometime," she said. She walked out of the diner, trying to clear her head with huge gulps of the cool March air. She got in the car and pulled out into the parking lot, trying to shake off the desire to put her hand on her hip—to feel the place where Walker's fingers had been.

Deep in her subconscious, a warning flag waved at her, trying to get her attention. Something about the picture in her mind wasn't right. She studied it—the curve of his palm against her jeans, the definition in his forearms, the way his bicep flexed the tiniest bit as he'd stopped her.

His bicep. His smooth, perfect, bicep . . .

There were no inky dots! No marks at all. Whatever she'd

seen on his skin at the music store had disappeared without a trace. Again.

Keira started to pull out onto the street. She was so distracted, she didn't even realize that someone had appeared in front of her car. She caught a glimpse of a guy in a strange, full-length coat; his crooked nose and haunted eyes peered out from beneath his hood. The world around her went dark. For a minute she couldn't see the street, the buildings—nothing. Only some guy standing in front of her car.

Instinct took over. She jerked the wheel sharply to avoid hitting him and swung the car into traffic.

She didn't look back to see if he was okay.

She couldn't. Not after she'd noticed the SUV that was barreling toward her, skittering down the street in spite of its squealing brakes.

The squealing gave way to screaming as the seat belt locked tight against her chest and the crunch of metal against metal ripped through the car.

Chapter Seven

KEIRA STARED AT THE blue SUV that had smashed into the side of her car. Through the glittering remains of her window, she could see the metal of an enormous fender. A cracked headlight. The driver's-side door of her car was pressed against her, the armrest handle shoved uncomfortably into her ribs. In front of her, the steering wheel jutted out at a jaunty angle, as though it had decided to glance out the passenger window.

She tried to sort through the jumble of events. She remembered twisting the wheel to avoid the fool who'd stepped in front of her car, and the SUV tearing down the street like a blue mountain on wheels. She remembered the pained, animal noise her door had made as the SUV slammed into it. The shock of the impact still screamed through her, like a fire alarm blaring long after the smoke has cleared.

Keira twisted around, searching for the hooded figure, but the street was empty except for cars. The parking lot, too.

Oh, shit, did I hit him? If he was lying on the ground, she wouldn't be able to see him. *Oh, God, please no.*

The seat belt strained against her shoulder through the fabric of her coat. She reached down, fumbling for the buckle, when her passenger door flew open. Keira shrank away from the figure that slid into the car next to her, sure it was the guy from the street, or the driver of the SUV, ready to yell at her for pulling out into traffic. Instead, the smell of peat smoke and flint filled the car as Walker leaned over and unbuckled her seat belt.

"Did I hit him?" she whimpered.

"He hit you, looks like," Walker said grimly.

"What? No—not the car. The guy. There was a guy—is there anyone on the ground?"

He frowned. "Keira, there's no one else here but you and the other driver." His eyes turned appraising. Suspicious. "Are you hurt?" he asked. His hands skimmed her shoulders and down her arms, like he was looking for an injury.

She shook her head. "I'm fine, I think."

A squat man with a phone pressed against his ear climbed out of his car and peered at her through the broken window.

" . . . just pulled right out into traffic," he said.

He looked at Keira like she'd vomited on his shoes. "Police," he said, pointing to the phone. "They want to know if we need an ambulance. You okay?"

She nodded. "Fine, I think."

He looked down at her car. "The way this thing looks, I'd say you got damn lucky."

Keira looked him over. "Are you okay?"

"Oh. Yeah. I had the airbags and all." He turned his attention back to the phone. "She pulled out of the lot and there was no way to stop before I hit her."

Free of her seat belt, Keira spun all the way around in her seat. "Did you see him? The guy in the weird coat? He didn't go into the diner, did he?" She scanned the sidewalks.

"Weird coat?" Walker's question was measured as a drumbeat.

"Yeah. Dark hooded coat, crooked nose. Dark eyes—kind of like yours, actually."

As soon as she said the words, the buzzing heat of embarrassment swept over her. Had she imagined the person standing there? Had she been so caught up in Walker that she'd hallucinated some guy who looked vaguely like him and then *wrecked her car*?

"Which way did he come from?" Walker asked, worry thickening his accent.

She grabbed the cuffs of her coat, twisting the fabric beneath her fingers. "I didn't see him come from *anywhere*. He just appeared. He was *there*, and then the accident happened, and then he was gone." She shook her head. "Maybe he crossed the street." There was a drugstore and a vet's office across the way. She desperately hoped that he'd gone into one of them. It was possible.

Barely.

"That's probably it." Walker leaned close to Keira. He lifted her arm and wrapped it around his neck, then slid his other arm beneath her knees.

"What are you doing?" She tried to pull away from him, but he curled his arm around her more tightly.

"Lifting you up?"

"I can get out by myself," she insisted, turning to slide across the bench seats. He reached out, stopping her.

"Keira. There's broken glass everywhere. Let me help you."

She glanced down at the upholstery. Tiny, glittering cubes of safety glass lay scattered across it like diamonds. She hadn't noticed them.

Crap. Get it together. You're fine. You didn't hit the guy. The other driver's fine. The car is . . .

She shut her eyes. The car was obviously not fine, but she had insurance. Cheap, crappy insurance. But still.

"Are you *sure* you're okay?" Walker asked. "Did you hit your head?"

Keira frowned at him. "I'm *fine*," she insisted. "I don't need help." Besides, every time Walker touched her, it was like a fog drifted into her head—it was the opposite of helpful. Tingly and distracting and wonderful, but not helpful.

Carefully, she picked her way across the seat, grabbing the dashboard and the top of the front seat to steady herself as she eased over the gearshift. Walker heaved a sigh and reached out, catching her around the ribs. He lifted her easily, moving her over the remains of the glass and spinning her so that she landed in his lap.

She froze, stunned that he'd actually had the audacity to grab her. For one brief moment, they sat that way, Walker's broad chest sure and warm against her back, his hands still circling her ribs. The whisper of his breath against her neck shot through her like an electric shock.

"You are the most stubborn person I think I've ever seen." He let go of her and Keira wriggled around to face the open door and slid off his lap. Her shoes landed against the pavement with a slap. When she took a step, though, her knees weren't as steady as she'd expected them to be. She wobbled, grabbing blindly for the door. It swung beneath her grip, throwing her even more off balance. Walker reached out a hand, his eyebrows lowered in concern. Instinctively, Keira slid her hand into his. He curled his fingers around hers and all she could feel was their skin touching. Her knees steadied underneath her and the world righted itself.

"Okay?" he asked softly, squeezing her hand.

She swallowed hard before she returned the pressure of his

fingers. "Yeah. Thanks." Reluctantly, she slid her hand out of his and walked around the front of the car to examine the damage on the driver's side. There wasn't enough room for a person in all the dented metal and splintered glass. "I . . . wow. I should be *hurt*." She ran a hand over her ribs as though she might have somehow missed an injury, but as shaken as she was, she seemed to be undamaged.

Walker stood next to her, close enough for their arms to brush against each other. "Yeah. You should. But I'm glad you're not."

"I guess I need to call my insurance company," she sighed.

He nodded. She opened the back door and pulled her bag off the seat, digging her cell phone out of the front pocket and her insurance card out of her wallet. The police pulled up before she could find the phone number. When Keira gave them the story about the disappearing pedestrian, the shorter and squatter of the two officers narrowed his eyes at her, like he thought she was making up the whole thing.

She wanted to curl up and die.

When the police finally left, she called her insurance company and worked her way through the automated system until an actual person came on the line. Walker sat on the passenger seat, lining up cubes of safety glass on the dashboard.

"Thank you for calling Equitable Insurance. My name is Molly. May I please have your name and policy number?"

Keira closed her eyes. This was going to take forever.

Chapter Eight

WALKER LOUNGED IN THE passenger seat, arms crossed over his chest, watching Keira talk.

She moved the phone away from her mouth to talk to Walker while the customer service representative babbled. "You can go. I appreciate your . . . Good Samaritan-ness, but I can take care of this."

"I can wait. You're gonna have to call a tow truck, too."

Keira grimaced. She hadn't even thought of that yet. She was going to lose a whole afternoon of piano practice—it was already almost five o'clock. Her fingers itched at the thought. She flexed her free hand. Her arm could have been crushed.

Missing a day of practice was bad, but if she'd been hurt . . . that would have been unimaginable.

Eventually, SUV guy got in his car and drove away. Keira and Walker were alone at the edge of the nearly empty parking lot. As the sun dipped low, so did the temperature. Tired of the cold, Keira opened the car's rear door and sat down. At least this way, she was out of the wind.

The tow truck was due to arrive any minute. She tried to call her parents, to see if one of them could come get her, but neither of them answered their cells. Susan was still at her flute lesson. Keira tapped her phone against her leg, irritated.

"Need a ride home?" Walker asked casually. "My car's over there." He nodded his head toward a black car parked in the corner of the lot.

"Maybe the tow truck can drop me off," she said, crossing her arms to mirror his posture.

He dropped his arms and gripped the seat back that stood between them like a wall. "I get it. I do. You're proud and fierce and strong and you're not one bit interested in me." The thrill of hearing him call her "fierce" kept his amusement from bothering her. "But getting into a truck with some man you don't know just so you don't have to accept a ride from me? Come on."

Keira felt some of the pride leak out of the set of her chin. She wanted to accept Walker's offer . . . that was part of the problem. She wanted him to drive her home. Saying yes felt too much like giving in.

A dented, rusty tow truck pulled up next to her car. The guy behind the wheel was as stringy and greasy as day-old fried chicken. He noticed Keira and a smirk spread across his face.

She turned to Walker. "Okay. Yes, please," she said. "I'm stubborn but I'm not stupid."

Walker looked both smug and relieved. "Good."

"Hey. Bad day, huh?" said the tow truck driver. The embroidered name patch on his coveralls read *Shrimp*.

Keira stood up, grabbing her backpack. "You could say that."

"Dispatch says I'm takin' this over to Brutti's Body Shop?"

"Yes, please." Keira looked around, hitching her book bag up onto her shoulder.

"Need a ride?" Shrimp asked. His eyebrows lifted slightly, the tip of his tongue wetting his bottom lip in a way that made Keira's stomach turn.

She felt Walker behind her—not stepping in and not taking over, but still behind her. Still watching.

"No, I'm good, thanks." She was glad to be able to say it.

"A'ight," he sighed. "They'll call you when they's got an estimate."

Keira nodded and headed for Walker's sleek black Mercedes sedan. She couldn't wait to get away from the twisted remains of her own car and in front of her piano, where she could forget about the whole disastrous day.

"You sure you're okay?" Walker asked as Shrimp loaded

the remains of her car onto the back of the tow truck. "I can't believe that you got out of there completely unhurt like that."

Keira followed his gaze, seeing how deeply the driver's side was bowed in. She shivered, holding her ribs where the door handle had slammed into them. But they felt fine. Perfect, even.

"I'm just tough, I guess," she said. It would have sounded a lot more convincing without the quiver in her voice.

"Yeah, I got that. You're not gonna let me open your door for you, are you?" Walker hesitated for a moment at the back of the car. The fading sunlight tangled in his hair, glimmering around his head like a halo.

Keira slipped around him to the passenger side. "Not a chance."

"One step at a time," he muttered, clicking open the doors with his key fob.

Keira slid into the car. The smell of Walker surrounded her. A steel travel coffee mug sat in the cup holder, and the floor was littered with paper napkins and straw wrappers.

Walker climbed in next to her and started the car. The engine turned over on the first try. Keira tried not to be jealous.

"Nice car," she said mildly.

"Thanks," said Walker, slinging an arm behind her leather seat. He turned to look out the back window as he pulled out of the parking space. "You'd think someone would've noticed that I'd stolen it by now."

Keira froze in her seat. "You're—are you kidding?"

"Um, yeah. I am."

A muscle in her jaw jumped as she clenched her teeth.

"Do I really look like someone who would steal a car?" he asked incredulously.

"Listen, I barely know you," she said defensively.

"Fair," he said, hesitating at the edge of the parking lot. "But that's only because you tried to go running off before we finished talking earlier. Which way?" He gestured toward the street.

"East to Madison and then right," she said.

"So, no, the car's not stolen. I came here with . . . I mean, my parents left me enough money for a lousy car and a decent apartment, or a nice car and a crappy apartment."

"And you picked the *car*?"

A wash of pink in Walker's cheeks revealed a hint of embarrassment. "I'm a guy," he said. "Of course I picked the car."

Seeing his bravado momentarily waver softened Keira.

"I guess everyone has that one thing that they can't resist spending money on, huh?" she said. "Susan's always harping at me about how I could have better clothes or a decent car if I didn't spend so much money on music."

"Exactly." He relaxed, looping one hand through the steering wheel. "But I don't think you need better clothes. You'd only be torturing the male population of Sherwin."

He wasn't the first guy who'd told her she was hot, but he was the first one who'd ever said it in a way that made her feel beautiful. He made it sound like something obvious. The compliment warmed her more quickly than the heat streaming out of the air vents.

Walker turned onto Madison and Keira gasped.

There was a door in the middle of the road. A door, standing there all on its own, like the entrance to some sort of grand house that had moved away and left it behind. It was intricately carved, with a pattern of circles and interconnected lines. It had a worn metal handle, but with only the bleak meridian of Madison Street behind it, there didn't seem to be any reason to open it. In front of the door, a swath of impossibly dark shadow lay like a doormat.

Or a threshold.

Walker drove straight toward the door, completely oblivious to it. Part of her wanted to scream that she was about to be in a second car wreck in as many hours, but she watched the car in front of them pass through it like a mirage.

Because I'm hallucinating. Again. It was exactly like what had happened with the fruit in the kitchen. *Oh, God.*

She reached up to touch the side of her head. Maybe she had smacked it when the SUV hit her car, after all. If she had a concussion, that might explain the sudden appearance of a door that no one else could see.

A shocked yelp slipped out of her mouth as the door handle whipped through the car between her and Walker, then disappeared through the backseat. Keira bit her lip.

"Uh . . . you okay?" The rumble of Walker's voice shook her back to reality. He leaned forward in his seat, like he was on alert, as if she might throw up or freak out. It was the same way people in school looked at Kendall Philips last year, after her boyfriend dumped her and she'd lost it and smashed in his locker door with a softball bat.

She glanced in the rearview mirror. The door was gone— the only thing behind them was a rusted-out Cadillac. Keira dropped her hand from her head. Her scalp wasn't tender at all—no lumps. No bumps. Whatever was wrong with her was obviously not from the wreck.

Obviously.

Anxious, she launched into a finger exercise, playing the notes on her lap. "I don't know. I guess maybe I did crack my head, after all," she said. "I'm seeing—my vision's kind of funny."

Walker's next words were as careful as a Bach composition. "Funny how, exactly?"

She shook her head. She didn't want him to think she was crazy. The thought of him shaking her off like some sort of lunatic he'd found muttering on the street corner made her ache.

The entrance to her neighborhood loomed on the right. "This is my turn." She pointed. "Take the first two lefts and we're the second house on the right."

He fixed his eyes on the street in front of them and put on his turn signal. A muscle in his jaw jumped, and she noticed that his knuckles had gone white around the steering wheel. "Seriously, Keira—if something's wrong with your head, you can tell me. You *should* tell me."

His sudden intensity sent a shiver through her. He didn't seem cocky anymore, and there was an edge in his demeanor that she hadn't seen before. She licked her lips, weighing her response. In her bag, her phone began to ring. The ridiculous ringtone broke the tension in the car.

"I bet that's my mom." She bent and wrenched open the front pocket of her bag, digging frantically until she came up with her phone. Keira had never been so grateful for a distraction—even if it did mean dealing with a thousand questions from her panicked mother.

Chapter Nine

"KEIRA?! I JUST GOT your message." Her mother sounded frantic. Keira could hear the slip-slosh noise of papers being thrown into desk drawers. "What happened? Where are you? I'm coming right now."

"Mom, *calm down*. I'm fine. I called the insurance company and a tow truck, and Walker's driving me home. The car . . ." She hesitated, seeing the damage in her mind's eye. "The car's pretty bad."

"I don't care one whit about that old car, as long as you're not hurt. And who on earth is Walker?" Her mother demanded. "I haven't heard that name before."

"He's just a friend, Mom. From the music store."

Walker shot her a sly look when she said the word "friend." The way his lips quirked up at the corners said that he had every intention of making a liar out of her, but then his face darkened. He cracked his neck uncomfortably.

Keira watched him out of the corner of her eye. "We were having coffee before the guy ran into me. Walker stayed to help."

Her mom made a skeptical noise. She always made little "oh, it's too bad you're not going to the dance with all of your friends" comments when homecoming and the winter ball rolled around, but Keira knew that her mom was secretly relieved that she didn't date. It was one less thing to worry about.

"Well, I'd like to meet him. I need to thank him, anyway. I can't believe I wasn't available when you called. The *one* time I had to take shorthand all week, and *this* happens. And where is your father? Did you try him at work?"

"I did, but it went straight to voice mail."

"Oh, nice," her mom snarked.

Walker pulled into the driveway, and Keira felt a rising flood of embarrassment lapping at her ankles. She saw the faded siding and the wild tangle of untrimmed bushes with fresh eyes. It was all so shabby.

"Mom, we're here. I'm gonna go, and I'll see—"

"Wait," her mother interrupted. "I'm in the car. Have Walker stay for a few minutes. I want to meet him."

"Mom, we're just *friends*. And I'm sure Walker has other stuff to do tonight, besides hanging out until you get home."

Walker turned off the car. "Nope," he said, loud enough for her mother to hear. "I'd be happy to stay and say 'hi' to your mom. Besides—" He lowered his voice enough that the phone wouldn't catch it. "If your 'vision's funny' then you shouldn't really be here alone." He raised his eyebrow pointedly.

"Good," her mother chirped in Keira's ear. "I won't be more than fifteen minutes. Twenty, tops, if there's traffic. See you then!"

Keira ended the call and closed her eyes. When she opened them, Walker was staring at her expectantly.

"Well, are you going to invite me in?"

She grabbed her bag off the floor without even bothering to zip it shut. "Fine. Come on in. But when my mother starts with the fake Junior League act and the snippy comments about the mistakes people make when they're young, don't expect me to rescue you."

Walker's charcoal eyes widened. "Hey. I *did* save you from having to ride home with Shrimp."

Keira's shoulders sagged. He was right. He'd done her a favor and she was being prickly as a thistle. Just because he'd managed to slip through all her hot-guy defenses didn't make it okay for her to act like a brat.

"Sorry. You're right. Mostly, I'm embarrassed about what my mother's going to put you through when she gets here."

"Mostly?"

Keira paused. "Yeah. The rest of it is that I don't get exactly what's going on here." With her finger, she drew an oval in the air between herself and Walker. "I don't like that feeling. It makes me grumpy."

Walker stretched his hand toward her, slow enough that she had time to back away if she wanted to. But she didn't want to move away from his touch. She stayed where she was and let him brush back a strand of hair that had escaped her ponytail.

"If it makes you feel any better, I don't know exactly what's going on here either. You're not the only one whose plans *this*"—he drew the same oval in the air that Keira had—"might be messing with."

Keira cocked her head to the side. "Really? What are your 'plans,' anyway?"

"You know, get a degree in music engineering, total domination of the human race—the usual sort of stuff." With the same devilish smile he gave her every time they shared a joke— the smile Keira was already starting to think of as *her* smile— Walker swung open his door and stepped out of the car.

Things looked even worse inside the house. Her father's breakfast dishes were congealing on the kitchen counter, and a pile of laundry was strewn across the dining room table. A pair of her underwear, decorated with hot-pink polka dots, lay draped across the top like the flag at the summit of a mountain. She shoved the pile onto one of the chairs, burying the underwear beneath a couple of T-shirts.

"Sorry—it's not usually this messy in here. My parents have both been working a lot." She was babbling.

She hated babbling.

She shut her mouth and turned to Walker. There was a twinkle in his eyes that made her wonder if she hadn't been fast enough with the laundry.

"So. This is the wonder that is my house," she said. "We can wait for my mom in the living room, or sit at the kitchen table . . ."

"I want to hear you play."

"You—really?"

Walker stepped close to her. The tips of his black boots brushed against her shoes and he took her hand. Her fingers curled around his, and she let him lead her toward the gleaming piano.

"This is gorgeous," he said, running his finger around the curve at the back of the piano.

"Thanks. My uncle left it to us when he died. It's pretty much the only nice thing in our house."

Walker peered at the rows of strings and hammers beneath the open top. "It's so . . . complicated."

"Not really." Keira slid onto the bench, feeling more comfortable than she had all afternoon. "But wait until you hear how it sounds."

She positioned her hands above the keyboard, hesitating for a moment while she decided what to play. She'd been practicing the new Beethoven piece so often that it was waiting in the tips of her fingers, but it didn't fit what she was feeling right then, and it wasn't 100 percent perfect yet. She didn't play anything for anyone unless it was perfect.

Finally, something came to mind. She hadn't practiced the piece in ages, but it would be exactly right. Rachmaninoff. The Prelude in C-sharp minor. With her fingers poised on the keys and her feet on the pedals, she started to play, her left hand reaching way down the keyboard for the low notes that marked the first lines. The music flowed through the piano, filling the room with its dark, sweet sound. Her eyes closed for a moment as the tempo built, rising in intensity until the room crackled with it. Her fingers flew over the keys, and the rhythmic thrum of her foot against the pedal was as natural as breathing. The music carried her up, sweeping her into the crescendo, washing away all her tension and uncertainty.

The final, rising chord sang in the room even after she'd taken her hands from the ivory keys and dropped them into her lap. With a satisfied sigh, she looked up, flipping a strand of hair out of her eyes.

Walker stared at her, pale as snow.

"That's the most incredible thing I've ever seen anyone do." His voice was gravelly. "That was unbelievable, Keira. *You're* unbelievable."

She smiled. "Thanks."

Holding her gaze, he stepped around the keyboard and sat

down next to her on the bench. "No, I mean it. I'm not giving you some random compliment." He swallowed hard. "Where I come from, music is *everything*. And no one can do anything remotely like what you just did. Growing up, I spent years trying to play. *Years.* Piano and violin and dulcimer—whatever I could get my hands on. And it never worked. I was terrible at everything."

"It's not for everyone," Keira offered, slouching into herself as though she were protecting her talent. As though Walker might want it badly enough to twist it right out of her.

"I know. That's the problem. But you . . ." He shook his head slowly, his eyes never leaving hers. "Do you know how you look when you play? It's like you're making the music from scratch. I could almost taste it."

The compliment washed over Keira. "I guess we're all good at different stuff. I mean, I suck at math and history. And I draw like a three-year-old."

The intensity of Walker's iron-hard expression cracked. A laugh slipped from his mouth like steam. "Really?" He eyed her. "I'm not sure I believe you."

"Believe it," Keira said. "Stick figures are about as good as I get." She leaned against the edge of the keyboard. "So what about you? You must have a talent of some sort. What are you good at?"

Walker tipped his head to one side. The inviting set of his shoulders, the way his hands slid across the wooden curves of her piano—it was a reply all its own, and it sent an ache through her. "Numbers. Sleight-of-hand. Making you blush." He ticked them off on his fingers, his lips curving up when the hot flush in her cheeks proved him right.

In the hall, the front door flew open and Keira's mom came rushing into the house and dropped her briefcase with a thud. "Keira! Thank goodness you're okay. Let me look at you."

Walker slid off the bench and stood with his hands in his pockets while her mother checked her hands and peered into her eyes. "Are you sore anywhere? Any bruises?"

"No, I'm fine."

"She was complaining about her vision being weird," Walker offered.

Keira shot him a dirty look, then turned back to her mother—and immediately panicked.

Her mom's tired, dark-ringed eyes and bobbed hair were the picture of normal. It was the enormous black tree that had appeared behind her mother that freaked Keira out.

Chapter Ten

OH, SHIT. NOT AGAIN.

The tree trunk was covered in deep-ridged bark and the lowest branches were thick with wine-red leaves and the same strange, oblong fruit she'd seen on the kitchen counter. Obviously, that had *not* been some sort of gourmet banana. The tree seemed to be growing straight up through the ceiling. Keira couldn't see the upper branches—the tree looked like it had been neatly sliced off by the second story of her house.

She was too shocked to speak, too shocked to move. Even her blood seemed to hesitate in her veins. Part of her was convinced that she was losing her mind. Normal people didn't see fruit that wasn't real. Doors in the middle of the street. Strange trees in the living room. But she felt so *sane*.

"Keira? You do look paler than usual. Are you sure you didn't hit your head?"

"I'm *fine*," she insisted. "If I'd hit my head, I'd probably be throwing up or seeing things that weren't there, right?" Saying it out loud was a sort of test. To see how crazy it sounded.

Her mom let out a thin laugh, but behind her, Keira heard Walker suck in a sharp breath. She shifted in her seat, glancing at him out of the corner of her eye.

He stood rigid, staring at her, his eyes round as a shark's. He looked like he was seeing her for the first time—like he suddenly recognized her somehow. Her eyebrows lifted in response, but before she could say anything—before she could even think of what she might say, her mother pounced on Walker, shaking his hand like he was some sort of minor celebrity.

"And you must be Walker! I'm so glad that you were there to help Keira this afternoon."

Walker blinked, sliding his most charming smile into place like a shield. The tree loomed over them, shivering in a wind that Keira could neither hear nor feel, but that nonetheless chilled her to the bone.

Walker cleared his throat. "Well, Keira actually didn't seem to need much help. Even after a bad car wreck . . ." His words slowed, like he was turning them over, looking for some

sort of secret hidden underneath. "A *terrible* car wreck . . .
Keira's very . . . capable. Independent."

"But you stayed with her, *and* you gave her a ride home,"
her mother insisted. "That was way above and beyond. I'm
grateful for that."

"It was my pleasure, really," Walker said, his gaze shifting
from Keira's mother back to her.

"Well, I'm glad Keira was with someone so considerate."
Behind her, one of the fruits fell from the tree. The instant it
would have landed—should have landed—on the carpet, it disappeared, taking the vision of the tree along with it. There was
nothing abnormal left in the living room—Keira had a perfect
view of the sagging couch and the dusty picture frames on the
mantel.

The simultaneous relief and embarrassment overwhelmed
her. Keira felt herself start to flush. "Mom! Please."

"All I'm saying is that I appreciate that he's being nice to you!"
Keira's mother snapped. She turned back to Walker. "I'd invite
you to stay for dinner, but I think Keira should probably rest, and
we need to call the body shop before they close." She tapped her
knuckle against her forehead, thinking. "Oh! And I should call
the insurance adjuster too. Maybe dinner one night soon?"

"I'd like that." Walker looked straight at Keira. "A lot."

Heat spread through Keira that had nothing to do with
being embarrassed. All at once, her mother was incredibly *in
the way* and Keira just wanted her out of the room.

Walker started for the door. "I'll head out," he said, sticking his hands back in his pockets, which made him look almost vulnerable. He looked over at Keira's mom. "It was really nice to meet you, Mrs. Brannon."

"You too, Walker." Her mom followed him toward the door, but when Keira stood up to go with them, her mother raised a warning finger. "Oh, no you don't. You stay right there. As soon as I see Walker off, I'm going to get you settled on the couch and you are going to take it *easy*, young lady."

Walker waved as he headed out the door.

"Handsome *and* charming," her mother said as she watched his car pull out of the driveway. She sighed. "Don't let him turn your head, though," she warned Keira. "You don't want to end up stuck because of some guy. Trust me. I wasn't that much older than you when I met your father. We shouldn't have gotten engaged so young. We were just babies."

The story had gotten more bitter over the last couple of years. When Keira was little, her mother's cheeks would bloom pink when she got to the proposal bit, and the pinprick diamond of her engagement ring would sparkle as she spun it around her finger. Back then, the story went that Keira's dad's love was even bigger and stronger than her mom's singing voice.

The phone rang and Keira's mom hurried across the room. She glanced at the caller ID. "Speak of the devil," she muttered.

"Hello? Dennis?" Her mother headed into the kitchen. "Yeah, she's fine." She dropped her voice, but it didn't stop

Keira from hearing. "What I want to know is where the hell *you've* been all afternoon."

While her mother banged pots and cracked open cans, Keira sneaked back over to the piano. Nothing hurt, and she knew that the visions had nothing to do with hitting her head. Not when they'd started before the accident.

Slowly, quietly, she started to play the Goldberg Variations. It was calm. Logical. It was good music for thinking and she had so much to think about—like the possibility that she was losing her mind. Or whether Walker could have seen the same visions, which seemed even crazier. Superimposed over all of it was the thrill that went through her every time she thought of Walker—the feeling that something had begun between the two of them that Keira wasn't going to be able to stop.

She stayed at the piano while her parents argued over the phone and dinner simmered on the stove. The music soothed her, but no matter how long she played, it didn't answer any of her questions.

Later that night, when she was supposed to be in bed, Keira called Susan.

Susan answered, sounding vaguely out of breath.

"Hey," Keira said. "You busy?"

"Nah. I just got home. I was literally one minute past curfew."

"Did your mom freak?"

"A hundred percent. I'm actually not allowed to see Tommy

alone anymore. Which is completely ridiculous. Oh—there was one good thing, though. My flute teacher loved 'Syrinx.' She was—and I quote—'impressed' with me for picking it."

Susan's flute lesson sounded so normal—so impossibly normal and far away from everything that Keira had been worrying about with Walker and the accident and the strange things she was seeing. It took her a minute to remember picking out the music in the first place, which startled her. Music was always the first thing on her mind. It was *supposed* to be the first thing on her mind. And now it wasn't.

"Oh—oh, good," Keira stammered.

"You sound kind of weird," Susan observed. "Did everything go okay with Walker? Because I was really hoping the two of you would go to dinner with me and Tommy next weekend, what with the whole no-more-solo-dates dictum my parents just handed me."

"It's not Walker—I wrecked my car. Some moron in an SUV slammed into my door like I was invisible." Absentmindedly, Keira ran a hand down her left side, feeling her impossibly intact ribs.

Susan's gasp crackled through the phone. "Oh, my God! Are you hurt? Is your car okay?"

"I'm fine, which is kind of a miracle, because my car was— is—totally smashed up. Walker thinks the insurance company's going to total it." She sighed, wondering if the payout would be enough to buy her another car, or if she'd be stuck begging rides and catching the bus.

"Wait—this was before or after you met Walker?"

"After. I was actually leaving the diner when it happened. He stayed while I waited for the tow truck. I think he wanted to make sure my brain wasn't going to start leaking out of my ears or something."

"That's totally sweet." Susan sounded pleased.

"It was pretty helpful," Keira admitted. "He saved me from having to get a ride home with the creepy tow truck guy."

"So you got a ride with the helpful hot guy instead?" Susan asked pointedly. "He *rescued* you, Keira. You have to see him again after that, right?"

The desire to pretend that Walker didn't mean anything to her rose up in Keira, curling around her like some sort of fast-growing vine. Still, the way she'd felt when they touched, and how he'd stared at her after she'd played for him—she couldn't act like those things hadn't meant something.

"He didn't 'rescue' me. He gave me a ride home. Which actually isn't all that uncommon at the end of a date."

"So it *was* a date!" Susan crowed. "And you like him enough to see him again next week. Just once. For me?" It wasn't really a question. "I'll plan it all. Dinner and a movie. You won't have to do anything except call and tell him when and where."

"I'm not sure I can give up that much practice time," Keira hedged.

Susan ignored her. "I'll check with Tommy about what day, and then I'll call you back."

"I'd rather make plans just with you," Keira insisted. "Speaking of which, do you want to come over this weekend? I could accompany you on 'Syrinx,' if you want to practice."

She rubbed her forehead, hoping Susan would take the bait. All she'd wanted was to call her best friend and moan about her wrecked car. And maybe, God forbid, talk her way through the confusion that Walker had stirred up inside her. Instead, here she was trying to keep Susan from forcing her into an faux relationship with someone Keira wasn't even sure she had room for in her life—no matter how scaldingly hot he was.

"That would be great, actually," Susan said. "My teacher was happy, but she seemed a little worried about whether I'd be able to pull it off. If you help me, though, I know I'll be able to get it. What about Sunday afternoon?"

"Perfect," Keira said. "I'll see you then."

They hung up. With the phone still in her hand, Keira flopped back on her pillow and threw her arm over her eyes.

There was no way she was getting out of this double date. And, in the darkest little corner of her heart, she knew she didn't really want to get out of it anyway.

What am I thinking?

She was thinking about his low-note voice.

She was thinking about his knowing grin.

But mostly, she was thinking about the things he'd told her after she'd played for him, and how much she wanted a chance to talk to him again. Even if it meant breaking her own rules.

Chapter Eleven

THE NEXT MORNING, KEIRA wandered into the kitchen, her eyes gritty with sleep and the bitter taste of yesterday's weirdness still thick on her tongue. Her mom was sitting at the table. She'd obviously been waiting for Keira.

"Hey, sweetie. How'd you sleep?" she asked. Her hands were curled tight around her coffee mug. There was something overly alert about her—like she was spring-loaded. Keira was surprised to see her. Usually her parents both evacuated the house early on Saturday, like refugees fleeing a coming war.

"Fine, I guess." Keira opened the pantry and blinked at the boxes of tea.

Her mother relaxed the grip on her cup a bit. "Oh, good. I was worried. I didn't want to leave until I knew you were okay."

"I'm okay," Keira said, doubting every word, but telling her mother she was seeing strange stuff wasn't exactly something she was going to throw out there first thing in the morning. She stumbled over to the cupboard and got out a mug. "Is Dad here too?" Her parents hadn't *both* stayed home on a Saturday morning since last fall, when they'd simultaneously come down with the stomach flu.

"Um, no. He isn't."

Something in her mother's voice made Keira freeze with her hand halfway to the faucet handle. Her mom was strangling her coffee cup, staring down into its depths like it was going to tell her what to say.

"Is he playing racquetball?" Keira asked, slowly setting her empty cup on the counter. Her dad had a standing racquetball time on Saturday mornings.

"I'm not sure," her mother said, still not looking at her. "He didn't come home last night."

"Okaaay." Keira's voice was slow and thick as honey. "Why?"

Her mother's eyes traced the pattern of the placemat in front of her. "We had a fight."

"You have a lot of fights," Keira pointed out.

Her mother blanched. "It was a particularly bad one. I'm sorry, honey. I hate that you see so much of this."

"So, where is he now? Where did he stay?" Keira asked.

"I don't know." Her mother's lips pressed into a thin line.

"When is he coming home? He—he is coming home, right?"

Her mother stood up from the table abruptly. "I'm sure it will all work out," she said. "I'm going to take a shower. I didn't get much sleep last night and this coffee isn't cutting it. Be out in a minute, okay?" Keira heard her mother's voice crack on the last word, but she was already halfway down the hall. The shower thrummed to life a moment later.

Keira slumped against the kitchen cabinets, trying to make sense of everything her mother had just told her. She'd known things between her parents were bad, but not *that* bad. Her mother hadn't even said for sure that her dad was coming home at all.

Keira abandoned her tea-making and headed into the living room. She sat at the piano with her hands in her lap, staring at the keys. She put her fingers in position and started running scales, but they sounded wooden.

How could she not have realized things were so terrible in her own family? Her parents were on the verge of splitting up and she was losing her mind.

Fabulous.

Shaking out her shoulders, Keira launched into one her favorite études. Something simple, that she'd been playing since she was thirteen. It was like the musical version of sweatpants. Soft. Comfortable. Easy. But three lines in, her fingers froze.

Her hands didn't know what to do next, the muscle memory pushed aside by the worry ringing in her head.

Dad slept somewhere else last night.

And probably better than he'd been sleeping at home, what with her waking him up in the middle of the night while she tried to grab exotic bananas that didn't even exist. She wondered if that had been the last straw, but as soon as she'd thought it, she knew it wasn't about her at all. That her parents' problems had been building for years—she just never thought they'd actually get to this point.

Growling with frustration, Keira launched straight into the Allegretto movement of the Beethoven sonata she'd been working on. It was the hardest, most mind-consuming piece of music she knew. She flew through the first twenty bars without a hitch, but just as she was starting to relax into the music, the shower shut off. In the sudden silence, Keira heard something small break in the bathroom, and then her mother's teary voice, swearing at whatever it had been. Keira's fingers slipped and the music turned into a discordant mess.

Shaken, Keira rubbed the back of her neck and tried again, but the notes wouldn't come. She remembered the wrong bars at the wrong time—her fingers hit the keys next to the ones they should have touched.

She never had trouble getting into her practice. It never sounded this bad. This *amateur.* In the bathroom, her mother's hair dryer began to whir.

As Keira put her fingers back against the keys, the house phone started to ring. Grateful for the interruption, she hurried to pick it up, hoping it might be her dad.

Her stomach sank when the number on the caller ID wasn't one Keira recognized.

Chapter Twelve

"HELLO?" SHE SNARLED INTO the phone.

"Are you always this cheerful in the morning?"

The accent was rich and smooth and foreign.

Walker.

"Uh, this is Keira, right?" He suddenly sounded uncertain.

"Yeah, it's me. You caught me off-guard. I don't remember giving you my number."

"You didn't."

"So how did you get it?" Doubt flooded Keira. Maybe he was creepy—tracking down her number seemed kind of stalker-ish.

"There's this remarkable thing called a phone book." He half stifled a laugh. "I looked you up. There are only two Brannons in Sherwin. An old lady's voice mail answered at the other number. I hoped this one would be you."

Keira perched on the arm of the couch. "Sorry. I didn't mean to snap at you. It's been a weird morning."

"Really? What happened?"

Immediately, Keira wished she could take back her admission. She didn't want to talk to Walker about her parents. "It's complicated."

"Isn't it always?"

Keira laughed. She picked at a loose thread on the couch. "Yeah. True. So, what's up?"

"I wanted to hear what you sound like in the morning."

Keira felt her blood begin to hum just beneath her skin. Her voice froze in her throat.

"You sound nice, you know. Your voice is rougher. I like that."

Keira cleared her throat self-consciously. "Thanks, I guess. Uh, if that's all you needed—"

"You also left your driver's license in my car," Walker cut in.

"I did?" Keira dove for the front pocket of her bag, where the contents of her wallet lay in chaos. "Oh, God, how could I have done that? I'm sorry," she apologized.

"Don't apologize. I wanted an excuse to see you again, anyway. It worked out perfectly. Are you busy this afternoon? I could bring it over."

Keira let out a long, slow breath. She knew she should say no. But she needed her license.

And she wanted to see him again too. Even if it was only for a minute.

"I really have to practice, but I could take a break. A short one. And—I'd appreciate it. I don't want you to have to go out of your way."

"It's not out of my way. I'll be there about three."

"Sounds good," Keira whispered.

"See you then."

Keira tossed the phone onto the front hall table and went back to her abandoned tea. Three o'clock seemed much further away than it should have. If her stomach stayed this fluttery until then, it was going to be a very, very long day.

She spent the day drifting back and forth between the piano and homework. She couldn't focus on either of them. It actually felt better to be staring uselessly at her homework—she was used to that. The crawling need to glance over her shoulder while she sat at the piano, to see if the creepy tree had reappeared in her living room—that was new. And terrifying. Even scarier than the thought of losing her mind was the idea that she might lose her music. She couldn't handle that.

When she was ten, her dad had a minor heart attack and spent a couple of days in the hospital. To cope, she'd managed to lose herself in Clementi's sonatas. The week before she'd started high school, she was nearly blinded by the anxiety of facing grades that "counted" and small-minded girls who'd judge her clothes instead of her music. She'd still managed to shrug it all off with Chopin.

But now her music wasn't working. She tried the first harsh chords of a Stravinsky piano concerto, but the keys felt dead against her fingers. She swept her music off the stand, the pages scattering against the floor.

She pushed away from the piano in disgust, nearly knocking over the bench as its legs snagged on the carpet. She caught it right before it fell, remorse spilling through her. She carefully set the bench in front of the piano, as if that could apologize for her outburst.

It wasn't her instrument's fault that she was so screwed up.

Briefly, she wondered if apologizing to a piano was as crazy as it sounded. She'd always talked to it in her head the way other people spoke to their cars or their dogs. But maybe it was a warning sign—proof that she'd never been completely stable to begin with.

The front door clicked open, and she whirled around, half expecting to see Walker. He *would* just walk in uninvited.

But it wasn't Walker who stepped through the door. Her dad crept into the house like he was sneaking in after curfew. He glanced at the living room and noticed Keira, still bent over her piano bench.

She straightened, swallowing hard as she took in his

day-old clothes and the stubble that darkened his chin. They were both reminders of the time he'd spent elsewhere—away from their house, away from his things. Away from *her*. It made the distance between them seem much larger than a few steps across the living room.

"Hey, sweetie." Her dad cleared his throat. "I didn't mean to interrupt."

She wanted to know where he'd been and what was going on and what would happen next. Instead, she nodded.

Her dad reached up and rubbed the back of his neck.

"I'm sorry I wasn't here after your accident. When I got your message, I was so worried—I'm so glad you're okay. I couldn't stand the thought of anything happening to you."

"It's okay. I'm fine. See?" Keira held her arms out as evidence.

"I know it's probably been a weird morning. I'm sorry. I really need to speak to your mother. As soon as we have things sorted out, you and I will talk, okay?"

More nodding. As much as she wanted to know what was going on, she didn't really want to *talk* about it. She didn't want to hear the gory, confessional details that lurked in her dad's eyes.

He headed to the back of the house, where Keira could hear her mother opening and closing dresser drawers.

She glanced at the clock above the mantel. It was two thirty. Walker would be there in half an hour. Suddenly, his visit seemed like the only bright spot in an otherwise miserable day.

Especially when her parents started yelling at each other.

By five minutes to three, Keira was hovering next to the front door, watching for any sign of Walker's car. There was no way she would let him set foot in the house. Not with the shouting and cursing that was streaming out of her parents' room.

When his car bumped over the curb and into her driveway, Keira slipped out onto the front porch and closed the door behind her. She shivered in her thin sweater.

"Were you waiting for me?" Walker's low voice swept through her like a brush fire. "I'm touched."

Keira rolled her eyes at him, matching his bravado. It felt good. Like a shield that sprang up around her, protecting her tender insides. It made her wonder what Walker was hiding under his pearl-smooth shell.

"Hardly," she said. Her parents' room faced the front yard, and the cracked window barely muffled her mother's angry voice.

"*Bastard!*" Her mom shouted. The wind chime sound of something breaking followed the epithet.

Keira winced, catching her bottom lip hard between her teeth.

Walker's gaze raked over her, and though every bit of his iron-cool attitude stayed in place, something in his eyes shifted.

"You wanna get out of here for a while? We could go for a drive," he said.

Her father's voice cut through their conversation. "I never wanted to come back here in the first place!"

Keira squared her shoulders and swallowed the tears that blocked her throat. "Yeah. Let's go," she said. "I've just gotta grab my stuff."

"You want me to wait out here? Or . . . ?" She could hear him trying to say the right thing. Not wanting to push her, which only pulled her in more. If he'd been falling all over himself with apologies and concern, she would have sent him away without a second thought.

"No, I'm good." The lie was brittle in her mouth. She darted through the door, snatched her bag off the floor and hurried back outside. She headed straight for the car.

"Can I open your door today?" Walker asked.

A snarky comment about having two perfectly functional hands melted on her tongue. She'd had such a disturbingly bad practice session this morning that maybe her hands weren't so functional after all.

Instead, she smiled at him, though the edges of it felt cracked and artificial. "I think you've been chivalrous enough today. I can open my own door."

He laughed at her, then his eyes went wide. "Oh! That reminds me." He reached into his jacket and pulled out her license, flipping it expertly over the roof of the car. Keira caught it as it sailed toward her.

"Nice reflexes." He gave her an approving nod.

She shrugged. "Nice throw." They climbed into the car. "So, let me guess. You played Little League?"

"Nope," Walker said. "No baseball. I've always preferred card tricks."

"Like, 'pick a card, any card'?" Keira asked. As the wet pavement of the street slipped beneath the car's tires, Keira felt herself start to relax.

"Exactly. I don't do them much anymore, but my fingers still have a feel for it."

"Muscle memory," Keira said.

Walker cocked his head to one side. "That's precisely what it feels like."

"That's what it *is*. The technical term for it. It's part of piano playing too—how your fingers know where to go to hit a major seventh, or how far to stretch for the D-below-middle-C key."

"Ironic."

She glanced at him out of the corner of her eye. "Ironic? How?"

"That's what always kept me from being able to play an instrument. I would be looking at the notes on the page and my fingers would freeze." He looked over at her, the gray of his eyes soft—honest. "I hated it. I could see the music—I could hear it, even, in my head. But I couldn't make my hands do what they were supposed to do. It was so frustrating."

"That's how I feel when I try to do pretty much anything besides playing the piano," she admitted.

"This is the whole 'I draw like a three-year-old' thing, isn't it?" he asked. The teasing was gentle.

Keira laughed. "Yeah. But that's not the only thing. I had a seriously bad incident involving juggling in the eighth grade. I gave the gym teacher a black eye."

Walker turned the car onto the highway. "Your laugh is gorgeous," he said.

The compliment blazed across the skin of her neck, making her insides molten.

"Um—thanks," she stammered, staring out at the highway markers that flew past her window. "Where are we going, anyway?"

Walker glanced over at her. "We could go get coffee. Or . . . there's this other place. I love to go there when it's foggy like it is today. But it's all the way down by the coast. And it's up a pretty decent climb. I don't know if you'd be up for it."

The challenge in his words made the idea irresistible to Keira. A little voice in the back of her head said that Walker had known it would do exactly that.

"I don't think my parents are going to care if I'm gone for a while." Her voice was bitter. It was the closest she'd come to mentioning the death spiral of her parents' marriage. It was the closest she thought she *could* come to mentioning it.

Without taking his eyes off the road, Walker nodded. "I know what you mean."

His parents were gone—she couldn't even imagine how

much worse that would be than having parents who didn't love each other. Part of her wanted to say something, to cluck and sympathize, the way the other girls at school would have. But she knew that if she did, the wall he'd been taking down, brick by brick, would go flying up again in an instant. It was exactly what Keira would do, in the same situation. So she kept her hands folded in her lap and stared down at her feet.

"Well, I'm glad I wore my boots," she said.

Walker turned to look at her, his face lit with a deadly sexy grin.

"Me too." Hitting the accelerator, he slung an arm around the back of her seat, not touching Keira, but close enough that she could feel the heat of him against her neck.

She still wondered what the hell she was getting herself into, but the reproach was gone. The only thing left in its place was a tingling excitement.

Chapter Thirteen

KEIRA STARED OUT AT the jagged pile of rocks. The muddy green-gray of the waves crashed against the spit of land like they wanted to pull the rocks down into the sea. The thin, empty-sounding cry of the seabirds wheeling overhead made her quiver. She didn't like seagulls. When she was five, one had dive-bombed a sandcastle she was building, spraying sand in her face. Her dad said it was only trying to get the mussel she'd used as a flag, but that hadn't made the sand in her eyes sting any less.

"That's not good." Walker frowned at her, and Keira felt her stomach drop.

"What?" She wrapped her arms around herself. The wind coming off the ocean cut straight through her sweater. The sooner they started climbing the rocks, the sooner she'd warm up a little.

"You're not wearing a coat," he said. "It's cold out here."

She shrugged. "I'll be fine as soon as we start moving."

Before she could even finish the sentence, Walker had shrugged off his jacket. He stepped close to Keira and wrapped it around her. The fleece was butter soft and it was still warm. Plus, it smelled like him.

Reluctantly, she slid her arms into the fleece. The cuffs flapped at her fingertips. "But now you'll be cold."

He shook his head, plucking at his thick, charcoal-gray thermal. It clung to his chest in a way that made Keira's heart-beat leap in response.

"This is super warm," he said. "I'll be fine. And either you're wearing the jacket or we're leaving."

Frowning, Keira looked up at the rocks. She wanted to know what the view looked like from the top.

She relented, heading toward the end of the point. "Okay, fine. But if you get sick or something—"

He interrupted. "If I get sick it'll have been worth it." He gestured at the stones. "Ladies first. Unless you want me to show you the way up."

She shook her head and scrambled up the rocks. She'd been climbing around the Maine coast since she was a kid—her dad used to bring her down for lobster rolls and tide-pool watching on Saturdays. The memory made her eyes sting. She blinked hard, focusing on the salty sting of the cold rocks beneath her hands and the smell of flint and peat smoke that drifted up from Walker's jacket.

It only took a few minutes of hard climbing before Keira found herself up at the top, standing on a broad, flat rock. The fog was thicker up here, obscuring the ocean that crashed below.

Walker pulled himself up behind her, his cheeks flushed pink with the cold air and the effort of the climb.

"What do you think?" he asked.

Keira looked at the fog swirling around them like tattered gauze. She couldn't even see where the point joined the mainland. The keening birds were lost in the white overhead, and the dark, seething ocean was barely visible below. It was like being on the inside of an egg. She could hear everything that happened outside the thin, cream-colored shell of the fog, but the only thing she could see were the gray rocks beneath them.

And Walker.

A violent wave crashed against the point, and the rush of noise thrilled Keira.

"It's like the ocean's sneaking up on us," she said.

Walker's face lit up. "I love that. I think it feels like playing hide-and-seek with the universe." He stared out at the invisible horizon. "When I discovered it, I felt like I'd found the perfect hiding place."

She'd never seen him look so relaxed. The corners of his eyes even crinkled up when he smiled. She took a step closer to the edge of the rock. The wind caught her hair. It whipped around her face, stinging her eyes and pasting itself across her mouth.

"Don't get too close to the edge," Walker warned. "The spray makes it slippery."

Just then, another wave bashed against the rocks and the ocean spat square in her face.

"Ugh!" She spun away from the spray, putting her arm across her eyes. She wiped at the salty mess, but the dangling jacket sleeves made it hard to get the hair and salt water off her face.

"Let me help." She felt the brush of fabric against her face, as he used his sleeve to wipe her forehead and cheeks.

Keira looked up at him, filled with an electric flood, like she'd touched a live wire.

With his gaze locked on hers, he smoothed her ponytail and tucked it into the jacket collar. Keira's knees felt uncertain beneath her.

"Thanks," she whispered.

He cocked an eyebrow at her. "Sure."

Keira swallowed hard, acutely aware of the blood coursing through her veins. Walker moved a degree closer, his arms sliding around her shoulders.

Behind him, Keira saw a dark wall of round bricks spring

up. A hook-studded ladder leaned against it. A strangled cry leapt out of Keira's mouth.

Walker pulled her away from the edge of the rocks, and the red-sheened hallucination faded in front of Keira's eyes. Walker followed her gaze into the swirling fog, not letting go of Keira.

"What happened?" he asked.

For one second, she let her head dip against his chest, shaking off the vision.

I am not losing my mind. I am not. I. Am. Not.

Walker kept his arm around her shoulders, a furrow of concern between his eyebrows.

Keira shoved her hands into her pockets. "It was a gull," she lied. Her voice wobbled like a buoy in an uncertain sea. "It flew out of the fog right behind you." She forced a little laugh. "It scared the crap out of me. Obviously."

Walker stared at her uncertainly. "A gull? I'm surprised I didn't hear it crying."

Keira nodded. "Sorry. I swear I'm not usually that girly. I kill my own spiders and everything."

Walker threw back his head and laughed. "I'll remember that. Maybe I'll have you kill *my* spiders. I'll deal with the gulls and you can handle the eight-legged things."

"That sounds fair." Keira relaxed. The point had gone back to being another jutting bit of the Maine coast, without any unexplainable walls or mysterious ladders. It was easier to believe she was still sane when everything looked normal.

"I think I'd better take you home," Walker said.

Disappointment swept through Keira, but it washed away when Walker reached down and took her hand. His warm fingers curled around her cold ones.

"I have to work tomorrow, but I want to see you again. Soon. Preferably in a seagull-free environment." A wicked smile crept across his mouth.

The wind had tugged Keira's hair free of her collar, and it danced around her face. She let it slide across her neck and stream past her cheeks. It made her feel stronger—more free.

Like she could say yes.

"I'd like that," she said, her words half-lost in the wind.

Walker's eyes narrowed, the gray in them darkening like a wet stone. "You do know that I'm asking you on a date, right?"

"I know. What part of 'yes' are you not getting?" she shot back at him.

He shook his head, but the smile on his face was genuine. "You confuse the hell out of me, Keira Brannon. I like that."

"You're not exactly a typical guy."

"You have no idea how atypical I am," he said, looking down at her.

The rocks under Keira's hands suddenly felt colder, but the heat in his gaze made the biting chill feel almost pleasant against her fingers.

"Well," she said with more confidence than she felt, "I look forward to finding out. Now quit distracting me or I'm gonna fall and break my wrist and then I'll be screwed."

"And you can't play the piano with a broken wrist," Walker said.

"Yep," Keira agreed. "Now shut up!"

Walker laughed and then obediently closed his mouth. The only sounds she heard as they picked their way down the rocks were the rush of the ocean and the call of the seabirds overhead.

Chapter Fourteen

THAT NIGHT, KEIRA SAT in her silent house and stared at her cell phone. Her parents had "gone out to dinner," though if she had to guess, they'd hit a drive-thru and were continuing their screaming match in the car. There was no way she could have Susan over tomorrow, not with her parents locked in their own private war.

Keira called Susan to cancel their plans, but she got dumped into voice mail.

Keira was ready to cut off the call without leaving a message, but she couldn't do it. She put the phone back up to her ear.

"Hey, Suz—it's me. Listen, about tomorrow—something's happened. My parents are fighting again. It's pretty bad. Can we reschedule for sometime when they won't be home? I know you're working Monday—maybe Tuesday afternoon? Anyway. I'm sorry." She hesitated, wondering if she should say something else, but the words caught in her throat. She ended the call before she started to cry.

Keira wandered over to the piano and sat down. Keira hated bailing on plans—plans she'd been looking forward to—on account of her parents' drama.

Speaking of unresolved . . .

Her miserable practice session that morning loomed over her like a storm cloud. On the floor around the piano, her music lay scattered like the last, stubborn patches of snow in the spring. She didn't want to pick them up. She didn't want to play any of them.

But she did want to play.

Keira put her hands on the keys. She thought about Walker, and the dark, salt-rimed rocks on the coast. The memory tugged at her fingers, and a simple, eerie melody sprang from the keys. Surprised, Keira played it again, stretching her pinkie up to reach a high note that echoed the sound of the seabirds. The resulting harmony made her catch her breath.

She snatched a piece of scrap paper off the coffee table and scribbled down the notes. With the pencil tucked behind her ear, she positioned herself at the keyboard and waited. She didn't know how to turn those haunting sixteen bars into a song. She'd never composed her own music before. It hadn't held any appeal, not when there were already thousands of gorgeous pieces waiting to be played.

But she wanted to remember the way she'd felt this afternoon, for that split second before her strange vision had ruined the mood. If she could catch that moment in a song, then she could have that feeling back anytime she wanted.

She played through the short little snippet again and again, thinking of the way the ocean had sounded. How the wind had felt when it caught at her hair, and the heat of Walker's hands as he'd swept the salt water off her face.

Her fingers struck a different set of keys. A yearning tone crept under the eerie melody, lifting the song up into something hot and light. Keira grabbed the pencil and scratched the next notes onto the paper. She barely noticed that the room had grown dark. All that mattered was getting the music down on the page, because finally—*finally*—her hands felt right on the keys again.

She ran through the piece again, letting her memories drift across her mind's eye. When she thought of the bizarrely dark wall that sprang up behind Walker, she stiffened. The music pouring from her fingers became discordant. Keira slid her hands off the gleaming keys. She didn't want to write the last bit down. It didn't sound the way she wanted to—it didn't sound *right*.

But maybe, if I hadn't had a stupid hallucination . . .

Tentatively, she played the first bit of the song again, remembering how Walker had leaned in close to her. If she hadn't imagined that wall, she would have swayed toward him, until there was no space left between them. Until . . .

The music soared, so graceful that Keira's foot quivered on the pedal.

The notes came so easily when she imagined kissing him. She hadn't played like that . . . well, ever, actually.

Keira scribbled the last few measures onto the scrap paper and looked at the song that had taken shape. The evidence of her feelings for Walker lay in front of her, separated into notes and bars and rests. It was like the universe was giving her a sign that it was okay to date him. Like the music itself wanted them to be together.

Jesus. Now I really am *losing my mind.*

Keira slid the sheets of newly written music into the bottom of her basket. With a sigh, she stood up and stretched, heading into the kitchen for the most sane thing she could think of: a cup of tea.

Sunday passed in miserable silence. Susan called and invited her over, but Keira could hear Mrs. Kim clucking and hovering in the background. She didn't want to deal with Susan's overinterested mother. Mrs. Kim would have too many questions and Keira didn't have any answers.

Walker didn't call, which disappointed Keira and she spent most of the day locked in her room, avoiding her cranky parents. The one time she ran into her dad, he gave her a twenty-dollar bill, in case any "expenses" came up while she was stuck riding the bus to and from school. It was obviously guilt-money, meant to make him feel better about having been gone after her accident. But without a job, she needed the money too badly to refuse.

School was a relief on Monday, even though she had to take the bus. Susan was supposed to give her a ride, but she'd called indecently early and announced that, as part of her punishment for coming in past curfew, Mrs. Kim had forbade Susan from using her car. She'd hinted none too subtly that Keira should call Walker and ask for a ride.

As if.

Susan flopped down across from Keira at lunch.

"Hey." Keira waved her half-eaten sandwich in Susan's direction.

"Hey, yourself. Sorry I couldn't give you a ride this morning. How are things with your parents? Are they still miserable?"

"Yeah."

"That sucks. Did you at least get some good practice in?"

"No. I couldn't focus."

"Oh, that sucks! And you were stuck in the house all weekend. Maybe today'll be better, since you've gotten out and all, even if it *is* just for school."

Keira hesitated. "Actually . . . I was gone almost all after-noon on Saturday, and it didn't make any difference."

"You were gone? Where?"

Keira shut her eyes. There was no sense holding back now. "I was with Walker. We drove down to the coast and hiked around on the rocks."

Susan stopped with a pretzel halfway to her open mouth. "Like on a *date*?" The last word was a squeal.

"Yes. No. I don't know."

"What's this about a date?" Jeremy leaned over her and put his hand down on the table. She could smell his musky cologne and she wrinkled her nose, moving her sandwich away from his hand.

"Hi, Jeremy," Susan said. Keira watched as Tommy stepped up behind Susan and wrapped his arms around her. Susan jumped in surprise and then cracked up. "Hey, you," she said, tilting her head up to kiss him.

"What's going on?" he asked.

"It sounds like Keira went on a date." The singsong tone in Jeremy's voice made Keira grit her teeth.

Susan frowned. "Jeremy, you are totally butting in on a conversation that has nothing to do with you."

Tommy pulled his arms away from Susan. "Hey, Jeremy only came over to say hi," he insisted.

"Then he's way over his word limit," Keira snarked.

"Come on," Tommy said to Jeremy. "Let's get some food before they close the line.

"Fine." Jeremy put his mouth so close to Keira's ear that she could feel his breath. "But if you're open for business, I am totally taking a number."

Before Keira could think of something smart to say, the guys had disappeared into the lunch line. She settled for a disgusted groan.

"So, putting Jeremy's jerk-wad tendencies aside, what *did* happen with Walker this weekend?" Susan asked.

A wave of warmth swept through Keira. She loved Susan. "I left my license in his car by accident. When Walker came to drop it off, my parents were . . . well. I was pretty desperate to get out of there."

"Oh. Oh, wow. That's so bad. And so good."

The memory of how amazing it had been stole the words from her mouth.

"Susan?" Tommy reappeared next to their table, his voice breaking through Keira's reverie.

"Yeah?" Susan asked.

"Can I talk to you for a minute? Alone?"

Susan pursed her lips in exactly the same way that her mother did when she was pissed.

Keira swept the remains of her lunch into her bag. "I was just leaving anyway." She looked pointedly at Susan. "I'll be in the music room if you need me."

Keira spent the rest of her lunch period alone at the piano, plinking out the melody she'd written on Saturday. The sudden desire to compose still surprised her, but she couldn't resist the urge to turn her memories into music.

The lingering melody tugged at her through the rest of the day, making it hard to concentrate. When the final bell rang, Keira raced for her locker. There was only one lame bus ride standing between her and her piano. She pushed through the stream of students flooding out of the school. The sudden sunlight made her blink.

"Keira!" someone called from the parking lot.

She squinted against the sun. It was Walker. She wanted to be irritated at him for not calling, but she couldn't stop the smile that swept across her face when she saw him leaning against his car. His answering grin made the pulse in Keira's neck beat furiously.

"Who's *that*?" Jeremy's venom-filled voice stung her.

"It's—he's—" She stumbled over her words. Her own feelings about Walker were so tangled up that she couldn't have answered the question if she'd wanted to.

Jeremy pressed in closer to Keira, and Walker straightened, pushing himself off the car and squaring his shoulders. It didn't matter that there were twenty yards between them, it was a protective gesture. A possessive gesture. And Jeremy spoke "guy" much too fluently to miss it.

"What d'you see in *him*?" Jeremy huffed. "You'd be better off dating someone who knows you. Someone who's friends with the same people you are."

"We're not dating," she protested.

Jeremy stepped around to face her. "The way he's looking at you? You're dating. Or, at least, *he* thinks you are."

Over Jeremy's shoulder, she saw Walker take a step toward them. She shook her head at him.

"It's not that I don't appreciate your insight, it's just that I don't care."

"Well, *I* care." Jeremy glanced back at Walker. "Seriously, Keira. Lots of guys would *love* to date you. *Lots* of them. Guys that are *right. Here.*"

Why was he *emphasizing* so many *words*?

"I'll, uh, I'll keep that in mind," she stammered.

She strode over to Walker, shaking out her hands as if she could shake Jeremy off her.

"You okay?" Walker asked, watching Jeremy wade through a sea of freshmen.

"Fine. I think Jeremy's trying to be protective. Or something. He obviously doesn't know when to mind his own business."

Walker's expression relaxed. "I can hardly blame him for wanting to mind your business instead."

She hitched her bag up on her shoulder, trying to hide that his comment had flustered her. "So, um, what're you doing here? I thought school wasn't your thing."

He lifted an eyebrow. "It's not. But I thought you might need a ride, since your car's in the shop. And on our way to your house, I thought maybe you'd get something to eat with me."

"An after-school snack?" she teased.

Walker laughed. "Something like that."

The twenty dollars her dad had given her sat in her back pocket, begging to be used. But she'd have to give up some of her practice time.

The music she'd composed whispered its melody in her ear, making the decision for her.

"Okay. Let's eat," Keira said.

Walker opened the back door. Keira pitched in her bag and the two of them climbed into the car.

Chapter Fifteen

TEN MINUTES LATER, THEY were at the diner. Walker ordered a slice of blueberry pie and coffee, but Keira asked for a cup of tea with hers.

While the waitress was busy getting the pie out of the glass-fronted dessert case, Walker picked up his spoon and twirled it, weaving it over and under his fingers, faster and faster, until it looked impossible.

Keira's eyes widened. "How are you *doing* that?"

Walker chuckled. "Are you kidding? You play the *piano*. This is way easier. Here." He passed her the spoon, which was warm from his hands.

"Put it like this." He reached across the table and gently lifted her fingers, weaving the spoon through them. The touch of his hands made it hard to concentrate. "Then you lift your index finger."

She followed his instructions, step by step, until the spoon was flying through her fingers almost as quickly as he'd done it.

"Who's got the tea?" The waitress appeared at her elbow, startling Keira. The spoon skittered across the table. Walker caught it just before it landed in his lap.

"I've got the tea," Keira grumbled. The waitress set down their cups and plates and plodded back to the kitchen.

Keira picked up her fork and frowned at her pie. "Well, I thought I was getting it," she said.

"You were," Walker said. "You picked that up really quickly. Wait—don't do that!"

Keira froze, her fork an inch above her pie. "Don't do what?" she asked, confused.

"Don't you know you're supposed to eat the point last? Then you make a wish on it."

"Wow. So, I'm guessing you're superstitious." But even as she said it, she spun her plate around so that the crust was facing her.

Walker shrugged, stirring cream and sugar into his coffee. "I don't think you should waste a chance to make a wish. You never know, right? But the spoon spinning—seriously, you have fast hands. I should teach you some card tricks some time."

"I'd like that," Keira said, breaking into the flaky pastry with her fork and watching the purple-black blueberry filling ooze across the plate. "Why'd you quit doing them, anyway?"

Walker lifted his mug and took a long drink.

He was stalling. The wall that had been crumbling between them came inching back up.

"There didn't seem to be much future in sleight of hand," he joked, setting the mug on the table.

Keira pointed her blueberry-tinted fork at him. "You're always at your wittiest when you're avoiding something."

Walker froze. "Ouch."

Keira speared another bite of pie. "Just sayin'."

For a long moment, Walker stared at her. When he finally spoke, his voice was low. "All those years of trying to play music—and failing spectacularly, I might add—it wasn't totally my idea."

"Stage mom?" Keira guessed. She'd run into them at competitions before. Whenever she heard someone playing something with perfect technique and zero heart, there was almost always a grimly determined parent hovering somewhere in the background.

Walker shook his head. "No. The town where I come from—let's just say that the people who ran things were really counting on me to be some sort of musical genius. When it turned out I wasn't, they were disappointed. Hugely disappointed. The card tricks only highlighted the fact that my hands were gifted in all the wrong ways. My mother asked me to stop. It made her nervous."

"Were you mad at her? For making you quit something you loved? I'd run away from home before I'd stop playing the piano." As soon as she'd said them, Keira realized the words sounded unnecessarily harsh. He'd lost his mom, and here she was, practically accusing the poor woman of being a bad mother.

"I thought about running away, but I was ten. Where would I have gone?" He shook his head. "My mother was only trying to protect me. I knew it, and so I quit." The wicked grin she loved streaked across his face. "Well, mostly. I kept a deck of cards under my mattress. After my parents left, when I couldn't sleep, I would get them out and practice until my hands were numb. It was the only thing that helped."

"What happened to them—your parents, I mean? Where did they go?" Keira's voice was gentle, but she could see the question sink its claws into Walker.

"They were working for the government. I guess you could call it a scouting mission," he said bitterly, knocking back the last of his coffee. "But everyone knew they wouldn't find what they were looking for. It was a suicide mission. That's why no one was surprised when they disappeared."

Keira watched him struggle to restrain his fury—a cold, black rage that went bone deep.

"Do you have other family?"

"I have an aunt and a cousin," Walker said grudgingly. She could almost hear his teeth gritting against one another. "But they don't live in Sherwin. Smith, my cousin, visits once in a while. My aunt doesn't like it when he comes to see me."

"Why?" Keira was too curious to blunt the edge of her question before it shot out of her mouth.

Walker looked into his empty coffee cup. "Basically, my aunt thinks I'm a bad influence—that I take too many risks. She's convinced I'll follow in my parents' footsteps, and that I'm going to put her 'baby' in harm's way." He sighed. "Smith thinks that I have all the fun, and he wants in on it, you know? My aunt doesn't let him do *anything*."

Keira nodded. "Susan's parents are like that. Super overprotective." The corner of her mouth quirked up. "That's why they like me. They think *I'm* a good influence."

"Is Susan their only kid?"

"Yep."

"Smith, too. He's all my aunt Holly has. It's been hard for her. She was already a single mom, and then I came along. Who wants to be saddled with the orphaned black sheep?"

Keira turned the information over, shifting it around, fitting it into the Walker-shaped puzzle in her mind.

"What's so bad about what you're doing?"

Walker shrugged. "I'm away from home, running my own life without her input. I think she really believes that if my parents hadn't died, I wouldn't have become so independent, and Smith never would have seen me as a role model. I think she finds the fact that they're dead very *inconvenient*." The last word was so bitter that Keira could taste it on her own tongue.

"I'm sorry," she said. "But I'm glad you told me." She reached out and put a hand on his arm. Walker tensed as though he meant to pull away, but then she felt him relax. He put his hand on top of hers and shrugged. "I probably shouldn't have, but I can't see how it matters. Anyway, my parents—they thought they were protecting me. I know they really believed that it was the right thing to do. Sometimes, though . . ." He paused. His eyes met hers and his gaze prowled through her. "Sometimes it's hard to know which thing is the right one."

An obsidian tendril sprang from the table, rising into the space between them like a vine. It hovered in the open air for a moment before slithering around Walker's neck and sinking into his skin. The world seemed to slow and shrink around Keira, until all she could see was the darkness writhing against his throat. He leaned closer to her and stared, like he was watching her lose her mind. The black mark slipped out of Keira's vision, disappearing as quickly as it had come.

"Sometimes, there's more to something than meets the eye. Things not everyone notices," he whispered.

She pulled away from him. *Oh, God. He* could *tell*.

Struggling to regain her mental balance, Keira picked up her fork. Her hand hovered above the last bite of her pie. The point.

"Make a wish," Walker reminded her, signaling the waitress for the check.

Let me *be his right thing.*

There were a thousand things she should be wishing for instead of that. Sanity, for one. An acceptance letter from Juilliard. A million dollars. But instead of changing her wish, she scooped up the pie and put it in her mouth. Eating a bite of dessert had never been so terrifying. She'd just asked the universe for the most foolish thing imaginable, and even more foolishly, she didn't care.

Across from her, Walker dropped a few bills on the table. "C'mon. I'd better get you home." He offered her his hand, helping her out of the booth, but once she was on her feet, he didn't let go.

Keira didn't either.

Chapter Sixteen

As WALKER DROVE HER home, Keira snuck a glance at his profile. His dark eyes were focused on the road. In the set of his jaw, she could read the history that he'd worked so hard to hide. He'd given her something, by telling her about his parents. Trusted her. It drove her to give something back, to tell him one of her own secrets.

"So, something really bizarre happened this weekend." As soon as the words were out of her mouth, she wanted to suck them back in. They sounded so overdramatic.

"Oh yeah? What?" Walker glanced over at her.

Heat crept into Keira's cheeks, and she hated that he could

see how uncomfortable she suddenly was. But she was committed to saying something.

"I wrote a song." She stared out the window, turned resolutely away from Walker's gaze.

"Really?" he asked. There was genuine interest in his voice. "I didn't know you composed, too. Exactly how many interesting talents are you hiding from me?" There was an echo of double meaning in his voice—a question beneath the question—but it wasn't his usual innuendo.

"I don't know that I'd call it a talent. I've never actually composed anything before—that's why it was so strange. I was trying to play and it—it just wasn't *working*. And then, I don't know, it was like my fingers were making up this song on their own. Ugh. That sounds crazy."

"It doesn't sound crazy. It sounds amazing. What inspired that?" he asked.

You.

The word caught in her throat, refusing to come out. She'd wanted to share something with him, open up the way he had in the diner, but she wasn't ready to take it quite that far.

She shrugged.

"Well, I'd love to hear it," Walker said, turning on to her street.

"It's a long way from being ready," she told him, "but when it is, I promise to play it for you."

He answered her with a smile that caught her like an

undertow, dangerous and fast, dragging her toward him. Only this time, she was all too happy to go.

Inside the house, Keira dropped her bag in the front hall, wandered into the living room and hit the blinking button on the answering machine. She braced herself, waiting to hear her dad's newest excuse for missing dinner.

Instead, it was Susan. A suspiciously muffled-sounding Susan, whose voice cracked on every third word as she begged Keira to call her back.

What the hell? Why didn't she call my cell?

Keira scooped up her bag and dug out her phone.

Six missed calls.

Oh, shit.

Had it really been that loud in the diner?

Keira already had the phone to her ear and an apology on her lips.

"Wh-where were you?" The hitch in Susan's voice was unmistakably the sound of hard crying and a lot of it.

"I was . . ." Keira stopped. She'd been about to say *out with Walker*, but a sudden foreboding stopped the words before they could leave her mouth. "I'm sorry. I didn't hear my phone. What *happened*?"

"Tommy broke up with me."

"He *what*? Why?"

"After you left the caf, we went out to his car to talk. He

was pissed about the way you treated Jeremy at lunch."

"Huh? Are you kidding? He dumped you because I didn't play nice with Jeremy?" Keira sank onto the couch.

"Not exactly. It's more that I stuck up for you today, and at the store, too, when they got you in trouble with Mr. Seever. He said the way I kept taking your side instead of his made him realize he needed to find someone who—and I quote—'is interested in being part of *my* life.'"

"He . . . what? Is he serious?"

Susan let out a choked sob.

Keira got up, too full of anger to sit there and do nothing.

"So, do you think he's really an asshole and he's managed to hide it all this time, or do you think it's a quality he's just now developed?" Keira practically spat the words into the phone.

"He's not an asshole. I mean, he's right, in a way."

"Breaking up with you because you are friends with me and I don't want to go out with Jeremy is not 'right.'"

Susan sighed defeatedly.

Keira squeezed her eyes shut. "Look, there are lots of guys out there. Great guys who will want to date you in spite of the fact that you're friends with me."

"I'm not blaming this on you!"

"I know you're not. Dammit, I'm *trying* to make you feel better."

"Yeah." Susan sniffed. "Listen, I've gotta go. I think I'm getting a migraine. I need to take something and go to bed."

It seemed like everything that came out of Keira's mouth made things worse. "Okay," she said finally. "I'll keep my phone on the piano. Call me if you need me."

"I will. Thanks."

Keira scuffed over to the piano and dropped her phone next to her on the bench. She was already late in starting her practice on account of going out with Walker, but now she was doubly late and doubly distracted.

Professionals play through distractions all the time, she reminded herself sternly. With a sharp exhale, she put her fingertips on the smooth keys and ran her fingers across them in a perfect, chiming scale. The mindless rote soothed her, as she hit the patterns of flats and sharps.

Still, as the night wore on, she lost track of how many times she picked up her fingers in the middle of a movement, thinking she'd heard the first mechanized note of her phone's ringtone, but it never actually rang.

Susan never called.

The chime of an incoming message woke Keira the next morning. She'd fallen asleep without even unzipping her backpack full of homework.

Dammit. Maybe she could get her English assignment done in homeroom, and finish her math problems at lunch. Blinking the sleep out of her eyes, she dug her phone out from under her pillow.

Pick you up in 30?

Susan.

Wondering how she'd gotten her parents to give her back the car, Keira texted back a resounding "yes, please!" and rushed into the bathroom to shower.

Thirty-two minutes later, with a peanut butter sandwich in hand and her hair still wet, Keira climbed into Susan's Toyota.

Susan's eyes were swollen and her cheeks were blotchy. She'd pulled on a baseball cap, but her normally silky-straight hair looked stringy where it spilled out beneath it.

"Hey. You never called last night. I was worried," Keira said.

"Sorry. My mother took my cell phone. She said the 'waves' from it were making my migraine worse. Can you imagine? I think she really just wanted to see if Tommy would call me or if I was telling the truth and we'd actually broken up."

"And?"

Susan threw the car into reverse with a little too much enthusiasm.

"Nope. Why do you think I got the car back?" Susan's voice was harsh. "They don't give a shit where I go as long as I'm not out with a guy. Like I couldn't lie to them if I wanted to. Like I couldn't sneak off to the bathroom at school and do it during homeroom like Missy Bridwell and her boyfriend."

Now Keira really couldn't swallow her sandwich. "What? Are you—"

"I'm just being pissy. I never slept with Tommy. Jesus.

Don't you think I would have told you if we had?"

"Sorry. No, I get it." Keira looked down at her sandwich. "Do you want part of this?"

Susan shook her head, tapping her fingers against the steering wheel. "My stomach's still gross from the Imitrex I took last night." She wrapped her fingers tightly around the wheel, trying to get a grip in more ways than one.

"So, did you talk to Walker yesterday?" she asked.

"Actually, we went out. He picked me up after school and we grabbed something to eat."

"Wow," Susan said. "That's—that's like really dating. Huh. I never would have thought *you'd* have a boyfriend and *I'd* be single."

Keira sank down in her seat. "I wouldn't call him my boyfriend. We've only been out a couple of times. We haven't even kissed."

The admission felt too personal once the words were out in the open air of the car.

"Really?" Susan eyed her suspiciously. "Is there something wrong with him?"

Keira swallowed. She imagined Walker's arms around her, how it would feel to have him lean close, the smile fading from his lips. His arms would tighten around her enough so their bodies finally touched and the heat between them ... Jesus. She shook herself.

"Not at all," she said casually. "We just don't know each

other that well yet. Hey—we're supposed to work on 'Syrinx' this afternoon. You still game?"

"No, but I need to." Susan pulled into the school parking lot and Keira watched her best friend scan the cars to see if Tommy was already here. "Besides, isn't that how you get through everything? Put your head down and focus on your music until the world gets its shit together?"

"Pretty much," Keira admitted.

"Then I'm all for trying the Keira Method. Meet here after the last bell?"

"Yep." Keira looked over at Susan. "You gonna make it through today?"

Susan shrugged. "Don't have much choice."

"Sucky, but true." Keira grabbed her bag. "You ready?"

"You go ahead in. I'm gonna sit here for a second, I think." Susan fiddled with the cap of her lip gloss and Keira could see her trying to hold herself together.

"I can wait," Keira offered. "It's not like I'm dying to get to English."

Susan shook her head. "You get enough tardies on your own. I don't want you picking up another one on my account. Really. I'll be fine."

"Okay. Text me if you need me."

"I will."

Keira walked into school with her phone clutched in her hand and her heart aching for Susan. What Tommy'd done to Susan wasn't fair, and Keira didn't have any way to make it right. She wondered if tracking Tommy down and kicking him in the shins would make things better.

Probably not, she decided, *but it would still feel really, really good.*

Chapter Seventeen

AFTER THE DRUDGERY OF school, it was a relief to be at the piano, with Susan as desperate to dive into practice as Keira was.

Susan headed to the fridge to get a soda and brought one back for Keira.

"Thanks," she said, setting it on the floor next to the piano. "You got the music? We need to get you ready to knock your teacher dead with your amazingness."

"Here." Susan pulled it out of her bag and set it on the piano in front of Keira.

Keira scanned through it, her fingers fluttering against the edge of the keyboard in response to the notes slipping past her eyes.

"Okay," Keira said. "I think I've got it."

Susan stood next to her, the flute against her bottom lip, waiting.

Keira counted out a measure and then began to play.

They'd stumbled through two pages before Susan stopped midphrase. "I'm never going to get this!" she roared.

"You will. It's a run-through," she said.

"Nothing sounds right! Even your playing doesn't sound right, but I know that can't be true."

The words startled Keira. She knew she'd hit a few wrong notes, and even the ones she'd played correctly had sounded limp and lifeless. She hadn't realized that it was bad enough for Susan to have noticed.

"Neither of us are used to the piece yet, and we haven't done a duet in a while. We should start again, from the beginning."

Susan stared at her. "You're telling me my ears aren't broken?"

Keira shrugged, and turned back to her piano, overwhelmed with the desire to defend herself. "Everyone's allowed to have an off day, right?"

"Except you. You don't have off days."

Keira spun around, ready to challenge Susan.

The air in the room shimmered, like the sort of heat mirage that cropped up over the blacktop on a scorching summer day.

Except it was indoors. And it was March. Keira's stomach roiled in time with the shimmering. She stretched out a hand to steady herself and her fingers found the piano's keyboard. The clash of discordant, high-pitched keys made it sound like the instrument was shrieking.

"Keira?"

In a snap, the air in the room stilled.

Keira wanted to shake her head—to shake it off—but she was afraid if she did, she'd puke. "Sorry. I got . . . dizzy or something for a second. I probably turned around too fast. I'm fine."

Susan put a hand on her hip. "You are such a shit liar. Something's going on with you. It's *been* going on with you for a while now. What is it, Keira?"

Keira's eyes automatically sought the spot on the carpet where she'd seen—*hallucinated*—the tree.

"It's probably because I didn't practice enough this weekend. I mean, I spent almost that whole afternoon with Walker."

Susan frowned. "No one slips that much from missing one weekend of practice. Not even me, and I suck. So don't go blaming this on Walker. One of the things he likes most is your music, right?"

"Yeah," Keira admitted. "When I told him that I'd composed a piece over the weekend, he *wanted* me to spend time on it. He knows how important this is to me. He knows that I'd never give it up—not for anyone. I wasn't trying to blame him. My parents' crap is probably stressing me out, I guess."

Hurt was scrawled across Susan's face. "You composed something?"

"Yes," Keira said, her anger leaking out of her.

"And you told Walker before you told me?"

Oh, shit. Shit. Shit. Shit. Shit. Shit.

"It just came up," Keira said. "I'm sure I would have told you first if . . ."

"If Tommy hadn't sucked up all my attention." Susan's lip trembled. "Okay. Not being the jealous friend. That's amazing news. Is there anything else you haven't told me? You know, while we're catching up and all?" The joke was shaky. Susan's voice was too.

Keira wanted Susan to know that she *did* tell her things that no one else knew. And she really wanted someone to know the truth.

"I've been seeing some weird things the last couple of days," she admitted.

Susan quit fidgeting. "Like what?"

Keira shrugged. "Things that aren't really there—just flashes of them, for a second. But hey, going crazy is probably more distracting than my parents' fighting, right? At least I have a really good excuse for sucking at Beethoven." She tried to laugh.

"You need to see a doctor."

This was exactly why Keira hadn't told her parents. She didn't want to be dragged into their therapist's office and picked apart thought by thought.

"Seriously." Susan leaned in. "That's *exactly* how my migraines started. I'd see things out of the corner of my eye and then they'd be gone. And then a couple of hours later, *bam*, headache. All you need is some medication or something."

Keira thought about it. She had been sort of headachy, but she was pretty sure the sort of visual disturbances Susan was talking about were different than the things she'd been seeing.

"Yeah. Maybe. It's not quite—"

"Mine always happen when the weather changes," Susan interrupted. "Which is actually helpful, 'cause I know when to have my medicine with me. Low-pressure fronts. They're my biggest trigger."

God, she would love to chalk her visions up to the weather. All the strange things she'd seen played in her memory. The dark marks on Walker. The strange fruit in the kitchen, on that first day after she'd met him at Take Note. The door in the middle of the road while she was in Walker's car. The tree in the living room, after she'd played for him.

Holy shit. It's all happened since I met Walker. And most of that has been while I've been with him.

Why hadn't she put that together before? Relief flooded through her. Now that she could see the pattern, she could imagine explanations. Like maybe her subconscious was trying to force her away from Walker and keep her focused on her goals. Or maybe she was allergic to his fabric softener. Or—

"You're not going crazy. You know that, right?" Susan asked.

Keira's throat was thick with sudden tears. "I don't think I am, actually."

"There's a perfectly logical explanation. I totally think you're having migraines."

Keira was pretty sure that wasn't the answer. Something about Walker was. All she needed was some way to prove it.

"Thanks," she said, feeling more together than she had in days. "Now, do you want me to hack my way through this music with you, or what?"

Susan's expression twisted. "Not really. I'm just . . . not feeling it. I really think it's more than Tommy and everything. I don't like the piece. Could we go to Take Note and pick out something else?"

"Sure. How about tomorrow after school? I promise we'll go and find a piece you like."

"Yeah. Okay." Susan reached for her flute case. "I think I'm done with music for today, anyway."

"We could watch a movie or something?" Keira suggested. She willed herself not to look over at her piano. She needed to sort through whatever was keeping her from playing as well as she knew she could.

"Nah. I know you're dying to practice for real. I'm going to get a pint of ice cream, go home, and reread all the texts Tommy ever sent me." Her lip quivered. "And then I'm going to delete every damn one of them."

"I'm not going to let you wallow alone," Keira insisted.

"Yes, you are. Seriously. You should call Walker. And then practice. And then go on a date, because God knows one of us should see a hot guy tonight."

Keira hesitated. She did want to see Walker, mostly to find out if he was causing her visions.

But not when her piano playing was such a mess. Everything else was just going to have to wait while she worked on that.

Keira shook her head. "I'm going to be a twitchy mess until I get this music-block sorted out."

"So practice fast," Susan suggested, snapping her flute case shut.

"I'll try," she promised.

After Susan left, Keira went back to the piano and ran scales until her fingers burned as badly as the knot in her chest. The only way she knew how to unravel a knot like that was to play the right music, and, just then, none of the music was right.

I am so screwed.

Keira's parents both came home for dinner. Keira retreated into her room while her parents mixed themselves cocktails and ignored each other.

She shut her door. Maybe an hour of homework wouldn't kill her. Surely by then one of her parents would have cracked under the strain of so much politeness and left the house. There was no way she could practice with them slinking around, anyway.

She opened her chemistry book, flipped to the right page, and stared at the equations. The part of her brain that worked through music told her that there was a pattern here, too, but she couldn't see what it was for the life of her.

Her phone rang and Keira slammed the book shut before she'd even bothered to check who was calling. Anyone would be better than chemistry.

But it was better than anyone. It was Walker.

"Hey," he said. "You busy?"

"Not exactly," Keira admitted.

"Well, are you busy tomorrow?"

The flutter in her stomach was nothing like butterflies. "I don't have any special plans," she said carefully.

"A standing date with your piano?" Walker guessed.

"Yes."

Every time he did something to show how well he understood her, she fell for him a little bit harder.

"Do you have time for a date with me? If not, I demand a rain check. And I'll want it to be made of actual rain."

Keira laughed. "So you're telling me it'll take less time to go out with you than to make you a rain check?"

"Smart *and* pretty. You're too good for me. Want to see a movie with me in spite of that?"

There was nothing in her that wanted to say no. So she didn't.

"Sure. What's playing?"

"Dunno. Don't care. I just thought it'd be fun to sit in the dark with you for two hours."

Heat flooded Keira's cheeks. "You just want someone to hold your hand during the scary parts."

"True." There was a faint clicking on his end of the phone. "Ah. Perfect. *Alien Invaders IV*? Starts at seven thirty? That should have lots of scary parts."

"*Alien Invaders IV*? Really?" It didn't seem like his style. Or hers.

"It's that or some movie about a talking dog."

"Oh, God, aliens. Please. Aliens."

"That's what I thought. I'm working until six thirty—I'll pick you up after, okay?"

Keira remembered her promise to find Susan some new music.

"Actually . . . I told Susan that I'd help her find a different piece for her flute. So, um, we're coming to Take Note anyway— maybe we could time it so that you and I could leave after that?"

"Sounds great," he said.

"Okay," she said softly. "See you then."

Chapter Eighteen

AT SIX O'CLOCK THE next night, Keira and Susan walked into Take Note. Well, Keira walked in. Susan trudged. When she'd heard that Keira was ditching her for a date with Walker, all the light had gone out of her.

The door chimed as they pushed it open, and Walker turned to look at them.

He wasn't the only one.

At first, Keira's gaze skittered over the sharp-featured guy standing across the counter from Walker. Just another customer. Except . . . She looked back at him. His black hoodie and dark jeans were unremarkable, and his faded Chucks weren't noteworthy. His nose bent slightly, as though it had been broken before, which added an air of toughness to his face.

The thing that caught Keira's attention most was that, though his hair was stick-straight, it was the same shining ebony as Walker's curls. And when he looked over and caught Keira staring at him, his eyes were the same shade of charcoal that Walker's were.

The only difference was that Walker's eyes were full of concern, while Mystery Guy's held nothing but curiosity.

Keira stepped forward and held out her hand. "You must be Walker's cousin, huh?"

The guy looked down at her outstretched fingers and his slightly-too-thin lips pursed in confusion before he extended his own palm.

His handshake was limp enough that it made Keira want to wipe her hand against the leg of her jeans. She resisted the urge.

"Keira, this is my cousin, Smith. Smith, this is Keira." Walker sounded resigned.

Smith smiled at her. There was something about him that put Keira on edge. "It's so . . . *nice* to meet you." His words crawled across her skin.

"Yeah. You too. I didn't realize you were in town."

"Oh, I pop over from time to time." He laughed, but Keira didn't get the joke. He turned his gaze to Susan. The minute his eyes traced her dark hair, tiny nose, and pouty lower lip, Smith pulled his shoulders back. When he stood up to his full height, he was almost as tall as Walker. Susan straightened, her cheeks pinking up beneath the attention.

"Who's this?" Smith asked.

"Smith, Walker, this is my best friend, Susan."

"Hi." Susan didn't even turn her head to acknowledge Walker. Her greeting was solely for Smith.

Keira looked over at Walker. The strange insta-attraction that was happening between Susan and Smith made it seem like she'd known Walker forever. She could read him like a billboard.

Compared to the two in front of her, she and Walker had a history.

Walker caught her eye.

She shot him a *What the hell is going on?* look.

He shot back a *Haven't you ever seen two people flirting for the first time?* eyebrow raise.

She narrowed her eyes. *Smart-ass.*

Walker laughed. "So. Susan." Susan and Smith both whipped around to face him. "Keira said you need to find some music?"

"Oh. Yeah. Yeah, I do."

"You play?" Smith asked.

"Yeah, the flute, but not very well. Are you a musician?" Susan actually batted her eyelashes.

Smith waved his hand dismissively. "Not a musician. I like

working on machines. You know—gears and belts and fans and stuff." He pinned Susan with a look. "But that doesn't mean I don't know how to listen. What style of music do you like to play?" He stepped closer to Susan, separating their conversation from Keira and Walker.

Walker grimaced, and Keira cocked her head at him, confused. So they were flirting? So what? If his cousin broke her rebounding friend's heart, yeah, she was going to make Smith eat that grin, but other than that . . .

Unless that's what Walker's making faces about. Is Smith a player or something?

Smith didn't seem cute enough to collect notches in his belt, but what did Keira know? She stepped close to the counter while Susan and Smith inched toward the bins of music.

"Everything okay?" Keira kept her voice low, leaning her head toward Walker's.

"Fine. My cousin is—well, I told you my family situation is a little complicated." He brought his lips so close to her ear that she could feel the heat of his breath against the sensitive hollow beneath her jaw. She spread her palm on the chipped counter, steadying herself.

"Yeah. Obviously, I don't have any room to judge you on that," Keira tried to make her voice light, but it came out breathy instead. She pulled away from Walker enough that she could turn to face him. "What's he doing here, anyway?"

Walker glanced back at Smith and Susan, who were

completely engrossed in each other. "Seeing what I'm up to," he said.

"What? Why?"

"So that he can figure out how he's going to rebel." Walker paused. "My aunt is going to be royally pissed if she finds out he was in Sherwin."

"And you're not going to tell her?" Keira guessed.

"Something like that. Anyway. I don't trust tattletales, you know?"

"Totally. He's not going to hurt Susan, is he?"

Walker stared past her, watching Susan and Smith circle each other. "Depends on why he wants her, I guess." He sighed. "I'd try to keep him off her, but that would just make him more determined to chase her. I'm sorry."

"Not your fault," Keira said, watching them too. Each grin Smith and Susan shared tightened the muscles in her neck a little bit more.

"Hey!" Susan held up a book of simple concertos. "Look what I found! Do you think these will work?"

Keira squinted at the concerto numbers printed beneath the composer's name.

"That should work."

"Okay, kids," Walker smacked the counter, pushing himself toward the register. "I'm supposed to usher Keira out of here in about ten minutes. If you're buying something, now's the time."

Smith perked up. "Where're you going?"

Walker's eyebrows drew together. "The movies."

Keira noticed that he didn't say *which* movie.

"Oh." Smith drew a finger across one of the bins, stirring up dust. "I've been wanting to see *Alien Invaders IV*." Keira realized—for the first time—that his accent was the same as Walker's.

"I'm *dying* to see that," Susan piped in. She looked up at Smith. "I love those crazy, blow-stuff-up, use-all-the-special-effects-at-once sort of movies. Keira hates them, though."

"I'm a huge fan of anything with a high body count and bizarre weapons." Smith laughed. "Walker's not usually into it either. Sounds like he and Keira are more the sensitive foreign-film types?" He made a face and Susan echoed it.

"Ew. Subtitles." She turned to look at Keira and Walker. "So, what are you going to see?"

The answer stuck to Keira's tongue. "*Alien Invaders IV.*"

Susan let out a half-giggle, half-squeal. "Really?!"

Smith turned to her. "We should go with them." He glanced at Walker. "You wouldn't mind if we tagged along, would you?"

"You know I have a strict rule against going on dates with family," Walker joked. Except from his tone, it clearly wasn't a joke.

Keira watched the spark in Susan's eye fade to a dull, cold cinder. Susan's fingers curled around the book of music like it might suddenly slip away too. Keira couldn't stand it.

"Oh, come on. Rules are made to be broken, right?" She

turned to look at Walker, hoping Susan and Smith couldn't see the desperate look she shot him.

Keira never begged, but as long as she was insisting Walker break his rules, she might as well break her own, too.

There was a pause so thick that the moment seemed stuck. Finally, Walker blew out a long breath. "I think the saying you're looking for is that it's the *exception* that proves the rule." He eyed Smith. "Which as you know is quite true, and I wouldn't keep Susan from the wonder that is *Alien Invaders IV*."

Smith looked stung, but he smiled to cover it. "So, we'll all meet at the theater?" He glanced over at Susan. "May I take you to the movie?"

Susan bit her lip. "Um. Yes. Please." She glanced over. "Keira? Are you riding with me or Walker?"

Keira looked back and forth between her glowing best friend and her glowering guy. She wanted to know what was making his eyebrows pinch together like that.

"I'll go with Walker," she said.

It was only eight blocks from Take Note to the Cineplex, which didn't leave Keira much time to be subtle. They hit the first light just as it turned red, so she'd have an extra thirty seconds, at least.

"You seem kind of . . . pissed about this whole group-date thing," she said. She glanced in the side mirror. Susan's car was directly behind them and Keira could see her frantically putting on lip gloss.

"I don't like it when Smith shows up uninvited like this. He thinks it's a game, but it's not. Besides, I like it even less when he wedges his way into my life by asking to come along on our date."

"So you *don't* think he's really interested in seeing Susan?"

Walker rubbed a hand across his face. His usual mask of unflappable wit came away beneath his palm. Worried lines were carved around his mouth, and concern clouded his eyes. "I don't know for sure, but I have a guess. She's . . . she's not like the girls he usually dates."

"What sort of girls does he date?" Keira asked, desperate to sketch a mental picture of Smith's typical girl.

"The kind my aunt approves of. The kind who've always lived down the street, who hang out at the library for fun." Walker grimaced. "The kind who're so anxious to say *yes* that they don't care who's asking."

Keira curled her fingers around the armrest. Ew. "Wait—the library? I thought Smith said he was really into machines."

Walker blinked at her before he burst into laughter. "They have machines in libraries, Keira. He fixes them. Maintains them."

"Oh. Yeah. Sorry—I'm not much of a library goer, I guess."

"Me either," Walker admitted. "But Smith is, like, the vaguely badass deity of information services. Susan's not the sort of half-wilted girl he normally picks. I wish he'd go back home where he belongs, but no—if I'm seeing a girl from

Sherwin, then *he's* going to find someone to date here."

Back home . . . that was weird. Hadn't he moved from somewhere far away? It occurred to her that she didn't know where he'd come from, exactly.

"I thought you said your family didn't live close? Aren't they still in the town where you grew up?"

"They are. It's a long way from here, but depending on . . ." He cleared his throat. "Depending how fast you travel, it's not that hard to get back and forth."

"What's it called?" Keira asked.

"Have you ever heard of Higgstown?" he asked.

She shook her head. "Is it . . . somewhere in Nova Scotia?" she guessed.

Walker bobbed his head from side to side in a *maybe* gesture. "Sort of close to there."

He looked utterly worn out.

Keira glanced outside, trying to figure out exactly how many blocks she had left to decide whether she should let Susan go ahead and rebound with Smith or whether she needed to pry her away from him.

When they pulled up to the stop sign at Kendall Road, Walker ran a fingertip down Keira's temple and tucked a strand of hair behind her ear. He took his hand from her face, but the sweet jolt of his touch slid down her neck and twined through her ribs, sending an audible shudder through her breath.

"Didn't mean to scare you." Walker's voice was soft in the quiet car.

"You didn't." Keira met his eyes. The usual spark was still absent, but beneath his worry was an irresistible heat. "I'm not that easy to scare." She leaned closer to him, so intent on the unusually serious set of his full lips that the night itself seemed to darken around them. She looked up long enough to see Walker's eyes slide half-shut as his head tilted a bit to one side.

The impatient beep of Susan's car horn shattered the moment and Keira's stomach lurched. The streetlights brightened and the hum of the car engine rumbled through her in a sickening flash. Keira reached out a hand and caught hold of the dashboard, steadying herself against the strange vertigo.

"You okay?" Walker frowned.

Keira leaned back against the seat. "Fine," she said. "Sorry. I just had a weird dizzy flash—maybe I didn't have enough to eat."

"Well, let's get you to the concession stand, then." Walker pulled into the multiplex parking lot and the neon signs above the theater eased the spinning in Keira's head.

"That sounds good," she said.

As they got out of the car and headed for the ticket window, Keira's vertigo faded. But Walker's frown, she noticed, hadn't washed away at all.

Chapter Nineteen

SUSAN RUSHED UP TO the two of them in the parking lot. "Keira? Can we . . . um . . ." She glanced up at Walker. "Keira and I need to go to the bathroom."

Walker raised an eyebrow, but his amused grin came back beneath it, and Keira found herself smiling in response. "Go ahead. I'll grab the tickets and meet you inside."

"Oh. Wait." Keira dug in her pocket for her cash. Susan danced next to her, scanning the arriving cars anxiously.

Walker waved his hand. "I've got it."

"But I want to—"

"You can get the snacks or something. Go, before Susan explodes." He laughed.

Susan grabbed her arm and hauled Keira toward the doors. "Thanks, Walker!" Susan called over her shoulder.

The second the bathroom door swung shut, Susan spun to face Keira.

"You have to give me a ponytail holder and a breath mint." She ordered Keira.

Keira stood, frozen, staring at her best friend. "What?"

Susan turned to check her lip gloss in the mirror. "Do I look okay?" she asked. "God, I wish I was wearing something cuter. Oh, I also called my mom and told her we were going to the movies together. Just so you know. Don't mention Smith if she asks, okay?"

Keira blinked, pulled her spare elastic off her wrist and handed it to Susan.

"You seem really into Smith," she ventured. "That must have been some conversation you guys had at Take Note."

Susan shrugged. "Yeah. I mean, he seems nice enough." She smiled a wicked little smile. "But mostly, he's *hot* and a little bit mysterious. And he's eighteen. *And* he said he's already finished with school." Her eyes narrowed as she smoothed her hair into the world's fastest French braid. "And if anyone sees me here with him, there is zero chance I will still be 'that girl that Tommy dumped' at school tomorrow." She held up her hand, looking at Keira in the mirror. "Hot. Mysterious. Older. From away. Likes action movies." She ticked them off on her fingers. "Win. Win. Win. Win. Win."

Keira was way past shocked. Her tongue seemed stunned, so thorough was its refusal to form words.

Susan bounced over, bumping Keira's shoulder. "Come on. We have *dates* waiting for us."

The smell of stale popcorn and faux-butter soaked into her clothes as soon as Keira stepped out into the multiplex. Susan made a beeline for Smith, who stood against one of the poster-lined walls, arms crossed, waiting.

Walker wasn't with him. Keira's eyes swept the crowded lobby. She spotted him, bent over the concession counter in his familiar wool peacoat.

He passed some money across the counter and turned toward her. He didn't scan the crowd the way she had. His eyes didn't catch on the woman wearing an out-of-season halter top or the screaming toddler.

Walker looked straight at her.

He smiled, and it was like dawn had broken all over again. The colors in the room were suddenly brighter, the air warmer. His happiness washed over Keira and her own mood lifted in response. Before she knew it, she was standing in front of him. He had a packet of red licorice in his hand. Favorite candy wasn't a topic she remembered talking about with him. Had she forgotten?

"How did you know?" she asked, pointing at the candy.

He gave her a quizzical look. "Know what?"

"My movie snack. The red licorice."

Walker's eyebrows lifted. "Are you kidding? Red licorice is *my* movie snack."

Narrowing her eyes, Keira cocked her head at him. "You mean I have to *share*? Besides, I thought you said I could buy the snacks."

Walker handed her the bag of licorice. "I said you could get the snacks 'or something.'"

Keira rolled her eyes. "That's totally not playing fair."

He leaned in close. "Playing fair's no fun at all," he murmured.

The overhead lights were suddenly too bright and Keira blinked against the unexpected glare, not quite believing what she was seeing.

There was a tiny starburst of darkness pulsing at the top of Walker's cheek.

She blinked hard, willing it away.

"Are you dizzy again? You look pale all of a sudden." Walker reached out and caught her chin in his fingers. His thumb traced the tender spot beneath the curve of her lower lip. When his fingertips grazed her skin, the black mark on his cheek exploded like dark fireworks, shattering into a thousand tiny dots that sank back into his skin and disappeared.

Keira barely noticed, mostly because their sudden contact brought a row of strange, rounded huts into view. The small buildings shimmered darkly against the bright normalcy of the multiplex. A headache flared behind her eyes, throbbing against her forehead. Walker dropped his hand and stepped closer. The huts disappeared and the pain in her head let up, until it was nothing more than a twinge.

"I'm not dizzy. I just—I had a weird headache for a second there, but it's gone. Susan thinks I'm getting migraines." They headed for the theater, easily falling into step with each other.

"Why?"

Keira leaned her head toward her shoulder, stretching out the tension in her neck. "Mostly because my eyes have been funny. Susan sees halos and sparkly lights sometimes before she gets migraines. Actually"—the pieces clicked—"I think she gets dizzy, too."

Walker looked at her sharply. "And you see the same sorts of things Susan does?"

His dark eyes searched hers, like he could read the truth there, whether she lied to him or not.

"Not exactly. All the stuff she sees seems to be about too much light. Mine's the opposite. It's dark."

Something in his expression made her keep going. "And it always seems to happen when I'm with you."

Walker's jaw clenched. Keira immediately regretted saying it, even though it was true. "Maybe I'm allergic to the smell your shampoo or something," she offered.

Walker opened his mouth, but before he could say anything,

Susan came bounding over with Smith sauntering a step behind.

"Guys, come on! The last showing's getting ready to let out. We'll miss all the good seats." She grabbed Keira's arm and carted her toward the ticket taker.

She looked back for Walker—he still had their tickets.

He hadn't moved. Walker's hands were clenched into fists, his shoulders half turned toward the front doors. It looked like he was leaving. Keira pulled her arm out of Susan's grip.

Except he didn't leave. He stared straight at Keira and his teeth grazed his lower lip like a little boy gazing at a long wished-for present. Everything about him said he was in the middle of an impossible choice.

It was only a movie date, but Keira had the unshakable sense that the moment was suddenly much, much bigger than that. She just didn't know why.

"Walker? Are you coming?" she asked.

He closed his eyes for a split second. Then he opened his fists, loosening his grip on the tickets.

When he looked at her again, the pain had disappeared from his eyes. There was nothing left in his expression but wanting and determination. Lots and lots of determination. The combination sent a shiver through Keira's middle.

"Yes. Absolutely." He held out the crumpled tickets to her.

Vaguely dazed from the remnants of her headache and the strange scene in the lobby, Keira turned to face the meager crowd that trickled out of the prior showing.

A group of people from school walked out of the theater. Tommy and Jeremy were with them. The two of them froze. Tommy's mouth was actually hanging open. One of the girls whipped her cell phone out of her purse, fingers flying as she started texting furiously.

"Hey, guys," Keira said. She tried to keep the smirk out of her voice. She almost succeeded. Susan's wish had come true.

Jeremy took a step toward them. "You going to introduce us to your friends?"

Smith crossed his arms. "No."

Walker snickered at Smith. "Oh, come on." He looked at the two guys. "Don't mind my cousin. He's a little testy."

Susan slid her hand into the crook of Smith's elbow. "Too bad we don't have time to chat, but I never miss the previews." She strode into the theater, half dragging Smith along with her.

They slid into a row of seats, and Keira ended up between Walker and Smith. The two cousins glanced at each other over her head, both of them wound tight with warning.

Penned in, Keira glanced at the screen, where the previews had, in fact, started.

Smith glanced down at her. "So, how long have you been seeing Walker?"

On Smith's other side, Susan laughed. "In Keira-time? Forever. In reality? What? A week? Two weeks?"

Smith looked back at Walker, as if for confirmation. "Really? That long? I'd have thought you'd've mentioned it, then."

Walker shot Smith a granite stare. "Some things are too good to talk about right away."

Smith looked over at Susan. "He's always trying to hide all the fun he has. He's scared my mom will be pissed at him." Smith leaned closer to Susan. "She's kind of high-strung, but it's not that hard to get around her rules."

Susan's eyes sparkled wickedly. "Sounds like my parents."

"Aunt Holly's only trying to keep you out of trouble," Walker growled. "And fun isn't always free. Especially if you're *sneaking around.*"

Smith huffed dismissively. "You just worry about your own cookie jar."

Walker huffed back at him, but then his voice and gaze softened. He looked down at Keira. "Speaking of sweets, are you going to open those Twizzlers, or just cuddle them?"

"Smart-ass," she answered. But she tugged open the plastic and offered him the candy.

The movie started with a bang. Literally. A house exploded when the aliens landed on it. Keira sighed and looked over at Walker. He rolled his eyes.

Susan, on the other hand, was practically bouncing in her seat.

"That was amazing!" She looked over at Smith. "Can you believe the effects? Oh, my God!"

"I know," he agreed. "But look at the gun he's carrying. No way would it work if it were built like that." He leaned close to Susan, his finger tracing the weapon on the screen as he explained why.

The next ninety minutes were painful. The movie was terrible, but Smith and Susan seemed to be having a ball, judging from the number of times they bent their heads together to talk. Of course, there was no telling if it was the movie they were enjoying or ... something else.

When the credits finally rolled, Smith practically leapt out of his seat. "It's too early to go home. Susan and I are going to get coffee. Do you guys want to tag along?"

Susan stared hard at Keira. Even in the half-light of the theater, Keira could see the tiny twitch of Susan's eyebrows as she silently begged Keira to say no.

Walker was grumpy about Smith intruding on their date, but now Susan was clearly telling them that they were in the way of her own evening plans.

"It's getting late and I really need to practice," Keira blurted out. "Why don't you guys go?" She looked over at Walker, realizing that it sounded like she was ditching him, too.

He gave her a tiny, I-get-it shake of his head. "I have to work early anyway," Walker said.

"Too bad," Smith said to Keira. "If you matter so much to Walker, it seems like his family should get to know you." There was an edge to his voice.

Walker stepped in closer behind her. "Keira wouldn't be Keira if she didn't want to run back to her piano. That's the great thing about her. Well, one of the great things. There are a lot of them."

Smith's smile fell a bit, then spread wolfishly. "I guess I'll have to spend all my time on Susan, then. I'm not the least bit sorry about that."

Behind him, Susan's eyes glittered. "I've got more dish on Keira than you'll get out of her, anyway," she teased.

"Best of both worlds, then." Smith looked at Walker when he answered, which made the hair on Keira's neck stand up in an unexpected warning. "You kids get home safe."

"We will. I always do." Walker stepped out into the main aisle. "See you two later."

He and Keira picked their way out of the dim theater, avoiding abandoned soda cups and errant popcorn. They'd barely made it into the glare of the lobby before Walker blew out a long breath.

"Sorry. My cousin's an ass sometimes." He shook his head. "He seems way more interested in what's going on between you and me than he does in Susan. I hate to say it, but I don't think he's going to be all that good for her."

Keira laughed. Walker looked at her, his eyes wide with surprise.

"Not if she does him wrong first," she chortled.

"What do you mean?"

"When we were in the bathroom, she admitted that she's mostly interested in what he can do to erase the social damage of being dumped by Tommy. And since we ran into them, I'd say she's well on her way to accomplishing that mission."

Walker looked startled. "*She's* . . . using *him*? Ha!"

"That's about the size of it. I'd bet you she'll take him to the coffee shop where everybody hangs out, just to get the maximum number of people gossiping about it."

The smirk that spread across Walker's face wasn't entirely pleasant. "That would serve him right," he said.

Keira pushed open the door and the cool freshness of the night air spilled over her.

"Come on," Walker said. "Let's get you out of here. Do you really have to go home or were you just giving Susan space? We could get something to eat, or go for a drive. Whatever you want."

Keira sighed. She needed to practice. She hadn't spent enough time at her piano lately. But she didn't want the evening to end, either. The glow of the parking lot lights blotted out the stars and she looked up at the pure, dark sky. She had to curl her hands into fists before she could make herself say no.

"I really do need to practice. I'm sorry—I know that's lame."

Walker pulled his car keys out of his pocket and held out his hand. Keira slid her cold fingers into his warm ones. "You have nothing to apologize for," he said. "I know that no matter what happens between us, I'll never be your first love. I'd never be your only love, either."

The word—*that* word—sent an anxious thrill straight down through Keira's middle. He tugged on her hand, pulling her to a stop. "Your music comes first," he said. "It *should* come first. I'd be thrilled to be a close second."

Walker wrapped his arms around her and pulled her in close. The parking lot seemed to swirl away, leaving only the two of them. Keira's eyelids drifted closed. The smell of him surrounded her. He brushed a kiss against the corner of her mouth and Keira drew in an aching breath. Her lips parted as an enormous gust of wind came out of the dark, cloudless sky. It whipped through her hair and tugged at their coats. Instead of kissing her in earnest, Walker leapt away from her, his eyes raking the rows of parked cars that surrounded them.

His agitation was contagious. "What?!"

He shook his head. "That wind—your hair . . ." He touched his face, then looked at the confusion on hers. He let out a shaky laugh. "It startled me."

Keira crossed her arms in front of her. "Uh-huh. The unflappable Walker Andover got startled by a breeze?"

Walker stepped back over to her. "I was pretty distracted. I'll make it up to you. Besides . . ." He glanced over at the sidewalk beneath the marquee. "I don't want to kiss you with an audience."

Sure enough, a couple of guys were standing in the cold, staring straight at the two of them.

Ew.

"Come on," Walker said. "Let's get you home."

Chapter Twenty

THE PING OF AN incoming text woke Keira the next morning. She rolled over and dragged her phone off the bedside table. Her mouth was cottony and her eyelids felt swollen from the lack of sleep. She'd spent hours at the piano after she got home from the theater, but her fingers hadn't wanted to cooperate. She'd fumbled easy chords and misfingered arpeggios she'd had down cold. Finally, her dad had shuffled into the living room and looked pointedly at the couch, saying he needed to get some sleep. Keira couldn't say no, so she stumbled into bed. Which had only been—she cracked open one eye—three hours and five text messages ago.

Five texts. She should have checked her phone before she collapsed.

Keira sat up, blinked the sleep out of her eyes, and scrolled through them.

Susan, texting to say she'd seen six people from school at the coffee shop.

Susan, texting to say that Smith had kissed her.

Susan, texting to say she hoped Keira remembered that as far as Mrs. Kim was concerned, the two of them had been together ALL EVENING.

And, just now, Susan.

Texting to say that she wasn't going to school—with a little winky face—and asking Keira to bring home her assignments.

Keira sighed and texted back.

Of course she'd bring the assignments. But why wasn't Susan going to school?

As if she didn't know the answer. As if it didn't have anything to do with Smith.

Keira staggered through school, one class droning into the next. She almost forgot to check in with Susan's calculus teacher.

Right before lunch, she saw Jeremy at his locker, joking around with Tommy and Chip Maxwell.

Jeremy looked up and saw her. Instead of looking guilty for his snarky behavior at the theater last night, hope flared in his eyes. He tugged at the hem of his shirt and ducked under Tommy's hand.

"Hey, Keira," Jeremy called. "How's it going?"

She swallowed the fanged words that filled her mouth. "I can't talk. I have to go get Susan's homework."

Jeremy's face fell.

"Oh. Right. Listen, I thought you should know that Brian and Chip saw you and your boyfriend in the parking lot last night. And if that had been me? *I* would have given you an *actual* kiss." He slung his backpack onto his shoulder.

Keira was too stunned to answer.

Jeremy seemed satisfied. He gave her a small smile, spun on his heel, and sauntered off down the hall.

She shook herself. Kissing Jeremy Reynolds. Ew. She was going to have to put a fast stop to whatever was going on with him.

A really, really fast stop.

When the bus dropped her off at home, Keira had her phone in her hand, ready to call Susan and tell her to drive over and get her homework. Before she could dial, though, a jolt ran through her.

Her dad's car was in the driveway.

At three thirty in the afternoon.

On a work day.

What the hell?

Keira hurried the rest of the way up the walk, fumbling automatically for her house keys. The knob turned beneath her hand as she tried to slide the blade of the key into the lock. Of course—her dad would have left it unlocked.

Shoving her keys back into her backpack, Keira pushed her way into the house.

"Dad?" she called, dropping her things in the front hall.

Her dad leapt off the couch so fast that she took a step back.

"Hi, honey." His eyes darted between her bag lying on the floor, her half-removed coat, and her raised eyebrows.

"Uh, hi. You're home early," she said, wondering what was going on. If this was some sort of daddy-daughter bonding time the therapist had cooked up with her father, Keira was going to be really irritated.

"Yeah. I had some . . . things to sort out and—" He paused, running a hand through his thinning hair. "And it seemed silly to go back to the office *now* and besides," he offered, "you've been cooped up without a car for days. I thought you might have something you wanted to do. Somewhere you needed to go?"

Is he trying to get rid *of me?*

The thought was too slimy to touch. Her dad had always been thoughtful—nice. Just because her parents were fighting didn't mean she should be so suspicious. Keira shook herself. He was offering her the *car*.

"That's great, Dad," she said, sliding her arm back into her dangling coat. She could at least save Susan the trip over. And then maybe on her way home, she could stop at Take Note.

The thought made her mouth water. She could spend the rest of the afternoon looking at music, searching for something new that would end her streak of bad playing. And she could see Walker.

She wanted to pretend that it was only the thought of new music that cranked up her heartbeat, but it wasn't. She wanted to see him, too.

As long as she wouldn't look desperate. She wasn't one of those girls who couldn't leave a guy alone when he was at work. His job just happened to be at her second-most favorite place on earth, after her piano. That was different.

But it didn't seem like it should be quite so hard to convince herself how different it was. Still. Susan and music *and* Walker was more temptation than she was up to resisting right then.

"Well? The gas tank's full." Her dad dangled the keys in front of her the way other parents waved rattles in front of babies.

She plucked the fob out of his hand. "I need to take Susan her homework, actually. She was going to come here, but . . . yeah. This is better. And maybe I'll stop by Take Note too. See if they have anything new in." She bent to grab for her bag, but her dad reached into his back pocket and Keira froze.

He pulled out his wallet.

Keira swallowed.

He dug a crumpled twenty out and passed it to her.

"Here—find something fun. You've been working so hard on your Juilliard pieces—you deserve it."

Keira stared down at the limp bill. Something really was wrong. It was too much bribery—her dad had already given her "emergency money" once in the last week. Twice was more than they could afford and she knew it. She swallowed hard, pushing down the sick feeling that rose in her throat.

"Thanks, but I've still got plenty left from what you gave me before," she lied. She'd spent a chunk of it having pie with Walker. But she still had her last paycheck.

Her very last, not-going-to-get-another-one paycheck.

She scooped up her bag and cradled it in her arms. Her dad stuffed the money into the open front pocket.

"Just take it," he insisted. "And go have fun!" His voice buzzed, bright and fake. He stared behind her at the door, like he expected someone to come through it.

Of course. He was probably waiting for her mom. It would be like them to schedule a time to have their next horrific fight. At least he was giving her a chance to escape first.

Keira backed out of the house. "Okay. Well—thanks, then. I'll see you soon!"

Her dad shut the door so fast that he snapped off the end of his "Drive safe!"

Keira tossed her stuff into the car. She shook out her hands. Whatever weirdness was happening with her parents, it wasn't about her. She shoved her parents' problems out of sight, into some tight-closing drawer in her mind, and focused on what was ahead.

Susan. Then music. And Walker. And a whole afternoon with a car to herself.

Chapter Twenty-One

THE KIMS' DOOR SWUNG open. Susan stood there, freshly lip-glossed and glowing. Her eyes had dark circles underneath them, but the smile on her face was genuinely happy.

"Uh, hey," Keira said. "How are you?"

"Hungry!" Susan announced. "I overslept and missed breakfast."

The off-balance feeling that something was wrong spread through Keira. She shifted her weight from foot to foot, trying to get her equilibrium back. "I brought your homework."

"Oh, my God. How can you think about homework right now?" Susan dragged her into the house and up the stairs. Keira could hear the TV in the living room, chattering in Korean.

"So, I take it this means you had fun with Smith?" Keira asked, dropping Susan's assignments onto her dresser.

"Last night? He bought me a mocha and we ended up talking for almost two hours. Tommy *never* listened to me that much. Half the cheer squad was there and Smith didn't even look at them."

Keira tugged at the loop on the top of her backpack. "Wow. That's—wow. I thought all you wanted was to make everyone forget about you and Tommy? Is that . . . ? I mean, are you . . . ? Is it more than that now?

"I don't know. What do you think? He's totally cute, right? In an edgy sort of way?"

The words crawled over Keira like fat spiders.

The TV in the living room got quieter. Susan rolled her eyes at her mom's attempt to listen in to their conversation.

"My mom's thrilled that I'm not dating Tommy anymore," she said, loud enough for her mother to hear. "She said that I've finally got my priorities straight." Susan slammed her bedroom door and lowered her voice.

"Speaking of Tommy, did you see him today? Did he seem upset?" Susan looked up at Keira so hopefully that Keira sagged with relief.

"He and Jeremy seemed pretty put out about last night," she admitted. True, she hadn't actually talked to Tommy, but he hadn't exactly looked pleased about the whole thing.

Susan sighed. "Imagine how pissed he'll be when he finds out that Smith is taking me to dinner tonight."

"How will he find that out?" Keira asked.

"Because we're going to The Blue Plate. Smith's picking me up in a couple of hours. He *wanted* to spend the whole afternoon together, but I told him I had to come home so my mom would believe I'd been at school."

"Wait—you're going to dinner at the restaurant where Tommy works?" Keira looked at the spite that was stitched into Susan's expression.

Susan snorted. "He's off tonight. He's always off on Thursdays. But trust me, everyone who works there will be running off to text him."

"And your mom's letting you go?"

"My mom's letting me go to *work*, yeah." Susan pursed her lips. "What? I don't like lying to her, but I can't just sit here and let Tommy ruin my life. Smith's hot and he's fun and he's exactly what I need to keep the rest of my year from sucking."

"I think you should be careful, that's all. There are a billion guys you could use to prove that Tommy made a bad choice when he dumped you. Smith—you don't know him at all, and neither do I. Walker doesn't really trust him, and—"

Susan interrupted her. "You know, that's interesting." Her voice had a little set of teeth in it, pearly and sharp. "Because Smith doesn't trust Walker. He thinks Walker's in some kind of trouble, but he wouldn't say what." She looked pointedly at

Keira. "And I don't see why you're getting so overprotective all of a sudden. I'm just playing with Smith. You're the one who's falling for someone."

"Hey," Keira started to protest, but Susan lifted a hand, cutting her off.

"I don't want to fight with you. I'm just saying. You're in uncharted territory, here. That's the time to watch your step— when things are getting serious. My whole goal is basically to make out in public with a hot guy. Speaking of which," Susan glanced at the clock. "I need to get in the shower if I'm going to be ready by the time I have to leave to meet Smith. Thanks for the homework. I'm only going to be able to pull this off if I keep my grades high enough to satisfy my mother."

It was a little bit like a dismissal, but there was nothing to do except go. Keira left Susan to use up all the Kims' hot water. Outside, she took a deep breath of the damp air. The car keys felt unusually heavy in her hand.

It was time to go to Take Note.

She opened the door so gently that the bells hanging from the handle barely chimed. As reverently as if she were entering a church, Keira stepped into Take Note. The paper and ink and dust smell of the store washed over her and her eyes closed as she breathed it in.

The smell reminded her of all the afternoons she'd spent there, poring over music, humming as her eyes skimmed the staffs. Immediately, she was calmer. Immediately, she was happier.

A voice slipped out of the back room, interrupting her reverie.

"It doesn't matter! Mom wants to know what's going on. *I* find things out when she tells me to, unless there's some reason to avoid it. Can you think of a reason for me to avoid it, Walker?" There was a sneer in the question—an insinuation.

The accent was familiar, but the voice was a tenor to Walker's baritone.

Smith.

Walker made a disgusted noise. "You can't blackmail me into letting you off the hook, Smith. I told your mother that I would call if I had any news. If you're looking for something about Keira to go running back to your mommy with—"

"I'm just saying that if you tell mom about Susan, I'm not going to go quietly. I want to have a little fun. I want to see what things are like here on the wild side."

"This is *not* the wild side. It's not a game, Smith. What's going on with Keira is none of your business. Please, go home and leave it alone."

"From what I can see, what's going on with Keira is that you're too busy trying to get in her pants to worry about anything else."

Oh. My. God. I cannot believe he just said that.

"If you ever say something like that again, they'll be the

last words you speak with your teeth in their current arrangement." Walker's anger leaked through the open door and the unexpected emotion in his voice made Keira suddenly aware that she was eavesdropping. She took a step back toward the plate-glass door. She should leave.

She really should.

Keira accidentally knocked into the door, sending the bells clanging.

"Someone's here," Walker said. "Listen, we'll talk more later. In the meantime, *behave.*"

"Sure. I have to go pick Susan up for dinner anyway. I'm sure our conversation will be much more pleasant than this one." The derision in Smith's voice made Keira wince.

"Don't do that. I mean it."

Walker strolled out of the back room, his face pleasant, his eyebrows raised in a can-I-help-you look, which disappeared as soon as he saw Keira. His eyes flashed with pleasure but then he glanced back at the open door and she saw his jaw tighten.

"Fancy meeting you here," he said, light as spun sugar and nearly as sweet.

Keira shrugged. "My dad was trying to get rid of me, so he gave me his car keys and money for music. I dropped off Susan's homework first." Without meaning to, she glanced at the back room, burning with curiosity. "But—if it's weird, if I'm interrupting . . ." She didn't want to admit she'd been listening in, but she didn't want to lie, either.

"Not at all. Smith stopped by to brag about Susan. It sounds like they had quite the day together." Walker rolled his eyes. "It doesn't matter though. He was just leaving. And anyway, I'd ditch him for you any time. You're significantly more beautiful than he is."

Keira ducked her head as the compliment caught her off-guard.

She tried to piece together the conversation she'd over-heard and also peek into the back room for a glimpse of Smith. "It sounded like you guys were talking about me."

A little crease of confusion appeared between Walker's eyebrows. "What? I . . . oh. Yes and no. He's looking for ways to get me in trouble with my aunt. Or rather, ways to keep himself out of trouble—if she's busy being mad at me, it's a lot easier for him to get away with stuff."

"So, why did he sound so pissed off back there?" Keira asked.

Walker dropped his hands from behind his head and tore his gaze away from the ceiling. "He told my aunt that I'm dating you. She found out that he'd come to see me, and she was pissed, so he pretended he'd only come to check up on me out of *concern*. Aunt Holly's not happy." He rubbed his neck. "To put it mildly."

"But they don't even know me," she protested. She'd only been out with Walker a couple of times—there was no reason she should care what his family thought about her. Still, it stung.

"That's exactly what I said, but it's not really about you. It's about me. Aunt Holly doesn't trust my judgment. She assumes that I'm incapable of making a decent decision. So if I choose you, obviously, it must mean something horrible." Walker got up and headed for the bins of music, riffling through them restlessly. "She'll come around." He shot her a sideways glance. "And if she doesn't, I'll trade them both in for puppies."

Keira's forehead scrunched up. "Puppies?"

Walker nodded seriously. "Yep. Think about it—they're cute, cheap to feed, and they keep their opinions to themselves. It would be a hell of an improvement, don't you think?"

Keira laughed, but her insides still felt heavy and cold. She had a feeling that this was going to be a bigger problem than it looked like.

"So, is he just going to hang out back there?" Keira demanded. More than a little bit of her liked the idea of confronting Smith.

"No, he's already gone."

"Gone? How?"

Walker blinked. "Through the other door."

Keira squinted at him. "That door's been locked for years. Mr. Palmer always said if I could find the key, he'd give me any music in the store."

"It was taped above the doorjamb." Walker shrugged. "You should have seen the tape. It was ancient." Keira wondered if she was imagining the faint red tinge to his cheeks.

"So, Smith's taking Susan out to dinner?"

Walker tipped his head back, studying the dusty ceiling tiles. "That seems to be the plan, yes." He sighed.

"And your aunt's not mad about that?"

Walker raised his eyebrows. "What makes you think he's told her?"

Keira opened her mouth and then shut it again. "Oh. Right."

Walker stepped behind the counter and motioned for her to follow. "Come on, there are two chairs back here."

Keira bit her lip. That was exactly the sort of thing she'd wanted to avoid—the clinging girl routine. Hanging out with the hot guy at work. "Thanks, but I really did stop by to find some music. My dad gave me guilt money and if I don't show up at home with something new, he's going to think something's horribly wrong with me."

"He'll show up at your bedside with a thermometer and the therapist on speed dial?" Walker guessed, flipping through one of Mr. Palmer's catalogs.

"Forget the therapist. He'd probably skip straight to the exorcist."

Walker laughed.

Keira walked over to the shelves, glad that they were alone in the store.

"So, why was your dad so anxious to get rid of you?" Walker asked.

Keira flipped through the books of music hard enough to raise a sparkling cloud of dust motes. "Honestly, I think he was waiting for my mom to get there. I think they had planned a hot afternoon of fighting." She stopped the rest of the words before they tumbled out of her mouth. He'd heard them arguing before. The details were unnecessarily gory. She blinked, trying to get her eyes to quit stinging.

It must be the dust.

Even in her own head, the lie sounded hollow.

"Families suck sometimes," Walker said.

"Wow . . . that's, I mean, since your . . ." Her stammering sent a flush of heat through her cheeks.

"Funny attitude for an orphan, you mean?" His eyebrow was cocked but there was only the gentlest teasing in the set of his mouth.

Keira nodded, staring intently at the book in her hands. A collection of Viennese waltzes. The illustrated lady on the front had been drawn with an impossibly tiny waist, as though a single wrong move on the dance floor would snap her in two. Keira knew how she felt.

She looked up at Walker. "You're not talking about your parents when you say families suck, are you?"

He linked his hands behind his head and leaned back in his chair. "Nope. See? I knew you'd understand."

Keira slid the waltzes back onto the shelf.

"At least this time you're leaving the music neat," Walker observed.

"Very funny." Keira remembered that first day she'd met Walker. She could still see the mess of music-covered pages on the floor, hovering at her feet like ghosts.

Walker leveled his gaze at her. It was like being caught in an unexpected spotlight. She suddenly felt completely visible, all of her flaws and secrets laid bare beneath the beam.

"I don't want you to worry about my family." Walker's voice was even lower than usual—a rumble that made Keira shiver as it rattled through her chest. "They're not worth it."

Walker rubbed his forehead. His fingers left a smear of ink above the bridge of his nose.

"I'm not worried," Keira insisted. "My whole family's crazy, too, remember?" She smiled at him, reaching up to wipe away the smudge, but before her fingertips could touch it, the black stain sank into his skin and disappeared.

She froze, her hand inches from Walker's face.

His eyebrows drew together. "You okay?"

Her own words echoed in her head. *My whole family's crazy. My whole family's crazy.*

Keira swallowed hard and forced herself to nod. She pasted on a sheepish smile. "I thought you'd gotten some ink here." She stroked a finger across his forehead and Walker's eyelids flickered. "But I guess it was just a shadow."

He reached up and caught her wrist before she could pull her hand away from his face.

Her heart thudded so frantically that Keira was dizzy with it. He had to be able to feel her pulse racing beneath his fingers—it was like her blood was leaping up to feel his touch.

She hadn't realized she'd moved so close to him. She couldn't look away from his fathomless gray eyes and she didn't want to. There was nothing else worth seeing.

"I'm sure it was just a trick of the light," Walker agreed, each word slow and thick as molasses. He slid his hand along her wrist, his fingers lingering against her palm before he let go. Her skin tingled where he'd touched her and she pressed her arm against her body, holding the feeling there.

"Saturday night," he said, still pinning her in place with his eyes. "Will you have dinner with me? Somewhere with actual napkins and decent food?"

Keira smiled at him. The spell of the moment broke, but the cracked pieces still glittered with leftover magic. "Yes to dinner. But this is Sherwin. We might be able to find cloth napkins, but you've been here long enough to know that there *is* no decent food."

Walker laughed. "Close enough. Now let's find you some music. Might as well make one of our families happy today, right?"

The two of them walked back to the bins, but Keira struggled to pick some music. She was like a ship caught on a roiling sea, pitching helplessly back and forth between the delicious heat of Walker's touch, his invitation, and the cold horror of the fact that his family already didn't approve of her.

And why should they, when she couldn't even be counted on to have a simple conversation without hallucinating? She toyed with the idea of saying something—asking him why it was only when she was with him that she saw the bizarre darkness.

She thought about asking if Walker saw it too.

Her mouth opened barely wide enough to let the words slip through. The tip of her tongue traced her lower lip—

And then the clang of the door echoed through the store as an old woman minced into Take Note with a battered violin case under one arm.

Keira's mouth snapped shut. Walker sauntered up to the counter, and Keira turned her attention back to the music. Fine. Maybe this wasn't really the time to bring it up after all.

Chapter Twenty-Two

FRIDAY SCRAPED BY SLOWLY. When Saturday came, time barely seemed to be moving at all. Susan was distant—it was like she could smell Keira's disapproval. When they talked, Susan was vague, and when Keira asked if she wanted to hang out, Susan was "busy." Keira's parents went . . . wherever it was they went to escape.

Keira spent the day at the piano. She played the things she was supposed to play, but after an afternoon of uninspired, technical practice, she found her fingers wandering over the keys. Not playing anything she knew, but playing *something*, nonetheless. She felt the music taking shape beneath her hands, the same way she'd stumbled into the song she'd written for Walker.

This one was different. Staccato and choppy and repetitive, but suspenseful, too. She could hear—could *feel*—all the wanting trapped inside her, echoed in the spiraling measures and circling notes. The strangeness of hearing music, *making* music, without being able to see the notes on a page in front of her, quickened Keira's breath. It was like driving with her eyes closed, trusting that she knew the road and the car well enough to avoid a crash. As thrilling as it was, though, it wasn't going to get her into Juilliard.

With a sigh, she let the last chord fade into silence. Without bothering to transcribe what she'd just played, Keira picked up the music for the Beethoven sonata and positioned it on the music stand.

At least she could play again. It was still missing the spark that she felt with her own pieces, but she knew she'd get that back.

It would just take practice.

Lots and lots of practice.

That evening, Walker pulled into the driveway at five thirty. Keira was already dressed and ready to go, her stomach rumbling at the thought of dinner. She stretched her neck, easing out the kinks that had set in after the hours she'd crammed in at the piano before getting ready for her date.

Her date. The words were cool and sweet as ice cream and Keira shivered pleasantly. She was going on a date with a guy she liked, and she wasn't sacrificing her music to do it. She would have loved to call Susan and gloat, but she was pretty sure Susan was already out with Smith. That sort of interruption wasn't going to win her any points at all.

The thump of Walker's car door snapped Keira's wandering thoughts back in line. She shrugged into her jacket and turned to yell good-bye to her mother.

"Where are you going?" Her mom stood in the kitchen doorway, her arms crossed in front of her.

"Um, out to dinner?"

"With Walker?" her mother prompted.

Keira nodded. She wasn't trying to hide what she was doing. If her parents were too wrapped up in their own drama to notice what was going on in her life that wasn't her fault.

"The therapist said it was healthy for me to spend time with my friends, remember?"

Her mother winced, then recovered. "But Walker's more than a friend, isn't he?"

Heat flooded Keira's cheeks. The doorbell rang.

"Well?" her mother asked.

"Not yet," Keira whispered, keenly aware of the thin walls and flimsy door. "Are you telling me I can't go? Because Walker's standing out in the cold and that's rude."

Her mother sighed and dropped her arms. "Fine. Be home by nine."

"Nine? But it's Saturday!" Keira protested.

Her mother gave her a don't-push-me smile. "He's welcome to stay for a while. But *you* are to be back in this house by nine p.m." She stomped into the kitchen, muttering something about learning lessons the hard way.

Keira waited until her mother was gone, then opened the door. "Sorry! I didn't mean to leave you waiting in the cold."

Walker stood on the porch, his hands shoved into the pockets of a black wool peacoat. He shot her a grin that was wicked as the devil.

"Some things are worth waiting for."

The cold air between them vanished. Keira smiled back and stepped out onto the porch. She closed the door behind her, shutting out her mother's disapproval and her parents' inevitable Saturday night fight. She shut out everything except Walker.

"Good to know," she said, arching an eyebrow. "But if I have to wait much longer for dinner, I'm going to die of hunger."

Walker laughed, a low, black-laced chuckle that went through Keira like a hot knife. "Then let's go."

He put a hand on the small of her back. The tips of his fingers pressed against the curve of her spine and his touch set her skin on fire. They climbed into the car and Walker tossed her a thin silver rectangle.

"Since you're the expert—I thought you should get to pick the music. It plugs in right there," he said, pointing to a spot on the dashboard.

While he drove, Keira scrolled through the albums. The eighties rock bands made her want to giggle, but she resisted. There was plenty else to choose from—lots of alternative stuff that didn't make her want to scream, but didn't feel quite right for the night. She settled on an old Van Morrison album, clicked play, and leaned back in her seat.

Walker looked over at her. "Nice choice," he said. "And thanks."

"For what?" she asked.

"Not laughing at my pathetic music selections," he said seriously.

She didn't laugh, but she couldn't stop the smile that slid across her face. "Hey, no one's perfect, right?"

His gaze swept over her hair and lingered for a moment on her mouth before he turned his attention back to the road. "I'm not so sure about that," he said quietly.

With his words still ringing in the air between them, Keira's cell phone started to vibrate. She thought about letting it go to voice mail, but if it was Susan . . .

She slid the phone out of her pocket, glanced at the strange number, and hit ignore.

"Not important?" Walker asked.

"Nope," she said. "I thought it might be Susan, but it wasn't."

"Everything okay?"

Keira cleared her throat. "I think she's busy right now," she said. "And I kind of told her that I wasn't sure Smith was a good choice for a rebound guy. She doesn't want to hear that. It's hard. I mean, not everyone's jumping up and down about you and me, either."

"Ah. So your mom doesn't like me," Walker guessed. "She thinks I'm the Big Bad Wolf, coming to steal you away from the path of your True Calling."

"How did you know?" she asked.

Walker shrugged. "I get that reaction a lot," he said. He pulled into the parking lot of a tiny restaurant.

"I mean . . . it's not exactly like that," Keira stammered as he shut off the car and turned to face her.

He watched her fumbling for the right words, his eyes sparkling with mirth.

She covered her eyes with her hand, needing to hide before she could admit the truth. "Yeah. That's pretty much how it is."

His skin was warm against hers as he gently tugged her fingers away from her face. Their hands lay linked on the console between them.

"So, then, the question is . . . is it worth it? Am I worth it?" His voice was soft.

In the silence that followed, she could hear her heart thrumming double-time. The words caught in her throat, and she had to swallow before she could answer.

"I don't know," she whispered. "I want you to be."

His eyes widened. Narrowed. "I guess that means I haven't totally swept you off your feet, then. I'll have to work harder."

Keira tightened her grip on his fingers, matched his gaze. "I'm not trying to hurt your feelings. I like you." Saying it out loud was like taking off a pair of shoes that were too tight—she felt freer and more naked, all at once. "But I know what it means to do something that shuts other people out. I've dedicated my whole life to music—picked that over everything else. I don't know if there's room for you and the piano. I can't say yes—not just because I want to. I *do* want to. But I have to be *sure.*"

Slowly, Walker nodded. He ran his thumb across the back of her hand. "Then I'll have to find a way to make you sure," he said.

"You're not mad?"

He shook his head. "I don't know if you'll believe me, but that answer was better than a simple 'yes' could ever have been." He slid his hand out of hers and opened the car door. "Now, dinner. Before you starve."

Keira watched him slide out of the car and flip his collar up against the wind that tugged at his curls.

He turned toward the car with a smile, waiting for her in every sense of the word.

Chapter Twenty-Three

DINNER WAS INEVITABLY TERRIBLE. There were only three kinds of restaurants in Sherwin—fast food, "family friendly," and a few independent holes-in-the-wall that hadn't changed their menus since 1963.

Keira watched Walker poking at his pot roast suspiciously. "How is it?" she asked.

"Murdered," he answered. "In more ways than one."

Keira laughed. "Sherwin's not exactly the Restaurant Capital of Maine," she agreed, gesturing to her own dinner, which was more soggy breading and lemon sauce than chicken.

"It's a good thing I'm not that into food. Otherwise, I guess I'd have to learn to cook."

Keira shrugged. "I couldn't help you with that. I can make tea and peanut butter sandwiches, but that's about it."

"Too absorbed in your art to bother with the real world?"

It sounded so ridiculous, so *pompous* when he said it like that. She frowned. "It's not that. Not the way you meant it, anyway. I just don't care. If I have an extra hour, I'd rather spend it in front of the piano than hovering over some pots and pans."

Walker opened his mouth to respond, then he hesitated. His gaze flicked away from her face, looking somewhere behind Keira. Automatically, she turned to see what had distracted him. She should have seen a couple of empty tables and the fern-laced paper that lined the restaurant's walls. Instead, spread out behind her was a thicket of reddish black undergrowth. The leaves were round and dull, which only highlighted the thorns that stood out between them like needle-pointed fingers.

In the bushes, something rustled.

The noise passed through Keira like an electric current. It rattled her teeth and the fork in her hand clattered to the floor. She spun around to find Walker staring at her. His expression spun—suspicious, then horrified, then amazed, then relieved, and then back to suspicious. Keira was dizzy with it.

"What—what were you looking at?" she choked out.

"I thought I saw a cockroach on the wall," he said evenly.

"Will you excuse me for a second? I need to use the restroom."

Without waiting for her to respond, Walker slipped out of his seat and strode toward the back of the restaurant, almost angry.

The door closed behind him, and Keira had the oddest sensation that he was gone—not just in another room, but *gone*.

She sat and stared at her inedible dinner, trying to ignore the invisible hedge looming behind her. When Walker appeared beside her, she jumped.

"I didn't meant to startle you," he said. His smile was hot and lazy as a summer afternoon, but there was a tiny, worried crease between his eyebrows. "This place isn't nearly good enough for you. Maybe we should get out of here?"

Keira watched his face. His forehead relaxed. Maybe she'd been reading too much into his expression. Maybe he was only suspicious because *she* was acting so weird. She had to figure out what was making her mind play these tricks on her.

"Sure," she said. Her voice was measured. "I couldn't eat another bite. At least, not of this." She gestured to her plate.

Walker tossed some money on the table. "I shouldn't have eaten the *first* bite of mine. We could go back to my place. I have some ice cream in the freezer, if you're still hungry."

Curiosity swallowed Keira in a single gulp. She wanted to see his place, his things. She wanted to know what would happen if they were finally, really alone. She wanted *him*.

Her common sense took over. She couldn't go to his

apartment. There was no way that was a remotely good idea. Tempting, yes. Good . . . not so much. Keira checked the time and blew out a disappointed breath. "I can't. I have to be home by nine."

Walker's eyes widened. "Nine? What kind of curfew is that?"

"Big Bad Wolf curfew, I think."

Walker laughed. "Fine. But if this keeps up, I might have to start calling you 'Red,'" he warned.

Keira shot him her most murderous stare. Ever since she was a kid, people had been trying that cutesy, redhead crap. "Carrot Top" and "Red" and even, for a short but horrible period in the fifth grade, "Clifford," after the dog in the kids' books.

"You wouldn't dare," she said, slipping on her coat.

Walker pushed the restaurant door open. "I might," he teased. "Don't Little Red Riding Hood and the wolf eventually end up in bed together?"

The thought turned her blood molten, in spite of the cold damp air that twined around her.

"Yeah, right before he *eats* her," she shot back.

The look on Walker's face twisted her words until she was sure she would spontaneously combust right there in the parking lot.

Smug as a cat with a mouse under its paw, Walker opened her car door.

"Come on," he said, dropping the innuendo. "You can make fun of my music all the way home."

In spite of herself, Keira laughed and swung into the car. "Deal."

It wasn't until he was halfway around to the driver's side that Keira realized she'd let him open her door for her. She hadn't even noticed he was doing it.

Walker's triumphant expression said that even if she hadn't noticed what he'd done, he absolutely had.

Back at Keira's house, Walker turned off the engine.

"What are you doing?" Keira asked. She hadn't meant to sound horrified.

Oops.

Without missing a beat, Walker opened his door. "Trying to correct your mother's impression of me," he said. "Moms like guys who come in for a minute and say hi. Trust me."

Keira hesitated. If both of her parents were home, if they'd decided to "sort through some things" while she was gone . . .

"What?" Walker asked.

"I—it could be World War Three in there."

Walker nodded solemnly. "All the more reason for me to come in. I don't want to send you into the trenches alone."

Keira tried to smile, but it twisted and broke, dying on her lips.

Walker reached across the car and squeezed her hand. "Seriously. It's okay. If they're fighting, I'll leave. And I'll still call you tomorrow. It doesn't bother me, Keira."

The dashboard wavered in front of her as tears crept into her eyes. "It bothers *me*," she whispered.

"I know." His voice was warm and calm. It soaked into her, making everything okay.

Keira got out of the car. "You can't say I didn't warn you."

Together, they headed up the front walk and Keira opened the door.

The silence that poured out was more beautiful than music.

Walker, a half step behind her, put a hand on Keira's shoulder and squeezed.

"Hello?" Keira called. "We're home."

"In the kitchen," her mother called back. "And who's 'we'?"

Walker's laugh was too quiet for anyone except Keira to hear, but she smacked his arm anyway. It only made him laugh harder. The two of them wove their way through the dark hall.

"Oh, hi, Walker. It's been a while." Her mother wore her best PTA smile—the one she reserved for people she couldn't stand but needed to be nice to anyway.

"I know. Thanks for letting me take Keira to dinner tonight."

Keira's mother tugged the dishcloth through her hands.

If that thing had a neck, she would be wringing it.

"Why don't you two go in the living room? I've got some decaf brewing—I'll bring it in when it's ready. Walker? Do you take cream or sugar?"

"Both. And lots of them, please." Walker smiled sheepishly. Keira thought it looked very sweet. Her mother looked like she thought the sheepishness was nothing more than a wolf in disguise.

Keira and Walker left her mother fiddling with cups and spoons. They sat an awkward but polite cushion-width apart on the sofa.

"Will you play?" Walker asked, gesturing to the piano.

Keira hesitated. She wasn't ready to play the pieces she'd written herself—not for anyone else—but the rest of her playing had sounded so wooden lately.

"Coffee's ready!" Her mother's voice was painfully perky. Her polite veneer was so thin that Keira could see her seething underneath it. Her mom stepped into the living room. In that instant, the same tree that Keira had hallucinated before swung into existence, swaying wildly in a wind that Keira couldn't feel. The branches above Keira's head dropped fruit like enormous hailstones and she automatically ducked as one sailed past her head.

"What's wrong?" her mother asked, frowning. "You look like you've seen a ghost."

Keira struggled to pull herself together, but the two visions coming so close together had left her nerves splintered. "No ghosts. Imaginary trees, sure," she wisecracked pathetically, "but no ghosts."

Walker stared at her. His voice was light, but his face was dark as a coal mine. "Imaginary trees aren't that bad. As long as you can duck the falling fruit, you'll be fine."

The words rumbled toward Keira. They slammed against her eardrums, their meaning painting itself across Keira's mind.

Instead of popping out of existence, the landscape around the tree shimmered and grew, spreading across the living room floor.

Keira clutched the pillow next to her as her sense of balance evaporated. She couldn't tell which things were real and which weren't. The couch was firmly beneath her, but her mother wavered insubstantially in the doorway. Keira could feel the wind that howled around the tree. It slapped her cheeks.

There was only one thing in the whole room that looked normal, that looked right.

Walker.

His eyes caught hers for a moment before glancing up at the canopy of tree branches over her head. She saw his hand curl into a fist at his side.

He knew. The thought stole her breath. It also made air completely unnecessary. He saw what she saw. She wasn't crazy. The visions weren't hallucinations or messages from her subconscious.

They were real.

They were

fucking

real.

Chapter Twenty-Four

THE TWO VERSIONS OF the living room in front of Keira vibrated like off-key tuning forks. It felt like her skull would crack from the pressure behind her eyes. Only Walker stayed steady. She focused on him as a whimper slipped between her lips.

Walker shook his head.

"Look at your mom," he instructed her. His words were low and urgent, out of place amid the oceanic roar of the wind in Keira's ears. His voice was a life raft, and without thinking—without questioning—she grabbed for it.

Keira turned to see the frown spilled across her mother's

face. Mrs. Brannon clutched the tray so tightly that the tendons in her hands stood out. She glanced between Keira and Walker, like she'd missed the crucial point of a tennis match. Like one of their faces would tell her who had won.

In an instant, the tree and the world that went with it disappeared. The real world went back to playing its solo.

Keira sat, trembling and exhausted, still clutching the pillow. The fabric was damp beneath her hand.

Walker pinched the bridge of his nose between his fingers. She could see him deciding what to do. Keira wasn't used to seeing him have to think before he spoke. But then again, she'd never seen him this clearly.

"I mean, she's standing there holding that heavy tray," he said carefully. "And we're just sitting here watching her." He leapt up, taking the tray from Keira's mom. She was too busy staring at Keira to notice, much less protest.

"Sweetie, you look terrible."

At the sound of her mother's familiar voice, the world tilted and nausea lurched through Keira. She bolted off the couch with one hand clamped over her mouth. She barely made it to the bathroom before her dinner made a sudden reappearance.

Keira flushed the toilet and shuffled to the sink, her hands shaking as she turned on the cold water.

She didn't look in the mirror. She didn't want to see what lurked in the glass.

"Keira? Are you okay?" Her mother knocked frantically.

"I'm fine," Keira called back. Her voice rasped and broke, showing her for the liar that she was.

Her mother cracked open the door. "Oh, my God, you're *gray*. Where did the two of you eat, anyway? You look like you have food poisoning. Or—you weren't *drinking*, were you?"

"No!" Keira shook her head. "We went out to Kincaid's. I had the chicken." The word brought another stomach-wrenching spasm, and Keira stumbled back to the toilet, retching.

"You're going straight to bed," her mother declared.

"Keira?" She could hear Walker, standing at the end of the hall, the creaky floorboard complaining beneath him.

Keira sat up and wiped her mouth with the back of her hand. "I have to talk to Walker first," she protested.

"Mrs. Brannon, if you could give us one minute—" Walker started.

Keira's mother cut him off with a snort. "You two can talk tomorrow." She turned back to Keira. "You. Go get in bed. I'll see Walker out, and then I'm calling your father. He can pick up some saltines and ginger ale on his way home."

Keira heard the front door open, the surprised tenor of her father's voice and Walker's baritone response. Keira wavered on her feet.

"Oh. Speak of the devil." Keira's mom frowned. "I mean it. I want you *in bed*."

Her mother ducked out of the bathroom. Keira heard her

parents ushering Walker out the door. Keira staggered toward the living room. Each step was terrifying. The floor didn't feel solid beneath her feet, and she wasn't sure that she'd still be looking at the dusty family photo at the end of the hall after her next blink. If the utterly foreign forest appeared in its place, she would start screaming.

She needed Walker. She needed to talk to him. To find out what the hell was going on and why, all of a sudden, it looked like crazy-land was a real place after all.

Her cell phone was in the living room. She just had to get to it.

Her mother intercepted her in the foyer, her coat half on, her face fury-clad.

"What do you think you're *doing*?" she demanded. "You need to be lying down. Why will no one in this house *listen* to me?"

While her father crept into the kitchen, Keira reached into the open coat closet and slipped her cell out of her coat pocket. "I was just getting something," she said vaguely. "I'm going to bed now. Swear."

The phone nestled in her hand like a lifeline.

Her mother reached out, tugged Keira's fingers off the plastic case, and slipped the phone into her massive, many-pocketed mom purse. "I don't think so. You're to stay off the phone. It won't kill you to wait until tomorrow to talk to Walker." Her mother snapped her bag shut and stormed to the door. "I'll be back with some ginger ale."

Keira stared after her.

Her mom was wrong.

If she couldn't talk to Walker, it might very well kill her.

She tiptoed into the living room and picked up the house phone. When she clicked it on, an unfamiliar woman's voice filled her ear.

"Hang on—hello?" her father's voice interrupted.

Suspicion squirmed through Keira, making her nauseous all over again. She dropped the phone back into its cradle and went, as instructed, to her room.

Keira lay awake, waiting for her mother.

Her eyes were closed so tightly that she could feel her lashes against her skin. Behind her lids, there was nothing but darkness, shot through with colors like the northern lights. As long as she stared at that emptiness, as long as the pillow stayed smooth beneath her cheek, she felt okay.

She wondered if Walker was calling her. Texting her. She wondered what her mother would think. If Keira's phone went off incessantly, her mom was likely to label him a stalker before she'd even paid for the crackers and soda.

I'll lie here until they go to bed. And then I'll find a way to talk to Walker.

Her brain ached from trying to wrap itself around what had happened tonight. The headache pounded relentlessly against her temples, a steady bass beat of pain. She felt herself shutting down as the terror and postvomiting weakness tugged at her. She slid into a sleep that was more protective than restful, her body pausing reality in the hope of letting her mind catch up.

When she woke, it was instantaneous—a sudden leap into consciousness. Keira sat bolt upright in the dark bedroom. There was a glass of ginger ale on the table next to her bed. It looked flat, like it had been sitting there for hours. The clock beside it said 3:22 a.m. Keira swung her feet over the edge of the bed, thinking only of getting a phone—any phone.

It wasn't until she had a hand on her doorknob that she heard the television murmuring in the living room. The sound of her mother, coughing quietly, rattled down the hall.

She was still up?

Dammit. God DAMN it!

Raking her hands through her hair, Keira threw herself into bed, flopping back against the pillows. She wondered briefly if Walker was lying awake, as confused and scared as she was. Maybe he wasn't. Maybe he actually knew what was going on.

Keira lay in the dark with her hands tucked behind her head, listening to her mother wandering around in the night. She waited. She drank the mostly flat ginger ale. Her mom couldn't stay up forever.

But she might as well have—Keira slipped back into sleep before her mother went to bed, if she ever did.

Then next thing she knew, there was light filtering through

her closed eyelids, and a hand on her shoulder, shaking her awake.

"Honey?" Her mother's voice was catastrophically quiet.

Keira opened her eyes. Her mother looked haggard.

"Unnh ... yeah?" Keira managed, struggling to sit up.

"I'm sorry to wake you. I have to run out for a minute, and I wanted to make sure you were okay before I left." Her mother studied Keira. "How are you feeling? I didn't hear any more vomiting last night."

"I feel fine," Keira said as convincingly as possible. It was hard to focus with the voice at the back of her mind yelling, *GET THE PHONE. CALL WALKER. CALL WALKER. PHONEPHONEPHONE.*

"That's good. I'm glad." Her mother looked exactly no happier than she had when she woke Keira.

"Mom, what's going on? You look like someone died or something."

For one instant, her mother's face looked as raw as a scraped knee. "I wasn't going to tell you about this until later—until you'd had a chance to wake up."

The back-of-her-mind voice shut up about Walker for a minute. "Tell me about what?" Keira asked carefully.

"Keira, you know things have been difficult between your father and I for some time now. Yesterday, after I left to get your ginger ale, he made ... I came home and he was on the phone. . . ." Her mother cleared her throat. "Well. I'll spare you the details. Everything sort of came to a head. We're going to spend some time apart and see if having a cooling-off period will help us straighten things out."

Keira's vision swam. She recalled the strange woman she'd heard when she'd picked up the phone last night. Her parents had always had an up-and-down relationship. It was like hurricane season—periods of stormy ugliness followed by stretches of relative calm. She'd known that they weren't exactly in one of their blue-sky times, but she hadn't suspected that her dad was seeing someone else.

"Are you getting divorced?" The question came out as a squeak.

Her mother swallowed twice and began to blink hard. "I don't honestly know. We haven't made any decisions yet." Her voice strengthened. "We're having a trial separation. We'll just have to wait and see how things go." She looked at Keira, sorrowful and sincere. "This isn't your fault in any way, and I'm sorry, because I know that you're the one who ends up suffering the most from all of this."

Keira nodded. She hadn't felt like she was responsible for her parents' bickering, but she loved her dad, too, and she didn't want to be stuck shuffling between her house and some crappy bachelor apartment. A lump swelled in her throat. "It's . . . I mean, it's not okay, but if you have to—"

"We have to," her mother said firmly. "One way or another, things are going to get better around here. If you're sure you're okay, I'm going to get cleaned up and head out. Your dad's going to come over and get some of his things. If you want to come with me, you can, but you don't have to. It's your choice, and I don't mind either way, but I'd rather not see him right now."

Keira stared at the empty glass that sat on the night table. She wondered what would have happened if her mother hadn't gone racing out to get the ginger ale last night. "You go ahead. I'll stay here and . . . I kind of need to think for a little while."

"I understand, sweetie." Her mother stood up, smoothing the rumpled spot she'd made on the comforter.

"Where's dad going to stay?" The question slid out before Keira could stop it.

Her mother's expression turned flinty. "I don't exactly know. I have my suspicions, but he hasn't said where he'll be. If you want to get ahold of him, he has his phone."

The words slipped over Keira's skin like an ice cube, leaving her goose-bumped and shivering. "Okay," she said. "Thanks." Her mother nodded without looking at her and headed toward the bathroom.

Mechanically, Keira got out of bed and headed to the kitchen. She filled her mug with water and put it in the microwave. She watched it rotate, echoing the spinning in her head. Her parents were separating.

It wasn't like they were ever home together, anyway.

It wasn't like they were ever *happy*.

It wasn't like it should have come as a surprise.

Still, she found herself standing in the rubble of her life and hating every second of it. She could practically feel the sharp edges under her bare feet. She glanced down and froze. Running through the middle of the kitchen was a path of black, glittering stones. And she was standing smack in the center of it. Out of the corner of her eye, she saw a shape—a person—dart into the kitchen and disappear through the refrigerator. Keira shrieked, whirling around and stumbling onto the familiar worn linoleum. As the floor reverberated with the impact, the path faded like a shadow in the sunlight. The refrigerator stood, white and impassive, humming contentedly. Keira's heartbeat, staccato and erratic, rose into her throat, choking her. After last night, she knew that somewhere, somehow, everything she'd just seen was real.

And whatever world—whatever reality—she was seeing . . . it was inhabited.

"Keira?" her mother called. "Are you okay?" Her voice was thick. In a flash Keira knew that she was crying. That she was using the shower to hide her breakdown from Keira.

"Sorry. I burned myself on my tea," Keira lied, hiding her own breakdown. She couldn't say anything to her mother. Not right then. Not when her mom was already crumbling.

"Okay." Her mother shut the bathroom door and Keira tried not to listen for the sound of her sobbing.

With a shaking hand, Keira dropped a tea bag into her mug and scurried into the hall to steal her phone back from her mother's purse.

She'll never notice, anyway. Not in the middle of this chaos.

Chapter Twenty-Five

SHE PULLED THE FAMILIAR phone out of the front pocket of the purse and growled in frustration. The battery was dead. Of course. She usually charged it overnight.

She half ran to her room and jammed the cord into the phone, watching as the screen began to glow in slow-motion. The voice mail icon appeared in the corner.

Two messages.

That's it? Two messages and no texts?

Maybe he was trying not to be suspicious. Not to be creepy.

But the first message wasn't even him. It was the insurance agent's office—the call she'd ignored on the way to the restaurant last night. The adjuster announced in a bored voice that the body shop had called with a damage estimate, and they'd had to total her car. She was supposed to call to discuss "next steps."

Right then, she didn't give a shit about the car. Right then, all she cared about was the next message.

Walker's voice filled her ear. "Hey. Listen, I know things got kind of weird tonight. I don't know exactly how to say this. I don't want to hurt you, Keira." There was a long pause, during which Keira's heart did not beat. "I'd give anything to have things be different, but they just . . . I'm sorry. I hope, maybe someday, you can forgive me. Call me when you get this. We need to talk."

There was a click. And a pause. And then a mechanical female voice asking her to press one to hear the message again, press two to save, or three to—

Keira snapped the phone shut.

What the *fuck*?

Anger swirled inside her. Was he breaking up with her? Was he really going to dump her in the middle of all this insanity?

Jackass.

She wasn't going to let him off that easy—she deserved an explanation. She tried to call him, but got sent straight into voice mail. It was still early—maybe his phone was off.

Fine.

She texted him.

Got ur message. Call me back. NOW.

She hit send and paced the room. Normally, the first thing she'd do in a crisis would be to call Susan, but what was she going to say? "Hey, I know you're busy with Smith, but my parents are getting divorced and I think there's another world out there that no one can see but me and Walker?"

Susan would think she'd lost her mind.

There was no way she could say that—not even to her best friend.

But Keira had one other friend she could turn to. A friend who didn't care how early or late it was, who didn't mind her snarled hair or morning grogginess, and who never accused her of losing her mind.

She carried her tea into the living room, put it on the floor, and sat down at her piano. Keira stretched out her neck and shuffled through the basket of music, nodding absently as her mother peered around the doorway and announced that she was leaving.

In the silence that followed, Keira knew that she wouldn't be able to play any of the pieces she held in her hand. She knew each note on every page, and not a single one fit her mood right then.

Tossing them aside, she put her fingers on the keyboard. With her back to the room, she could feel the visible-invisible tree, lurking there, like it was waiting for her to start playing. She shivered.

She let the fear slink through her, let it slide down her

arms and into her fingers, which twitched against the keys. The music that slithered out of the piano was terrifying. There was a simple melody woven through, but layered on top of it was something discordant and jarring.

Keira poured all of her unmanageable feelings into the music. Without the weight of so much emotion pressing down on her, she was finally able to breathe. When the notes dwindled, and she could hear the end of the song approaching, her eyes fell closed.

The last, quavering note still hung in the air as Keira slid off the bench and padded back to her room to check her phone. She felt braver after playing.

She dialed Walker again. She was going to *make* him talk to her. He *was* going to give her an explanation. If he wanted to up and walk away after that, then he was a bastard, but she'd let him go.

She wasn't going to deal with a world that only the two of them could see all by herself. Not when he obviously knew more about it than she did.

His phone went straight to voice mail.

She dialed him again and again, not caring that in any other situation, she'd look desperate and obsessed.

The fourteenth time she called, he picked up.

"About time," she greeted him.

"I'm sorry! I fell asleep!" He sounded exasperated. "How many times did you call, exactly?"

"How many times did it take you to answer?" Keira snapped. "You're the one who disappeared after you left me that *message.* I don't know what your plans are. Quite frankly, I don't care. But before you tell me that we can't see each other anymore, I need some answers from you."

"What? Keira, I'm not telling you that we can't see each other. Believe me, if I thought you'd be safer with me gone, I'd already be *gone.* But that wouldn't keep them from coming for us. Both of us."

A tendril of fear sprouted inside her, but she brushed it aside. "Jesus. Is the mafia after you, or what? This is Sherwin, Maine, Walker. Not Sicily."

Walker's laugh was rough. "They're much worse than the mafia. Please, Keira . . ."

Please, nothing.

He was not going to beg his way out of this. Her insides turned to flint. "I don't know what kind of game you're playing, but I know that you saw what I saw last night. I *know* it. And it's . . . Walker, that's not the only time I've seen something like that."

He groaned. "Shit. I was worried that was the case. When you said there was a shadow on my face at the theater . . . when you didn't burn yourself on the tea that afternoon at the diner . . ." He half growled. "I should have known then. I should have walked away and never looked back."

She interrupted him, ignoring the grief that sliced through

her when he said *never looked back.* "I'm not exactly trying to hold you against your will," she countered. "But you owe me an explanation. I want to know what I'm seeing. I want to know what it means and why it's happening more often, and then I can *deal with it myself.*"

"It's happening more frequently," he echoed in a whisper. "Oh, no. No, no, no. This is all my fault."

Keira exploded. "*What's* all your fault? Enough with the cryptograms. *Explain it.* Now."

"I'm going to have to. But not over the phone. I don't know what will happen when I tell you. If they—you might need me."

Keira rolled her eyes. "Your confidence in me is breathtaking. Just . . . whatever. If you want to do this in person, then you'll have to come get me, Captain Secrets. The insurance company totaled my car."

"I'll be there in an hour," he said. His voice brimmed with regret and something that sounded an awful lot like he was saying he would have loved her, if he'd had the chance.

The sound spilled over Keira, breaking everything it touched.

It broke her open.

It broke her heart.

Chapter Twenty-Six

KEIRA STARED OBSESSIVELY AT the driveway, watching for Walker. The shadows lengthened in front of the house. As she turned on the lights, the phone rang.

She hesitated. It was tempting to let the machine pick up, but with all the crap that her parents were going through, she knew she couldn't do that.

She rushed to grab the phone. "Hello?"

"Keira. You're there. I hope I didn't interrupt your practice time." Her father sounded as wrung-out as an old mop.

"Hi, Dad. No, I was—" She glanced out the window, checking for Walker. She didn't want to tell her dad where she was going. If he had questions—any questions—she wouldn't have answers. "I was just hanging around."

"I know it's been a difficult day," her dad said. "I'm going to come by in a while and get some things. If you want to talk, I'd be happy to. If you need a little time, well, I understand that, too."

She really didn't want to sit down and have a heart-to-heart with her dad. Not yet, anyway, but it seemed like a flat-out "no" would be unnecessarily rough—like slamming a piano's key-cover just because practice had been hard.

"Okay. I don't know exactly what my plans are yet. I'll . . . if I'm here, maybe we can talk. I don't know. I'm sorry. It's not . . ." She heard her voice thickening as the emotions gathered in her throat.

"It's okay," her dad reassured her. "I understand. No pressure. I'll be there in a bit."

"Thanks." Keira sniffed back her tears and hung up. She stared out the window for a minute, shaking off the call. Everything was broken, and she didn't know how to fix any of it. She wanted desperately to dissolve into sobs, but Walker would be there any minute.

Pull yourself together. Pull. Yourself. Together.

Walker's car slid into the driveway.

Time's up.

Composing her best impassive concert-pianist mask, Keira grabbed her coat and went out to face Walker. Surprise fluttered across his face when she opened the car door.

"Hey," he said. "Um. I thought maybe we could talk here. At your house."

So he can tell me what's going on and then run away without having to drive me home first.

"Sorry," she said, slamming the car door. "But it turns out my dad's sleeping with someone else and my parents are separating." She jammed the seat belt into the latch. "He's coming home to get some of his stuff soon. I'd rather not be here when he does."

"Oh, Keira." The guarded expression on his face broke and Keira felt her own mask crumble in response.

She thought about her dad, stacking work pants and polos into his racquetball duffel. Emptying his shelf in the bathroom's medicine cabinet. Wanting to tell her all about where he was going and why he had gone.

"Is there anything I can do?" Walker asked quietly.

Keira bit her lip. She wanted him to wrap his arms around her. She wanted to bury her face in his jacket and block out the crashing noises of her life being demolished around her.

But she couldn't. Not when she was trying her hardest to prove that she was strong enough to handle whatever was going on—with or without him.

She looked up at Walker's gray eyes. "There is something you can do. You can get me out of here. And then you can answer my questions. I don't give a crap where we go, as long as it's away from this house." She hesitated. The desire to be somewhere familiar swept over her like an incoming tide. "Actually, I take that back. There is somewhere I want to go."

"You name it, I'll take you, kitten."

Keira wrinkled her nose. "Okay. Two things. One, don't call me 'kitten.'"

Walker tried to swallow his smile, but he didn't quite manage it. It made her want him more, which in turn made her even more angry with herself.

"What's the second thing, then?"

"Let me drive. It'll be easier than directing you." It was a test, and she knew it. She felt the imaginary red pencil in her hand, waiting to grade his response.

"You have major control issues, you know that?" The words were harsh, but his tone was gentle. Not quite worthy of an F, but close. A D-minus at best.

"Fine," she admitted, flicking her hair back over her shoulder and watching as his eyes followed the fiery strands. "I like being in control. Can I drive or not?"

He dragged his teeth across his bottom lip, considering. "Okay." He pulled the keys out of the ignition and spun them around his finger. "You can drive. But you had better be careful," he warned, patting the dashboard.

She plucked the keys from his hand. "Don't worry. I know how pissed you'd be if I put a scratch on your *baby*."

He grabbed her hand, curling his fingers around hers so that the sharp metal teeth of the key pressed against her skin.

"Keira." The bravado was gone from his voice. "I'm not worried about the car. I'm worried about *you*. It's my job to worry about you, to keep you safe. None of what's happened—what's going to happen—is me trying to be a jerk." He slid his hand up her arm and it was like flint against steel. Just like that, she was on fire.

"Safe from *what*?" She pulled her arm away, but it was too late. The flames had already spread. Everywhere.

Walker shook his head. "Let's get where we're going first. I actually *don't* want you to wreck the car when I tell you."

Normally, Keira would have rolled her eyes at that sort of drama, but something in his voice stopped her.

"It's really that bad?" she asked in a small voice.

He didn't respond, but she saw his jaw clench.

"Well. Let's go, then," she said, squaring her shoulders.

Keira climbed into the driver's side, sliding the seat forward and adjusting the mirrors while Walker folded himself into the passenger seat. She snuck a glance at him. He was pretending to be relaxed, but he kept pressing on an imaginary brake with his right foot.

Keira'd been to the little park so many times that the turns came as naturally as breathing. She wished she'd been able to calm down enough to enjoy driving his car. Instead, by the time they got to the playground, her shoulders were bunched up around her ears. She pulled into the quiet parking lot and shut off the car.

A few tendrils of mist curled around the slides and swings.

The park was deserted, but the bleak weather made it look lonely, too.

She turned to give Walker the keys, but he didn't notice her outstretched hand. He stared out the windshield, his fingers curled tightly around the door handle.

"*Here?*" He looked over, his eyes searching hers. "Why here?"

Keira shrugged. "It was my favorite park when I was a kid. I always felt safe here. Happy."

"Damn," he whispered. "It started that early."

"What started that early?"

He jerked his head at the playground. "C'mon. Let's go find somewhere to sit."

The two of them wandered between the metal cages of the equipment, heading for the merry-go-round. Walker sat down and patted the space beside him. There was enough room for her, but it seemed like it might be smarter to put one of the metal bars between them.

Wind whipped through the park, making the swings creak on their chains.

Screw it.

She squeezed in next to him, glad for the warmth. Still. Whatever came next was going to hurt. She could tell.

"Okay," she said. "Enough waltzing around. Talk."

Walker reached over and wrapped his hand around hers. "I'm trying. It's hard to know where to start."

Keira stared down at their linked fingers. A strand of darkness, thin as a thread, trailed down Walker's wrist. As she watched, it swirled across the back of his hand, like it was reaching for her.

Keira had spent hours staring at the backs of her hands. She'd watched her fingers move over piano keys and checked her wrists to make sure that they were in the proper position above the piano. She knew the pattern of the veins beneath her translucent skin, every tiny crease in her knuckles.

In one instant, that all changed. She watched a coal-colored ribbon unfurl beneath the base of her thumb. It stretched and spread until it touched the marks on the back of Walker's hand and nestled there comfortably, her own darkness rubbing up against Walker's.

"Can you see that?" Her voice shook. She didn't look up. "That dark stuff on our hands?"

"I see lots of stuff that other people don't notice," he said.

Keira tugged her hand out of his and stood up, turning to face him.

"What kind of stuff?" she demanded. "Like dark marks on your skin that come and go? Trees growing in my living room? What about the door in the middle of the road, when you drove me home after the accident? Did you see *that* stuff?" Saying the words was like walking to the very edge of the high dive. She'd left herself exposed. Vulnerable. One push and she'd fall. She wrapped her arms around herself, her marked hands curled into fists.

Slowly, Walker stood up. He stepped toward her, gently pulling her arms away from her body. He held her balled-up fists in his hands. There was something desperate in his eyes.

"What about now?" He inched closer. Her knee brushed against his leg. "Do you see anything like that now?" The desperation in his eyes changed tone, becoming another sort of begging.

Right then, Keira couldn't see anything but Walker. She shook her head slowly, the air around them so thick that she could barely move.

His hands slid around to the small of her back. She looked up at him, frozen.

Burning.

Both.

His lips were close enough that she could feel his breath against her mouth. Her eyes drifted nearly closed.

Just as her eyelashes tangled together, the park completely disappeared.

And that's when she screamed.

Chapter Twenty-Seven

WALKER LIFTED HIS FACE, but he didn't let go of her.

Keira wriggled out of his arms, spinning around disbelievingly. The park was only a faint, ghostly outline. Around it—around *her*—an enormous, vaulted room had sprung up.

Beneath the arched beams of the ceiling were rows of benches, arranged in a circle around some sort of machine that was all claws and points—a jagged row of spikes pushed out of the floor, reaching for a barrel that had been suspended in midair. The barrel itself looked like it was made out of coal—it glowed darkly, pulling the light that rippled across its surface into itself, rather than throwing it back into the room.

Gleaming teeth jutted out of the barrel at intervals, like a sort of horrible, mechanical grin. Keira shuddered.

"What the hell, Walker?" She didn't bother to ask him if he was seeing the same thing. It was obvious he was.

Filmy strands of darkness, like blackened cobwebs, hung from the machine and draped across the benches, undisturbed by the wind that buffeted the park. Walker wrapped his arm around her and tugged her closer to the mechanical monstrosity, ducking under one of the black wisps.

"It's a church," he said quietly. "Or, it used to be, back when our kind still thought that praying would fix things. There was a handle they'd turn, trying to get this thing to make music. Like a—"

"Giant music box," Keira finished, suddenly seeing the metal hulk in front of her differently. If the spikes in the floor had been even, and tall enough to reach the bumps on the spinning barrel, it would have looked a lot like the insides of the ballerina jewelry box she'd had when she was five.

"Exactly."

Her knees weakened beneath her, and Keira lowered herself onto one of the benches. Only the bench didn't stop her. She sank right through it, landing hard on the ground.

"Ow! Damn it!" She scrambled to her feet, brushing stray bits of mulch from the back of her jeans. "If I can see it, why can't I *sit* on it?"

Walker shoved his hands into his pockets. "Because even

though you can see Darkside—" He paused and shook his head, disbelief written across his face. "You're not *there*. It's like a mirage in the desert. Except this mirage is real. The world you grew up in isn't the only one out there, Keira."

Keira drove her hands through her hair, cupping her head like it was in danger of cracking. "That's crazy. You know that sounds crazy, right? The two of us having a shared hallucination is more sane than that. How do you know it's real?"

"When I told you I moved to Sherwin two years ago? I moved from *there*." Walker gestured toward the church. "I mean, not this church specifically. From Darkside."

Keira took a step back. "No."

"Listen, I know it's hard to believe, but it's not as bizarre as it sounds. There are scientists who've detected our world. They just can't *see* it yet. Did you take physics?"

Keira nodded.

"Have you ever heard of dark matter?"

Keira shook her head, too stricken to answer.

"Damn. Okay, well, you know there are particles—protons and neutrons and stuff—that make up everything humans see?"

"Yeeees," she said slowly, her memory reaching for the science lessons she hadn't paid attention to.

"Well, just because that's all humans can see doesn't mean that those are the only particles out there."

"The other ones are dark matter?" Keira guessed. Her face had gone numb, and she couldn't tell if it was from shock or cold.

"Exactly." Walker stepped toward her, closing the distance she'd created between them. "Darkside is even bigger than the human world. There's more of it. Dark matter, Dark*side* is everywhere. It's in everyone's living room, moving through their hands while they work, coexisting at the bottom of the ocean. The particles aren't built to interact. The worlds are meant to be completely invisible to each other."

Keira tried to swallow, but her mouth was too dry. "So, why can I see it, then? Why can you?"

Walker stared at her. "Because Darkside is part of you. It's your world too. That's why you see the marks on my skin, and now yours, too, when no one else can. You're as much Darkling as human, Keira. Your mother's human, but your father's a Darkling."

Her dad wasn't human? Was he serious?

She shook her head, her thoughts buzzing like angry bees. "That doesn't make any sense, Walker. If there are two worlds that can't interact, then how could my parents come together to make a *baby*?"

Walker's smile was sorrow-filled. "I didn't say they *couldn't* interact. I said they weren't meant to. A few Darklings have a flaw in their molecular structure, like a DNA mutation. It allows them to slip between the worlds and touch humans. But it turned out to be a really, really bad idea for them to do that."

"And you just—you just *guessed* that I might be one of their kids?"

Walker's eyes grew stony—cold and serious. "No. I saw that you'd developed an immunity to heat."

"What? I have? How did you know that?" She remembered the shirt, the one Jeremy had burned, that first day she'd met Walker, and shivered.

"That first time we were in the diner, the tea you had was boiling hot. You should have burned yourself on it, but you drank it without even blinking."

Something in Keira's mind slammed shut, like a mental security gate. "I don't believe you." She sounded like a petulant child, but she didn't care. "If you don't want to see me anymore, all you had to do was say so. Making me think I'm insane and trying to sell me this crazy story . . ." She backed away from him. "It's a real asshole move, Walker."

"Keira, I'm not lying to you." He reached for her. "I . . . look. *Look.*"

She waited. And waited. In the silence, she could hear the strangled panting of her own breath. Nothing happened.

"What?" she finally demanded. "What am I waiting for?"

Walker's mouth moved. She could see him talking, but there was no sound. He stepped over to her but he didn't stop. He walked right through her.

A sound somewhere between a sob and a shriek rattled in her throat. Keira spun to face him. She reached out to touch Walker's face, but her hand slid through his cheek.

Her voice was barely a whisper. "No." It was too much

to take in. It couldn't be. It *wouldn't* be. As long as she didn't believe it, it would all go away.

She stepped away from him and ran straight into the merry-go-round. "I don't believe you." Her voice grew loud. Shrill. "I don't *believe* you! Just leave me *alone.*"

Someone else appeared behind Walker in the gloom of the church. Beneath the figure's hooded robe, Keira saw a guy with a crooked nose and she recognized him in an instant. It was the disappearing pedestrian. From the day of her car accident. He was here.

And it turned out it hadn't been any old pedestrian. It was Smith.

Her panic anchored her to the ground.

Smith was Walker's cousin. That made him a Darkling too.

A Darkling who was dating her best friend.

Walker spun and his expression hardened. He said something to Smith. Keira could see now that it was a robe, and not a coat that Smith wore. Walker looked back at Keira.

Keira turned away from Walker's stricken expression. She watched as the church disappeared and the damp, gray park sprang up to fill the vacant space. As fast as she could, Keira ran. Walker's voice rang through the park.

"Keira! Keira, *wait.* Please, you have to listen to me!"

She ignored him.

She'd taken the footpath home from this park a thousand times. In ten minutes, she'd be home. She'd be inside the familiar walls of her familiar house, which felt a lot safer than the empty church that appeared and disappeared inside the park with no warning.

She wasn't going back there. Not to the park and not to the church. Not ever.

Chapter Twenty-Eight

HALFWAY TO THE HOUSE, Keira's phone started buzzing in her pocket. After three calls in a row from Walker, she turned it off. She raced up the driveway and into the house. Inside, the door to the front hall closet hung open. Keira could see the wedge of emptiness inside, where her father's coats had hung that morning.

"Hello?" she called, her voice half-choked, hoping her dad was still home. She wanted—*needed*—to see someone familiar.

The only response she heard was the furnace humming through the vents.

He was already gone.

And she was alone.

Keira shrugged off her coat, trying to get rid of the damp smell of the park. She staggered over to the piano and collapsed onto the bench, resting her head against the music stand. She sat, staring down at the keyboard, waiting for her breath to even out. For her heart to slow down. A blur of things she didn't want to examine slid through her head again and again.

She stumbled over to the ancient computer that her parents kept in the dining room. After it finally wheezed to life and plodded its way onto the Internet, she typed "dark matter" into the search engine.

The results brought her simmering headache to a rolling boil. There were university pages and online encyclopedias and astrophysics journals, but even the most simple-looking introductory sites were full of physics terms she didn't understand and numberless equations that didn't make any sense.

She picked through it like a dish of spoiled berries, looking for something worth eating. Here and there she caught a sentence, once or twice even a whole paragraph, that she could grasp.

Walker had been telling the truth. Scientists seemed to agree that for the universe to work the way it did, there had to be something more out there than the stuff that humans could see.

Something invisible.

Something dark.

Something that worked exactly how Walker said it had. The molecules moved through the regular world without anyone feeling them, hearing them, or seeing them.

Except Keira.

There were pages and pages about the experiments scientists were doing to find dark matter—smashing atoms together in Switzerland, arguing about theories at Berkeley—and part of her wanted to laugh, because she'd already found what they were looking for.

They might as well hand over the Nobel Prize now.

She flipped off the computer and went back to the piano. She didn't even put her hands on the keyboard. She just sat there, looking at the black keys nestled so neatly between the white ones, the same way Walker's world pressed up against hers. The difference was, she liked having both kinds of keys on the piano. She wasn't at all sure she liked having an extra world in her life.

Vaguely, she heard the furnace shut off, and then later kick on again, driving out the chill that had settled in the room. The house phone rang a couple of times. Once, Keira heard her mother leave a message, saying she'd be back later that night. The other times, the line disconnected after the machine picked up.

She knew it was Walker.

Finally, his voice drifted through the living room. "Keira, please. Call me back. I know this must be hard to understand, to accept, but—there are still things I need to tell you. Please." There was a pause, then a click as he hung up.

Her back stiff, Keira stood up from the piano and turned off the answering machine, setting the phone's ring volume to silent. Slowly, the trepidation seeped out of her and questions started to shape themselves around what little Walker had told her about Darkside.

If what he'd said was true, then did it really mean her father wasn't human? Was *that* why he and her mother fought all the time? And how the hell had Walker found her, anyway?

The danger Walker'd hinted at sent a shiver through her. She had to call Susan. There must be some way to warn her about Smith without sounding completely insane.

Keira grabbed her cell phone and turned it on before she could second-guess the decision. Or, twenty-second-guess the decision, more like. As soon as the screen glowed to life, she punched the speed dial for Susan's phone.

She picked up on the first ring.

"Keira. Oh, my God, I've been calling and calling. Are you okay?"

Keira's mouth went dry. Susan knew already? Had Smith said something himself?

"Keira?" Susan's worry poured through the phone.

"Sorry. I . . ." She forced back a crazed giggle. "I don't know if I'm okay or not, actually."

"I don't blame you. Why didn't you call me right away?"

Susan said. "My mom ran into your mom at the mall earlier. She told her about your parents separating. Keira—I'm really sorry. I knew they fought a lot, but I didn't know it was that bad."

Oh. Right. Her parents.

"I guess I was too shocked to talk." Keira blew out a long breath. "But yeah. I'm ninety-eight percent sure my dad's having an affair."

"Oh, crap. That's horrib—" A call-waiting beep interrupted Susan. "—ow could he do that to you g—" *Beeeeep.*

"I don't know. I don't think I *want* to know," she said over another beep. She knew without checking that it was Walker, calling again. She was tempted to dump him into voice mail.

"Who's beeping in?" Susan asked.

"No one," Keira said a beat too quickly.

"Walker?" Susan asked, her voice cooling.

"Yeah," Keira admitted. "We're—he's . . . Things got kind of complicated."

Susan sighed. "Smith said that might happen."

Keira finally understood what people meant when they said their blood ran cold. Her skin seemed to freeze from the inside out. "He did?"

"Yeah. I'm so sorry. But listen, Smith said something about having some friends who'd be really interested in meeting you. Guys who are way more important than Walker, he said."

Keira leaned her forehead against the wall. What guys was

Smith talking about? Susan had no idea what she'd gotten herself into. Actually, neither did Keira.

"Listen, I don't know how to tell you this, but Smith's not the guy you think he is and—" The beeping started again.

"Jesus. Is that Walker calling every thirty seconds?"

"Uh, yeah, actually."

"Wow. Stalker much?" Susan asked, but there was genuine worry in her voice.

"It's not that . . ." A thread of defensiveness stitched an edge into Keira's voice. "We're sorting some things out."

"Oh. Well. Whenever you're finished dealing with him, let me know. If you want to come over here, where he can't get ahold of you, that'd be okay. I'm leaving in a while to meet Smith, but you can come with me. We can all hang out."

Every cell in Keira's body felt too heavy too move. "I guess I need to answer him."

"Fine. Call me when you shake him off."

Keira switched calls, punching the button ferociously. "Hello?"

"Keira, thank God. Listen, I'm sorry about how things went in the park. I feel terrible. I understand why you're scared and pissed, and you have every right to feel that way. But there's more you need to know and—"

"You have five minutes," Keira snapped, willing herself not to melt under his apology. "Talk fast. And if I think you're screwing with my head, I'm hanging up." She paced in front of the window.

"So you know that you—we—aren't completely human. And obviously, you've started to see Darkside. The one thing we have going for us is that it doesn't seem like they've sent any Seekers after you. But that's not going to last long. When they realize what I've done, they'll—"

The glass windowpane next to Keira shimmered, and a black-gloved hand reached into the living room, grabbing the air less than an inch from her arm. She could hear the quiet slap as the fingers curled into a frustrated fist.

For the second time that day, Keira screamed. She leapt away from the window, and the hand blurred into nothingness. The water-spotted glass looked utterly normal. The evening outside was undisturbed and calm as a prestorm sea. But her heart rattled in her chest.

Walker begged her to tell him what happened.

"Someone tried to grab me. Someone reached through the window, right through the goddamn glass, and tried to grab me!" Keira edged out of the living room, her eyes scanning the yard for some sign of her attacker. "Oh, my God. I need to call the police. What if they come back?"

A door slammed on Walker's end of the line. "Damn. They know. Listen to me, Keira. The police can't do anything," he growled. "And whoever tried to grab you *is* coming back. I will be there in five minutes. *Five minutes.*" She heard the purr of his car starting. "Keep moving. Don't stand still. And whatever you do, you stay focused on the human world. Think about your dad. Your piano. I'll be right there." The line went dead.

Keira backed into the corner of the kitchen table and bit back a shriek of surprise. Her eyes darted over the room. There was no part of her that doubted what Walker had told her earlier. She still didn't want to believe it, but ignoring this other world wasn't going to make it go away.

It would just make it easier for them to come for her.

She edged her way around the table, crossing her arms. The light from the hanging lamp poured over her. Her forearms were bumpy with gooseflesh and marred by a series of black dots and dashes, like some kind of dark-matter Morse code.

The insides of her cheeks filled with the sour taste of bile and she squeezed her eyes shut against the marks. The second her kitchen was out of sight, terror blazed through her. With her eyes closed, she didn't know where she was. If she wasn't looking, she couldn't see them coming for her.

Her eyes snapped open and she stared resolutely at the glowing numbers on the microwave clock. Four minutes until Walker would be there.

The silence of the house pressed in on her.

Three minutes.

Her skin quivered, feeling a breeze that shouldn't have been blowing through the kitchen. Instinctively, she hurried over to the counter and grabbed a stray T-shirt her father had left on the counter, clutching it like a security blanket.

Two minutes.

How was she supposed to survive this? Walker had said "they" would come for her again. But who were "they"? What did they want with her? And how the hell was she supposed to hide from them if she couldn't even see where they came from?

One minute.

Outside, she heard the squeal of tires and a thump as Walker took the high curb into their driveway too fast. He was early.

Chapter Twenty-Nine

WALKER THREW OPEN THE door before Keira made it across the foyer. He strode past her, staring around the living room. A guttural roar of frustration ripped through his throat, startling Keira.

"There's no one in this part of Darkside but the Reformers' guards and Record Keepers. None of them can cross over. I don't get it!" He smacked the back of the couch before he spun to face Keira, who was too stunned to move.

In three strides, he crossed the front hall and stood in front of her. "What did they look like?"

"The hand?" she asked, confused.

"It was just a hand?" He blinked.

"Yeah. A hand, covered in something dark. Like a glove, I guess, but thinner, somehow."

Walker's shoulders sagged. "That's very smart, actually. They knew you wouldn't be able to identify the Seeker. And it also means they know I've turned."

Walker wrapped his arms around her and tucked her head under his chin. The security of being pressed against him, of not being alone, was like stepping into a hot shower on an icy morning. Even though it stung, bit by bit, she felt herself thawing.

He turned his head, his cheek resting against her hair. "At least you're okay. I swear, Keira, if anything had happened to you . . ."

"Anything like what?" she asked, her voice muffled against his shirtfront. His scent surrounded her and she breathed it in, letting it calm her. She stepped back, barely holding herself together as she stared at him.

She was dizzy with questions. "What's going on, Walker? I know this is my own stupid fault for running away today, but I need you to tell me exactly what's happening. What's a Seeker? Who are the Reformers? And what do you mean you've 'turned'?" Her voice rose higher, cracking on the last word. "And what about Smith and Susan? Are they coming for her, too?"

Walker stepped back a few inches and stared at her. "So

you believe me now, about Darkside?" he asked. "You're not going to freak out?"

"I don't want to believe you, but I do," Keira said. "And I'm not making any promises about the freaking out bit. I won't run away again, though."

"It's a start." He kept his arm around her as he steered her toward the living room.

They sat on the couch. Keira's eyes swept the room again and again, looking for signs that there was someone else there with them.

Walker reached out and twined his hand around hers. "You don't have to worry. I'm watching now."

"But what about Susan?"

Walker laced his fingers more firmly through hers. "Susan's human. She's of no interest to the Darklings. Well, except Smith, and I really think he's only seeing her in order to get more information about you. He might break her heart, but nothing in Darkside is coming for her."

"So . . ." Keira licked her lower lip, trying to get the words out. "You can see it all the time? That other world?"

Walker nodded, his gaze never leaving her face. "I don't *have* to see it all the time, though. It gets sort of schizophrenic trying to watch two realities at once."

Keira let out a bitter laugh. "I know. That's what I've thought, all these weeks, seeing all this weird crap. I thought I was losing my mind."

Pain streaked across Walker's features, like a burning star across the night sky. "Oh, Keira. I'm sorry. It'll get better." He ran a hand through his hair, tugging at his curls. "Well, actually it's going to get worse. But you'll learn to control it."

"Why is it happening all of a sudden? If I'm really not human, if I'm really like *you*, why haven't I always been able to see this stuff?" she asked. It seemed like as good a place to start as any.

"It might have something to do with you being raised here, in the human world. I don't know for sure, though."

"Then tell me what you *do* know for sure," Keira said.

"The whole mess is really about that. . . ." Walker gestured to the piano.

"My piano?" Keira felt her eyebrows shoot up in disbelief.

"Not *your* piano, specifically. Music. Didn't you notice, in the park? The whole church was built around the music box. Darklings worship music. It's their god—our god."

In spite of her terror and confusion, a little smile crept across Keira's face. Whatever this other world was, at least she understood its religion.

"So, I'm part of a race of musicians?" she ventured.

Walker shook his head. "That's the thing. Darklings can't create music. Humans have this one part of the brain that's missing in Darklings. At least, it's missing now. Like, a billion generations ago, we could make music, but eventually, the ability got lost. Once our kind realized what had happened, it was too late."

"How long ago was that?" Keira asked.

"About a hundred thousand years," Walker answered seriously.

Keira's mouth dropped open.

"Yeah. We've been around awhile." He shrugged. "But after we quit making music, Darkside started to fall apart. Disintegrating, particle by particle. A few generations later, some Darklings were born with a genetic mutation that gave them the ability to interact, at least a bit, with baryonic matter, the stuff your world's made of. And then your scientists started to see evidence of our world too. They're hunting for it now, smashing atoms and staring into the middle of galaxies, trying to see what should still be invisible." His jaw had tightened and Keira saw something angry glowing in his eyes.

"So, why come here at all?" she asked suspiciously. "I don't get it."

"About twenty-five years ago, the Reformers got this idea to start a breeding program. The few females of our kind who could interact with the human world would, uh, mix their genetics with musically talented humans." He raised an eyebrow at her and Keira flushed as understanding swept over her. "The Reformers' plan was for them to rebuild the missing part of our brains, so that we'd be able to create music again. That's why they're called that. Because it's their intention to re-form the Darklings. Literally."

"I can play music," Keira said slowly. "So it worked, right?"

Walker shifted uncomfortably. "Sort of. There were some problems with the crossbreeding. Big problems, actually. The Reformers called the new breed 'the Experimentals.' But none of them—the Experimentals—showed any musical ability. And the Darklings who could cross over into your world—it got ugly for them, too."

"Ugly how, exactly?"

"Crossing back and forth damaged the Seekers—that's what they called the Darklings who could cross, because they were 'seeking' mates. Eventually, it got so bad that the Reformers shut down the program."

"And what about the Experimentals?" Keira asked. "We're just living here, thinking we're crazy until someone like you shows up?"

All of the light went out of Walker's eyes.

"Actually, you're the only Experimental that's ever lived in the human world. You were the exception. Your mother is human, so you were raised on earth instead of being brought up in Darkside. The rest of the Experimentals were born to Darkling women, and raised in Darkside." His hands curled into fists. "And then they were destroyed."

The security she'd felt with Walker ripped away painfully. "You mean—the rest of them were killed?"

He nodded.

"Why?" she whispered.

"The Experimentals had the ability to pass back and forth

between the two worlds, the way you're starting to. Only it was different from when the Darklings crossed. Those Darklings, the Seekers, suffered for it, but Darkside itself didn't. Each time the Experimentals crossed, though, it created a rip in our world. It was destroying Darkside." He shrugged, uncomfortable. "It wasn't their fault. Most of them didn't even understand that they were crossing when it happened. Eliminating them was the only way for us to save ourselves. The Experimentals were created to save Darkside. Instead, they just brought more destruction."

"So, you're here because . . . Oh, God, you're a Seeker? You're here to take me—" She couldn't even choke out the question. There was no way she could outrun Walker. If he'd actually come here to kill her, then she was already dead. But he'd been alone with her so many times, he'd already had so many chances . . .

"Of course I'm not going to take you to them! I wouldn't do anything to hurt you." He slid off the couch, kneeling on the floor in front of her. "I couldn't." Beneath him, where the living room carpet had been, a strange, dark ground appeared. It looked like smooth-swept coal dust.

"Then why did you come find me?" she asked. "And don't try to tell me it was a coincidence."

He shook his head. The look in his eyes was torture. "I was supposed to bring you back. The Reformers sent me to find you. I'm not a Seeker, Keira, but my parents were. I was supposed to finish their job by finding you. I thought it was the only way to keep the rest of my family safe. The Reformers are our government but it's basically a panel of ten dictators, if you ask most Darklings. They tell us what to do and we do it. That's what I meant when I said I'd turned. I don't care about the mission anymore. I'm not doing what I've been told."

"What would happen if you brought me back?" Keira pressed.

Walker closed his eyes. She watched his Adam's apple bob as he swallowed. "They'd kill you. But I'm not going to let that happen. That's why their Seeker tried to grab you tonight. They've figured out that I'm not doing my job anymore."

He opened his eyes and stared straight at her. "They know I care more about you than I do about them."

A bulky, dark form appeared behind Walker, moving purposefully toward them. Before she could get her muscles to move, Walker's arms were around her waist. He pulled her to the floor and she landed on top of him in a tangle of arms and legs. The two of them rolled into the coffee table, and Keira cracked her shoulder against the wooden leg with a thud. As the blaze of pain shot down her arm, whatever—*whoever*— was sweeping through the room disappeared.

Walker leapt up and spun wildly. "I can't see him—there are too many goddamn trees!"

"That was a Seeker, wasn't it?" she whispered as she struggled to sit up.

Walker nodded, fumbling in his pockets and coming up with a handful of car keys. "I can't see him, but there are lots of places around here to hide." He hesitated. "If I crossed over, I could look for him, but then you'd be alone. . . ."

Keira quivered.

"Exactly," Walker said in response to her shiver. "And he's already crossed twice tonight. Crossing takes a toll on the Seekers. He'll be hurting . . . hopefully too much to try again for a while. But we need to get out of here." He looked down at her as she rubbed her throbbing shoulder.

She could feel the bruise blooming beneath the skin already.

"You okay?"

"Fine. Other than the fact that, you know, I'm not human, and I'm being hunted in my own house. Besides that, I'm just fucking great." Anger swept through her voice like a wave through a sand castle.

"I understand why you're mad—" Walker started, getting to his feet.

"Mad?" Keira interrupted, leaping up to stand so that they'd be on equal footing. Not that it made much difference. He still towered over her. "Mad doesn't even begin to cover it."

He ran a hand over his face. "Okay. I get it. You're infused with the righteous fury of the endangered and disenfranchised. Totally understandable. Right now, though, we need to get the hell out of here or the only thing you're going to be infused with is a bunch of the Reformers' guards."

"So, where am I supposed to go? How am I supposed to hide from something I can't see?" Her voice squeaked on the last word.

Walker's face was determined. "I'll keep them from finding you. I can see Darkside for both of us. If anything happened to you, I couldn't stand it. I understand if you hate me, but please let me help you anyway."

"I don't hate you." Keira paced, trying to hold herself together. "I want to, but I don't. I like you more than I should, Walker. A lot more. I always have." She looked down at the floor. "I know that I need your help. But I don't like being the kind of girl who needs a guy to save her. I want to be able to handle things on my own."

Walker stepped in front of her. "You're the kind of girl who does whatever she has to do to save herself. Even if that does mean asking for help." His eyes searched hers.

"It still seems weak, somehow."

He shook his head, his gaze never wavering from her eyes. "I've never met anyone as strong as you. Ever." His arms slid around her back. Keira's middle was like the July sun. Burning. Melting. Liquid.

He leaned in, his eyes reflecting the same heat she felt. Keira slid her arms around his neck as his lips met hers. The kiss shot through her, twining itself around her limbs, pushing her closer to Walker. She couldn't hear anything except the pounding in her ears and she couldn't feel anything other than

Walker—his mouth on hers, his hands pulling her to him.

The sound of a far-off shout startled her and her eyes snapped open. She and Walker were standing beneath the tree, sheltered by its spreading limbs. Her house, her reality, had completely disappeared. Shocked, she stepped out of his arms, staring at the foreign landscape.

More trees stretched into the distance, lining a path that glittered like crushed black glass. At the end of the path stood an enormous cube-shaped building with windows cut into it at irregular intervals. Huge twin lamps glowed on either side of the door, though the light seemed to be streaming into their glow, rather than shining out of it. It gave Keira a headache.

A second shout, closer than the first, jerked her out of her reverie.

"Oh, shit," Walker whispered, staring at her with something like awe, only more terrified. "We're Darkside. *You're* Darkside."

The sound of people running across dry grass whispered in the distance.

"They can see us?" she asked Walker.

"Not for long," he said. "Think about your house. Think in very excruciating detail about your house."

Keira imagined the carpet beneath her feet, the couch behind her and the piano gleaming in the corner. It wasn't working. Why wasn't it working?

"Don't move!" The voice was close, the words thick and strange, like a pattern of drumbeats more than an actual language.

Walker shielded her with his body.

"Keira, try again. Come on—your piano. The pictures over the fireplace."

She shut her eyes, blocking out the dark glimmer of the lamp in the distance, the trees around them—everything about Darkside. Instead, she smelled the dusty, burned-coffee scent of her house. Felt the glow of the piano lamp on her face. Imagined squishing her toes in the wall-to-wall carpet.

She opened her eyes and whimpered with relief. She was home. Walker's arms were still around her, but in spite of his heat, she was trembling with cold.

Walker didn't look cold. He also didn't look relieved.

"We have to go. Right now." He grabbed her hand. As his fingers wrapped around hers, she saw Darkside shimmering against the background of what she still thought of as the real world. Blurry forms darted madly through the room, their arms waving wildly. Outstretched. Grasping.

Walker paused in the front hall. "You were there. And they saw you. And they'll do whatever they can to get you. Even if it means making that Seeker cross a third time in one night." Grim lines appeared at the sides of his mouth. He yanked a coat out of the closet and threw it at her. It was her mother's dress coat, but something about the look on his face made her shrug her arms into the sleeves without protest.

She grabbed her bag and let him tow her out of the house, slamming the door behind them. The back of her neck tingled as she imagined being touched by unseen hands. She couldn't think about what would happen if those hands actually caught her. She put a lid on her rising panic, trying to keep it from boiling over. If she panicked, they'd get her.

She wasn't going to let that happen.

Chapter Thirty

"WHERE WILL WE GO?" she asked as Walker started the car. When he'd let go of her hand, her view of Darkside had disappeared. She thought that she could see it on her own if she tried—after all, she'd seen bits of it without touching him before—but she was too scared to try. She might somehow slip through. And if she did go Darkside, there was no way to know if she could make it back on her own.

Walker tore out of the neighborhood, drumming his fingers impatiently on the steering wheel as he drove.

"Okay. First we're going to drive around for a while. That way they'll have to figure out where we've gone before they send in the Seeker. They know the places you usually go—"

"How?" Keira interrupted.

Walker was quiet one beat too long. His silence answered the question before he spoke. "I told them." His voice was sorrowful. The rush of pleasure she'd felt when he kissed her faded. In its place, a sick, silent nausea settled into her middle. *He'd told them?*

"I was supposed to report back on anyone who might fit the Experimental's profile—anyone I suspected might be the One. I told them about you when we first met, before I really knew you. And then, once I *did* know you, once I started to feel ... the way I feel ... then it was too late. I'm so sorry, Keira."

He stopped at a red light and looked over at her. "I'm not loyal to them anymore, but I was. When I met you, my assignment—my *mission*—was to destroy you. And so I did what I was supposed to do. When I thought I'd found the Experimental, I reported my suspicions to the Reformers. Two days later, I was sorrier about that than I've ever been about anything. I tried to convince everyone that I'd made a mistake, but my aunt Holly didn't believe me. She sent Smith to snoop around. I can't change what I did, but I would give anything to take it back."

She stared at him for a long moment. It might be foolish, but Keira believed him. And she trusted him. Besides, it wasn't like there was anyone else she could turn to. "Don't betray me again," she said finally.

"Never," he swore. "I'll spend the rest of our lives making it up to you if I have to."

The rest of our lives.

The words reminded her of the fate that awaited her if she was caught.

Elimination.

Extermination.

Death.

"That might not be as long as it seems like, huh?" she whispered.

The light turned green and Walker hit the gas. "Don't talk like that. We'll get you hidden. And then we'll find some solution to this mess."

Keira longed for somewhere familiar to sit and collect herself. She wished she were spending the night at Susan's house, listening to Mrs. Kim rattling around the kitchen. Her spine stiffened.

"Susan." Her voice cracked. "I go to her house all the time. They won't go there, will they? Smith . . . he . . . is he a Seeker too? That's why he can come here, right?"

"Smith's not exactly a Seeker. When I told you my family was unusual? I meant Smith, too. He's a special case," Walker admitted. "The thing is, Smith's ability to cross over is a secret. A big secret. That's why my aunt is so protective of him. The Reformers have been looking for someone like Smith for ages.

If they ever found out what he can do, his whole life would be over. They'd put him in a lab and test his DNA and force him into experiments crossing the Darkling–human barrier. That's the last thing my aunt wants to happen."

"Then why does he keep crossing over? Isn't that, like, the opposite of hiding?"

"He thinks it's worth the risk, as long as he gets to be part of the human world. My life looks totally glamorous to him. He wants to live on his own, date a human girl, be out from under my aunt Holly's eight thousand rules."

"Oh." The pieces all fell into place and Keira blinked. The irony was that Smith and Susan had more in common than she'd thought. In spite of the fact that he wasn't human, they'd grown up in almost identical situations.

"That's why my aunt's so desperate for me to hurry up and finish my assignment. She wants to be sure I find the Experimental and bring it—you—back to Darkside. The thing is, once the Experimental is gone, there's no reason for anyone to cross between the worlds. The Reformers wouldn't be looking for Darklings like Smith, and the Reformers would finally leave our family alone. My aunt Holly wants that. Desperately."

"But you don't."

"Not anymore," he said.

She relaxed back against the seat. At least she hadn't put Susan in danger.

"So where will we go that they won't think to look for us? Jail? The library?" Keira mentally scrolled through the places she had never been in Sherwin.

Walker tapped his finger against his lower lip, thinking. "Oh! I've got the perfect place. Well," he amended, "it's actually pretty far from perfect, but it'll hide us."

"Where?"

"You'll see." Walker headed toward the outskirts of town. Keira watched the streets fly past and wondered, again, what the hell she'd gotten herself into. Even more, she wondered if there was any way out.

About five miles outside of Sherwin, Walker turned the car into the parking lot of the Steer Inn Hotel. Keira stared uneasily at the crumbling brick facade. Black shutters hung at the windows and white columns flanked the iron-grated office door. But the attempt at grandiosity failed miserably, as the paint flaked off the shutters like cheap mascara and the left-hand column tilted like it was drunk.

"We're staying *here*?"

Walker nodded. "Safest spot for miles."

Keira turned to him, mystified. "And can I ask how the hell you found this place?"

Walker cocked an eyebrow at her. "That you probably don't want to know."

Keira ignored the embarrassed heat that flared in her cheeks. She looked at all of the ordinary, human surroundings, waiting for something bizarre to appear. Like saying "bloody Mary" while staring into a dark mirror. It seemed insane to think she'd see something, but that didn't stop her from looking. Which was crazier—believing in something no one else could see, or ignoring the proof that it existed?

"Are you sure no one followed us here?" Keira reached to unfasten her seat belt and her shoulder throbbed painfully.

"As sure as I can be. We're safe for now. I'll show you why once we're inside," Walker said. "So, do you want to come in with me and endure the knowing looks of the night clerk, or wait in the car while I get us a room?"

They were going to stay in a hotel. Together. As tempting as the thought was, Keira's instinct was to insist on having her own room. She was grateful for Walker's help, but that didn't mean she was going to sleep with him. Then she remembered that she'd run out of the house with only her backpack and her mother's coat. Keira had about twenty bucks to her name. And no pajamas, either.

"Um, I'll come in with you, I guess. I want to pay for part of the room."

Walker shook his head. "With what money? You carry your life-savings around in your bag?"

"No," Keira admitted.

"I've got this one," Walker said. "We'll call it even. I ruined your life, so I pay for the fleabag hotel. Now come on. We'll be safer inside."

"We will? Why?"

"You'll see."

The clerk eyed them sleepily when they pushed into the office. Overhead, the fluorescent light buzzed unpleasantly.

"We need a room for the night," Walker said. "One on the east side of the hotel."

"One with two beds," Keira piped up.

"Jesus Christ, what d'you think this is, the goddamn Ritz?" The clerk shook his head. "The rooms on that side of the building all got one king bed."

"That'll be fine," Walker said smoothly.

Keira frowned, wondering why it was so important to be on that side of the hotel. The clerk handed Walker a key and a set of sheets that looked reasonably clean.

The two of them walked down the hall, which smelled of mildew and old fast food.

"Three-A," he said. "Home sweet home."

Walker opened the door and flipped a light switch. The room was shabby, with threadbare, mismatched furniture. There was an old-fashioned television bolted to the dresser, and a water stain shaped like the State of California on the ceiling.

"Wow. This is bad, even by Sherwin's standards," Walker said.

Keira squinted at him. "I thought you'd been here before."

"I've never been *in* here. I've only, uh, taken the lay of the land." He glanced around. "At least the bed looks decent."

At the mention of the bed—the one and only bed—Keira felt herself blush.

For a moment, Walker's eyes glittered with the sexy, joking-but-wanting look that made Keira's legs feel unsteady beneath her.

"So," Keira said as breezily as she could. "You want to tell me exactly why we're safe here?"

"Let me see if I can show you." Walker sat on the edge of the bed and gently pulled her down beside him.

The surprise must have showed on Keira's face because Walker laughed. "Don't worry. I'm not putting the moves on you."

She hoped her disappointment wasn't as obvious as her surprise had been.

"At least, not yet," Walker added.

Keira rolled her eyes. "You know that saying 'putting the moves on you' is about as unmovelike as you can get, right?"

Walker's lips curved in amusement.

"Okay." He tipped his head up so that he was staring at the ceiling. "Look up."

Keira obediently scanned the plaster. "What am I looking for?"

"Darkside," he said, wrapping his fingers around hers.

His warm palm should have distracted her completely, but instead it seemed to bring the invisible world closer to her. Uneven black walls rose around them, pressing in on either side of the hotel room. They rose up through the ceiling. Squinting,

Keira realized that she could see all the way to the top of the walls, even though her view of her world ended at the ceiling.

The hotel was at the bottom of a Darkside ravine.

At the top was the sky, filled with a river of stars so thick and clear that it made Keira's breath catch. They moved and swirled, literally dancing across the slice of sky that she could see between the close-pressed cliffs.

"Oh, my God," she whispered. "That's amazing. I've never seen anything so gorgeous in my whole life."

"I feel exactly the same way." Instead of complimenting the stunning sky, Walker's voice was directed straight at Keira.

Immediately, she was more aware of his weight next to her on the bed, the heat of his skin, than any star in the universe. She turned to look at him, drawn like a compass needle to the north.

He brought his lips to hers. This kiss was more certain than their first—insisting, when the other had been hesitant. Walker wound his hands through her hair and she pulled his shoulders toward her, swinging her legs across his lap.

Without warning, they crashed through the mattress, landing hard on the rocky ground.

"What the hell?" Keira looked around.

The hotel room was gone.

Chapter Thirty-One

"OH, SHIT," SHE WHISPERED, struggling to stand. A gooey black sludge coated the back of her jeans. "Walker, what is this stuff?"

"It's . . . I guess it's sort of like what you'd call mud. Listen, we've got to get out of here. Can you see the hotel room if you try?"

Keira stared at the black cliffs, trying to see the dusty drapes, the battered nightstand, but there was nothing besides the oozing mud and the rocks and the stars. "I can't," she whispered to Walker. "Can you?"

"Of course," he said. "Let me see if I can pull you back over with me. We did it once before, right?"

"Yeah." She stepped into his open arms and pressed her face against his shirt. Beneath her cheek, his heart beat furiously. She closed her eyes, focusing on the rhythm. There was a pressing sort of squeeze, and the uncomfortable sensation of something viscous running over her, like cold egg dripping down the back of her neck.

And then it stopped.

She opened her eyes.

First she saw the plaid of Walker's shirt, and then, beyond that, the stained green carpet of the hotel room. She let out a shaky breath and stepped away from Walker, spinning around so she could see the whole room.

She stared at him, shuddering with cold. "That's twice. This whole time I've seen Darkside, I've never gone there. And now, I've been there twice in one night. You kiss me and I end up there. What gives?"

"I don't know," he said slowly. "Here." He held out his hand. Keira took it, and the cliffs shimmered into view. Her mouth fell open.

"It's us." An aching certainty filled Walker's voice. "The more we touch . . ." He pulled her into his arms and Darkside came into sharp focus around her. Keira had to close her eyes against the two equally real worlds. It hurt to look at them simultaneously. "The more contact there is between us, the more access you have to Darkside."

"So when we kissed, *if* we kiss . . ." She bit her lip, not wanting to say it. As though it wouldn't be true if she didn't say it.

"If we kiss, you end up where the Reformers' guards can see you. Where they can catch you."

She let her head fall against his shoulder. "We can't *kiss*?"

Walker laughed bitterly. He stepped back and caught her chin, tipping her face up to his. A tiny smudge of darkness slipped into view at the edge of his jaw, pulsing like a heartbeat.

"Believe me, we can kiss." His eyes burned. "That was the most mind-blowing, reality-bending—" He stopped. "We *can* kiss. It's just not *safe* for us to do it again."

Keira shivered, still cold to the bone and aching for the warmth of Walker's mouth on hers. "Unbelievable."

"I'm sorry about the cold," Walker said. "It goes away after you've been back and forth a few times. Until you get used to it, crossing between the worlds messes with your metabolic systems. You're probably going to be—"

Keira's stomach growled.

"—hungry, too," he finished.

"Yeah. Oh, my jeans!" She twisted around, looking for evidence of the black muck that she'd fallen into, but there was nothing on her.

"With the exception of the Seekers, dark matter stays Darkside," Walker said. "But you can sort of take baryonic matter—the stuff that makes up your world—into Darkside. Clothes and instruments. That sort of thing. As long as it's been impregnated by enough dark matter by being in close contact with a Seeker. Or"—he looked at her—"by an Experimental."

She could have been stripped naked each time they'd crossed. God. It was a pretty slim silver lining, but she clung to it anyway.

Wait . . .

"So if dark matter has to stay Darkside, how come the Seekers aren't naked when they come over here?" she demanded.

Walker's mouth twitched with amusement. "At first, they were. Now they keep a stock of things from this world to wear when they think they're going to cross. It's not easy."

"So they can take clothes back to Darkside—what about people? Can a Darkling bring them across? They're baryonic." The word felt strange in her mouth.

Walker's face twisted like she'd suggested microwaving a puppy. "Uh, yeah. Humans are made of baryonic matter. The thing is, once baryonic matter's in Darkside, it disintegrates. The environment's too foreign. It's one reason music is such a challenge. Even if instruments are coated in dark matter, the baryonic stuff underneath disappears, and the materials we have in Darkside can't re-create the sound they make." He shook his head. "Anyway. The point is, stuff disintegrates. So if *people* come Darkside, they—"

"Disintegrate too. You can stop there. I get it." Something snippy had crept into Keira's voice. It was too much to absorb all at once, and she was full to the brim with surprises.

"I know this isn't easy for you," Walker said gently. "Why

don't you go take a hot shower and I'll go hunt down a vending machine so that you'll have something to eat."

"Fine," Keira agreed miserably. Realizing that she was being nasty to him while he was trying hard to take care of her, Keira turned back to Walker. "I mean, thanks. I'm sorry."

Walker shook his head. "You don't have anything to be sorry for."

He slipped out the door, leaving her alone in the threadbare room. She turned and headed into the bathroom, intending to stand in the shower until she'd used all the hot water in Sherwin or the world ended, whichever came first.

When she was finally warm, Keira climbed out of the shower and stood, wrapped in a towel, in the steamy bathroom. The reality of spending the night in a hotel room with Walker came crashing down around her. She had nothing to change into. And her mom was going to expect her to be home in a couple of hours—to be crawling into her own bed for the night.

She could hear the staccato chatter of Walker flipping through the television channels. She pulled on her shirt and underwear, wrapped a dry towel around her waist, and stepped out of the bathroom.

Walker looked over at her, his eyes widening in appreciation at the amount of thigh visible beneath the inadequate towel she was wearing.

"Wow." He cleared his throat. "So, I got you some stuff to eat.

The choices were pretty pathetic, but it's better than nothing."

She picked a package of cookies off the dresser and looked for somewhere to sit. She noticed that the bed had been made.

"Did you do that?" she asked.

"Yeah, I put the sheets on while you were showering," Walker said.

It was so domestic—so *cute*—that Keira had to wrestle down a desire to run across the room and throw herself into his lap. Instead, she pulled a cookie out of the cellophane and perched on the edge of the bed.

"Aren't you going to eat?" she asked.

Walker stared at her appraisingly. "I don't need to."

Keira swallowed the cookie carefully. "You mean you're not hungry right now, or you don't ever need to eat?"

"Of course I need to eat—you've seen me do that plenty of times," he said. He still sounded guilty, somehow.

Keira stared down at the package of cookies in her lap. "But crossing back and forth doesn't make you hungry anymore?"

Walker leaned back in the worn chair. "True. I've done it too many times. And to be honest, I don't really like the food here. Darkside stuff tastes way better. It's nothing to look at, but it's *delicious*."

"What's it like?" She recalled the fruit she'd seen in her living room.

"Fruits and vegetables, I guess you'd call them. There are huge orchards near here where we grow a lot of . . . well. You don't have a word for them, I don't think. But they're sweet and kind of creamy. I guess you'd call us vegans?"

"You don't eat meat? Wait. You had pot roast the other night."

"Yeah. It's not that Darklings don't *want* to eat meat. There are hardly any animals Darkside, and even if you could find one, you wouldn't want to eat it." He shuddered.

"So, you miss it?"

"I miss the food, yeah. But there's not much else left for me over there. My parents are gone. I never had many friends, since no one else's parents approved of my family." His eyes were rueful. "It was so easy to say yes, when the Reformers got ahold of me after my parents died. They made it seem like finding the Experimental would fix everything. That I'd be important. That I'd have a place in the world again. And by the time I realized they were wrong, I was stuck."

It took Keira two tries to swallow the cookies in her mouth.

"Stuck how?"

"Stuck between, I guess. I don't belong there, and I don't belong here." His shoulders slumped. "And then I found you. You're beautiful and talented, but other than that"—he gave her a small smile—"you're just like me. You know what it feels like to be stuck. To not belong wherever you are."

He was right. Keira'd never felt like she was in the right place. She'd been working her whole life to get out—to get away. It had never occurred to her that she might feel equally misplaced once she got out of Sherwin.

Walker looked at her, spreading his palms open. "When I found you, *really* found you, it was the first time since my parents died that I didn't feel alone."

"Oh. *Oh*." It was so exactly how Keira felt that she could barely breathe.

"*Oh* good or *oh* bad?"

"Good. No, really good. I hadn't put it into words before. But that's exactly it."

Walker looked so relieved that it made her chest ache.

"Did you really think I'd break all of my own rules just because you were cute?" She sighed. "I wish we weren't both so stuck. And I'm not talking about Sherwin."

"I know. But we *will* figure it out. I swear."

Keira stared around the room, her head full of questions she didn't want to ask. She wanted things to be as normal as they looked. A shabby bed. A dented brass lamp. A glowing digital clock.

"Oh, crap! Is that really the time?!" Keira leapt off the bed, barely catching the towel before it fell.

"Yep," Walker said. "So, what are we going to do about your mom?"

The way he said *we* made Keira feel calmer. Whatever happened next, she wouldn't have to deal with it alone. She'd always pictured herself facing the hard things in her future on her own. Partnerless. Practically friendless. Sure, Susan would be in the background—a phone call away, if they needed each other.

Keira sure as hell needed Susan now. If Susan covered for her, then Keira's mom wouldn't freak out when she didn't come home that night.

"Call her and ask," Walker said.

Keira jumped like he'd slid an ice cube down her neck.

"Jesus Christ, don't tell me you're psychic, too."

"Nope. But if you're trying to pull one over on your mom, who do you call? Your best friend. I just did the math." He tapped his temple.

"I don't know if I can ask her to lie for me like that."

Walker shrugged. "If you want, you can tell her you ran away to join the circus. But it's your call. If you'd rather tell her the truth ..."

The thought turned Keira's stomach. "She'd send me off to the mental ward before you could say 'schizophrenic.' I'll call Susan."

With each ring, her heart beat lower in her rib cage. When the voice mail message came on, Keira squeezed her eyes shut.

"Hey, it's me," Keira said. There was no way to even begin to explain what had happened. "God, I didn't want to leave this on a voice mail. Things are really screwed up. I need your help. I mean, really genuinely life-or-death need your help. If either of my parents call you, please, please, *please* tell them I'm at your house. I can't say why right now but ..." She bit her lip. She was asking a lot of Susan. Maybe she did owe her some of the truth. "If you can call me, I swear I'll try to answer. I have a lot of things to explain to you. Until then, please cover for me. I'm begging you."

She ended the call and looked at Walker. "How much can I tell her?"

He spread his hands in an I-don't-know gesture. "As much as you think she can handle without freaking out, I guess."

Keira chewed on her lip, considering that. She'd always trusted Susan with everything, but everything had never included something this bizarre . . . or this deadly.

"Do you think she'll cover for you?" Walker asked.

Keira shrugged. "I hope so. I'm gonna call my mom now."

She dialed her house, praying that the ancient answering machine would pick up.

"Hello?" her mother answered.

Shit.

"Um, hi," Keira said.

"Honey. Where are you? It's getting late—I was starting to worry."

"I know. Sorry. Listen, I'm at Susan's. I'm going to stay here tonight."

Walker made a *longer* sort of gesture with his hands.

"Actually," Keira said quickly, "I might stay for a couple of days."

"You want to stay at Susan's? For a couple of days?" Her mom sounded confused.

Keira knew what she had to say. She didn't want to do it, but hurting her mother was the only way to keep herself safe.

She'll be more upset if I end up dead.

She took a deep breath. "It's just been so tense around the house, with you and dad . . ." It was true, but it was also a complete lie. "It's making me crazy. I need to get away from it for a couple of days."

There was a long pause. On the other end of the phone, Keira could almost hear her mother crumbling.

"Oh."

Another pause.

"Well."

Silence.

Keira finally cracked. "Mom?" She was on the verge of retracting the whole thing and saying she'd run away to play piano in a blues band, when her mother finally spoke.

"I understand." Her voice was an octave higher than usual and quivered with tears. "I wish it wasn't this way. I don't want the stress at home to affect you, but—" She stopped abruptly. "Okay. You can stay with Susan for a few days, but then you need to come home so that we can sort this out. As a family. We're still a family, Keira, we're just different now."

Ain't that the truth.

"Thanks," Keira said, with honest relief in her voice. "I'll call to check in."

"I love you, Keira."

Crap. She could hear her mother crying. Keira was acutely aware that she was leaving her mom broken and alone, in a house full of Darklings.

They can't find her. She's human. She's why I'm *half human.*

The question that had been humming around the edges of Keira's thoughts came soaring in.

So why hasn't my dad ever bothered to tell me I'm half Darkling?

Her mother took a shaky breath on the other end of the phone. Keira had to finish dealing with this. Now.

"I love you too, Mom. Thanks for understanding."

She hung up before her mother could start sobbing. Keira wasn't sure she could have held on to her lies in the face of that kind of breakdown, and right then, she really, really needed her mother to believe that she was safe.

Wordlessly, Walker came over and sat next to her on the bed. He wrapped an arm around her and Keira leaned her head on his shoulder.

"Well," he said softly. "That sounded like it sucked."

"Pretty much," Keira said. "I've never really lied to my parents. Not about anything that counted. I never had to."

"Me neither. That's one of the only good things about losing my parents. I never had to hurt them. All the stuff I've done, the people I've used, trying to find the Experimental, to find *you* . . ."

Keira lifted her head and he looked down at her. Sadness pooled in his eyes.

"At least they didn't have to see it." His voice was barely more than a whisper.

"I'm sure they would rather have been around to see it," Keira said.

Walker looked down at their legs, pressed against one another on the bed. "After they disappeared, after they died, I was so devastated. It seemed like things would never be good again. Eventually, I quit hoping they would be. When the Reformers told me to find the Experimental at any cost, there didn't seem to be any point in fighting it."

Goose bumps rose on Keira's skin. He was supposed to have dragged her Darkside to be killed. If things had been different—if the attraction between them hadn't been like some sort of electromagnetic miracle, pulling them together—she would already be dead.

Walker's expression mirrored her thoughts. "I never expected to find *you*."

Keira's lips moved toward his, her body insisting she show him how perfectly their feelings matched. For a moment, he leaned in, but then he backed away suddenly.

"We can't." He sounded like it hurt to say the words. "Not when it means going Darkside. You can't get out on your own."

"We're at the bottom of a ravine," Keira reminded him, her mouth tingling with the desire to kiss him.

Walker reached out and traced the shape of her bottom lip with his thumb. The longing in his touch made Keira dizzy. "I know. But each time we cross over, we put a rip in the fabric of Darkside. The more times we cross in one place, the bigger the tear gets. The bigger the tear, the easier it is for the Reformers and their guards to trace, and—"

"The easier it is for them to find us," Keira finished for him.

"Exactly." He laughed.

"What?" Keira demanded. "I don't think this is funny *at all*."

"It's not funny," he agreed. "It's horribly ironic. I've kissed a lot of girls I didn't care about one bit, and now that I've found one I care about a great deal, I can barely touch her."

His words were better than a kiss could have been, but that didn't stop Keira from wanting it.

Walker stood up and paced the tiny room. "So, what do you want to do? Watch TV?" He yanked open the nightstand drawer and his eyes lit up. "Oh, look! Cards! I could teach you some tricks...."

The weight of the day came crashing down on Keira. She ached with fatigue, and her overwhelmed mind begged to shut down for a while.

"Actually, would you mind if I went to bed? You can watch TV or whatever. It won't bother me. I need to crash. It's been kind of an exhausting day."

"Oh, sure. Of course," Walker said. "It *is* pretty late."

Keira waited.

He stared back at her, confused.

"I, um, need to take my towel off. I don't think it's going to work for sleeping." The blood pounded against her cheeks.

"Oh. Right." Walker turned around to face the curtains

that covered the window, muttering something about chivalry being better off dead.

Keira slid off the makeshift skirt and tossed it on the end of the bed before sliding between the neatly made sheets. They were thin and worn, but they smelled reassuringly of bleach and she snuggled deeper into the pillow.

"Okay," she said, her voice already heavy with sleep. "I'm decent."

Walker spun and looked down at her. A slow grin spread across his face. Keira's sleepiness evaporated, leaving a pounding desire in its wake. She was instantly and acutely aware that she was lying in a hotel bed, barely dressed, with Walker staring down at her like she looked delicious.

"You are completely indecent," he said. "But since there's nothing we can do about that, I'm going to go take a shower."

He will be naked in the shower, a voice in her brain informed her. Like she needed reminding.

Keira was suddenly too hot beneath the covers, but she didn't trust herself to move them. It might look like an invitation. It might *be* an invitation.

Walker's face softened. The tenderness in his eyes turned her desire into something deeper—something more important. Something Keira couldn't even bring herself to name, much less think about.

"Sleep well," he said quietly.

"You too," she managed to whisper. Then she shut her eyes

on him, on the room, on the screwed-up double worlds—on everything. The shower hummed to life on the other side of the bathroom door.

Keira tossed and turned on the lumpy mattress. If she'd been at home, she would have padded out to the living room and played her piano until the music pushed her thoughts aside, leaving sleep a space to slip in. But there was no piano here. Frustrated, she flopped onto her back and squeezed her eyes shut against the view of the water-stained ceiling. Her piano sprang to life in her mind. She could see every key, the gleaming wood—even the single scratch from the time her metronome fell, glancing off the piano on its way down. Just looking at her piano, even if it was only in her memory, made her feel calmer.

Her fingers began to move against the scratchy sheets, but Keira could have sworn she felt the cool, smooth faces of the keys beneath her fingertips. She played. It didn't matter that the music was only in her head. It didn't matter that her piano was miles away. She could feel the notes, moving through her blood, relaxing her muscles. Her thoughts quieted.

Before she could even finish the first étude, Keira's exhaustion claimed her. Her fingers slowed their drumming and finally, she slept.

Chapter Thirty-Two

KEIRA'S OWN SCREAM WOKE HER.

In the darkness, it seemed entirely possible that it was real—the hooded figures, the cylindrical stone they'd pressed her neck against, the graphite-colored scythe swinging above her.

Keira struggled against the tangled covers, kicking a leg free and sitting up with a choked cry. The freezing air cut through her T-shirt.

"Keira, shhh! You're okay." Walker sat up next to her.

"Oh, God. It looked so real. I saw . . . I thought . . . they were going to kill me." Her voice shook. The icy covers slithered against her, making her quake with cold. The room had turned wintry while they slept.

Walker pulled her against him and she buried her face against his neck, wrapping her arms around his back. He was shirtless, and his skin was bed-warm beneath her fingers.

"I'm not going to let that happen." He stroked her hair, her terror fading beneath his touch.

"I want you to teach me how to get back from Darkside on my own," she said. He tensed, pulling away from her. In the dim glow from the digital clock, she could see him looking at her. His curls were wild with sleep.

"I will teach you. But we can't do it until we're ready to run. Each time we cross, we'd tear a bigger hole in Darkside. Going back and forth in one spot like that would bring the guards in a heartbeat."

Then the nightmare wouldn't be a nightmare anymore. It would be real.

"Tomorrow, then. I can't be totally dependent on you to take care of me."

"I want to protect you, but you're right, you should be as prepared as possible. Who knows? I might even need you to save me."

"Exactly. If I can learn to go back and forth, then I can escape if I need to. We'd be safe."

"They do have ways of keeping you from escaping," Walker said. The warning poisoned his voice. "We'll never be completely safe."

"Well. That's a super nice thought. Thanks." She yanked the covers straight and slithered beneath them, flipping onto her side. Away from him.

"Keira. I'm not trying to make you mad," he said quietly.

After a long moment, she let out the breath she'd been holding. She wasn't really angry with him. She was angry at everything; at the unsolvable situation, at the disaster it had made of her carefully planned life. Walker just happened to be there too. It wasn't fair to blow up at him.

"I know. It's not your fault. I'm sorry."

"You don't have to apologize." The bed shifted as he settled himself.

They lay next to each other in the dark.

"I'm sorry too," he said.

She shivered, drawing her knees up beneath the covers. So they were both sorry. And she was still screwed. She sniffed once, swallowing back tears.

"Keira . . ." Walker's voice was hesitant.

"I'm fine," she said, shivering again.

"I know you are." There was as much sadness as admiration in his words. Then he slid across the bed, spooning himself around her. He draped an arm over her and their bare legs pressed against one another. His warmth drove the chill from the sheets and took Keira's fear with it.

The contours of the Darkside ravine appeared, shining with a different sort of blackness against the dark of the hotel room.

Keira stared at it. She knew if she pulled away from Walker, it would disappear.

But it wouldn't really be gone.

And she would be cold and scared and alone.

It didn't seem like such a hard choice anymore. She squeezed her eyes shut and snuggled back against Walker's chest. His arm tightened around her waist.

Keira relaxed. Her thoughts began to drift, and when Walker murmured something into her hair, the words were lost in the fog of her almost-sleep.

"Mmm . . . what?" She struggled to open her eyes, wondering what he'd said.

"Oh. Sorry. Nothing. I didn't mean to wake you," he said.

Her curiosity was no match for her exhaustion, and she drifted off to sleep.

Her cell phone rang early the next morning, waking Keira. She'd rolled toward Walker in the night, and they were so tangled up in each other that it took her a minute to extricate herself. She grabbed for the phone a moment too late. It was Susan. Keira swore.

The sharp wolf whistle from the bed made Keira jump.

She glanced down and realized that she was standing in the middle of the room, wearing only her T-shirt and panties.

Hot-pink, polka-dotted panties.

She yanked the hem of her T-shirt down.

Walker propped himself up on his elbows. The sheets pooled around his waist, highlighting his shirtless state. She hadn't realized how muscular he was. He looked more slender when he was dressed. Her mouth went dry.

He arched an eyebrow at her. "I hoped I'd get to see you in those someday."

"Huh?" She was so confused, she wondered if she were still dreaming.

"The laundry? That first day at your house?" He grinned at her. The look on his face made Keira feel more naked than standing in the middle of the room in her underwear.

She felt herself blush, embarrassed by the memory.

"You're gorgeous," he said softly.

Every inch of her was aware that Walker was even less dressed than she was, that he was lying in a warm, rumpled bed, that there was nothing stopping her from getting in next to him and answering that wanting look on his face.

Nothing stopping her at all. Aside from the fact that it might get both of them killed.

"I'm getting dressed," she said, cutting off her wandering thoughts. She ignored the low, pained chuckle that came from the bed and hightailed it into the bathroom. She tugged on her jeans, then brushed her teeth with her finger, wishing she had a toothbrush. And clean clothes. And a comb.

Her hair was hopeless. The best she could do was to snarl it into a low knot. When she opened the bathroom door, she was relived to see that Walker had gotten dressed too.

Though she hated to admit it, the more layers of clothes there were between them, the better. If she hadn't been so angry and terrified in the middle of the night, who knew what might have happened?

"My turn," he announced, sliding past her into the bathroom.

She flopped down on the bed. Her phone still showed Susan's missed call, but there was no voice mail. Keira called the school, lowering her voice enough to pass for her mother. One quick case of fake strep throat and she was off the attendance hook for the day.

She sat on the bed and flipped the phone between her fingers. What could she possibly tell Susan that wouldn't make her best friend worry that she'd lost her mind? How could she explain what had happened? What she *was*?

Keira couldn't think straight. She didn't miss her parents, couldn't care less about being away from her house, but her piano was a different story.

"Why are you grinding your teeth?" Walker's voice split the stillness of the room and Keira leapt to her feet.

"You scared the crap out of me!"

"Uh, sorry? I didn't realize I had been so ninjalike."

Keira laughed, surprising herself.

Walker nodded approvingly. "Laughing in the face of mortal danger. I'm proud." He motioned toward the phone lying on the bed. "So, did you talk to Susan?"

Keira sat back down on the bed. "Not yet." She looked up at Walker. His hair was damp, and stubble shadowed his chin. It made him look more rugged than usual. Keira wondered what it would feel like against her skin—she wanted to run her lips across his jawline to see exactly how rough it was.

"Why?" he asked, interrupting her blossoming daydream.

Keira closed her eyes. Her fingers drummed imaginary scales against the bedsheets, forcing her thoughts into line. "I can't figure out what to tell her," she admitted.

"Yeah. I can see that. What we really need is a plan. Like, a good plan."

The conversation they'd had the night before wound through Keira's thoughts. It had been easier to talk to him in the dark. The morning sun that poured into the room made her feel exposed.

"That would be nice," she agreed. "Since 'run like hell' is going to be impossible to maintain. There must be something we could do. Someone who would be willing to help us over there? What about my dad? I can't figure out why he never told me I'm a Darkling; why he never said anything about Darkside."

Walker swallowed. "Your dad's human. You know that, right?"

"What? But you said my *mom* was human. You said that's why I was raised here, instead of Darkside!"

"Keira. I thought you'd realized—" He shut his eyes. "Your dad, the man who raised you, is human. But your real father is a Darkling."

The news crashed into her with such force that the room seemed to tilt around her. Her father wasn't really her father?

No. No. Oh, God, please no.

Chapter Thirty-Three

"WHAT?" THE WORD WAS little more than a whisper.

Walker licked his lower lip. "Keira, someone else, a Darkling, got your mother pregnant. Your dad isn't your father. I'm sorry."

All her parents' fights tumbled around in her memory. No wonder things were so bad between her parents. Her dad knew that she wasn't his daughter. Or he must suspect, at least. She had a vague memory of him joking about her being the first redhead in their family, and her mother snapping at him to quit.

She shivered. "Do you know who my real father is?" Saying

the words felt like a betrayal. Her *real* father was the one who'd been to every one of her recitals. Who'd checked under her bed when she'd had little-girl nightmares. Who'd gotten choked up when she'd gone to get her driver's license. *That* was her father.

"Are you hungry?" Walker asked suddenly.

Keira's vision narrowed until all she saw were his eyes, darting around the room, looking for an escape.

"Why are you changing the subject?" she asked. Her stomach twisted, reminding her that she *was* hungry. That package of cookies the night before had been totally insufficient. She ignored it. "Do you know who my father is?" she asked again.

"I have a guess," Walker admitted. "But I'm not totally sure."

"So, he must know I exist. We should find him. Maybe he'll help us."

"There are a couple of problems with that," Walker said softly.

"Oh, yeah? Like what?"

"Like it would mean taking you Darkside, for one. And for another, no one knows exactly who your father is. Your birth records were incomplete—they only discovered the discrepancy after the head of the Experimental Breeding Program disappeared."

"Why did he disappear?" Keira's words were careful, her voice measured and even.

Walker crossed the room and knelt in front of Keira. His eyes begged her not to be angry. "He had to. He was supposed to take you from your mother and bring you back to our world to be raised. But he didn't. And even when the extermination started, he wouldn't tell anyone where you were. He claimed to have 'lost' you, but no one believed him. He became the most wanted man in all of Darkside."

Her mouth went dry.

"I think he was your father. I think that's why he left the records blank. Why he hid you here."

"They were going to kidnap me?" Keira asked, horrified.

Walker frowned. "It didn't seem like that. Darklings—they don't think of humans as equals, Keira. To them, it was like picking up a puppy from the breeder. Humans do that all the time—take dogs away from their mothers. The Darklings saw it the same way."

Keira shuddered, thinking of the abandoned dogs who died in shelters every day. Her death wouldn't mean any more than that to the Reformers.

"You were the only Experimental who was ever raised in the human world, Keira. Because of him. And no one's seen him since. There was some evidence that he crossed between the two worlds a few times during the first years after he went into hiding, but then his trail dried up. The Reformers never found him. And believe me, they searched. Seekers died looking for him. Eventually, everyone realized that he must be . . ." Walker pressed his lips together, like keeping the word in would make it less true.

"He's dead," Keira said flatly. "He's the only one who knows where I come from, who I *really* am, and he's dead."

Walker sat next to her on the bed. "I'm sorry." He slid his hand through hers. The dark stone that shimmered into view drove Keira's ache deeper. She'd lost her history before she'd ever really found it.

Even though it brought Darkside closer, she squeezed Walker's hand. In spite of the sun pouring into the room, a chill wrapped around her. "I need to talk to my mother. I can't believe she never told me."

"Keira, he wouldn't have told her he was a Darkling. And can you really imagine your mother sitting you down and announcing that she'd had an affair?"

The idea of talking about her mom's sex life was disgusting. "No, I guess not."

"That doesn't mean it doesn't hurt. Being without your parents makes the universe feel like a lonelier place," Walker said.

Keira looked over at him. He'd lost both of his parents. If it hurt this much to be without someone she'd never even *known*, how much pain had Walker been through? She couldn't imagine.

He cupped the back of her neck. "Maybe I can take some of that away? The universe doesn't feel so empty since I found you."

He stared at her. Without taking her eyes from his face, Keira wound her fingers through his.

His hand tightened around the back of her neck in response, and Keira's stomach dropped. In that one instant, their connection deepened immeasurably. It felt like a free fall.

"I definitely don't feel empty," she whispered.

The pull between them was irresistible. It felt wrong not to kiss him, not to create some physical evidence of the way she felt. His lips were so full and so soft and so close.

Walker's thumb traced the curve of her cheekbone. He leaned in until Keira was dizzy with his nearness.

"I swear to you, the second it's safe, I am going to get you alone."

He shifted his weight, sliding her back and lowering her onto the bed. He braced himself above her, his arms framing her head. Keira was vaguely aware that he was very carefully not touching her, but right then, she would almost have traded being found by the guards to feel the press of his weight against her.

"We *are* alone," she murmured.

He shook his head, growling in a pained way. "You know we can't. But when we can—" He dipped his head. His lips barely brushed her ear, but the touch sent a sparkling explosion of fireworks through her. It also brought the Darkside ravine back, close enough that Keira could smell wet stone. She closed her eyes, focusing only on the bed beneath her, Walker's weight above her, and the hot press of his breath against her ear.

"When we *can*," he whispered, "I am going to kiss you until you catch fire." For a white-hot second, his teeth caught her earlobe and Keira gasped. "I am going to make up for every single second we've lost. I swear."

"Oh, my God," Keira whispered, half-desperate with wanting him. "Then can we please hurry up and get to that part?"

"Good idea," he said against her neck.

He pushed himself away from her. His cheeks were flushed.

"I need to look at the records again," he said. "Maybe there's something there—something I missed. The program notes got pretty cryptic toward the end. Now that I know more about *you*, maybe we can find something that would convince the Reformers to spare you."

It was too much to wish for, but the possibility still crashed over Keira in a hopeful crescendo. "So, where would we find that sort of information?" she asked.

Walker squirmed. "The Hall of Records. That's where all of our information is. There are only four halls in all of Darkside, one for each quadrant. They house all the historical information, all the records of births, taxes, scientific programs—everything. They're the most important places we have, now that the churches have been abandoned."

"Is it far from here?" Keira asked. She was on her feet, throwing the few things she'd brought into her bag.

"Uh, not really."

Something in his voice made her stop dead.

"Where is it, Walker?" She searched his face.

"You know that really big building behind your house? The one in Darkside?"

"Yeeeeaaah." The word stretched between them. If the Hall of Records was anywhere close to her house, it was going to be beyond risky. Her whole house had been swarming with the Reformers' guards less than twenty-four hours ago.

"Well, that's it—the Hall of Records."

"It can't possibly be safe to go back there," she said.

Walker rubbed his forehead. "We don't have much choice. I don't want to take you with me, but I think it's more dangerous to leave you alone. We'll just have to find whatever we can and fast."

A little crinkle appeared between Walker's eyebrows. He wasn't telling her something.

"What's the catch?" she asked.

His eyes widened. "How . . . ?" He didn't finish the question.

Keira shot him a rueful grin. "Your poker face isn't as perfect as you think it is."

"Probably true. I've never gotten to know anyone well enough for it to matter." He rubbed his hands against the legs of his jeans. "There is a catch. The Experimental records are kept in a restricted section of the Hall of Records. Locked cases. Special permission required."

"And we don't have special permission," Keira guessed.

"Exactly. But we might have a way around that."

"Like a cape of invisibility?" she joked.

"Like my cousin," Walker said.

"Smith? But how?"

"Smith works there. He's a Sorter; like a librarian?"

"So when you said he fixed machines, and that they have machines at the library . . ."

"I meant the Hall of Records, yes. It's the closest thing we have to a library. That's where all of Darkside's information is stored. Darklings don't have books, the way you do here. It's . . . well. You'll see."

Keira crossed her arms. "You expect Smith to sneak us into a restricted area to find information that might save my ass?" Keira stared at him. "What are the odds that might actually, oh, I don't know, *work?*"

"There are reasons for Smith to help me."

"You mean because of his secret. The fact that he can cross back and forth."

Walker stared down at the horrible green carpet.

"I think this might be Smith's big break. It's his chance to have something to hold over me. He'll love that. There's no way I can go tell my aunt that he's hanging out in Sherwin after this."

If her life weren't in imminent danger, Keira might have been bothered by forcing Smith to help them. Actually, she was bothered by it, but she couldn't afford to say anything. She wasn't in any position to refuse Smith's assistance, even if it came from a twisted arm.

"I don't like doing things this way," Walker said quietly. "But I don't have a choice. Please believe me when I tell you that I wish Smith would stay Darkside and leave Susan and everything else in the human world alone. If he's ever caught, my aunt Holly will never forgive me. Hell, I'll never forgive myself." His shoulders sagged with unwanted responsibility. "I don't like being underhanded. But the only way I can make Smith help us ensure you're around for your next birthday is by *making* him."

Keira watched his knuckles whiten with tension. "I understand," she said. "Then before we go, I just need you to teach me how to cross back and forth."

Walker nodded. "You're right. But not here—we're too far from the car, and the car is our only chance of outrunning the Seekers and the Reformers' guards."

"So, where?"

He held out his hand. "Come on."

Chapter Thirty-Four

THE PARKING LOT BEHIND the hotel was deserted except for a couple of Dumpsters. Walker pulled the car up alongside them and got out. Keira climbed out too, watching as he shaded his eyes from the sun. Beyond the asphalt was an overgrown lot with a faded FOR SALE sign in the middle of it. Past that was a stand of scrubby trees. If they stood on the far side of the Dumpsters, there was little chance they'd be seen.

At least, not by any humans.

"This looks pretty good," he said.

Keira squinted, trying to see Darkside. "Are we out of the ravine?"

Walker laid his hand on the small of her back, and as the pressure of his touch traveled through her, Darkside sprang into view. Keira gasped and swayed toward him. They were out of the ravine, but barely. With the two worlds layered over each other, it looked like the very back of Walker's Mercedes was hanging over the lip of the chasm. Keira's inner ear spun with the sensation of simultaneously being at sea level and forty feet above.

"Sorry. I should have warned you that the view might be a little disconcerting." Walker slid his hand around her waist, wrapping his arm securely across her back.

"Yeah. Well." Keira cleared her throat, fighting back the vertigo that threatened to bring her to her knees. "Whatever it takes to find out if my . . . my father's still alive, right?" The word 'father' was incredibly difficult to say. "So, how do I cross?" she asked, changing the subject.

Walker pulled his arm away, and while she managed to see Darkside, the details went fuzzy without his touch. It looked like a watercolor rather than a photograph.

Walker bit his lip. "What seemed to work last night was when you really pictured yourself in your living room—the way it smelled and felt."

Keira frowned. "But I don't know how Darkside smells. Not really. And everything looks hazy. I can't see the details."

"Well, what can you see, exactly?"

"The ravine," she said.

"Okay, but what else?" he prompted her. "Describe it to me. Pretend I can't see it at all."

She squinted. "There are bushes on the other side of the ravine but they're tangled and fuzzy. And then there are trees past them. It looks like they're growing in rows, sort of, and—" Keira jumped as everything came into sharp focus. A sudden wind slapped at her arms.

"Congratulations," Walker said. "You made it. Welcome to Darkside."

Keira stared at the trees. "There are . . . what are those three lumps back there?"

"Huts. It's where the orchard workers live."

"Will they see us?" Keira asked.

"No," Walker assured her. "And even if they did, they wouldn't recognize us. They're pretty much the lowest rung of Darkling society. They live in the trees, they work in the trees, the only education they get is how to harvest what grows on the trees."

"That sounds awful," Keira said.

"Yes and no," Walker said. "Come on, let's cross back. I'll feel more comfortable explaining when I know we can get away if we need to."

"Oh. Right." Keira turned so that the wind was at her back. She concentrated on the shiny black curves of the Mercedes, the unpleasant smell that wafted out of the Dumpsters.

"Keep trying," Walker said.

Keira squeezed her eyes shut. Even though it was barely April in Sherwin, there was a first kiss of heat in the sun's rays. The back of her neck arched toward that warmth and the faint chirp of a bird reached her ears.

Her eyes popped open. Darkside was gone and the parking lot was back beneath her feet.

"Nice job," Walker said. "Wanna try it again?"

"No. Yes. I mean, not really, but I know I need to," Keira stammered. She was shivering violently. She couldn't imagine how cold she'd be after she went back and forth a second time. "What's the deal with the hut dwellers?" she asked, stalling.

Walker laughed.

"What?"

"Pretty much all Darklings are 'hut dwellers' in one sense or another," he said. "The Reformers have been in power for . . . sixteen thousand years?" he said doubtfully, his eyes rolled up in thought. "Yeah. Sixteen thousand years. That's right."

"You mean—they're like a separate species? Or an ethnic group or something?"

Walker shook his head. "They're definitely separate, but what I meant was that everyone else is so far beneath them, we might as well be orchard workers. In a lot of ways, the Reformers are ordinary Darklings. They're just more important. You remember how I said that the orchard workers' kids are only taught to be orchard workers?"

Understanding broke over Keira. "So—the Reformers' kids

become the new Reformers? Like royalty or something?"

"Exactly. Forty thousand years ago, the priests ran most everything in Darkside, but they got more and more restrictive about what kind of music was right to worship, and who could play it and when. Eventually, the Darklings quit listening to the priests. As the years passed, the Darklings quit believing in music and lost the ability to make it at all . . . then the priests slowly disappeared. For a long time, there was no one ruling Darkside. It was just little groups of Darklings, fending for themselves and trying not to fight with their neighbors. But as Darkside itself became unstable, Darklings had to move away from the damaged bits. Which meant they encountered other Darklings who didn't want to give up their land. There were fights—wars. Eventually, the Reformers came to power. They ended the wars, gave everyone a role, a job to do. Everyone did as they were told. The ones who didn't were killed. In return, the Reformers provided for all the Darklings. Everyone had enough food and a place to live."

Keira's skin crawled. "It sounds awful."

Walker shrugged. "It's all anyone has ever known. The Reformers aren't kind, but they're powerful. They have history and tradition on their side too. Plus, the lower you are on the Darkside social scale, the less likely they are to notice you. That's what I meant when I said that being one of the orchard workers wasn't all bad. Those Darklings can pretty much live how they want, as long as they pick their quota of fruit. They're almost free."

"But you work for the Reformers."

Walker nodded, his gaze holding hers. "The more educated and important your family is in things like science or art or record keeping, the more careful you have to be."

The puzzle pieces slid together. "Your *aunt*—that's why she's so worried all the time."

"Yep. She—" Walker stopped and stared at the back of the Dumpster.

Keira followed his gaze, trying to see Darkside. If she concentrated, let her focus go soft, like she was looking at an optical illusion, she could see the ravine, even without touching Walker. The stars had disappeared. Now the sky above it was streaked with black and gray, like an ever-changing piece of marble.

"What?" she asked. The shifting sky gave her the chills.

"Can you hear that?" he asked.

Keira listened, holding her breath. It reminded her of when she was little, and strained to hear the footsteps of the monsters she imagined creeping toward her bed in the dark.

Only this was much more terrifying.

"I can't hear anything," she whispered. "I didn't think you could hear Darkside if you weren't there."

Walker looked surprised. "Of course you can hear Darkside." A furrow appeared between his eyebrows. "You haven't?"

She shook her head. "But then again, I just started *seeing* it. Maybe I just need more time?"

"Or a different focus. You have a musician's ear, Keira. Just listen for a minute." Walker held out his hand. Keira took it, thinking of hearing Darkside, rather than seeing it. She focused on the sounds of Sherwin, trying to hear something layered underneath the noise, the same way she saw Darkside and her own world simultaneously.

Her breath caught.

In the distance, she could hear a clinking noise, and it was getting closer. She'd done it. She could hear things that were happening in Darkside. The hair rose on the back of her neck.

"What the hell is *that*?"

"The Reformers' guards. It's their vehicles. They're not good at getting through the trees."

"They found us already?" Keira asked, tightening her grip on her backpack, ready to run.

Walker looked over at her. "We crossed last night. They probably started to trace us hours ago." His face was so pale that even his lips had lost their color. "Damn. We have even less wiggle room than I thought. We need to get out of here. *Now.*"

Keira let go of his hand and the sound disappeared. The silence that surrounded her was almost worse than the sound of the vehicles. Now she couldn't hear them coming for her.

And they were definitely coming for her.

Chapter Thirty-Five

TECHNICALLY, THE HALL OF Records was three houses away from Keira's, through the backdoor neighbor's and one to the south. Right by Jeremy Reynolds's house. The thought of him living in a library of any kind made Keira's lips twitch into an involuntary smile.

"So, how are we going to do this?" she asked, wadding up the wrapper of her greasy, drive-thru breakfast sandwich. Instead of making her feel better, the food sat in her stomach like a lump of clay.

Walker pulled the car over to the side of the empty street, running his hands around the steering wheel. "I think—if I go through to Darkside and you stay here, then you'll be able to see what I'm doing, but you'll be safe. Well, saf*er*."

"Okay," Keira agreed. "In and out before they can track us?"

"Something like that."

"Well, let's go wheedle some information out of unsuspecting family members, hmm?"

"Excellent plan."

Keira scanned the street. There were faded garden gnomes, vinyl siding, Christmas lights that were months past needing to be taken down—but behind all that, Darkside hovered, just beyond the normal world. She caught glimpses of enormous trees that were twisted and gnarled and unnaturally black. She saw the facade of the Hall of Records. But no people. No guards. No movement.

"Where is everyone?" she asked. "Surely they haven't stopped looking for us?"

Walker shook his head. "No. But since they seem to have found the tear we made in the ravine, they'll probably have most of their forces out there. I'm sure they left a scout around here, but that's another reason we need to do this now—they'll be distracted."

Walker parked two blocks away. As soon as the car came to a stop, Keira grabbed the door handle. If she waited any longer, she was probably going to lose her nerve.

"Then what are we waiting for?" She stepped out onto the

soggy spring lawn next to the car. Her ballet flats squelched unpleasantly in the mud.

"Okay," Walker came to stand next to her. "Ready?"

"Yep," she said.

They hurried down the sidewalk in silence and stopped in front of the spot where the Hall of Records lurked. Their hands found each other effortlessly. Comfortably.

Darkside came completely into view and the dizzying sensation of being caught between two worlds swept over Keira. She squeezed Walker's hand, steadying herself.

"Stay quiet and stay close," he reminded her.

"Got it. Let's go."

Hand in hand, they walked into her neighbor's backyard. Keira stared uncomfortably at the houses around them. She'd been so worried about what might happen if someone caught them Darkside, she hadn't really stopped to think about what could happen if someone caught them trespassing. Still, as long as they were outside, it would be easy to pretend they were headed back to her house.

"We're here." Walker's voice was low.

Keira dragged her attention back to Darkside, ignoring the headache that blossomed behind her eyes as her focus shifted. The size of the building that surrounded them was overwhelming. They stood in a massive central room, ringed by huge pillars that supported a series of archways. Above them, tiny rooms, like the cells of a beehive, stacked on top of one another, all the way to the ceiling. She could see into some, but others were covered by doors that looked like they were made of leather. Beyond the pillars were hallways that lead deeper into the building, twisting away so that whatever lay at their ends was hidden from view. Keira wondered what secrets might be hidden in the dark bowels of the Hall of Records.

She dragged her attention away from the dizzying expanse of the Hall. Directly in front of them was an ornate table littered with tiny boxes. Oblivious to the fact that he was being watched, a robed figure bent over the small containers, stacking them according to some system that Keira couldn't understand. A few of the boxes lay open, revealing gleaming black objects that looked like needles.

"What are those?" Keira whispered.

"Needles," Walker murmured back.

The one time I really wanted to be wrong . . .

She hated needles. She'd almost fainted the last time she had a shot. And she didn't even want to think about what the Darklings might be using them for.

Walker glanced around the Hall. Keira watched as his eyes followed a Darkling's robed back. When the room was empty except for the guy at the desk, Walker let out a long breath.

"Okay, I'm going over." He let go of her hand and Keira's headache intensified as she struggled to keep Darkside in focus on her own. His expression was grim as he stared at her. "You be careful. I don't want anything to happen to you." The end of the last word snapped off as he crossed.

Across the desk, the guy's head snapped up. It was Smith. Keira saw his strangled cry at Walker's sudden appearance, but all she heard was the gasp that came from her own throat.

Her surprise broke her focus and blotted out her view of Darkside. Keira was left staring at scruffy grass and worn vinyl siding.

Crap. She focused on Walker, then Smith behind the desk. She concentrated with everything she had, until the hush of the enormous Hall overshadowed the distant-traffic-and-small-animals noise of the yard.

Smith looked like a very large and unpredictable dog had cornered him. "Walker! What in discord are you doing here?" His words were intelligible, but just barely. She understood him in the same instinctive way she understood the rhythm of a drumbeat. "I thought you were allergic to this place."

"Good to see you too, Smith," Walker said. His speech had taken on the same pattering rhythm as Smith's. All at once, Keira realized that they weren't speaking English, and yet she still understood every word.

Shivering, Keira stepped closer to Walker. If they'd been in the same world, she would be near enough to touch him. It was like being a ghost. He knew she was there, but Smith stared straight past her—straight *through* her—without even a flicker of recognition. The invisibility should have calmed her. After all, she didn't want to be seen Darkside. Being seen meant getting caught. In spite of the logic of it, she felt more vulnerable, more exposed, when she didn't know exactly who could and couldn't see her.

Smith rose behind the desk. He wore a robe. It was shaggy and graphite-colored, like someone had shaped a pile of iron filings into a garment. "You really shouldn't be here," he hissed. "Up until last night, the Hall's grounds were *swarming* with guards. They *know*, Walker. They know about Keira. I heard them talking. You should get out of here before they come back."

The fear in Smith's words buzzed through the air like a swarm of wasps, but Walker stayed remarkably calm.

"I'm not planning on staying long, but yeah, I am having just the *tiniest* bit of trouble." Keira could see the line of his jaw sharpen, but that was the only sign of his tension. "That's why I came to see you."

Smith narrowed his eyes, but Walker looked like he wasn't bothered at all by the challenge in Smith's face.

Pride swept through Keira, drowning her in a high tide of new feeling for Walker. Every time she got used to the intensity between them, something deepened it.

"Walker, it's not that I don't want to help you, but my mom would kill me."

"She'd kill you if she knew about Susan, too."

Smith stiffened and crossed his arms. "This is bigger than

me seeing a human and you know it. I'm not worried about getting grounded. The *Reformers* want you. I can't fix that."

Walker put his hands on the desk, carefully avoiding the boxes of needles, and leaned toward Smith. Keira crossed her arms, watching as a thread of darkness snaked into view under her skin and slithered around her wrist. Walker's voice jerked her attention back to Darkside. "The Reformers need me. They're not happy, I get that, but I'm too valuable to lose. Unless, of course, there was a replacement at the ready?" The threat was sharp. It pierced Smith and the sneer slid off his face.

"You wouldn't." His eyes went round and sad as an abandoned puppy's.

"I don't want to, but I'm telling you that right now, there's *nothing* I wouldn't do to get what I need. Come on, Smith. You've been risking your life for years. What's one more time?"

The resignation that dropped onto Smith's face was a relief to see, but something else lurked behind his slumped shoulders and defeated-looking mouth.

Right then, he hated Walker.

But he owed him more.

Keira could see it, clear as day, in the way he grunted at Walker and offered him his choice of needles with a wave of his hand.

"What do you need?" Smith asked. "I'm assuming it's restricted, or you would have pulled your little appearing-out-of-the-ether act in front of the records you wanted."

"Your powers of observation are sharp today," Walker said. There was an edge of irritation in his voice. His calm veneer was wearing thin. "I can see why they put you in here with the needles."

"Ha." There was no laughter in the word.

Walker picked up two boxes and checked the sides. A series of crosshatched lines were etched there, and he scanned them like he was reading.

"I need to see the records from the Experimental Breeding Program," Walker said, like it was a completely normal request.

Smith recoiled. "Why? You already saw them during your training. What *is* going on, Walker?"

Walker shrugged. "I need to see the records. And I need you to keep your mouth shut about it. If you don't, I won't be the only one the Reformers are disappointed in. I'll have you signed, sealed, and delivered to them before you can say *harmony*."

Smith's face twisted unpleasantly as he weighed the seriousness of Walker's threat. Whatever secret Walker held over Smith, it was big enough to make Smith give him what he wanted.

With far more force than necessary, Smith bent and opened a small door in the side of the desk. Keira stretched up on tiptoe to see over the desk, and nearly lost her balance when she reached for Walker's shoulder to steady herself. For a moment, she'd forgotten that they weren't together, in spite of being right next to each other.

Stupid.

She laughed to herself, and Walker's head whipped around in her direction, his eyes wide.

Smith looked up at Walker with a vinegary expression on his face. "What's funny?"

Keira froze. *Oh, shit. Oh,* shit. *Had he heard her?* She hadn't slipped over, had she? She glanced down at the mud beneath her shoes. Shimmering over it was a gleaming floor that looked like a single, enormous slab of stone. She curled her hands into fists. It was getting too easy to see Darkside.

"Easy, there. I only cleared my throat," Walker said.

Smith's eyes narrowed suspiciously, but he went back to hunting through the desk's contents. Behind the desk door hung a series of small black discs, each the size of a quarter. They all looked identical to Keira, but Smith grabbed one and rubbed it between his fingers. Smith glanced up at Walker's hands, wrapped around the small boxes he'd selected.

"One needle per patron," Smith scolded.

Walker hesitated. "I know," he said slowly. "I hadn't decided which one would work better for this. Don't want to have to come back and *bother* you again if I need a different depth."

Keira shuddered. She didn't exactly know what the needles had to do with getting the information they needed, but she had a sneaking suspicion she should have brought some Band-Aids. Big ones.

"Fine," Smith snapped. "But you bring them all back in *perfect* condition, and if you tell anyone—"

"I wouldn't tell anyone, Smith. You should know that by now. I'm *excellent* at keeping secrets," Walker spat back. "Speaking of which, how are things going with Susan? Have you told her everything? Bared your soul? Or are you just trying to get her to bare her ass?"

"There's nothing 'going' with me and Susan. Not anymore."

Walker snickered, but the set of his shoulders tightened. "Wow. She dropped you already. Exactly how bad a kisser are you?"

Keira automatically reached for her phone, wondering why Susan hadn't called again. What exactly had happened between her and Smith? But her pockets were empty. She'd left her phone in the car.

"That's none of your fucking business. Let's go," Smith said. The tips of his ears turned red.

He and Walker strode across the smooth floor and Keira hurried to keep up. The guys crossed the large, open main room. They passed straight through the Reynoldses' chain-link fence, but Keira had to struggle over it, then run to catch up to them.

Which she did.

Just before they disappeared into a little hallway. A hallway that was *inside* Jeremy Reynolds's house.

Chapter Thirty-Six

KEIRA CURSED AT THE wall of vinyl siding. She focused, seeing Darkside. Walker and Smith were at the entrance of a small room lined with what looked like glass-fronted cases, only the glass shone in the same light-absorbing way as the lamps. Keira couldn't look directly at them without the ache behind her eyes becoming unbearable.

She was going to have to break into Jeremy's house. Fabulous. He'd practically begged her to come over, and now she was sneaking in like a criminal.

Thank God it was Monday. His parents would be at work and he'd be at school.

She hurried around to the Reynoldses' back door. It was locked. Of course.

She glanced around frantically, knowing that Walker couldn't see her and wouldn't know she was stuck. That's when she saw the dog door.

The Reynolds had an ancient golden retriever, and if the door was big enough for him, just maybe . . . Keira knelt down, wondering if she were really desperate enough to try it. She looked Darkside again and saw Smith and Walker standing in front of one of the cases.

She didn't have any other choice.

With a last glance around to make sure none of the neighbors had spotted her, Keira shimmied into the house. Her shoulders stuck in the small opening and Keira panicked. The Reynoldses' dog, Buddy, came bouncing around the corner, barking. He stopped in the kitchen door, his tail wagging as he saw Keira. In three bounds, he'd crossed the linoleum floor and started licking her face enthusiastically.

Keira twisted and squirmed, trying to avoid his slobbery greeting. In the process, one of her shoulders popped into the house. She slithered through as fast as she could, landing in a heap on the dirty floor.

She ran to the back of the house, into the cluttered spare bedroom. She stopped with her nose inches from Walker's back. The dog bounced around excitedly, distracting her and making it hard to hear Walker and Smith.

"—not like you'd ever let me forget," Smith said.

"Just unlock it," Walker said, his frustration showing.

Smith spun to face the cabinet and pressed the small disc he'd taken from the desk against the glassy front. Keira watched, stunned, as the surface disappeared like clearing smoke. On the newly visible shelf stood a row of what looked like wafer-thin books, their impossibly skinny spines etched with the same sort of crosshatch symbols that decorated the needle boxes.

Smith leaned against the other cabinet with his arms crossed. Waiting.

Walker mirrored his posture. "This might take a while."

"I can wait," Smith said.

Walker dropped his arms, carefully setting the needles on a small, circular table that stood near the doorway. "You're allowed to unlock the doors, but that doesn't mean you're allowed access to the information in here. You know that."

"Oh, come on. I'm curious. We're already breaking the rules, so what's one more? No one has to know," Smith half challenged and half begged.

Walker stared at him until Smith's shoulders fell. He edged back toward the main hall.

"Fine. I've gotta get back to my desk, anyway. I have a bad feeling about all of this, Walker. You need to be careful."

"Now you sound like your mom," Walker said lightly. "But I appreciate your concern." He reached for the door, which looked solid but fell into place with the same rustle and shimmy as a curtain being pulled closed. When it had settled, shutting Smith out, Walker turned to face the room.

"Okay, Keira," he whispered. "Time to go hunting."

Keira watched Walker rifle through the books on the shelf. The double vision of the Hall of Records and the junk-filled spare room throbbed against the backs of her eyes. Walker finally found what he wanted, and when he pulled out a large, square case, Keira realized that the books in the case weren't books at all. Walker carefully shook a flat circle, the size of a large plate, out of the protective square sleeve.

Oh, my God, it's actually a record.

Keira hadn't seen one in ages. Mr. Palmer had a stack of them in the back room of Take Note, but she never paid any attention to them. Walker put the record into a round depression on the tabletop. It had been carved into the surface of the table and it fit the record exactly.

Walker selected the smaller of the two needles he'd taken from Smith and held it above the record.

At least no one's stabbing themselves, Keira thought with relief.

Walker looked up at her. "It's really weird, not being able to hear you," he whispered. She was uncomfortably aware that he was supposed to be alone in the little room. If someone heard him talking, that was bound to draw suspicion. "You can hear okay?"

She nodded.

"Okay, here we go." He lowered the needle, tracing the irregular grooves in the surface of the record. "You have to feel the bumps to know what it says—it's like . . . what do they call it? What blind people use to read in your world?"

"Braille," Keira answered, even though he couldn't hear her reply.

"Anyway, I'll read it to you." He cleared his throat.

Walker scrolled the needle around and around the record, reciting snippets of sentences as he looked for information.

" . . . six two six, parentage Poppy Gates and human Mike Hannaford . . ."

" . . . discord apparent, combined with lack . . ."

" . . . failure of musicality . . ."

" . . . four seven declared insufficient . . ."

" . . . experiment officially at an end, the subjects are being eliminated in order of birth date, beginning with the eldest." Walker slowed the needle and Keira guessed, from the mix of anticipation and dread on his face, that he'd found what they'd been looking for.

His voice got quieter. "After the integrity of the records was compromised by the program's head, Dr.—"

The thump-swish of a door crashing open echoed through the Reynoldses' house, breaking Keira's concentration. The dog raced out of the bedroom, his tail wagging furiously.

"Hey, Buddy!" Jeremy's voice bellowed in the kitchen.

Panic spread through Keira. What was he doing home? Why wasn't Jeremy at *school*? She had to get out before he found her. The room's only window was blocked by a dresser. The sound of paws racing down the hall made her spin back to face the door. Buddy the dog stood in the doorway and woofed at her.

"Buddy?" Jeremy called, concern tingeing his voice.

Keira looked over at Walker, who was bent low over the record, frowning in concentration. She waved her arm, hating the swishing noise the fabric of her shirt made. It sounded impossibly loud.

Buddy galumphed back down the hall. Keira heard his nails clicking against the linoleum back in the kitchen. He woofed again, and she could hear him racing back and forth between the kitchen and the bedroom. She was trapped. The closet was open, stuffed to bursting with shoeboxes. All the hiding places in the room were already full.

"What's your problem, ya dumb dog?" Jeremy sounded irritated. She heard him start down the hall, as Buddy burst into the room dancing around her excitedly.

"Sssh," she hissed, shooing him toward the other bedrooms. Her skin prickled with fear and she ducked behind the open door, pressing herself flat against the wall.

Jeremy's footsteps stopped.

"Hello?" Jeremy called as he came down the hallway. The question had a lot of threat and no welcome in it. Buddy whined and darted back into the hall, twisting around to look at Keira. She glanced behind her.

Walker was still in the Hall of Records, tracing the patterns in the record, oblivious.

"Sonofabitch." Jeremy stomped away for a moment. "If there's someone back there," he called, over the sound of a door swinging open, "you're gonna be sorry. You picked the wrong house."

The ringing *thunk* of something heavy and metal dinging against the doorjamb echoed down the hall. A crowbar? A baseball bat?

Keira looked at the protected little room in the Hall of Records. There was no time to make a good decision. Jeremy would be swinging something heavy at her head in a matter of seconds. She wished she'd had more practice going Darkside on her own, but it was too late for that now. Crossing over was the only way she could save herself.

Chapter Thirty-Seven

KEIRA SQUEEZED HER EYES shut and focused on Walker. She felt for the hard floor of the Hall of Records, the scratching sound of the needle against the record.

The sensation of being squeezed and something cold and viscous sliding over her skin were immediately followed by Walker's strangled cry of surprise.

Keira sagged against the table, gripping its smooth edge.

"Oh, shit." Walker stared through the wall behind Keira and she knew that he could see Jeremy, baseball bat and all, back in her world. Walker looked at her. "I didn't think about you getting caught. I didn't even notice that you'd gone inside a house." He ran a hand through his hair. "I'm sorry, Keira. I was so wrapped up in the crap with Smith that I didn't realize—"

"It's okay," she said. Her voice shook and she cleared her throat. The noise shivered against the locked cases and she winced. It sounded so loud in the tiny room.

He picked up the record and slid it into its protective sleeve, putting it back on the shelf. Keira didn't like the rising note of alarm in his voice. "We have to get out of here. Legal studies is only two rooms over. If we can make it that far, then we can get out of Darkside without running into Jeremy's bat." He crammed the needle back into its box and left it on the table.

His hands were shaking.

The bottom dropped out of her stomach. Keira had never seen *anything* make Walker's hand shake.

"I'm sorry," she whispered. "I didn't know what else to—"

"You have *nothing* to be sorry for." He stepped in close, catching her face between his hands. "It's not your fault. Coming here was better than getting whacked with a blunt object."

He didn't add *I think*, but Keira could see it in his eyes.

Walker leaned down and brushed his lips across hers. The heat of his skin melted her knees and she swayed into him, wrapping her arms around his neck and pressing her mouth against his.

Walker slid his hands up her arms, gently breaking her hold on him.

"We can't," he whispered. "There's no time. Oh, God." He

dropped another quick kiss onto her mouth, catching her lower lip gently between his teeth. "We have to go. *Now.*" He spun her so that she was facing the door and then he carefully swept it aside. His shoulders relaxed a fraction of an inch as the sight of the empty vestibule came into view.

He motioned for Keira to follow him. "This way," he whispered, heading right.

Keira stepped around the corner in time to see Smith pull Walker out of view of the main hall.

"They're coming. Dozens of them. You have to go *now*," Smith panted. Walker looked over at Keira and Smith followed his gaze. They both looked scared, but Smith's eyes glittered with shock. She froze.

"Oh, shit! Keira." Smith looked from her back to Walker. "So she really is the Experimental?"

Walker nodded.

"And you brought her *here*?" Smith gaped. "Have you lost your mind? You have to get her out of here, Walker." Sweat glistened on his pale forehead, making him look ill. "The guards, they—"

From across the Hall, a shout rent the air like a bullet.

"It's the Experimental! Hey! You—Sorter! Stop them!"

Keira looked at Walker, whose face filled with terror.

"Cross!" He whispered.

She tried, but she was so flustered that she could barely remember what her piano looked like, much less Jeremy's spare room.

She shook her head mutely.

Then you need to run. Now! he mouthed.

She nodded, sprinting off toward the main part of the Hall.

"Sorter!" the guards called. Smith's head snapped up. "Get them!"

Smith grabbed Walker halfheartedly, and a quick glance over her shoulder confirmed for Keira that it was a ploy. With a roar, Walker tackled him, sending Smith sprawling against the floor.

Keira ducked behind one of the enormous curtains that had been pinned back against the wall, and peered around it, looking for a way out of the Hall. She nearly screamed when one of the guards tore past her, headed for Walker and Smith, who were rolling around on the floor in a very effective fake fight. She was stuck—there was no way she could make a run for it without someone seeing her.

The guard pulled Smith off Walker. Walker's arm gave a gut-wrenching snap and he screamed. With one enormous, booted foot, the guard kicked the back of Walker's head, sending his face smashing into the stone floor. Walker stopped moving. The sight made Keira sway on her feet. She wanted to run, but how could she leave him like that? And then she saw his ribs move, just a little.

He was breathing at least.

"Leave the traitor for now," the guard shouted. "We've lost the Experimental! You, Sorter," he barked at Smith. "Check the other rooms in this annex." Smith scrambled away while the guard dashed into the listening room where Keira and Walker had been moments earlier.

The antechamber was empty.

This was her chance.

Keira sprinted out of the vestibule. She skidded into the main hall and stopped short at the sight of another black-robed figure running toward her across the main hall.

Another guard. It had to be. A couple of Darklings had emerged from other little rooms in the Hall, and they shrank back against the pillars and walls, as though they could become invisible. As though getting chased by the guards was the worst thing they could imagine.

The guard's leathery robe flapped around him like bat wings, more intimidating than Smith's shaggy robe was. He shouted at her and Keira took off, her shoes sliding against the floor as she fought for traction. There were two other small rooms set into the walls of the main hall, but they offered nowhere to hide. Up ahead, Keira could see a long, dark hall, lined irregularly with openings. She ran for it. Behind her, she heard someone yelp with pain, but she didn't look back. The sudden silence in the antechamber was just as terrifying as the slapping of the guard's feet against the floor.

Her chest ached as she ducked under the archway that led to the darkened hall. She needed Walker to be okay, and not only because she was entirely too panicked to get out of Darkside without him.

In the hall, the doors were mostly shut. She peered down the black corridor, looking for an exit, but the passage twisted abruptly, hiding everything beyond the bend.

At least it would hide her, too.

The guard's footsteps drew closer.

She had to move.

The first door she tried opened into an empty room with a domed ceiling. Something about the musty scent of the air and the dark glitter of the smooth walls made the back of her neck prickle in warning. She dropped the door back into place and sprinted down the hall.

Her lungs and thighs burned with the effort of running. Her feet slipped against the floor again. She rounded the bend in the corridor and kicked off her ballet flats in frustration. In the newly visible part of the hall, she could see two new doorways. She sprinted toward them, wincing at the iciness of the floor beneath her bare feet.

She stopped in the middle of the hall, between her potential hiding places. Her palms were sweating and she wiped them against her jeans automatically.

What she could see of the room on her left was nearly filled by an enormous machine that was covered with levers and dials. She glanced to the right-hand room and saw stacks of boxes. It would have been perfect to hide behind them, except they were pressed up against the walls. Behind her, the timbre of the guard's footsteps changed as he crossed from the main hall into the hallway.

The hallway she was standing in.

Her time was up. She'd have to take her chances hiding with the machine. She darted into the room, ducking behind a panel of switches that was waist-high. If she knelt down, she'd be invisible from the door.

Above her hung a row of the same sort of needles that Walker had used in the little record room. They dangled from a mechanized-looking track like a row of dark icicles. Keira shuddered.

The guard's footsteps slowed, and she could hear the creaking, leathery noise of the doors down the hall being opened and closed. Keira wrapped her arms around her knees and closed her eyes. She tried to wish herself back to the normal world, but it didn't work—she didn't even know where she was in that world, whether she should be feeling for grass or Berber carpet or asphalt beneath the soles of her freezing-cold feet.

Keira opened her eyes and stared around her as she huddled behind the machine that filled most of the room. She longed for the headache that came with seeing both worlds at once. She caught a glimpse of blue sky, but the sound of the footsteps inching closer swept it away.

Focus. Focus or get caught. Those are your two choices. And if you get caught, they get Walker, too.

Crossing over was her only chance. Keira blocked out everything but a tiny ripple in the black stone of the room's walls. She looked for the familiar sights of her neighborhood with her peripheral vision, trying to see even the edges of something normal.

The tall, litter-strewn grass of an empty lot drifted into view. Keira knew that lot—it was two doors down from the Reynoldses'. It would be muddy beneath her. And she could see the grass moving. It must be breezy. She struggled to feel those things. Keira welcomed the almost familiar press of sliding between the two worlds. Her skin had begun to go clammy with the feeling of going home when a light flared to life above her.

A guard stepped around the side of the machine, his robe swirling out in front of him. The fabric was the same as what Smith had worn, only this looked finer. It moved like magnetic dust, shifting and re-forming as if it were alive.

The guard yelled when he caught sight of her.

His shout broke Keira's concentration and for a horrible moment, she felt herself catch in the thin place between Darkside and home.

Unable to move.

Unable to breathe.

Her gaze was locked on the guard. Beneath his hood, she saw two eyes, pure black as a spider's. They glittered in the strange antireflection of the ceiling light. Keira tried to scream, but she had no air to scream with. The guard reached for her with his unnaturally long fingers. He brushed her shoulder and she jerked, every molecule in her body pulling away from him.

She landed on her side.

In the mud.

In the empty lot.

Home.

Keira let out a choked sob as she rolled away from the spot where she'd come across from Darkside, afraid that the guard would be able to reach into her world somehow. She knew they couldn't cross through the fabric of their reality, but she also knew that she'd made a new rip in Darkside. She wasn't taking any chances. Keira stood up and picked her way across the debris-strewn grass. Her bare feet slowed her down as she tried to look for Walker in the Hall while still avoiding the broken bottles in her world.

She stopped near the edge of the lot. Cautiously, she looked for the other world she knew was there. The world that was more than the leafless trees and suburban grass and cracked sidewalks in front of her.

Keira dug her toes into the mud, keeping her physical awareness in Sherwin while she looked for Darkside. A swirling dark mark twirled on the top of her naked foot, reminding her of the place she'd just escaped; luring her back.

The machine-filled room was gone. From her spot at the edge of the lot, she found herself looking at a Darkside wall.

She wasn't inside the Hall of Records anymore. She couldn't see anything except the building's smooth facade.

She had no idea where Walker might be now, but he was in the Hall of Records somewhere, and she'd be damned if she was going to leave him to fend for himself.

Chapter Thirty-Eight

KEIRA THOUGHT FRANTICALLY, TRYING to come up with some sort of plan. She couldn't wander around the neighborhood, peeking into the Hall of Records while she searched for Walker. For one thing, Jeremy was home and already hot to use his baseball bat. For another, she didn't have any shoes. Someone might notice a muddy, barefoot girl roaming the sidewalks.

She wanted to plunge back into Darkside but she'd barely gotten out the last time. What if she got stuck? They'd catch her, and then who would save Walker? The memory of the guard's eyes ghosted through her like a recurring nightmare.

She needed to find Walker while keeping herself from

getting caught. Her thoughts were impossibly tangled and her vision swam—she was having trouble shaking the effects of passing between the two worlds. Her fingers ached for her piano. She needed to play—to use the rhythm of the notes to quiet her mind. It was the way she'd always worked through her problems and without it, she felt lost.

But then again, she'd never had this sort of problem. There was no time to pick through a sonata when a life hung in the balance.

Suddenly, Smith appeared in front of her. Keira would have staggered back if he hadn't grabbed her shoulders.

"He's still there, Keira, on the floor. You have to go get him before the guards decide they can spare someone to drag him away."

Now she knew what people meant when they said their hearts had leapt into their throats. She couldn't breathe, couldn't swallow through the thudding fear that filled her neck.

"What about you? Why didn't you bring him across?" she croaked, both worried for him and also desperately wanting his help.

"I couldn't! They would have seen me. I'll go to another part of the Hall and create a distraction." Smith's face was grim, but determined. "If we both get caught trying to get Walker out, they'll take the three of us in front of the Tribunal for sure. If they're busy watching me throw a fit, though, we might all make it out alive."

"Okay," she agreed. "Go, then."

Smith disappeared as quickly as he'd come, and Keira strode toward the last place she'd seen Walker—facedown in the vestibule in front of the records . . . which was probably somewhere in the Reynoldses' living room. Somehow, she was going to have to get back into Jeremy's house.

She hurried across the cracked sidewalk. She was muddy, barefoot, and disheveled—maybe she could use that to her advantage. Not even Jeremy could find her sexy when she looked like she'd just rolled through a ditch. In front of the Reynoldses' house, Keira squinted, looking for the Hall. Her skin crawled in warning, but she couldn't tell if it was because she was close to the guards or because Jeremy was watching her from his living room window.

Keira curled her hands into fists as the Hall came into view. She was right next to one of the pillars that ringed the open floor of the main room, and even though she wasn't Darkside, she felt more secure—more hidden—with the enormous column at her back. She didn't see Walker, but she also didn't see anyone moving toward the spot where she'd last seen him.

Keira dropped her view of Darkside, and hurried toward the Reynoldses' front path, hoping she looked more pathetic than crazy. The door flew open as she raised her hand to knock. Keira yelped.

"Keira?" Jeremy's face was pink as an Easter ham and his eyes gleamed with unspent adrenaline. He squinted at her like he wasn't sure he was seeing things properly.

"Um. I'm glad you're home," Keira said.

"Yeah?" A smile slid across his face. "So, how come you're not at school?" He leaned against the door frame, confidence replacing his confusion.

"I had a dentist appointment," Keira lied. "My car broke down back that way"—she waved her hand in the direction of the empty lot—"and my cell phone's dead. Could I use your phone? Please?" When he went to get his phone, she'd duck into the house and take a quick look around Darkside. She couldn't see around the walls in the Hall of Records from where she was standing.

Jeremy's lips twitched. "Sure." His voice was oily. "I'd let you use my cell, but I'm pretty sure the battery's dead too. Why don't you come in? You can use the phone in the kitchen."

The heat in his eyes made her think twice about being alone in the house with him, but she didn't really have any choice. She was the only one who could save Walker. She couldn't leave him to fend for himself. And if Jeremy tried anything funny, she could always cross into Darkside, even if it would mean facing the guards.

Crap. Why did all of the possibilities end up with her risking her own ass?

The longer she paused, the more eager Jeremy looked.

"Okay," she said, stepping across the threshold. "Thanks." She struggled to stay calm as the musty, messy house surrounded her.

Leaning against the wall next to the door was the baseball bat. It gleamed dully, radiating danger. Keira swallowed her fear as Jeremy's dog came bounding into the room, greeting her like a long-lost friend.

Jeremy shoved the dog aside. "Get off her, moron." He glanced sideways at Keira as he gestured toward the back of the house. "Kitchen's that way," he said.

Keira strode into the kitchen, trying to look as competent as she could. Walking the way she imagined someone who'd taken extensive self-defense courses would walk.

"Hey!" Jeremy said. The accusation in his voice stopped Keira midstep. "You're barefoot," he observed. As if, just because her feet were bare, the rest of her clothes might slither off her too.

"I, uh . . . yeah." Keira cleared her throat, flipping through a list of possible excuses. "I like to drive barefoot."

Jeremy snorted disbelievingly. He looked at her through half-lidded eyes. "I know you wrecked your car, Keira. And I saw it sitting at Brutti's body shop two days ago, still completely bashed up." His eyes narrowed. "So. Why are you *really* here?"

Oh, shit. Oh shit oh shit oh shit.

"I'm driving my dad's car," she stammered. "It's the one that broke down."

"So why don't you just walk home?" He smiled like he'd caught her.

"I tried, but I'm locked out," she lied.

Keira hurried across the kitchen and reached for the phone before he could ask her any more questions. She dialed Susan's number, hoping for once that she *wouldn't* pick up. While she listened to it ring, Keira let her gaze soften, searching Darkside to see how far she was from the antechamber. There was no way to tell if Smith had made it back, or whether he was distracting the guards. She could be missing her chance to get Walker out while she dicked around in Jeremy's kitchen, making sham phone calls.

Fuck.

Darkside ghosted into view, and she could see the archway that led into the anteroom at the edge of the kitchen. Walker lay on the floor, facing her, his arm twisted at an unnatural angle. His head was bleeding, but it wasn't like anything Keira had ever seen. It pooled beneath his nose, black as oil, and moved like liquid mercury, tiny droplets breaking off and skittering across the floor as the puddle grew.

The sound of Susan's voice mail message broke her concentration, and Keira realized that Jeremy was watching her intently.

"Hey," she said, instinctively acting like someone had actually picked up the phone. "Yeah, dad's car broke down and I'm stuck."

Pause.

"Near Temple and Newbury. Can you call a tow truck and come unlock the house?"

The nasal auto-voice of the voice mail service cut her off and Keira prayed that Jeremy couldn't hear it.

"Thanks," she said quickly. "I really appreciate it."

Keira hung up the phone, her hand trembling. Walker was only a few feet away, injured and unconscious in Darkside, but Jeremy's stare was boring holes into her back in the normal world. She was going to have to go back into Darkside and get Walker out somehow, without both of them reappearing in the Reynoldses' kitchen. Or getting caught by the Darkside guards before they made it back.

Great.

"Well, I guess I'll be going," Keira said. "Thanks for letting me use the phone." She turned around. Jeremy was standing a lot closer to her than he had been before.

"You might as well wait here. You can have a soda. Or something. We'll talk." He took another step closer to her, and Keira edged toward the back door.

"Um, about what?"

"About Walker. His name's Walker, right?"

Keira nodded.

"He's an asshole. You and I make so much more sense, Keira." His eyes glittered. "If you'd think about it, I'm sure you'd see what I see. We'd be good. *Really* good."

"You and . . . you and *me*? Jeremy, that's . . . I'm . . . very flattered but . . . ." The words barely made it past her stammering lips. Keira shook herself. "Listen, I should probably get back to my car. My mom's on her way home from work and it won't take her that long to get here. I have to go."

Anger flashed across Jeremy's face, sudden and hot as a grease fire. "You haven't even given me a chance to finish. We *do* make sense. I can prove it to you." Jeremy reached out and caught hold of her sleeve.

Every alarm bell inside Keira went off at once. The only thing she could think of was getting out of the house. She yanked her arm away, but instead of letting go, Jeremy's grip tightened and the shoulder seam of her shirt ripped.

Jeremy didn't seem to hear the threads tear. Still holding her by her mangled shirt, he pulled her close and kissed her, forcing his tongue into her mouth. Keira turned her head to get away from his kiss. He ended up licking her cheek.

Trying not to gag, Keira wrenched herself out of his grip and ran toward the back door.

"Wait!" Behind her, Jeremy stepped forward, but the dog darted between the two of them, barking excitedly. Jeremy tripped over the dog and cursed. In the spare second the dog had given her, Keira flipped the lock and yanked open the door, careening out into the backyard.

"Hey!" Jeremy shouted after her, as she raced around the corner of the house. Vaguely, she heard the phone in his house ringing, followed by a string of curses.

She might have gotten away for the moment, but she wasn't at all sure Jeremy was going to let her go for good.

Chapter Thirty-Nine

PROTECTED FROM VIEW BY the wall of Jeremy's house, Keira crouched down on the scruffy grass and reached for Darkside with everything she had. She crossed over so quickly that it hurt. It was like she'd been shoved through a meat slicer, chopping off her connection with one reality and dropping her into another.

She found herself pressed up against the exterior wall of the Hall of Records, the stone stealing her body heat with shocking speed. A scream of frustration rose in her throat and Keira gritted her teeth against it. There was no way into the Hall from this side. It was windowless. Doorless. Impenetrable. And there was no way she was going in through the Hall of Record's main door. She couldn't risk that.

She'd just have to go back to her world and try again. Squeezing her eyes shut, she felt for the grass beneath her bare feet. When she could feel dirt beneath her fingertips, she opened her eyes.

Home.

There was no time to be relieved, not with Walker bleeding and Jeremy convinced that he just needed to keep kissing her until she realized that she wanted him too. Keira crawled up to the house, pushing against it until the cheap siding pressed painfully against her back. She had to be close enough now. If she wasn't, she and Walker were both screwed. Briefly, she wondered if it were possible for her to materialize halfway through the stone wall of the Hall of Records. The thought made her shudder. Right then, though, she didn't have time to worry about it. She had to try, no matter what might happen.

One more time, she told herself, reaching for another reality. Sweat sprang up on her scalp from the effort of going Darkside again, and the chill that came over her when she passed through turned her damp skin to ice.

But she was *through.* That was all that mattered.

Keira found herself at the very back of the listening room.

The door was open and she could see Walker's feet just beyond it. In the main room, shouts echoed. She peered around the doorway in time to see Smith dart out through the main doors, followed by a swarm of guards.

Keira scrabbled across the floor, keeping herself as low as possible. Grabbing Walker's ankles, she dragged him into the room, grateful for the glass-smooth floor. His right arm flopped as though his hand wasn't attached to his elbow. Keira's stomach rolled. She shook his good shoulder.

"Walker. Walker, wake up!" His head lolled. The blood from his nose had dried into dark, shimmering flecks.

"Walker!" She pinched him, hard, but his face remained blank. In the main room of the Hall, Keira could hear the rustle of activity. She couldn't wait for Walker to regain consciousness. There wasn't time.

She pushed him across the floor so that he was flush against the wall. She had to get Walker out of here, and if he were any farther inside the listening room, they'd end up in the Reynoldses' spare room when they crossed over.

Keira crawled halfway on top of him, buried her face in his shirt, and wrapped her shaking arms around him. She closed her eyes, blocking out everything about the Hall of Records. She concentrated on the scraggly grass and the cold, gray siding of Jeremy's house. The rusted, chain-link fence around the yard. The blue sky and the sun glowing overhead, radiating outward, the way light was *supposed* to.

Something unpleasantly wet swept along her bared arm, and Keira opened her eyes, ready to scream. Ready to fight.

The golden retriever looked at her quizzically, like he couldn't understand why she kept disappearing just when he was ready to play. Beneath her, Walker stirred.

"Oh, holy discord, are we back in Sherwin?" He sat up and Keira blinked, staring at him. The blood was gone from his face, and he leaned back on his arms. His arms, which were obviously not broken. She had a million questions, but none of them burned as brightly as her desire to get the hell away from the Reynoldses' backyard.

"Yes," she whispered, climbing off him and grabbing his hand. The dog danced in front of Walker, whining to be petted. "We have to get out of here. *Now.*"

"Keira, the guards can't get us here."

"No," she breathed, yanking Walker to his feet, "but *he* can." Walker paled at the sound of heavy footsteps against the Reynoldses' concrete patio. The two of them sprinted toward the fence. Walker grabbed Keira, lifting her over it like she was as light as a leaf, then vaulted it easily himself.

They ran back toward the car, ducking beneath trees and behind parked cars until they had put enough distance between them and Jeremy's house that they couldn't be seen.

Walker tugged her behind a fir tree, his hands reaching up to stroke her face. His thumbs skimmed over her eyebrows and across her cheekbones. They hovered over her lips like a place-holder for an impossible kiss.

"You're okay?" he asked. "No one hurt you?"

The memory of Jeremy's unwanted kiss, of the guard reaching for her shoulder, made her want to crawl right out of her skin. There had been nothing but near misses that morning, but in the end, she'd managed to slip away each time.

"*I'm* fine," Keira panted, out of breath from all the running. Hours and hours at the piano didn't exactly count as cardio.

"Where's Smith? What the hell happened?" he asked.

"I hauled your unconscious ass out of the Hall of Records, that's what," Keira said, her adrenaline-fueled fear exploding into anger. "Smith ran out the front door with a bunch of guards behind him. I don't know where he is now."

"Smith can take care of himself," Walker reassured her.

"I hope you're right, because one of those guards broke your arm and kicked you in the head. Once you were unconscious, he left you bleeding on the floor. At least, I think it was blood."

Walker rubbed the back of his neck uncomfortably. "Yeah. It was probably blood. The dark matter particles that get mixed in make it look different. I remember one of the guards smashing into me . . . he broke my *arm*?"

"It was flopping like a fish," Keira said.

Walker dropped his hand from his neck and held out his hands, twisting them from side to side, showing her that he was fine.

"How is that possible?" she asked with a croak of surprise.

"It's the crossing," Walker said. "In the same way it messes with your metabolism—the molecules in your body shift as you go through the barrier—it sort of resets them. You go back to the way your genes say you are supposed to be. I'm surprised you didn't notice that the other night with your shoulder."

Keira reached up and felt her shoulder, the one she'd painfully slammed into the coffee table when she'd first seen the Seeker at her house. It seemed like weeks ago, but it had been less than a day. She tugged the neck of her shirt aside, examining the skin. There was no bruise. She'd been sure it was going to bruise.

"How did I not notice that it was better?" she asked.

Walker wrapped his arm around her, sliding her shirt back into place. "You were maybe too busy freaking out about the fact that you'd crossed into another reality?" he suggested.

His teasing was gentle. She laughed shakily, letting his humor calm her.

"Speaking of which," he said, "you must be hungry."

She was. Her stomach twisted with hunger, but it was bearable. "Yeah, but I can wait awhile if we need to."

Walker's eyes widened in surprise. He pulled the keys from his pocket and aimed the fob at the car. "You're adjusting fast. That's . . . good. Surprising, but good."

"Why is it surprising?" Keira asked, as she sank into the passenger seat. She reached down and flipped on the seat warmer. The leather heated up beneath her and after the cold concrete of the sidewalk, even the scratchy floor mats felt heavenly beneath her feet.

"The others who crossed—the other Experimentals—they

always came back practically incoherent with hunger. Like you were last night, but even more. Eventually, they'd get a little better, but before any of them could . . . well, you know what happened."

"The Extermination Program," Keira said.

"Exactly," Walker said. Keira saw him swallow, eating the words he didn't want to say. "I think we should take a quick drive past the Hall on our way out of the neighborhood," he said. "As long as you're okay with that? I want to know just how many of the guards they called back."

"There were an awful lot of them," Keira said. "I saw at least a dozen, which was sort of surprising, because I thought they were all out at the ravine."

Walker's grip tightened on the steering wheel. "It's my fault. I heard the transport vehicle and assumed they'd sent most of the guards to examine the new rip we'd made. I didn't think they'd leave so many at the Hall. It's like they knew we'd be back. . . ."

"Well, I do live right behind it," Keira said. "It makes sense that I'd come home sometime. Maybe that's what they were waiting for?"

"Maybe," Walker said, though he didn't sound convinced. He slowed the car, idling on the side of the street. "Oh. *Shit.*"

Keira struggled to make Darkside visible. She could see Jeremy's house, the darkened windows staring at her. Someone was in there, watching.

Jeremy.

Keira could feel it.

Beside her, Walker's breath grew ragged, and she refocused, trying to see what he saw. Darkside appeared so quickly that, for a moment, she was afraid she'd actually crossed over. She grabbed the armrest, reassuring herself that she was still in her own world. Guards streamed past the car, along with people she assumed worked in the Hall of Records, since they were dressed in the same sort of robes that Smith had worn. Everyone was running.

Not just running.

Running *away*.

The building itself listed slightly to one side, like a ship against a sandbar. In the distance, robed figures stood against the trees that ringed the Hall with their heads in their hands. A few of them actually knelt, having collapsed into dark heaps on the ground.

Keira turned to Walker. "What's happening?"

Walker looked almost exactly like her mother had, the day she'd announced that she and Keira's dad were separating. His face was a wide-eyed mask of worry and suspicion and surprise.

Keira's insides swirled and dropped.

"The building's not safe anymore," he said. "The whole area's unstable."

Keira watched as a few guards, each carrying a bundle of sharp-tipped spears, crept toward the building. They stopped in unison about twenty yards from the Hall and began driving the spears into the ground, point first, creating a makeshift perimeter.

"It's all my fault." His voice was quiet. "If I hadn't dragged you here, hadn't been stupid enough to let the guards catch us . . ." He stopped for a moment, pulling himself together.

"We crossed back and forth too many times in places that were too close together," he explained. "All the rips—it's making lace out of Darkside. This area's too fragile now. It's dangerous. Going in the Hall would be like walking out on thin ice. One step in the wrong place, and the whole thing might collapse."

Keira thought of all the squeezing in and out of Darkside.

How many times had she *crossed that morning? Six? Eight? Plus, Walker and Smith had crossed too. . . . Oh, sweet Jesus.* She stared at the wounded building, drowning in the knowledge that she was the reason it had been ruined.

"Will they be able to fix it?" she asked.

Walker ran a hand through his curls. "It might settle where it is, if the fabric of Darkside is strong enough to hold it. There's a chance it won't sink any farther than that."

Relief spread over her and Keira loosened her grip on the door handle.

"But they'll never be able to use the building again," Walker said. "The records . . ." His voice was thick. "They won't be able to get to the records. One Darkling stepping into an area that weak could destroy the whole thing. It's happened before, in other places. Never with a Hall of Records, though." His cheeks were ghostly pale.

Keira's hope shattered, as broken as the bit of Darkside spread out in front of her. Only four Halls of Records in all of Darkside, and they'd destroyed one of them. That sort of tragedy wasn't going to go unnoticed.

"The Reformers," she whispered.

Walker nodded. "They're going to spend the next several months consoling the Darklings—and looking for someone to hang for this."

Keira shuddered. "But we didn't mean to destroy it."

"It doesn't matter. We did. And they want us anyway, so we're ready-made for blaming." Everyone in Darkside had their attention pinned to the Hall of Records, which made the sudden movement toward Keira and Walker that much more noticeable. No one in Darkside was looking at them.

But Jeremy Reynolds obviously was.

Chapter Forty

THE FRONT DOOR OF the house stood open and Jeremy took a half step toward the street, shading his eyes with his hand. He had his cell phone in his other hand and he tapped it against his leg.

Keira pressed herself back against the seat, hoping the glare of the sun against the windshield was enough to keep her invisible to Jeremy. Walker just stared through the houses and past the lawns, his attention still fixed on the tragedy unfolding in his own world.

"Walker," she whispered, as though Jeremy would somehow hear her even through the steel of the Mercedes, "he's watching us. We have to *go*."

Walker jerked around, his focus shifting away from the Hall of Records. He stared at Jeremy. Then Walker clenched his jaw and stomped on the gas pedal. In a bone-jarring second, they were racing for the stop sign at the end of the street. "I don't like the way he looks—or the way he looks at you. At all. I'm glad you got out of his house before he saw you."

Keira froze. Walker didn't know. Of course. He'd been unconscious.

"Um, actually, I sort of had to go through his house again, to find you. After the guard beat you up."

"You went into his house, *alone?*" Walker asked. "What were you thinking?"

Keira crossed her arms, squaring off against him. "I thought I was rescuing *you*. And besides, I knew I could cross over if anything happened."

Walker pressed his head back against the head rest. "How would you have explained it if you'd up and disappeared? You're lucky he *didn't* try anything."

Keira's silence lasted a heartbeat too long.

Walker's eyes cut over to her. His gaze lanced through her bravado.

"What happened?" His words were measured with restraint.

"Nothing, really. He said some stuff about how he and I should be together. And then he shoved his disgusting tongue in my mouth."

"He *what?*"

"Listen, I handled it!" Keira insisted. "I got away, didn't I? I ran out the back and crossed over into the Hall. I found you and I got us both out. That's all that matters."

"He could have . . . he could've—" Walker struggled with the words.

"What? Raped me? Hurt me?" Keira spat. "So could the guard who caught me in the Hall. Pretty much everyone in your world thinks I'm an experiment that needs to be ended, so what's one more asshole who thinks he owns me? I took care of myself. I took care of *you*. A little gratitude wouldn't be completely misplaced here."

Walker pulled the car over to the side of the road and killed the engine. For a long moment he was silent, staring out the windshield at the empty street. A single slash of darkness appeared on the side of his neck, fading almost as quickly as it had come. Finally, he turned to look at Keira, his eyes sorrowful. "You're right. You are so, one hundred percent right. I know you saved me. If you hadn't come back, the guards would have taken me, and probably Smith, too." He shuddered. "Thank you. I'm sorry I didn't say it sooner."

Keira's anger leaked out of her and she leaned back against the seat, limp. "It's okay. I didn't mean to freak out. I'm really not the freaking-out type. I just—"

"You've just had people trying to kill you all morning," Walker interrupted her. "You're not *supposed* to be all calm and composed after that, Keira. Let's agree that we might both need a little help in the saving our own lives department, okay?"

Keira closed her eyes briefly, shutting out the disbelief and despair that she was even having this conversation in the first place.

"Okay," she agreed. She would get through this the same way she'd gotten through every hard piece of music she'd ever played—by focusing on the next line, and nothing more. Not the movement she'd just played, not the hard crescendo that came later. Only what was in front of her. One finger stroke after the next. It was the only way through. The only way out.

"So, what next?" Walker asked.

Keira looked down at her bare, muddy feet. Her naked toes were mottled with cold.

"I need shoes," she said. "And food. Let's start with that."

Three quarter notes and a rest. Food and shoes.

One thing at a time.

Keira had inhaled the bag of fast food almost before Walker disappeared into the shoe store. She'd shoved some money into his hand and instructed him to get whatever he could find in a size eight that was less than thirty dollars. She knew he hadn't wanted to take her money.

She also knew that he could read her face well enough to realize that arguing would be pointless.

Alone in the car, she counted up the cash left in her wallet. It was barely enough to buy food for the next couple of days, much less enough for a place to stay or new clothes. And her clothes were starting to stink.

She was going to have to go home. The thought made her scalp prickle. It was so close to the Hall. The whole area was *swarming* with guards. But where else was she going to get clothes?

Her phone rang and Keira dug it out of the bottom of the bag, noticing that her battery was getting low.

It was Susan. Susan, who wore almost exactly the same size as she did. Who could save Keira now in more ways than one.

Oh, thank God.

"Hello?"

"Hi. It's me. Why are you not at school? Have you heard from Walker or Smith?" Susan's voice was all wrong and it sent a chill down Keira's spine.

"What do you mean?" she asked.

"I think I need to talk to my parents. Or maybe even call the cops. I don't know. I just talked to Smith and I think he's lost his mind."

Susan's choice of words made Keira's throat seize.

"What happened?" she choked out.

"We had this really amazing night last night, and he was totally saying all this stuff about how he hadn't expected to feel the way he did. I was like, 'Okay, I need to think about whether I want this to be more than a rebound.'"

Keira gagged silently.

"But then he called and was saying all this weird stuff about how he and I couldn't be together and it wasn't Walker's fault, but that he still hated him for it. It didn't make *any* sense, but I figured Smith was just being a drama queen, because, you know, he's sort of a drama queen. But I still want to know what's going on. Did I get dumped? Again?"

The burger Keira'd eaten swam unpleasantly in her stomach. There was no way out of this except to explain it to Susan.

"I don't know what to say. I do think we need to talk, though."

"Hang on, I'm getting a text." When Susan came back on the line, her voice had gone squeaky. "I'll say we need to talk. Apparently, word is out about you and Jeremy."

"What do you mean? There is no 'me and Jeremy.'"

"Not according to this. Tommy just texted me that Jeremy said the two of you hooked up this morning."

Keira's stomach dropped. The cell phone Jeremy had in his hand before she'd driven away with Walker—the horrible look he'd had on his face . . .

Oh, no.

Oh, no, no, nonono.

"It's not true," she said adamantly. "I mean, I'm with Walker. Why would I hook up with Jeremy?"

"So, why aren't you at school with the rest of us? It's not that I don't believe you. I do. But it looks really bad."

It was a reasonable question, but she still hated that Susan had a reason to ask it.

"I've been with Walker. Mostly." She rubbed a hand over her aching eyes. "We got separated for a little bit while we were looking for something. I ended up at Jeremy's. And yeah, he told me he liked me. And yeah, he kissed me. But he also ripped my shirt trying to force me into that kiss."

"I . . . oh." Susan sucked in a long breath. "But wait, I still don't get why you were there in the first place."

"I really, really want to tell you," Keira said. "But it's complicated. Listen, this is serious. I'm in trouble. Can I come over when you get home from school and borrow some clothes?" She thought about Walker buying her shoes . . . she'd still need those. Susan wore a six and a half.

"Don't tell me you're running away. Not because of a few lying texts and our school's lame gossip obsession." Susan sounded horrified.

"No, it's not like that," Keira insisted. "So, can I come over? Please? I need your help. I need you to trust me. Please."

"Of course," Susan sighed. "I'll help you. But I want to know what's going on. If there's an explanation for all this, you know I'm behind you a hundred percent, but everything's *weird*, Keira. I'm not okay with that."

"I know. I understand, I really do." Keira leaned her cheek against the cool glass of the car window. Susan was going to help her. It was a start.

"Okay, then. I'll see you later."

The phone went dead in Keira's hand.

Susan wasn't okay with things being weird. So how the hell was Keira supposed to tell her about Darkside? Everything about Keira's life was weird now. Everything. And she couldn't see any way that things would ever be normal again. She sat in the car, her chest tight, trying very, very hard not to cry.

Chapter Forty-One

WALKER PULLED UP IN front of Susan's house.

"I can buy you some clothes," he said. Again. "Your pride is awesome and all, but in a life-and-death situation, it really doesn't matter."

Keira shook her head. He didn't get it.

"It's more than that. I can't abandon Susan. First of all, I already asked her to lie for me about where I've been staying. And secondly"—she stared up at Susan's bedroom window— "she's my *best friend*. I trust her. I'm not going to walk away from her. She deserves an explanation, and not just 'I have a new boyfriend and some stuff's going on and I can't tell you anything else about it.' I don't know if she can deal with the truth, but I have to try to tell her. It's the only way I can live with myself."

She looked over at Walker.

Walker ran his hands over the sides of his jeans again and again. If she hadn't been able to see that his eyes were dry, Keira would've sworn he was about to cry.

"What's wrong?" she demanded. Not a single thing she'd said should have made him look so distraught.

"You called me your *boyfriend*." He sounded horrified.

Keira felt stung. Her skin throbbed with it. After everything they'd been through—he didn't want to be her boyfriend? Was he really so used to this bizarre life that their relationship didn't mean anything to him?

Feeling painfully uncertain, Keira unbuckled her seat belt and reached for the door.

"After last night?" She could feel herself blushing. "If you're not my boyfriend, then fine, whatever. I was just illustrating a point." Keira angrily swung open the door, but before she could step out of the car, Walker caught her wrist.

Time itself seemed to slow. Her indrawn breath lasted for a tiny eternity.

"Keira, stop. I don't think I *am* your boyfriend," Walker said.

The world dropped out from under Keira. She hung there, waiting for the fall. "You . . ." She couldn't bring herself to finish the sentence.

"After everything we've been through, the way I feel when I look at you, when I think about losing you—" Walker shook his head. "I don't know *what* we are. I don't know that there's even a word for it. Not in either of our worlds. But I do know that it's a hell of a lot more than *boyfriend*."

The words tumbled over Keira, cracking open the air around her like an unexpected and very loud chord. Her head rang with it, filling her with its own rhythm and color and light.

She stared at Walker. She couldn't voice the feeling spilling through her. It was something she could have played on the piano, maybe. Something she could have made him feel with notes and sounds. But without a piano all she could do was hope that he could see the joy in her eyes.

"Okay," she whispered.

Walker brought her hand up to his mouth and turned it over, exposing the inside of her wrist. He pressed his lips against the road map of blue veins visible beneath her translucent skin. The kiss was a risk, throwing into view a hilly, forested section of Darkside that was studded with rocks. Keira closed her eyes against the vision, trying to focus on the smooth door handle in her palm and the scent of the Maine air flowing into the car. Trying not to slip into Darkside. When she opened her eyes, she saw only the car, Walker, and Susan's house.

"Go on in," he said, releasing her hand. "I'll wait here."

Feeling light-headed, Keira swung herself out of the car, her new shoes chafing against her sockless feet. As she trudged up the familiar front path to Susan's house, she tried to clear her head, to get rid of all the chaos, so that she could be the same Keira she'd always been. The sort of Keira that Susan was expecting.

And then the door was in front of her and there was nothing to do but lift her hand and knock. Keira'd done it a thousand times before, but now it seemed like the hardest thing in the world. Still, she'd never been one to back down from a challenge.

She took a deep breath and rapped on the door.

Susan opened the door. The pinched expression on her face evaporated into surprise when she saw Keira's disheveled hair and filthy clothes. *Those* hadn't gone back to their original state when she'd crossed back and forth from Darkside.

Keira watched her best friend take in her ripped sleeve. Verifying Keira's story.

"Can I come in?" Keira asked.

Susan glanced behind Keira, her gaze riveted on Walker's sleek car, waiting at the curb. "I can't believe you ditched school to be with him. That's not like you at all! Is he just going to lurk out there?"

"You skipped last week to hang out with Smith," Keira said simply. "And he's not lurking. He's my ride."

"I know. Sorry. I'm just really freaked out. Smith won't answer my texts, you're acting weird *and* you asked me to lie to your parents. You've never done that before. I want to know what's going on."

Smith wasn't answering Susan's texts? Worry nibbled at her as Keira sagged against the door frame. "Susan, I'm sorry. I never meant to put you in this position. Please, let me come in and explain? And maybe change out of these clothes?"

Susan wrinkled her nose. "Those clothes need to be burned. What have you been doing, exactly?"

Keira paused, sorting through the lies she could tell. None of them seemed believable. Besides, she was going to ask Susan to give her clothes, to cover for her, and more than that, she was asking Susan to trust her. To understand. A lie wasn't going to earn her any of that. Not even a good lie.

There was only one way to solve this—only one way that Susan would understand why she'd done all the inexplicable things she'd done. After all her insistence that she could trust Susan, it was time to act like she actually did.

She had to tell her best friend the truth.

Keira looked Susan straight in the eye. "Let's go upstairs. I'll tell you everything."

Susan glanced at the kitchen, where her mother was pointedly banging around pots and pans. "Fair enough."

The two of them trudged up the stairs and Susan pointed to a pile of clothes on the bed.

"That's all the stuff that's a little bit too long for me. Help yourself."

Keira felt her chin quiver as she stared at the neatly washed and ironed fabric, smelling like the floral detergent Mrs. Kim loved. It didn't seem like anything to get upset over, but the sight of something so simple and familiar made her realize how far from normal her life had become.

Keira pulled a pair of black yoga pants and a long-sleeved shirt out of the pile. She shucked off her filthy jeans and T-shirt and slid into the clean clothes with a groan of relief.

Susan handed her a hairbrush. "You look like you got caught in a hurricane," she said. "So? You were going to tell me what was going on? Since apparently Jeremy's story that you slept together isn't true?"

Keira froze halfway through pulling the ponytail out of her hair. "He said *what?*"

Susan winced. "He texted Tommy that he'd 'done you'"— she added air quotes with her fingers—"but that it, um . . ." She trailed off, squirming uncomfortably in the chair.

"It what?" Keira asked, biting off the end of each word.

"He said it was like humping a dead fish." Pink bloomed in Susan's cheeks. "And then Tommy sent the text to me and well, pretty much to everyone, actually."

"God. What a lying asshole." Keira smacked the hairbrush against her thigh. "After everything that happened this morning, the last thing I want to deal with is Jeremy Reynolds's crap. You don't believe him, right? I don't care what everyone else thinks, as long as you know the truth."

Susan hesitated. "I don't think you slept with him. Especially not since I know you spent last night with Walker."

Keira's jaw clenched. "We did spend the night together, but we didn't . . . you know . . ."

Susan looked at Keira like she wanted to believe her, but she couldn't quite do it.

"Sure. Okay. I still don't get why you were at Jeremy's, though. What's really going on?"

Keira sighed and yanked the brush through her hair. She wanted to tell Susan. She was *going* to tell Susan.

The only trouble was figuring out where to start.

"Okay, when I met Walker a couple weeks ago?"

"Yeah?" Susan said, perching on the little wooden chair at her desk.

Keira winced as the brush caught in a knot of hair. She pulled the bristles out and started working at it more slowly.

"Well, the more time we spent together, the more I noticed that there were all these strange things happening."

Susan stopped bouncing her knee. "What sort of strange things?"

"I started seeing stuff. Like, weird things where they shouldn't be. Black marks on Walker's skin that would move and disappear. Stuff like that." She laughed uncomfortably. "I thought I was losing my mind from all the stress from my parents' fighting and my practice not going well. I thought I was starting to crack."

"And are you still seeing these strange things?" Susan asked, frowning.

Keira put the brush down on the bed. She felt better, in clean clothes and with neat hair. More in control. "Yeah. There's another world out there, Susan. All around us. Everywhere. It's made of something called dark matter, and pretty much no one can touch it or see it. But I can. And so can Walker."

Keira watched as Susan went from shock to panic to anger faster than a piano string vibrates.

"That is ridiculous. I can't believe you would make up something like that, just to avoid telling me the truth."

"I'm not making it up!" Keira insisted.

"Then you were right before and you're insane."

I have to show her. I didn't believe Walker until he showed me.

"I'll prove it to you. I can cross over. Watch."

Keira squinted, looking for Darkside. It shimmered into view and Keira caught her breath, her fingers curling tight around Susan's bedspread.

Oh, shit.

She'd forgotten that Susan's bedroom was on the second floor. Keira was sitting a good twenty feet above a cluster of Darkside rocks. They grinned up at her like a mouthful of teeth, waiting to chew her up and spit her out. There was no way she could cross over. Besides, the rip would draw the guards right to Susan's house. She should have thought of that earlier.

"Damn it. I can't cross here. There's a huge drop; I'd break my neck. You have to believe me," Keira begged. "It's a real thing—dark matter—you can look it up!" But Keira knew that wouldn't be the same. Susan wasn't the least bit convinced and Keira knew it.

Susan shook her head. "If you'd told me that you'd fallen in love and lost your head, *that* I'd believe. If your parents' problems had gotten to you, I could have bought it. But *this*? Come on, Keira. Just—" She stood up so fast that the chair wobbled.

"Just take the clothes and go. I'll lie for you. I'll help you. I'm not going to stop being your friend because you're in a tough spot." The hurt rang in her words, a painful counterpoint. "But I'm not going to listen to you feed me some ridiculous story that you and Walker have cooked up so that you can run away together to New York or something." She swept the clothes on the bed into a ball and shoved them into Keira's arms.

"Susan, it's not a story. I'm trying to tell you the *truth*."

A tear sparkled at the corner of Susan's eye.

"Come downstairs with me," Keira begged. "We'll go across the street, somewhere you can see what I'm talking about. I swear, I'm not making this up."

"Just go," Susan whispered. "Call me if you're ever actually ready to talk."

Tears blurred Keira's vision as she clutched the wad of fabric to her chest. Susan turned away from her. Keira slunk out of the room, her head low. She crept down the stairs, half crushed by Susan's reaction and half worried that she'd change her mind and decide Keira wasn't worth helping.

She let herself out the front door and ran across the street to the car.

In the middle of the damp blacktop, Keira came to a complete stop. Walker wasn't in the car. He was leaning against it. And he wasn't alone.

Chapter Forty-Two

SMITH'S EYES WERE RED-RIMMED and wild, so full of anger that Keira could barely bring herself to step closer. She glanced back up at Susan's window, wondering if she'd seen her ex-fling standing with Walker, but the blinds were closed.

"She was right all along—this is all my fault. I never should have gotten mixed up in any of this!" Smith spat.

Walker put out a placating hand. "Smith, you didn't mean for this to happen. I know you're upset about your mother—"

"His mother?" Keira interrupted.

"My aunt Holly was taken by the Reformers this afternoon," Walker said. "They found out that Smith can cross over."

Keira held the bundle of clothes against herself more tightly. "What?! How did they find out?"

"I was trying to create a distraction for you guys. One of the guards came around the corner of the building when I crossed back into this world. He saw me do it."

"No," Keira whispered. No wonder there had been so much shouting and running in the Hall when she'd gone back in to get Walker.

"I got away," Smith said. "I mean, I can cross and they can't. Once I made it back to Sherwin, I thought I'd be okay." His voice broke. "I didn't think about them taking my *mom.*"

Walker's voice was grave. "They're holding her until Smith agrees to work for them . . . until he proves his loyalty."

"They caught me while I was looking for my mom. I thought for sure they would toss me in a cell and leave me there, but they said they want me to follow you, to spy on you," Smith said. "I don't want to do it, but I have to. It's the only way to save my mother." He fixed his gaze on Walker. "I'm sorry. I can't live with myself if they hurt her, or . . ." He swallowed hard. "I know what you meant now, back in the Hall, when you said you'd do whatever you had to do to save Keira. I snuck over here to warn you that they're coming, before I go tell them where you are. I'm giving you a head start. It's the best I can do. The two of you need to get the hell out of Sherwin." Smith swallowed hard. "I can't let them have my mom, Walker. Not even if it means handing you over to the Reformers."

Walker tipped his head back and looked at the sky. He blinked, hard and fast. "I'd like to tell you there's nothing to worry about. That you should tell them to go fuck themselves and that Holly'll be fine." His voice roughened and he cleared his throat, leveling his gaze at Smith. "But you know that's not true. *I* know that's not true."

Keira's legs wobbled underneath her. This had already happened to Walker once before.

"Walker—" Smith started, but Walker shook his head.

"You have a shot at saving your family. Do you know what I'd give for the same chance?" The pain in Walker's voice was so fresh that Keira's eyes filled with sympathetic tears.

"So you'll leave Sherwin?" Smith asked.

Walker looked over at Keira.

She wanted to nod, but she couldn't bring herself to do it. She was going to abandon her family, so that Smith could save his.

None of us asked for this. And you've been dreaming of getting out of Sherwin for years, she told herself.

"I'll need to say good-bye," she croaked. "To my parents, I mean."

Walker flinched. Smith's eyebrows pinched together.

"Be quick about it," he advised her.

"We'll go as fast as we can," Walker assured him.

"Good." Smith nodded, sniffing back tears. "That's good."

Keira had never seen someone look as utterly lost as Smith did in that moment. She stepped toward him and hugged him awkwardly with one arm, on account of the clothes she still held in the other. Smith started, but she held on and in the next instant, he folded her into a brotherly embrace that made her wish she'd never doubted him.

"I'm sorry," she whispered.

"Me too," he said. "Run fast, okay?"

Before she could answer, Smith disappeared beneath her touch.

The second he was gone, she could feel time start to slide away from her. She unfroze and climbed into the car, the clothes in a bundle on her lap. A little row of black dots popped up on the back of her hand. Keira watched, her head aching, as they danced toward her palm and disappeared. It was like the darkness was taunting her, snuggling down into the—what had Walker called the particles that normal things like clothes were made of? Baryonic matter? She'd never wanted to know that much about physics. Not the physics of the real world, not about Darkside physics, and certainly not the mess that got made when they mixed.

Walker slid into the car next to her and let out a grim sigh.

"You okay?" she asked, knowing full well that he wasn't.

"Not really. You?"

She shook her head.

"So, you saw Susan," he ventured.

She shrugged. Her throat was too tight to talk.

"It didn't go so well, huh?" he guessed.

Keira shook her head again.

Walker put the car into gear and sped away. Keira didn't know where they were going, but it didn't really matter. As long as it was away, it was right.

Keira tossed the clothes into the backseat, and dug her phone out of her pocket. There was only a sliver of life left on the battery icon.

Keira glanced at the clock. Her mom should be home from work by now.

Please, let her be home.

She dialed. Her heart felt uncomfortably large in her chest.

"Hello?" her mother answered.

Walker shifted in his seat and Keira motioned to him to be quiet.

"Hi, Mom," Keira squeaked.

"Hi, sweetie." Her mom sounded sad and worried. "I was just getting ready to call you. You haven't checked in for a while."

"I know. I'm sorry. It's been a rough day." Keira was telling the truth, but she knew her mother would misinterpret her words. She *wanted* her to.

The silence on the other end of the phone became too uncomfortable to bear.

"We just left Susan's. I was hoping we could swing by the house and say"—the word "good-bye" almost slipped out of her mouth—"hi. Is that okay?" Keira asked.

"I was hoping you'd say that. I thought we could talk

over dinner. Even if you're thinking of staying at Susan's again tonight, you must need some clean clothes." The idea of clothes—her own clothes—sent a horrible pang through Keira. She'd have to take some things. Pack for wherever they were going. And then leave everything else behind.

Including her piano.

The thought of leaving her instrument sliced through her. She hadn't played in almost two days. The last time she'd been away from her piano for that long was freshman year, when she'd come down with mono. She'd thought she'd go crazy, lying there in bed, too tired to walk the seventeen steps to the piano. Her fingers ached for the smooth feel of the keys beneath them.

Keira gave herself a mental slap. "Dinner sounds great, but Walker and I have to . . . be somewhere. We won't have very long."

"Walker? I thought you were with Susan." Her mother's voice turned suspicious.

Keira winced. She hadn't said exactly *who* was driving her. It wasn't her fault her mother had assumed the ride would be with Susan.

She pinched the bridge of her nose between her fingers. "He picked me up from Susan's. We're going out to dinner. Or we were. And then to a movie. Later." Keira'd never been good at lying. She obviously needed to get better at twisting the truth, and fast.

Her mother cleared her throat. "I think having dinner

with Walker sounds like a lovely idea. I'd like to spend a little more time with him, since he's obviously spending a lot of time with you."

Keira's palms started to sweat. There was an accusation in her mother's words, taut and sinewy as tendon. Like she knew, somehow, that Keira'd spent last night with Walker. If her mom tried to force her to stay home tonight, then what would they do?

"Um," she said, but her mother barreled right over her.

"Bring him over. You can pick up some clothes, Walker can stay for dinner, and then after he leaves, I'll drive you back to Susan's." Her mother's voice was brittle.

The air in Keira's lungs all came rushing out at once, in a little *ugh* of surprise.

"See you soon." Her mother hung up, leaving Keira with a silent phone pressed to her ear.

She wanted to scream, but she settled for a frustrated growl.

"That good, huh?" Walker asked.

"It seems my mother is suddenly dying to see you. So much for thinking you're the Big Bad Wolf," Keira said, exasperated.

Walker laughed in the low, gravelly way that went straight through Keira's middle, warming her.

"I'm pretty sure she wants me to come precisely *because* she thinks I'm the Big Bad Wolf."

Keira threw herself back against the seat and gave in to her black mood. "She wants to drive me to Susan's after. I don't think she believes that I'm staying there."

Walker stopped at a red light. He shifted his weight, leaning in until his forehead rested against her temple.

"Don't worry," he whispered. "We'll figure something out. If I have to, I'll just huff and I'll puff"—he blew a trickle of cool air into the sensitive hollow behind her ear and Keira shivered—"and I'll blow the house in."

He was so close. She wanted to kiss him. She *needed* to kiss him.

But she couldn't. As soon as he'd touched her, she'd heard the susurration of the Darkside trees, as their leaves shifted against one another in the wind. Kissing him would drop them straight into the forest. It would make another rip in Darkside.

It would call the guards.

As if he could hear her thoughts, Walker sighed and pushed himself away from her.

"Dinner won't be all bad. You've got to be desperate to play, right? Having a little time with your piano won't be so horrible."

It would be wonderful, if I weren't trying to say good-bye.

And her dad wouldn't even be there. She pulled out her phone again and called him. His office and cell numbers both went to voice mail.

"Please call me back," she said, struggling to keep her voice even. If she could talk to him, maybe she could figure out a way to meet up with him.

At least for a minute. Long enough for one more hug. A few last words before she ran away from Sherwin.

Her throat closed up, her panic choking her.

"So, do you want to tell me what happened with Susan?" Walker asked gently.

"I told her the truth."

"You did *what*?"

"Don't worry," Keira growled. "She didn't believe me. Not for a second. God, she barely believed that I didn't sleep with Jeremy Reynolds."

A muscle jumped in Walker's jaw and she watched him struggle to stay focused.

"You didn't believe me about Darkside at first either," Walker pointed out.

Keira opened her mouth to contradict him, but he was right. That was the whole reason why she'd wanted to cross over in front of Susan in the first place—to prove herself. Why should she expect Susan to believe something Keira herself hadn't wanted to accept? Especially when Susan wasn't having the same strange visions of Darkside that had plagued Keira?

She rubbed her burning eyes.

"Everything is so screwed up," she said.

She felt Walker's hand on her knee. "Not *everything*," he said.

Keira cracked open an eye.

"Okay," she relented. "*Almost* everything. How can you turn into Mr. Silver Linings at a time like this?"

Walker cocked an eyebrow at her. "Because it's necessary." His face grew more serious. "I can't have you sliding off into the abyss of despair. If we're going to stay ahead of Smith and the Reformers, I need you on your toes."

Keira stared out the window as the familiar streets slipped past.

"Where will we go?" she asked.

"I thought maybe New York," Walker said. "The Darkside terrain there is difficult—it's all steep mountains. They're older and more stable than the part of the range that runs up north, but they're still considered uninhabitable. I hear the same about Manhattan," he joked, "but I know you've always wanted to go there. Juilliard may be out of the question, because it would pin us too publicly in one place, but we could find some way for you to play, and let the crowd hide us. It's a start, at least."

"Yeah. Okay. That makes sense."

New York. It should have been a dream come true.

Instead, it was just another waking nightmare.

Chapter Forty-Three

THE SMELL OF TOMATO sauce wafted over Keira as soon as she walked in the door. Her mother hadn't wasted any time starting dinner.

"We're here," she called.

"Oh, good. I was about to put some water on to boil for the pasta. Come on in and say hi," her mother called back.

Walker touched Keira's arm, stopping her as she headed for the kitchen.

I'll go talk to your mom, he mouthed. *You,* he pointed a finger at her, *go watch what they're doing over there*—he gestured toward the Hall of Records—*and see if we need to be worried.*

Keira's eyes widened. She shook her head. What kind of chivalry was that, anyway? Hey, babe, why don't *you* go check out the creepy noise in the basement?

She pointed back at Walker, her gesture telling him to do surveillance instead.

"I can't," he whispered. "It would look incredibly weird if I hung back while you went in the kitchen."

Crap.

He was right. Keira heaved a sigh and nodded. Fine. She would go back to her bedroom and look Darkside. She was tough. She was independent. She could do this.

Walker headed into the kitchen. "It smells amazing, Mrs. Brannon."

"Thanks, Walker, but please, call me Julia."

Keira winced, immediately reminded of her parents' problems. She wondered if her mother's last name would even *be* Brannon much longer.

"Where's Keira?" her mother asked.

"I think she went to change and get some clothes and stuff together." Walker's voice was a shade louder than was absolutely necessary and Keira knew he'd intended for her to hear the comment.

No time like the present, she thought. She walked down the hall to her room and stood next to her bed, facing her closet. She started to reach for Darkside and yelped as she felt the familiar squeezing chill of moving between two worlds. She braced her feet against the carpet, willing herself to stay in her room. It took all of her effort to push back the magnetlike draw of Darkside. With a soft *pop* of broken suction, she was back in her bedroom. What the hell? She hadn't had any trouble staying out of Darkside this morning. Why was she slipping over so easily?

"What's with the shrieking? You okay back there?" her mother called.

"Fine," Keira called back. "I stubbed my toe."

Much, much more carefully, she looked for the other world, barely dipping a fingertip of her awareness into it. It snapped into view immediately, sharp and clear as broken glass.

The Hall itself was still listing to one side, but the scurry of activity around it had stopped. The fence that she'd seen the guards constructing earlier had been finished and reinforced, and guards stood at regular intervals around it, their backs to the building.

Watching.

Waiting.

The one closest to her lifted a hand. Keira was sure he'd seen her somehow. He seemed a breath away from pointing at her and shouting, but instead he adjusted the shoulder of his robe and dropped his hand back down by his side.

Keira shuddered. The Darkside wind that always seemed to be blowing ruffled her hair.

Keira pulled herself all the way back into her bedroom. She realized with a shock that she was having trouble keeping

Darkside *out* of view, instead of the other way around. Before, it had always been something that disappeared unless she was focused on seeing it. Or unless Walker was touching her. The sudden effort of keeping only her own world in view sent a wave of worried nausea through her.

Walker could see both worlds any time he wanted to. Was this what it was like for him?

Sympathy clanged through Keira, making her head ache. It was horrible. How did he do it?

Her mother's voice floated in from the kitchen, followed by Walker's rumbling laugh. Keira shook herself, remembering that she was supposed to be changing. She pulled off Susan's clothes and wondered if it would look weird if she showered.

She decided it would.

With a sigh, she pulled on a clean bra and underwear, trying not to think about it too hard as she reached for the prettiest ones in her drawer. Maybe it was just wishful thinking, but what the hell. Maybe Walker would see them. Who knew? She was owed a little optimism, right?

Trying to hurry, she pulled a pair of jeans and a white cami out of the closet and added a purple corduroy shirt on top. The purple of the shirt and the dark denim of the jeans would be decent for hiding Darkside if she had to. The cami was practical—layers seemed practical.

She threw on socks and a pair of running shoes, remembering the ballet-flat disaster from that morning.

Fine. She was dressed.

Keira grabbed an empty bag from the corner of her closet and stuffed in a few extra pairs of everything, a hairbrush and her deodorant, and threw the bag on her bed.

Before she zipped it, Keira reached to snatch the car charger for her phone off of her desk. Her gaze landed on the little framed picture next to the cord. In the photo, she was about ten. Her parents had taken her to the beach for an impromptu picnic and her mother had asked a nice-looking girl to take their picture. Keira and her parents stood, their arms tangled around each other, squinting into the sun. They had matching sunburns across their noses, matching windblown hair, matching smiles. It was the smiles that broke her heart.

Keira snatched the picture off her desk and slipped it into the bag too. She wiped her eyes. They'd be wondering what was taking her so long. It was time to go, and she turned to leave her room. She tried not to think about everything she was leaving. She tried not to think about saying good-bye.

It was just too terrifying.

Keira stopped in the bathroom to grab her toothbrush and splash some water on her blotchy face before she headed back to the kitchen. It didn't matter. Walker and her mother still looked worried when they caught sight of her expression. Keira dropped her bag in the corner.

"You okay?" Walker asked quietly.

"Fine," she said. Her mother turned to open the pantry and Keira shot Walker a look that she hoped said, *Oh, my God, we are in seriously deep shit*. He looked alarmed, which—ironically—left her feeling relieved.

"Oh, no!" Her mom spun around, her eyes scanning the counter.

"What?" Keira and Walker asked in unison.

"I'm out of spaghetti." She glanced desperately at the simmering tomato sauce and boiling water. "Shoot. Um, let me, uh . . ."

Keira watched her mother flail for an answer. "Walker and I could go get some more?" she suggested.

"No, no," her mom snatched her purse off the counter. "Just keep an eye on the sauce for me. I'll be back in fifteen minutes. You can play for a bit—I know Susan doesn't have a piano." It sounded a little bit like an apology and Keira glanced at Walker, wondering exactly how hard he'd had to work to charm her mother out of her suspicions.

The garage door slammed and Keira looked at Walker.

"Oh, my God, Walker, it's *right there*." She kept her voice low, aware that her mother hadn't driven away yet. "There's practically nothing between us and Darkside." Her voice rose and Keira stopped, fighting for control. "I have to work *not* to see both places at once. It's making my eyes hurt. How do you *do* that?"

She pressed her fingers to her temples, trying to slow the beat of her pulse.

Walker crossed the kitchen in two enormous strides and wrapped his arms around her.

"It's not easy. I know," he whispered against the crown of her head. She could feel the worlds sliding beneath them like the shifting of dry sand. Walker's breath puffed out, stirring her hair. He was the one keeping them from crossing over and she knew it. Keira tried to focus, to help him, but it was too hard. As comforting as it was to feel his chest beneath her cheek, the effort of staying out of Darkside made her head feel like a pincushion. She pulled away.

His smile was bittersweet. "Come on," he said, reaching for her hand. "I know exactly what will make you feel better." He tugged her toward the living room.

Keira stood in the doorway for a moment, staring at her piano. The wood gleamed in the evening light. It looked for all the world like it was beaming at her—like it was as excited to see her as she was to pull out the bench, flip on the lamp, and play.

More than her room, this was what she thought of when she pictured *home*. Leaving her belongings behind was hard; leaving her piano behind was impossible.

"I don't know if I can," she whispered. "I don't want the last time I play it to be . . . like this."

Walker put his hands on her shoulders. He stepped in close behind her, his body pressing against hers, warm and solid.

The touch made her shiver in spite of his heat.

"If you pass up your last chance to play your own piano just because you don't want to say good-bye, you'll wish a thousand times that you had this moment back." He leaned his head against hers. "Come on—I'll be right there with you."

Keira let him guide her across the room. She couldn't bear to play, but he was right. Not playing would hurt more. The pain was worth it if she could have one more memory of her piano.

Chapter Forty-Four

Keira trailed her fingers silently over the flat whole notes and the intimate ridges of the black half-step keys that interrupted them. She was vaguely aware of Walker, leaning against the windows, over her shoulder, just out of sight. Taking a breath, Keira rocked forward and ran a set of scales at lightning speed. The stiffness vanished from her fingers and her shoulders relaxed. Darkside didn't seem quite so close with her focus fixed on the piano, and as it receded, so did her headache.

The Beethoven sonata was open on the music stand and Keira launched into it, feeling herself strengthen with each note. The arpeggios wrapped around her, weaving her frayed edges back together. Her skin hummed with the music, alight with the feeling of coming back to herself.

This was where she belonged.

This was who she was.

She didn't care about Darkside. She didn't care about Susan. She didn't care about her parents. She didn't even care about Juilliard. All that mattered was playing herself back into one piece. A tiny thread of her awareness stretched behind her to where Walker stood.

With a start, she realized that she still cared about him, even as the notes swept away everything else. Instead of weakening her connection to the music she played, he made it stronger. She was playing for both of them. She needed him to hear the music as much as she needed to create it.

She reached the end of the second movement, but as she turned the page to begin the Allegretto, Walker quietly cleared his throat. Keira glanced at him, the question in her eyes but not on her lips.

"Play something of yours?" he asked. "Please?"

The heat in his eyes was like nothing Keira had ever seen before. It made the glow that came with his wanting little jokes look dim. This was a bonfire. A solar flare. A supernova.

She nodded and turned back to the piano. When her fingers dropped onto the keys, she felt exposed, vulnerable, more than if she'd been standing in front of him naked. Her body was just her body. Her music was part of her soul.

The scariest part was how badly she wanted to give him her music—to give him all of her.

She closed her eyes and began to play. Her fingers automatically found the melody from the day he'd taken her to the shore. It spilled out of the piano, crashing through the room the way the waves had battered the rocky point. Keira couldn't hear Walker's steps over the music, but she could feel him drawing closer. She perched on the edge of the piano bench and reached for the soaring, twisting notes that brought back the memory of the two of them alone in the fog. The music stretched up toward its peak as Walker slid onto the bench behind her. His legs rested on either side of hers and his arms wrapped around her middle, loose enough to leave her room to play but tight enough that they supported her too.

The intense, yearning arpeggio that represented the kiss she'd imagined happening that day rang through the room. Walker pressed his lips against the back of her neck as her fingers moved against the keys. The sensation of his mouth against her skin shot through her, like the last tumbler of a lock falling into place with an enormous *click*.

It wasn't until she realized how completely still Walker had become that Keira's fingers slipped off the keys.

The *click* hadn't been in her head.

It had been an actual sound, as real as the notes from her piano.

Walker stood and Keira spun to face him. Something was

different, and it took her a moment to figure out exactly what that was.

Her headache was gone. She wasn't struggling to keep Darkside out of view. Stunned, she reached for it, looking for the tree that should have stretched over her like a canopy. No matter how hard she battered against the membrane of her reality, she couldn't see past it.

"It's gone," Walker gasped. "I can't—" He snapped his head around to look at Keira. "I can't see Darkside. Can you?"

She shook her head.

"Hang on." He ran for her bedroom as Keira waited in the eerily empty living room. A tiny corner of her mind was amused that she'd gotten to a point where she was disturbed by *not* seeing strange, dark visions. But it was a very tiny corner of her mind.

The rest of her was freaking out.

"I can still see it in here," Walker called. He sounded relieved, but there was an edge to his words.

"What's wrong?" she asked.

"Well, for one thing, I don't know why I can see Darkside in your bedroom but not in the living room. And for another, the guards are panicking." He strode back into the living room, his handsome face twisted into a grimace. "They're all running."

Keira looked around the room, feeling blindfolded in spite of her sight.

"Running where?" She sat down on the edge of the piano bench.

"Away, for now," Walker said. "They're just *scattering*. But I'm sure they'll be back." He shook his head slowly. "Nothing like that has ever happened. I don't know exactly how, but something pulled Darkside back together. It's all rippled and thick, like a scar. But it looks more solid than any part of Darkside I've ever seen." His face was white as bone.

"It happened while I was playing," she said. "Do you think maybe . . . ?" The end of her question died in her throat.

The muscles of Walker's throat jumped as he swallowed. "If you did that, somehow, then we have a way to save you. The Reformers would never kill someone who could undo the damage the rest of the Experimentals did to our world."

"But I've never done anything like that before—at least, I don't think I have. If I don't know how I managed to stitch Darkside back together, how will I be able to do it again?"

Keira ran her hand over the wood trim beneath the keyboard. Besides the scratch from her metronome, the bottom of the keyboard was the only damaged place on the piano. It was scarred by a long row of slashes and crosshatches that had been scratched into the wood. They'd been there when Keira had gotten the piano. She used to rub them when she was nervous, feeling the pattern of them against her fingers.

Keira's fingers stopped. Her breath hiccuped in her throat.

She hadn't looked at the scratches in so long, she'd almost forgotten what they looked like. In one swift movement, Keira pushed the bench out of the way and ducked beneath the piano.

It felt awkward—she hadn't sat beneath the instrument since she was a little girl. She had to twist her neck uncomfortably in order to see the scratches. The sight of them made her mouth dry and her palms moist.

"Keira?" Walker sounded worried. "What are you doing?"

"I think you need to see this," she said simply, unable to find the words to explain.

Walker folded himself into the space beneath the piano, next to her.

"Look." Keira pointed at the etchings above them. "Is it the same as what was on the outside of those needle boxes in the Hall of Records? It is, isn't it?"

"Yeah," Walker said, his eyes traveling back and forth over the slashes and crosshatches. "It's writing. Darkside writing." He looked at her, biting his lip uncertainly. "The message is addressed to you."

Keira stared up at it. "Who's it from?"

"Pike Sendson," Walker said.

Keira wrapped her hand around the wooden post that connected the brass foot pedals to the piano. "Uncle Pike?"

"What do you mean, 'Uncle' Pike? Keira, Pike Sendson was the head of the Experimental Breeding Program."

She choked on the words. "Uncle Pike was the head of the Experimental Breeding Program?"

"Yes. And according to this"—Walker ran his hands over the marks—"he's not your uncle, Keira. Pike Sendson is your father."

The cry that escaped her lips was utterly involuntary. Pike was her *father*? All his mysterious comings and goings shifted in her memory, aligning with her parents' bouts of fighting. The hugs and good-byes and the promises he'd made to take care of her . . .

He was her father.

"Pike is a Darkling?" she croaked. "But he was here—if Pike is my father, then my mom *must* know something. He and my mom were best friends."

Walker cocked an eyebrow at her.

Obviously, they'd been more than friends.

"I have to talk to my mom. Tonight. As soon as she gets back." The frustration of so many missed opportunities built painfully in her chest and she growled. "I can't believe she never told me any of this before. If she had, we might already know where Pike is! We might already be safe."

"Keira?" The warning in Walker's voice snapped her out of her hysteria.

She braced herself. "Yeah?"

"That's not all it says. It tells us where he is. Uh, sort of. This says that when he disappeared, he went—" Walker stopped, frowning.

"What?" Keira demanded, impatient. "He went where?"

"It says 'somewhere thin as thread, a rocky haven in a watery grave.'"

"Where is that?" Keira asked, her mind spinning.

Walker shook his head. "I don't know. It says, 'I'll wait there. My only hope is that these words below and the keys above will both make sense to you. Your music is my only salvation. It will save us all.'" Walker looked over at her. "He knew you could play?"

"Yes and no. I used to go with my mother when she had choir rehearsals. Pike was always there. The accompanist showed me how to play the melody lines and stuff when there was a break. I couldn't have been more than three, but I remember it. I'd play what she played. Pike was excited that I learned it so fast. That's one of the reasons I remember it so clearly, I think."

"So he knew, before he left. He knew you were his and he knew that all the experimenting had finally paid off." Walker's voice faded. "But it would have been too soon. Your talent wouldn't have been developed enough to prove him right. No wonder he ran off. Staying here would have gotten both of you killed. His only chance of survival—for both of you—was to hide. And hope you found him later."

The words sloshed over her, cold and heavy. "But it sounds like if we find him, he thinks we can fix the whole mess. Like he knows a way we could get the Reformers to let us *all* live."

Walker nodded. "I agree. This could be the answer to everything, if we find him. But if we fail . . ." His voice trailed off.

The squeak of the back door startled Keira so much that she nearly banged her head on the piano.

"Hello?" her mother called. "I'm back. Sorry it took me so long—I figured if I was already holding up dinner, I might as well pick up some things to make a salad."

Walker scooted out from beneath the piano, reaching down to help Keira. She opened her mouth to respond to her mother, but she couldn't think of anything to say. It was like all the words had been shaken out of her.

Chapter Forty-Five

"We're in here, Mrs. Brannon," Walker called. "Keira was just playing for me."

Keira's mom appeared in the doorway. Her hair was limp and there were harried lines tracing the corners of her eyes, but her smile was genuine.

"Walker, it's Julia. I insist." She turned her smile to Keira and it dimmed a shade, a wash of sadness sliding over it. "I'd love it if you played something while I'm finishing dinner. I miss hearing you play more than anything."

Walker put a hand on the small of her back and Keira leaned into it. There were too many pieces of too many questions fluttering around her head and the effort of putting it all aside to pretend everything was normal for her mother was more than she could handle.

One thing at a time. That's what she'd promised herself. All she had to do was play one piece for her mother. That was the next thing.

She could play one piece of music.

"Sure," she said, stepping away from Walker. Pulling herself together, she slid onto the piano bench. "Anything particular you want to hear?"

It was all she could do to keep her hands away from the message carved below the keyboard. How many hours had she spent with her fingertips inches from the truth?

"How about that Brahms piece you were working on? That one is so pretty," her mother said.

Keira put her hands on the keys, reaching for the start of the sonata that she'd been planning to play for her Juilliard audition, until she'd found the Beethoven piece that day at Take Note.

The day she'd met Walker.

At the time, it had just seemed like a strange day, something she'd never remember in a month's time. Now, she could see her whole life spread out, before and after, resting on that day like a fulcrum.

That day had changed *everything*.

The timbre of her mother's waiting shifted, and Keira

realized she'd been drifting through her thoughts in silence.

She lifted her hands again, but the notes weren't there. She couldn't hear them through the static in her mind. The only thing her fingertips could feel was the message scratched beneath the piano.

Keira tried to start the Brahms piece, but she couldn't feel the shape of it in her hands. She couldn't remember which keys to hit. A ribbon of panic traced the shape of her spine. The awful memory of her inability to play when she'd first met Walker rose in her mind's eye. Clearing her throat, Keira bent awkwardly to sift through her music basket.

"It's been a while," she said by way of apology. "I think I need to find the music."

"Oh." Her mother's surprise made Keira wince. "Well, you can play whatever you were playing for Walker, if it's easier."

The horror of the suggestion shot through Keira, speeding up her hands as she riffled through the pages. She didn't mind playing her own music for Walker. It had been exhilarating, drawing them closer in a way she could never have imagined. There was no way she could play something she'd composed in front of her mom. It was way too intimate.

She found the Brahms in the bottom of the basket and straightened, holding it in her hands like a shield.

"No, it's fine. I've got the music right here." She showed her mom. "I should play it. Obviously, I've let it go too long." Keira spread the pages open on the piano.

"Okay, then," her mom said. "I'd better get back to dinner. Thanks, honey."

Keira nodded vaguely, squinting at the notes. Her fingers jumped in recognition and her shoulders dropped as she began to play. The music was still there. She'd only needed a reminder.

The soothing notes floated through the living room, filling the space. Her own thoughts settled under the weight of the music.

Somehow, Darkside had repaired itself. That had to be a good sign—one less thing the Reformers could blame her for, if she and Walker got caught. And there *was* a chance they'd get caught, because she was determined to find her uncle Pike.

She shivered. She really had to stop thinking of him as "Uncle" Pike. He was the Darkling who'd fathered her and he'd been the head of the breeding program. If there was anyone, anywhere, with a way to keep the Reformers from exterminating her, it would be him.

But first, they had to figure out exactly where he was.

If he was even still alive.

Keira glanced over at Walker. He was watching her play but his gaze was empty, utterly lost in thought. *He must be trying to piece things together too.* She turned back to the music before she lost the thread of the melody.

She followed the song through to the end, letting the notes replace the words floating through her head. When she took her hands off the keys and slid her foot off the pedal, her mother reappeared in the doorway.

"That was absolutely beautiful. Come on, you two, dinner's ready." She turned back to the kitchen, tossing a dishcloth over her shoulder.

Keira lingered on the bench for a moment, savoring the emptiness of her thoughts. She could already feel the worries and what-ifs tapping at the edges of her awareness.

Walker's hands slid onto her shoulders, his thumbs tracing the sweep of her neck. His voice was quiet as a cat. "Come on. We'll eat, and then we'll figure this out. First things first, right?"

Keira nodded. First things first.

Quarter note. Half note. Rest.

She stood up and followed Walker into the kitchen. She was willing to sit at the table and make nice, but she had no idea how she was going to force herself to eat when her stomach was snarled into such a hopeless knot. If her mother knew something about Pike and Darkside, she had to find out what. And if her mother didn't know anything about Pike and Darkside, Keira had to keep from making her suspicious.

It was a very fine line, and Keira wasn't looking forward to walking it.

In the kitchen, the sight of the Hall leaning toward the healed bit of Darkside slid in and out of Keira's vision. It was nearly impossible to push it away completely, when the barrier in the kitchen was still so thin. Her head throbbed from watching both worlds at once, but she curled her hand around the cold edges of her fork and kept looking. She wanted to know what was happening in Darkside too desperately to quit. She could see robed figures in the woods, pointing at the newly healed rip and shaking their heads. The whole scene hummed with curiosity, the resonance of the impossible. At least the Darklings didn't seem to be looking for Keira.

She managed to choke down a few bites of pasta, then pushed the rest around her plate. She thought about Pike—where he was and how they were going to find him in the immensity of Darkside, with only a few vague clues to go on. She tried to keep her thoughts hidden, but she wasn't the only one at the table keeping secrets.

Maybe her mother didn't know about Darkside. If she did, could her mom really sit there, making small talk with Walker, and not suspect anything?

The questions buzzed in Keira's head, demanding she ask them. How could her mother have cheated on her dad? How could she have had another man's baby? How could she have kept the truth from Keira all these years? And what if her mother knew something about Pike that might save Keira's life?

"Mom? How did Uncle Pike die? I can't remember."

Keira wasn't sure who looked more stunned by the question—Walker or her mother.

Her mom's eyes held a curious mix of stale sadness and fresh pain. "No one knows exactly, honey. His lawyer called one day and said that Pike had passed away and that he'd left you his piano and, of course, the college fund. He traveled a great deal for his work, and it was very dangerous."

"What did he do?" Keira pushed. Walker kicked her under the table, his eyes darting furiously between Keira and her mom in a please-don't-make-her-suspicious sort of way. Keira shot him a glance that she hoped said, *Shut the hell up,* and looked back at her mom, who was twirling spaghetti around her fork in slow motion.

"Something for the government, I think. He said he wasn't allowed to tell me the details. He'd warned me that if something went wrong at his job, it would be the end of . . . everything," her mother finished awkwardly.

She looked up at Keira, her eyes narrowing. "Why all the questions about Pike? You haven't asked about him in years."

Keira spun out a lie as fast as she could. "Walker was asking about the piano. I couldn't remember all the details." She speared a carrot from her salad, as nonchalant as if she'd been asking about the weather.

"Ah." Her mother patted her lips with her napkin and then tucked it neatly under the edge of her plate. "Well. It was a hard time. Things were . . . things were never the same after Pike died." She pushed her chair back, clearly hoping to end the conversation. "Walker? More pasta?"

"No, thank you. It was delicious, but it's getting late." Walker gave Keira's mom his most shining smile and picked up his plate, carrying it over to the sink. He glanced over his shoulder at Keira.

"What's your plan?" he asked casually. "Do you want me to drive you to Susan's, or are you going to stay here awhile?"

The thought of staying—when the living room was a blind spot and the reality in the rest of the house was slick as an ice rink—no. Just no.

Keira grabbed her bag from the corner of the kitchen. "I'd love a ride," she said.

Her mother's face crumbled. "But we had such a nice visit. And things have settled down around here. Keira, I really think it's time you came home."

Crap.

There was only one way out of this and it meant hurting her mother. Keira curled her hands into fists. Her nails were barely long enough to cut into her palms and she tightened her grip, wanting the pain. Punishing herself for what she was about to do.

"I couldn't even play the Brahms piece without having the music in front of me," she said. "Everywhere I look, I think about Dad and the fact that he's not here and he's not coming back." Her voice shook with the double meaning of her words. Neither of her fathers were there. Neither of them were coming back. "I need more time. Susan likes having me stay there, Mrs. Kim doesn't care—I have to get my head together."

Her mother leaned back against the kitchen counter, wrapping her fingers around the edge. Keira could see her mother's loneliness. The long, empty night ahead shone in her mother's eyes. It cut through Keira.

This is the only way. If I don't go . . . if I don't find some way out of this, she'll lose me forever.

The thought crashed into her like a rock through a window, cracking her into pieces. Her terror rose through the mess, leaving her feeling wounded and helpless.

"I'll call you as soon as I get to Susan's, okay?" Her voice was quiet. "And I promise you, as soon as I can, I'll come home for good."

Her mother sagged. "Fine. I'll drive you, though."

"I have to go right past Susan's," Walker said. "It's really no trouble for me to drop Keira off."

Keira's mom hesitated, glancing between the two of them. Her gaze landed on Keira.

"If Walker drives you, you're to go straight to Susan's and stay there."

Keira nodded. She felt like she'd gotten away with something, and relief slid over her, guilty but sweet at the same time.

Her mom lifted a warning finger. "I have had my trust broken too many times these past few days. If you betray me too, I will be beyond disappointed. Do you understand?"

"Yeah," Keira said. The word was hard to say. She'd violated her mother's trust before she'd even promised not to. She couldn't go to Susan's, even if she wanted to. Susan didn't want her there.

There was nowhere for her to go, and Keira felt trapped. She needed out—out of the house, out of this hopeless situation, out of this mess of her life.

Walker tried to help her with her bag, but Keira hitched it over her own shoulder.

"Thanks, but I've got it," she said.

"Proud," he accused, but there was a light in his eyes that made Keira feel the smallest bit better.

"I'll call you," she promised her mother again. She wanted to make one she could actually keep.

"You'd better," her mother said, turning to the dishes. It was probably supposed to be a warning, but it sounded more like a plea.

Before she could lose her nerve—or her mind—Keira turned for the front door. She glanced at her piano. The keys seemed to smile at her. She couldn't remember a time when she hadn't gone to her piano to solve her problems.

Pike's words echoed in her mind. If the music made sense to her, it would save them. Nothing in the world made as much sense to her as the piano. If Walker could figure out where Pike was, then they had a real chance at figuring out how to satisfy the Reformers and stay alive, too. She was sure of it.

Keira held on to that tiny kernel of hope as she hurried out into the failing light with Walker. The night crept around them, and Keira worked to keep Darkside out of sight. Proving to herself that she was still strong enough to do it.

Proving that she could still see her life however she wanted, wherever she wanted.

"So, which is it?" Walker asked, opening his door. "Hunt for Pike or go to New York?"

Keira looked over at him, blinking as Darkside flashed behind him for a moment before she forced it away.

She wanted this not to be good-bye. She wanted to come home again.

"Pike," she said. "I know it's risky. But let's go anyway. I don't want to run forever."

She got in the car and buckled her seat belt.

Ready or not, she thought, *here I come*.

Chapter Forty-Six

WALKER DROVE THROUGH TOWN, weaving through neighborhoods. Keira could see him thinking. A familiar little furrow had appeared between his eyebrows, and she kept her mouth shut, concentrating on plugging her phone charger into his fancy dashboard while he thought things through. She turned her attention to Darkside, letting it slip into view. Though the sight of two worlds moving past the car window turned her stomach, it eased the ache of trying to hold Darkside at a distance. As they reached the edge of town, the Darkside forest gave way to rockier terrain. Beyond it, where the edge of Maine trailed off into the ocean, Keira could see the Darkside mountains. They were craggy and treeless, the Darkside stone glimmering beneath the strange, ever-moving stars.

"Isn't there an ocean Darkside?" she asked, forgetting her plan to let Walker think uninterrupted.

"Not here," Walker said. "Those are the Novitiate mountains. They go for a long way, and beyond them there's another forest, like the one here. There's another city or two on the other side of the mountains, but they're in the middle of the Atlantic in this world, so it's pretty much impossible to cross back and forth from there."

Walker stopped talking as abruptly as if someone had clapped a hand over his mouth.

"What?" Keira asked.

Walker ran a hand through his hair. "At the north edge of the mountains, there are these caves. They're beneath your ocean and the peaks are really unstable, because the fabric of Darkside is still weak from when the mountains formed. No one goes there. It would be like camping on top of a lake covered with paper-thin ice."

"Thin as thread," Keira said, the pieces falling into place.

"A rocky haven," Walker agreed. "No one goes in or out of the caves."

"In a watery grave," she finished, "because crossing over would put you under the Atlantic Ocean. That's where he is. It has to be!"

Walker was silent.

"We're likely to get killed trying to find him there," he finally said.

"You don't have to go. I'm the one the Reformers are after. Take me as far as the coast, and I can go the rest of the way myself." Keira's chest felt empty as she said the words, but she meant them. She didn't want Walker to get hurt again. The memory of him lying bleeding and broken on the floor at the Hall of Records stung her.

He put on his turn signal.

"Not a chance." His voice was steely. She'd never heard him sound like that. He looked over at her. The *tickticktickick* of the turn signal measured out the seconds as he stared at her. "I threw in my lot with you ages ago," he said. "The Reformers want me as much as they want you, now. I betrayed them when I chose to protect you. Please don't question that."

She swallowed hard and his eyes softened.

"Please," he said.

She reached for him, grateful and apologetic at once, but as her fingers grazed his neck, headlights illuminated the car from behind them.

"Time to go," Walker said, his voice low and sweet.

He headed toward the coast. Fear and excitement bubbled up in Keira so quickly that it felt like she was going to explode. She wrapped her arms around her ribs, holding herself together.

They knew where Pike Sendson was.

Now they just had to figure out how to get there.

. . .

Walker drove north, staying as close to the coast as he could. Keira watched as the Darkside mountains got more ragged. They looked newer—more raw. When she could catch glimpses of the ocean, the surging waves coursed hungrily beneath her view of the Darkside mountains. Keira had never seen anything so forbidding. She tapped her fingers nervously against her legs, playing the Beethoven sonata in time with the rhythm of the tires as they thrummed over the pavement.

Their progress was slow. They had to get off the interstate to get close enough to the coast to watch the Darkside mountains. Even then, the view often wasn't good enough to see the mountains well. The thick darkness of the night wasn't helping things either. Despite stopping for coffee, Keira's eyes began to feel gritty, and her shoulders ached with exhaustion.

Predawn light began to shimmer over the water, and Keira realized they were so far north that she was actually looking at the Bay of Fundy.

Finally, they got to a spot where the road kissed the coast. Signs cheerfully pointed them toward a "scenic overlook" ahead and Walker pulled into the tiny, deserted lot.

Keira looked over at him. His hand was wrapped around the gearshift, the ridges of his knuckles echoing the mountains that loomed ahead of them. The two worlds overlapped in Keira's vision so that the dark crags seemed to rise straight out of the ocean. The peaks looked smooth and unbroken. She slumped down in her seat, wondering if they were going to drive off the tip of Maine before they found the caves.

"We're here," Walker said, his voice rough and tired. He opened his car door and the chilly, salt-rimed air rushed in.

Keira scrambled out of the car and followed Walker to the edge of the overlook.

"But—where are the caves?"

"Down there." Walker pointed.

Keira stared into the maelstrom of purple-black waves. She looked through the sea, dipping her consciousness into Darkside. The base of the mountains appeared, at least thirty feet below the surface of the water. She'd been expecting fat, round holes to mark the cave mouths. Instead what she saw was a collection of slashes in the rock face, like open wounds.

She shivered. "How are we going to *get* there?"

They had no boat, and no SCUBA equipment, not that Keira would know how to use it. Her family had never had enough money for that sort of thing. The sea was too cold and rough for her freestyle stroke to be helpful.

"We'll have to go through Darkside," Walker sighed. "It's the only way."

Keira blanched. "But won't that give the Reformers' guards time to catch up with us?"

Walker shoved his hands into his pockets. "Yep. We'll just have to hope they're slower and more scared than we are."

Keira stared down at the crashing waves. "Well, then," she said sarcastically, "what are we waiting for?"

"We could still run," Walker offered. "We've done a decent job of staying one step ahead of the guards."

Staring at the maze of death that spread out in front of them made the idea of running seem almost tempting. After all, they *had* succeeded at it so far.

Except she'd barely touched her piano.

And she'd barely touched Walker.

Running meant giving up those things for good, and it wasn't worth it.

She shook her head. "No. I may be able to stay alive if we run, but I can't *live* that way. Not if it means going without the piano. Not if it means never really touching you. I'm not going to give up the things that make me who I am just because it would be the safer choice." She turned to face Walker and he wrapped his arms around her waist. The wind coming off the water howled around them, pushing them closer together.

Keira glanced down. Their feet were on solid ground in Maine, but they hovered above the Darkside slope that lead down to the base of the mountains. The ground in Darkside was five or six feet beneath them. Crossing over was going to hurt.

She looked up at Walker.

"Let's go the nice way," he said, his arms tightening around the small of her back. Her pulse thrummed against the hollow of her throat as he leaned in toward her.

"I promise you," he whispered against her lips. "We're going to get out of this. Together." He ducked his head a fraction of an inch, pressing the words against her lips, sealing them there with his kiss. The taste of him filled her mouth and Keira's stomach dropped out beneath her.

Too late, she realized that it was the fall, as much as his kiss, that had sent her stomach plummeting.

Chapter Forty-Seven

KEIRA LANDED HARD ON the Darkside slope. Beneath her, her ankle crunched viciously and collapsed, sending her sprawling. Walker had managed to land on his side and Keira fell on top of him, crying out as the pain in her ankle bloomed and spread, setting her whole leg throbbing.

Keira rolled off Walker and he struggled to sit up. She curled into a ball on the rock, feeling it slide beneath her. It was hard as iron but it shifted like something not yet settled.

"What hurts?" he asked, crouching in front of her.

"Ankle," Keira gasped, gritting her teeth against the pain.

Moving carefully on the unstable slope, Walker gently pulled up the hem of her jeans. Keira hissed as the denim brushed against her skin, sending her already screaming nerve-endings into an agonized shriek.

"Sorry," he whispered. "This is probably not going to feel so good."

Keira squeezed her eyes shut as his fingers slid over her ankle.

"It's swelling," he said. "You definitely sprained it. It might be broken. I can't tell."

"Shit," she whispered.

She couldn't run on a broken ankle. Keira looked up. The streaks of light that soared across the Darkside sky blurred as tears pooled in the corners of her eyes.

They were so close. They'd been *so close*. And now here she was, like an injured rabbit lying in the wolf's path.

Anger screeched through her, cutting through the pain and disappointment. She hadn't come this far to give up now.

Keira pushed herself into a sitting position, facing Walker. "It'll be fine. I'll . . . I'll just cross over and heal it."

Walker raised his eyebrows. "Keira, we'd be underwater. Literally." He stared at the Darkside terrain. "We can't cross back over here. To get to a place where the terrains of earth and Darkside line up, we'd have to hike a couple of miles to the east." A crease appeared between his eyebrows. "It's probably almost as far to the caves, but we could try to get back to a good crossing point. We might have time. I think."

Keira shook her head. "Never mind, we're not wasting time with that. I can walk it off."

Walker stared at her. "You can't walk off a sprain, Keira. Much less a break."

"It isn't *broken*," she roared. Her voice echoed strangely in the mountains, some of the syllables bouncing back to her while others disappeared into the rock. Keeping her weight on her good foot, she hauled herself up to stand.

The incessant Darkside wind fluttered her shirt like a flag. Walker watched her, frozen. Silent. He'd always accused her of being stubborn, and right then, she was counting on him being right.

"I'm going down to the caves and nothing is going to stop me," she announced, taking a step down the incline. When her weight reached her foot, her ankle exploded in pain. She tried to move the pressure back to her good foot but the rock shifted beneath her and suddenly nothing was holding her up.

Keira landed hard on her hip and began to slide down the scree. She heard Walker's shout above her but it was too late. The rock moved around her, slipping into new shapes as her weight pushed against it. Loose bits of gravel pinged past her, and Keira closed her eyes against them as she tumbled to the bottom of the hill.

The thud of her body hitting one of the boulders that littered the mountain's base rang through the range like some sort of strange thunder. It stopped her fall and her breathing, simultaneously. Keira's lungs burned for the want of air, but she was unable to draw it in. The wind had been knocked out of her. She gave a ragged, painful gasp and suddenly she was breathing again.

"Keira! Are you okay?" Walker was at the bottom of the hill and running toward her.

She lay there, thinking about it. Her ribs and hip were sore, but not unbearably so. Her ankle still throbbed with a steady drumbeat of pain, but it didn't seem any worse. Carefully, she sat up.

"I'm okay," she answered, her voice shaking.

"Holy—" Walker stopped, letting out a long breath. "Don't do that again, okay?"

"I wasn't planning on it," Keira said, "but it worked, didn't it? I made it to the bottom of the hill." Her face itched and she reached up to scratch it. When her hand came away from her temple, it was coated in Darkside dust. It was like being covered in the prickly bits of hair that drifted down during a haircut.

"Here," Walker said. He lifted the hem of his shirt and wiped the mess from Keira's face. She swallowed hard at the sight of his bare skin. There was nothing stopping her from touching him—nothing but the time that ticked away. They'd been Darkside long enough that the guards would have noticed the new rip. She knew the longer they were out in the open, the more likely they were to get caught.

Still, the temptation to run her hands over the smooth skin

above his waistband was almost too much to bear. When he dropped his shirt, slapping the dust from it, Keira had to shake herself.

He gave her a quizzical look, his eyes becoming heavy-lidded as he took in her expression. "What're *you* thinking about?" he asked. The honey in his voice said that he had a pretty good guess.

Keira matched his smolder. She had nothing to lose and nothing to prove and no reason to pretend she didn't want him terribly. "Just remembering why I'm doing this," she said. "About all the things I'll be able to do if—*when*—I find a way around this death sentence."

The last two words sucked all the heat out of the moment, leaving a desperate cold in its wake. The truth—the deadly seriousness of the situation—was too close to the surface to ignore.

Walker pulled her arm around his shoulder and lifted her gently to her feet.

"I'm gonna hold you to that," he said. "And I mean that very, very literally." Keira heard the innuendo in his voice, the tantalizing taunt he'd mastered, but there was more beneath it. Something deep and aching that made Keira have to wait until her heart was steadier in her chest before she could speak.

"Okay," she whispered. "I think I can walk if I lean on you."

"I won't let you fall," he said, brushing a kiss across her temple. "We'll take it a step at a time."

• • •

Slowly they made their way over to the crags. Keira's ankle hurt with every step. The ridges that rippled across the ground were smooth enough that it was hard to keep her footing, even with Walker supporting her.

Keira struggled to keep herself upright, clutching Walker's shoulder. Darkside itself was as delicate and slippery as a soap bubble. It took all the focus she could muster to keep from bursting through it.

Step by step, they picked their way across the landscape of boulders. The silence that surrounded them was nearly unbearable. It waited, huge and ominous, like it was hiding something.

By the time the rock started to incline again, Keira's forehead was damp with sweat. The effort of walking, the pain that swept up her leg, the thud of the headache she had developed from keeping her world out of view—it was exhausting.

Walker stopped near a small rock formation that had an unusual vein of stone, like luminous quartz, running through it. His breathing was labored.

"Okay, I think we need to stop here for a minute," he said. Carefully he helped Keira sit on a flat bit of the stone. She whimpered with the relief of being off her feet and propped her bad ankle on another rock.

The mountains rose behind them like a protective curtain and the boulders shielded them in front. They wouldn't be able to see anyone coming for them, but then again, it was unlikely that they could be seen.

Standing next to her, Walker rolled his shoulders uncomfortably. The fabric of his shirt was damp and wrinkled where she'd been gripping it.

"You okay?" Keira asked, acutely aware that he'd half carried her the entire way.

"Fine," he brushed away the question. "Just stretching." Walker crossed his arms and looked up at the mountains looming above them. "Darkside is thinner here than anywhere else in the whole mountain range. If your father's still here, he's probably not that far away." He frowned. "Still. I didn't realize there were so *many* caves."

"He must have picked one that he thought I could find, right?" Keira offered. She looked hopefully at the lowest, biggest cave openings.

"Yeah, but he would have wanted to make sure he was hidden if anyone else came poking around," Walker countered.

Keira frowned. Which of these caves would stand out to her but not to the guards? The headache thrumming behind her eyes made it hard to sort out her tangled thoughts.

The headache.

The headache that she had because she could see both worlds at once, which the guards couldn't.

"*Oh.*" She looked up at the mountains. "I bet one of these lines up with something on the other side," she murmured.

Carefully, she let her vision double. The pain behind her eyes spiked suddenly as the murky ocean swept into view. The dawn light didn't penetrate that far down, but Keira could see rocky outcroppings pushing up from the ocean floor, reaching for the watery light.

A fish swam past her and the surprise of it shifted Keira's focus.

In an instant, she was no longer Darkside. She was home.

Home, and thirty feet beneath the ocean swells.

Terrified, Keira opened her mouth and it immediately filled with the salty seawater. She held on to the last breath she'd taken as the current slammed into her, carrying her away. Frantic, she stared around, looking for the Darkside mountains, trying to see the strange, swirling stars overhead instead of the eddies of murky water.

Her lungs screamed in her chest.

The cold, dark water buffeted her, dragging her toward a rocky mound with an opening in it like a vacant, staring eye. Fighting the force of the current, Keira spun, her hair and clothes tangling around her. She caught sight of Walker, standing on the Darkside ground, panicked and helpless, his arms outstretched.

His reaching hands shot through her memory. The feel of them, cupping her ribs as he helped her across the rocks, was stronger than the chill of the dark ocean, stronger than the press of the water against her.

She slid through the barrier into Darkside and lay gasping on the blissfully dry ground.

Her mouth tasted like the sea and Keira pushed the thought out of her mind. She wanted nothing to remind her of the world she knew—nothing to risk sending her back.

Walker dropped beside her.

"You are impossible! *Impossible!*" His voice was as rough as the mountain peaks above her. "We can't keep the Reformers from killing you if you kill *yourself* first."

"Sorry! I was just trying to see if any of the caves lined up with something on the other side—something only you and I would be able to see," she said, sitting up. Her clothes and hair were nearly dry. The water was evaporating much too quickly. She should have been sodden.

"Where's the water going?" she asked.

Walker shook his head. "It's baryonic matter, like everything else over there. Remember? It only came over because it had a bit of your dark matter in it. Like your clothes. Only it's even less stable, so it's already fading—disintegrating." He waved his hand like it didn't matter. "Did you see anything, at least?" he asked.

Keira stood, turning to face the direction that the current had been dragging her. She gingerly put a bit of weight on her ankle and was stunned when it didn't hurt anymore. She'd been so shocked over her near-drowning that it hadn't occurred to her that she was no longer in pain. There was nothing but sweet, quiet relief.

Of course. She'd crossed over. Automatic genetic reset.

At least something good had come of her slipping back into her world.

Two good things, actually, she thought, facing the mountains. There was a small opening about a quarter of the way up the rock face. It was narrow and short, crammed between a ragged outcrop of stone and a smoother, sheared-off looking bit on the other side of the cave's mouth.

But Keira was pretty sure it lined up perfectly with the opening she'd glimpsed in the sea stone.

"I think that cave up there is in the same spot as something I saw underwater." She crossed her arms tight, shivering. "But I'd need to look at it again, to be sure."

Walker wrapped his arms around her. "I don't think we can both look, or we're likely to slip over again. Do you want me to give it a shot? Or do you want to see while I try to hold you here?"

Keira knew that he was better at keeping himself in one world or another than she was. But if Walker crossed, she wasn't sure she could pull him back. The thought of the dark water taking Walker made her quiver.

"Can you swim?" Keira asked.

A sheepish expression crept across Walker's features. "Um, not exactly," he admitted. "But I *can* hold my breath."

Keira rubbed a hand across her eyes. It was her father they were looking for. It was her life they were trying to save.

"I'll do it," she said. She faced the cave, craning her neck so that she could see the opening.

Walker kept his arms around her and she looked for the looming rocks that lurked beneath the ocean. As the water shimmered into view, she felt the touch of Walker's lips on her neck, reminding her where she was. Keeping her grounded. His mouth traced a path toward her shoulder, and Keira let her guard down the smallest bit, seeing the light of the rising sun bounce off the water. Walker reached up and tugged her shirt to one side. He hooked a finger beneath the straps of her bra and cami, sliding them down her arm, baring her skin to his mouth. Above her, the rock formation appeared, the round opening lining up exactly with the black slash in the side of the Darkside mountain.

"I see it," she said, her voice breathy as Walker's other hand slid beneath her cami, tracing the curve of her waist. "It's right there."

In spite of Walker's touch, her internal balance wavered and Keira felt herself slip, hovering between the two realities for a horrifying moment. The weight of the sea crashed over her, yanking her away from Walker—carrying her out of Darkside.

Without letting go of her, Walker spun her around and crushed his mouth against hers. One of his hands cupped the back of her neck, pulling her tight into his kiss. The other, splayed against the skin of her back, held her against him tightly enough that she could feel the button of his jeans pressing into the bared skin of her stomach.

He was all she could feel, all she could smell, all she could taste. The places where their skin touched burned and Keira melted into them, wanting more. Walker was everywhere and everything and she was with him, completely. The ocean slipped away like an outgoing tide, leaving only Darkside in its wake.

Keira whimpered with desire and relief. Walker broke the kiss, slid his hands up to cup her face, and leaned his forehead against hers.

"I felt you slip. Is it gone?" he asked. "What did you see?"

"It's gone." She closed her eyes, breathing in the mineral, almost metallic smell of the rock around them. "And yes, the cave mouths line up. I think it must be the place."

Something thundered through the air, beating against Keira's eardrums like a shock wave—noiseless but unbearable, a sound she felt rather than heard. She clapped her hands over her ears, trying to block out the pulsing that rolled across the Darkside landscape.

"What *is* that?" she asked, wincing as the aural assault battered her hearing again and again.

Walker's lips pressed into a grim line. "It's the alarm," he said. "They only trigger it during large-scale emergencies. Everyone's supposed to stay where they are until they can be accounted for. Only the Reformers' guards can travel."

Keira struggled to think beneath the soundless wailing of the alarm.

She had crossed over. Multiple times. Enough to cause a rip that would most certainly be noticed.

"The alarm is for us, isn't it?" she asked.

"I think so, yes. I think they've realized where we are."

"Then why not just come for us without setting off an alarm?" Keira lifted her hand from her ear to wave toward the reverberating sound. It was a mistake to leave her ear unprotected—her brain itself seemed to pulse with the alarm.

Walker grimaced. "I don't know. But I think we'd better start climbing, and fast. It won't take the guards long to get here." He looked at her, a question glowing in his eyes. "Unless you want to double back? We can get to the beach near where we parked the car if we go that way—"

She interrupted him.

"No! What are you talking about? If we leave now, we can never come back—you know that. They'll search for us and what about my father? If they find him . . ." Keira shook her head, unable to finish the sentence.

The soundless waves came to a sudden stop. Keira's ear drums thrummed in relief. With her head feeling clearer, she looked Walker in the eyes. "It's too late for me to turn back now."

He stared at her for a long moment before nodding. "Then it's a good thing your ankle's healed."

The two of them turned in unison, faced the jagged rocks in front of them, and began to climb.

Chapter Forty-Eight

THE SLOPE STEEPENED ABRUPTLY, and Keira grunted as her shoes scrabbled for purchase against the slippery rock. The irregular face of the mountain at least offered hand- and footholds, though she felt more like she was crawling up the incline, rather than climbing it.

She could hear Walker behind her, his breathing heavy with exertion. By the time the cave seemed within reach, Keira's arms shook with the effort of the climb. She paused, clinging to the rocks. Her gaze jumped from handhold to foot-ledge, measuring gaps and drops and spans of smooth, flat rock. She needed a path. A connect-the-dots way to get to the black mouth of the cave.

Come on—just find a pattern—like notes on a staff.

She squinted at the rocks, trying to see the right outcroppings to grab while keeping the ocean—the whole crushing, rolling enormity of the ocean—out of view.

And then it appeared, the same way she could hear music when she rolled her gaze over the notes.

Walker pulled up short behind her, panting hard. "You need to head to the le—"

"I see it," she said, reaching for the first handhold in the chain, holding her breath the same way she did when she reached for the first note in a piece of music.

"Okay. I'll add free-climbing to your list of skills, then."

They climbed the rest of the way in silence. Keira moved from rock to rock, pretending the whole way that she was simply playing a new concerto, or an unfamiliar étude. There were the expected hesitations and near misses, the fear of the unknown combined with the need to keep going at the expected pace. As long as she pretended her fingers were striking keys instead of curling around bits of rock and kept up the illusion that her feet were pressing pedals instead of feeling for toeholds, she would be okay.

She could keep her fear from swallowing her.

At least, until the floor of the cave appeared in front of her, interrupting her fantasy. Then, she hesitated.

"Go on," Walker said behind her. "The sooner we're out of sight, the better."

She shook herself, willing her frozen muscles to stir. In one fast move, she slithered into the cave on her belly. Inside, it was blacker than the devil's own heart. Leaving just enough room for Walker to come in, Keira curled up against the slippery stone of the cave's wall, shivering with fear and the exertion of the climb.

He pulled himself in next to her and they both turned to face the darkness at the back of the cave.

"Hello?" Keira called hesitantly.

The walls seemed to soak up her voice. Nothing responded to her—no answer. Not even an echo. The silence that followed was the most heartbreaking sound Keira had ever heard.

In the noiseless dark, a sob rose in her throat. She hadn't realized how deeply she'd believed Pike would be waiting for her.

Walker pulled her against his side.

"It's okay," he whispered. "This is a good place to hide. We'll wait for the chaos to die down and then we'll figure out a new plan. We can keep traveling, find some way that you can keep up with your music. . . ."

Keira's hands curled into fists at her sides. She could feel her whole life slipping through her fingers like sand. Juilliard was gone. Her family, Susan—all of it, gone. Just like that.

There was a snapping sound at the back of the cave. Before Keira could even ask Walker what it might have been, one of the peculiar Darkside lights began to glow in the recesses of the cave.

Keira leapt to her feet, ready to run, but clueless as to whether she should be running toward the light or away from it.

A figure stepped toward the lantern, shrouded in a heavy hooded cloak. Keira felt Walker's protective presence behind her as she willed herself to call out again.

"Uncle Pike? Is that you?"

A hand reached up to pull back the hood and Keira leaned in, struggling to see. In the strange Darkside light, the face that appeared was thin and aged, but it was distinctly familiar.

Pike Sendson grinned at her. In the gloom of the cave, it looked like a skeletal rictus, instead of the charming smile she remembered. But still, she smiled back.

"Keira. You made it." His voice was cracked and reedy, a long-unused instrument. He stretched his arms out to her, but when she didn't go to him, he looked so wounded that his arms began to shake. Keira's stomach knotted when she saw that he was missing most of the fingers on his right hand. "You look like Hope itself," he said. "I'd almost given up. All these years, hiding and waiting—I thought maybe I'd been wrong about you. Misjudged. That happens, you know. Bad judgment." He wrapped his arms around himself, rocking slowly back and forth in front of the lantern.

The desperation rolled off him in waves, pushing Keira back even though she wanted to run to him. Walker put a hand on her shoulder and Keira reached for it, covering his fingers with her own.

"Uncle Pike—"

"Uncle?" he interrupted her. His eyes cleared and he spoke with the same ringing confidence she remembered. "Don't you know? Can you really have come all this way and not *know?*"

Keira grimaced. It was one thing to think of Pike as her father—her biological father—in the abstract. It was another to acknowledge it to him in person. For all his flaws, her true father was Dennis Brannon. He was the one who'd always been there when she needed him. Pike was a memory; a myth. "I know that you're my father."

He smoothed the front of his tattered robe again and again. "I imagine it's not easy for you to accept that, but I hope in time you'll be able to. I am prouder of you than anything else I've done in my life. I knew you were special the first moment you smiled up at me from your mother's arms." His face darkened. "Keira, you're in a great deal of danger."

"I know. That's why we came. We read the note." She stepped toward him.

"We?" The suspicion in Pike voice was shrill as a siren. The muscles in Keira's legs bunched in response, begging her to back up—warning her to keep her distance. Pike's eyes darted around the cave and his hands clutched ineffectively at the sides of his robe as though he'd lost not just his fingers but his grasp on reality, too.

"We. Walker and me. Walker was the one who found me," she said.

Pike squinted at Walker, who waited outside the wavering lantern light. "I wanted a visitor, but I wasn't expecting two. Two might be too many. Who are you, exactly?" he asked.

Walker stepped forward. "I'm Walker Andover."

Pike wavered on his feet, stretching out an arm for balance. "Andover? But then you must be—that's not *possible*—" he stammered. His eyes rolled wildly.

The *thud, thud, thud* of something hitting the cave floor behind them made Keira spin like a jewelry-box ballerina. Three of the Reformers' guards stood in the doorway. Their long fingers curled around lengths of black rope. One of their hoods had slipped back, and Keira could see a pale, hooked nose and pitlike black eyes staring at them.

She couldn't feel her legs beneath her.

All this time.

All this running.

And now—*now*—they were caught?

"Shit," Walker said simply.

"Congratulations, Experimental," one of the guards said in his strange, rhythmic language. "It took longer to track you down than we thought it would."

Behind Keira, Pike began to laugh, burbling and bubbling in a way that made Keira's skin crawl. Her gaze raced around the cave, looking for an escape, looking for something to fight with. There were only three guards—maybe Walker was strong enough to—

The end of her thought snapped off like the tip of a too-sharp pencil. Walker had already turned and put his hands together behind him, surrendering to the guards. His instant submission shocked her.

He glanced up at her and the pain in his eyes was so sharp that it hurt Keira just to look at it.

"Turn around," he begged. "Turn around and hold out your hands."

She stared at him, dumbfounded. "We're giving up? Just like that?"

"This isn't a game, Keira. We have to go with them now. We can try to talk to the Reformers"—his words were coming faster and faster, and Keira's throat tightened in response—"but the guards—"

"Show no mercy," the guard hissed as he strode toward her, a black cord stretched taut between his hands.

Keira spun before it could touch her, stretching out her hands. In her blind reaching, the cave walls around her seemed to shift, and for a moment, she thought about letting herself go back to Maine. They weren't as deep beneath the ocean as they had been. She could swim for it, and as long as the currents didn't keep her trapped in the sea cave, she might even make it.

Before she could decide, though, the cords tightened around her wrists, cool and metallic, like unbelievably fine mesh. The ocean disappeared. She tried to see it, reaching for it in spite of the danger, but the metallic cord tugged at her wrists, anchoring her in Darkside. She couldn't see anything but the cave. Her own world had disappeared completely. She was trapped, stuck in Darkside and at the mercy of the Darklings.

Oh, fuck.

At the back of the cave, Pike kicked over the lantern, which went out with a *whuff*, throwing the cavern into sudden blackness. The guard who had bound Keira's hands tossed her to the ground next to Walker, who lay in a trussed heap. The three guards converged on Pike. He shot past them and leapt out of the mouth of the cave, swinging onto the rock face with the ease of a mountain goat. The guards scrambled to follow him. His shouts turned into a series of keening shrieks that made the hair on Keira's arms stand up.

"Can you get across?" Walker asked in an urgent whisper.

"No," Keira whispered back. "I can't even see it!"

"Damn. Me either. How did they get here?"

The scuff of a shoe against the cave floor made Keira lift her head. She squinted at the backlit figure, unable to see who it was. It turned out not to matter.

"I told them where to find you."

As soon as he spoke, she recognized Smith's voice, and she didn't think she'd ever heard anything so horrible in her life.

Chapter Forty-Nine

WALKER ROLLED TO FACE his cousin. "What the—how did you—we left . . ." His voice was slick with frustration. The impossible half questions slid off his tongue.

Smith crossed his arms. "You went too far this time, Walker." He sounded like an actor.

A bad actor.

He leaned over them. "I told you to hurry!" he spit the words at them. "You hung around Keira's house so long that I didn't have any choice. They were watching me watching you. I *had* to follow you guys."

Keira closed her eyes. If she hadn't been so desperate to

say good-bye, they might have escaped. Staying for dinner had used up too much time. They'd forced Smith's hand. She felt sick.

Smith straightened, resuming his booming fake stage voice.

"Besides, it turns out delivering both Experimentals to the Reformers came with quite a prize."

Keira choked on her own breath. Both Experimentals? She looked at Walker.

"What does he mean, 'both Experimentals'?"

Smith's laugh was as sudden and ugly as a misstruck note. He nudged Walker with his toe. "You didn't tell her? Wow. You're better at keeping secrets than I thought." His voice dropped and softened. "I can't believe you didn't say anything. You really did care about her after all, didn't you?"

There was a rough shout from outside the cave. "Seeker!"

Keira saw Walker flinch as Smith turned in response.

"Get out here and help us!"

Smith dutifully scurried to the mouth of the cave.

Walker and Keira lay alone on the cold stone floor.

Keira tried to breathe, but the air seemed too thick to get past her throat.

"Why didn't you tell me?" she choked out.

Walker was silent. In the blackness of the cave, with her own hands bound behind her, Keira died a thousand little deaths for every second he didn't speak.

By the time he finally responded, she was numb.

"I was scared," he admitted. "I was going to tell you. I was going to tell you every day. Every time I saw you. Not that I expect you to believe me. But I'd already told you that the Reformers wanted all the Experimentals dead. I'm not exempt from that, Keira. They let me live as long as I was looking for you. As long as I was doing their work, I was safe. When I did the seeking, it kept the other Seekers from being damaged by traveling back and forth between the worlds. That way, no one else would have to end up like Pike—eaten away, physically and mentally."

Keira sucked in an enormous breath, ready to rage at him for all the lies—for breaking the trust he'd always begged her to have in him. If he'd just *told* her, she would have . . .

Her breath hung suspended in her chest, her lungs stretched and aching.

What would she have done? Once Walker'd started helping her, he'd signed his own death warrant. She never would have let him protect her if she'd known. Not when the cost was so high.

Outside, Pike's shrieks turned into a slow, moaning whimper. The guards had caught him.

Between her clenched teeth, Keira snarled with frustration.

She wanted to be angry with Walker—to be scared of him, even.

But she wasn't. And there was no time to second-guess herself, either.

"If I weren't so damn stubborn," she growled, "I—"

Walker cut her off. "If you weren't so damn stubborn, then I wouldn't have found you nearly as interesting. Or sexy. Or worth risking so much for."

Keira thought about that. "So, you really are just like me?"

"Not exactly," he admitted. "For one thing, you're much prettier than I am."

"Walker, I'm being serious," she protested.

"I am too!" he insisted. "But there's other stuff. My mother was a Darkling—it was my dad who was human. Their relationship was more complicated than the other people's in the Breeding Program. They fell in love. And I was raised Darkside. So, we're not the same. You can play music. And I can't. So, if it comes down to it, you might have a way to save yourself. But after today—"

"Walker doesn't have a way to save himself." Smith swung into the cave. "Because the Reformers don't need him anymore. Now they have me."

The guards appeared in the cave's entrance. Two of them held Pike, who was hog-tied and disturbingly limp. They bundled his body into a mesh sack while the third guard reached up above the mouth of the cave and pulled down a rope. It dangled in the entry like an enormous leash, and the guard clipped it to the bag that held Pike's unconscious body. The guard gave the rope a sharp tug and it went taut.

Nausea rocked Keira as she watched Pike's limp form rise from the guard's grip, swinging into the open air, held only by the single thin rope. As he disappeared above the cave, Keira suddenly understood.

The guards hadn't followed them *up* the mountain at all.

They'd come down *over* it.

And they were taking Keira, Walker, and Pike back with them.

Terror filled her veins and crushed her thoughts and sang to her muscles. Keira struggled into a sitting position. The guards looked at each other. One of them nodded.

"Walker?" Keira gasped.

"Don't fight them. Don't ask any questions," he warned. He lay still, controlled.

The guards approached, pulling small bottles from their pockets. The urge to scream rose in Keira, irresistible and unstoppable.

Her mouth opened of its own accord, but as she drew in a breath, the guards cracked the bottles' seals with their too-long fingers and something hissed into the air, spraying across Keira's face. It filled her nose and mouth and she choked as she breathed it in. The earth and metal smell of it gagged her and the edges of her vision grew fuzzy. She closed her eyes against the undulating darkness in front of her.

When she opened them again, she was alone.

In a very tiny room.

With no way out.

Chapter Fifty

OH, CRAP, IT'S A CELL.

Keira sat up and the room spun around her. Whatever the guards had drugged her with hadn't completely worn off. She could still taste it lingering on her tongue. When the walls stopped their crazy dance, she slowly got to her feet. Someone had unbound her hands, but the tips of her fingers tingled numbly. She shook her hands, fighting the effects of the drug. There was no clock in the room. No windows. No way at all to tell what time it was or how long she'd been knocked out.

There was a bench along one wall of the room that was big enough to be a narrow bed. They could have at least left her there, instead of dumping her on the floor. But the guards had just thrown her on the ground, like a *thing*. Keira shivered. That's how the Reformers thought of her, as something to be disposed of, like a spoiled apple or a broken cup.

Keira made her way over to the bench and sat down. She set her hands on either side of her, drumming her fingers against the smooth surface. She ran imaginary scales for a moment, driving the last of the Darklings' drug out of her system. The best option would be to get out of Darkside completely, if she could.

Carefully, slowly, she lowered her guard enough to let the earth she knew slip into view. At first, it seemed out of reach, like it had been when the guards had bound her in the cave. Keira leaned forward, adjusting her focus. She saw something shift and felt an unbearable press of weight against her skin.

The last of the drug's fog swirled out of her mind as the answer became clear. She couldn't see anything on the other side because they'd gone over the Darkside mountain. Which meant they were who knew how far out in the Atlantic Ocean, lost in its featureless depths.

It really was the perfect prison. The only certain escape also meant certain death. Keira curled her fingers around the edge of the bench, letting the corners bite into her skin. It kept her grounded. Focused.

The familiar headache took up its pulsing rhythm behind her eyes as she pushed the ocean out of sight. When it was gone, Keira stared around the tiny room. There was a table in the corner with a square tray on it. On the tray stood a glass filled with a purplish liquid and a bowl of something mushy.

It had been so long since she'd had anything to drink. Her head throbbed.

Can I even eat things here? What if it's poisoned?

She stood up, relieved to find her legs steady underneath her. Carefully, she made her way over to the tray and lifted the cup. She sniffed it. It smelled like oranges and mint.

The Reformers already had her—why would they be sneaky about poisoning her now? Still, she stood for a long moment with the glass pressed against her bottom lip, deciding.

She was so thirsty.

Slowly, she tipped the glass until the liquid touched her mouth. It was cool and sweet, with a fresh, green edge to the taste. If it was poison, then death was delicious. Keira gulped down the contents of the glass, her head clearing with each swallow.

She set the glass back on the tray and looked at the unappetizingly gray mush. Leaving it where it was, she turned and paced the perimeter of the room, running her fingers over the walls, searching for something—anything—that might be a way out. She drummed her fingers against the strange surface and finally found a section near the corner that sounded more hollow than the rest of the room. She tapped carefully, listening as her knocks outlined an area big enough to be a door.

Hope stirred in her, like the first crocus pushing up through the long-frozen dirt, but she shoved it back down. It might mean nothing. Still, there was no vent to crawl through, no window to jump from. If she had a chance, this was it. She ran her fingers over and over the expanse of wall, looking for a bump, a ridge, a dip—anything. Up and down, across and back, she searched for a way to open the door.

She found nothing.

The cell was sealed like a tomb.

Is that what this room really is? A tomb? Have they thrown me in here to die?

The idea was terrifying. Keira hammered at the wall as though she could beat it down—as though she could push the lid off her own coffin.

And then, without warning, she was falling.

The sensation was so unexpected that Keira barely managed to brace herself for the impact. Her palms slammed against the ground and she instinctively wrenched her face to one side so that her right cheekbone, rather than her nose, smacked the stone. Pain exploded across her eye, sending a starburst of sparkles across her view of a long, featureless hall.

Get up, get up! The voice in her head was insistent. Instinctive. But before she could listen to it, a pair of hands curled around her upper arms, yanking her to her feet. Keira whipped her head around to see who held her. The sudden movement sent another flash of pain through her head and she bit down on the inside of her cheek, determined not to cry out.

The guard who held her made a noise like sandpaper scraping against metal. The realization that he was laughing at her only made the noise more awful.

"This way," he hissed in the same sibilant, heavily accented voice she'd heard the other guard use. Before she could even think to fight back, he was dragging her down the hall. She hung from his grasp, her face and shoulder screaming in pain while the tips of her shoes traced their path. Keira gritted her teeth. She forced back her screams, struggling against the shackle of the guard's grip, but it made no difference. Desperate, she swung her feet up, meaning to kick him or, better yet, trip him. As soon as she lifted her feet off the ground, though, the wrenching pressure on her shoulder brought her to the very edge of unconsciousness. She dropped her legs, letting herself go limp in his grasp.

She gave up.

The guard grunted in approval. He finally set Keira on her feet in front of a huge pair of ornately carved doors. They looked out of place in the otherwise featureless building. There was something familiar about the pattern on them, the way the circles overlapped and intersected—of course. The door she'd seen in the road, when she was in Walker's car, back when all of this started. It had been carved in the same style, if a bit less ornately.

Thinking back to those first visions was too much like thinking of home—too much like thinking of the life she was about to lose. Because if there was one thing she knew, bone-deep and absolutely, it was that the Reformers were on the other side of those doors.

She could feel them there, waiting with her death sentence in their hands. Eager to make her pay not just for her mistakes, but for her existence, too.

It was going to cost Keira her life, and there wasn't a damn thing she could do to stop it.

The doors swung inward, revealing a room filled with shadows. A long bench, like a church pew, sat against the back wall, illuminated from above by Darkside lights. Guards ringed the room, as evenly spaced as if they marked a clock face. They each held a staff that looked heavy enough to smash in a skull if need be.

Walker and Pike stood off to one side. Walker's hair was a tangled mess, but beyond that, he appeared unharmed. The relief of seeing him whole was so sweet it was almost unbearable. Pike stood behind him. His robes were ripped and he winced like something pained him, but if he was injured, she couldn't see it.

Walker turned and looked at her. His eyes widened at the sight of her cheek. It must've looked terrible. She wasn't surprised—it was throbbing like it had its own heart.

Still, at least it wasn't her hands. They stung a little, yeah, but as long as they were fine, she was fine. She tried to reassure him with a smile, but the guard prodded her in the back. Keira stumbled forward.

"With the others," he hissed.

She scrambled away from him, rushing to Walker's side.

She clung to him, burying her face in his chest. He stiffened beneath her touch, gently pulling her away from him. His reaction was so cold that she shivered.

She looked up at him and saw that his gaze was focused behind her. The sound of footsteps broke through her confusion and Keira turned to see five robed figures, their features ancient and angular, making their way over to the bench.

"It's the Tribunal," Walker whispered. "Half of the Reformers—they're Darkside's judges. And juries."

He didn't say "and executioners," but Keira heard it anyway. She swallowed.

The silence that filled the room was so thick that it seemed to slow time itself. The moment hung there, suspended. It was only the beating of her heart and the pumping of her lungs that kept Keira from believing the universe had stopped entirely.

One of the members of the Tribunal cleared his throat. Keira couldn't tell which of them it was—they were all as motionless as statues.

"We have in front of us," the Reformer said, "a trinity of failure." His voice rose and died oddly in the dark corners of the room.

There was a murmur of agreement from the rest of the

Tribunal. The noise passed over Keira, leaving a sick sense of foreboding in its wake.

The voice continued. "And so today marks a chance to wipe out our past mistakes."

Keira forced herself not to shudder as the center-most member of the Tribunal leaned forward to peer more closely at the three of them.

"Walker Andover."

Walker nodded.

Keira could hear his breath, fast and shallow. He was scared.

"You were charged with the task of finding the lost Experimental and bringing it back to us."

It didn't escape Keira's notice that they'd referred to her as "it." She bit down hard on the inside of her cheek to keep herself from protesting.

The Reformer paused. "The fact that you accomplished the first part of your task while abandoning the remainder is more offensive to us than if you'd simply never found the Experimental at all. What you have done is beyond disobedient. It is treason. Moreover, you knew that having more than one Experimental moving back and forth through the barrier would create unsustainable levels of damage to our world, but you wantonly disregarded that danger. You have ruined the Hall of Records in your home province. The information from entire *generations* is lost to us because of your careless actions. That alone would be enough to render you unforgivable."

Walker gave the smallest possible nod. Keira wanted to say something—defend him somehow—but she didn't understand the formalities of the situation. Any words she spoke would be as likely to damn him as they would be to save him.

"Walker Andover. As punishment for your transgressions, you are sentenced to die."

Keira couldn't breathe. Every detail in the room came into perfect focus. The sagging folds in the Reformers' robes, the way one of the guards had his head turned ever so slightly to the left—the details etched themselves into her mind. She would never be able to forget anything about this horrible moment. It didn't matter if they killed her now. Once they'd condemned Walker, she was already lost.

Keira managed to turn her face toward Walker.

Walker's lips parted as though he were about to say something but he stayed silent, clenching his teeth.

All along, Keira'd known that if the Reformers caught them, they would be facing death. Hearing the words said out loud, though—it was too much. The reality of it had a texture and weight that Keira wasn't sure she could endure.

Walker couldn't die. They hadn't had enough time to kiss yet. She hadn't told him about the time she'd fallen off her bike when she was five and cut her knee nearly to the bone. She hadn't played him the Beethoven Allegretto.

A sob rose in her throat, keening through her vocal chords and slipping out into the room.

"Silence!" The roar came from the tallest of the Reformers. "We have not invited you to speak."

So that was why Walker hadn't tried to defend himself. They hadn't invited him to speak. Keira lifted her chin. She was not going to be condemned to die without having a chance to explain herself. And if they decided to kill her—the thought dropped into her arms, too heavy to hold. She locked her knees beneath her and straightened her spine. She forced herself to think it.

If they decide to kill me, I'm not going to go without defending myself and Walker, too. They won't kill me without hearing me first. I won't let them.

Chapter Fifty-One

THE REFORMER WHO HAD sentenced Walker turned to Pike. "Your failings were nearly as great as his. It was you who created the Experimentals in the first place. It was your 'vision' that we followed, marching blindly toward our own destruction. When it became obvious that your Experimentals were wreaking havoc on our very existence, you refused to come before us and answer for it. What have you to say for yourself?"

Pike scurried forward. "Your Honors. Thank you for the chance to speak. I've been saving up my words. A whole pile of them."

He cleared his throat, rubbing his hand over his face

repeatedly. He looked even more unstable than he had in the cave.

"Your Honors," he began again. Pike's voice was stronger this time. "It's true. The early parts of the Experimental Breeding Program failed. They hurt things. Damaged Darkside. I regret that. Really, really more than almost anything in my whole life, I regret how much damage was caused. I still believed in the program, though. I could have fixed it. But the program was stopped before I could finish my experiments."

There was a dry murmur among the members of the Tribunal. Reddening, Pike barreled on. As he talked about his work, he seemed less scattered. More like the Pike Keira remembered—quick and intense.

"All of the Experimentals we'd created had been raised here in Darkside, force-fed music education. They were deluged with human-made instruments that deteriorated all too quickly in our Dark environment. As you know, the continual passage back and forth between our realities to bring new instruments only caused more damage."

"Even here!" The smallest of the Reformers had a distinctly feminine voice, though it creaked and popped. "When one of your fool Experimentals tried to cross over during his pre-elimination hearing, he created a rip in this very chamber. Do you have any idea how outrageous it is that your creations have damaged *our* compound?"

Keira knew there was nothing on the other side of the room—

the earth side—but the ocean. Crossing over would be suicide.

The fact that it had seemed the better choice to that Experimental made her shudder.

Pike glanced behind him and his gaze settled on Keira. She tugged self-consciously on the hem of her shirt and was shocked when it crumbled away to nothing in her hands.

She'd been Darkside long enough that her clothes were beginning to disintegrate. It seemed so terrifyingly final. Even this last bit of the life she'd known, the life she'd planned, the life she *wanted*—was crumbling beneath her fingers. It wouldn't be long before the Reformers would hand down their sentence and then she'd be nothing too. Gone. Like her shirt, and the instruments, and everything she'd ever known. A lump sprang up in her throat, impossible to swallow.

"But Keira was different." Pike's words cut through her thoughts and she blinked in surprise. He looked back toward the Tribunal but he pointed at her, his arm shaking.

"Keira was raised on earth. She had the best possible Darkside lineage. Her mother possessed tremendous musical talent. I myself heard Keira's fledgling ability—little musical birdie who hadn't learned to fly, plinking out the notes with her tiny, little girl fingers—I was proud. Proud, proud, proud as that thing— that funny thing—and birds. Birds with their wings and their beaks . . ." Pike's hands shook at his sides and his eyes wandered.

Keira curled her fingers tight against her palms. His mind was slipping again. Shit.

"Dr. Ssssendson?" One of the Tribunal members prompted him, "You recognized some ability in this earth-bound Experimental?"

Pike clasped his hands in front of him as though doing so would help him hold it together. "Yes. Even though she was so young, Keira was obviously able to make music. More than that, she seemed to have a real talent for it. I made sure she was provided with an instrument and money for the education she needed to develop her abilities."

He turned to Keira.

His face shone with pride.

She remembered Uncle Pike putting phone books on the piano bench for her so that she could reach the keys. When she pushed down middle C with a pudgy little finger, his face had shone the same way it did now. She could hear him saying, *That's my girl*, while he ruffled her hair. With a start, Keira realized that, in a sense, Pike himself had been her first piano teacher.

The ruined face that stared at her now was a ghost of that man.

Pike licked his lips.

"Your Honors, it was the goal of the Experimental Breeding Program to create a being with Darkling genetics who also possessed musical ability. To bring the music we worship back into our species. The damage the Experimentals did to our world was a deeply unfortunate side effect. But side effects are not the same as failures. I believe—" He clacked his teeth together, half choking on the insane giggle that Keira heard rising in his throat. "I believe that she can play. Let her prove her musical ability to you. She's not a failure and neither am I. I can feel it in my bones." Pike held up his right hand, shaking back his sleeve to reveal a mutilated hand, the stubs of his missing fingers offering physical proof of the damage that the Seekers caused themselves with too much crossing between the worlds.

Keira gagged.

The Reformers eyed her suspiciously.

Keira's blood began to burn like a signal fire. Pike was trying to prove her worth. It was a shame he was too far gone to realize what he was actually condemning her.

One of the Tribunal members tilted his hooded head, considering Pike. "If she can play, then perhaps you are right. It would be a mark in your favor to find out that all three of you were not wasted. If she can play, perhaps we have enough use for her to spare her."

The room bucked and spun as his words wormed their way through Keira's mind.

There was no way out of this now, because if they thought she couldn't play, they'd kill her. And if she proved she could, they'd still kill Walker. Those were the only two possible outcomes.

Walker caught her arm as she staggered. She looked up at him, but meeting his eyes was a mistake. Pain and loss burned in his gaze. She couldn't breathe through the ache in her chest; she couldn't see through the lake of tears.

"Well, then, Experimental," the Reformer rasped. "What instrument did Dr. Sendson provide you with?"

"A piano," Pike said proudly.

"Sssilenccce!" The hiss rose from the Tribunal in unison. Even the walls seemed to cower beneath it. "You were not invited to speak!"

Pike's skin turned pearly gray and he shook like he'd touched a live wire.

The female Tribunal member gestured to one of the guards.

He turned neatly and swept aside an enormous curtain, revealing an assortment of instruments in varying stages of decay. Among them was a scratched and worn upright piano.

Keira's stomach plummeted.

They didn't just expect her to play. They expected her to do it *right now*.

Chapter Fifty-Two

KEIRA STARED AT THE PIANO.

It was like a roulette wheel marked only with death. There was no way to win. Either she didn't play and she died, or she did play, and they killed Walker anyway.

As she stood there, being slowly ripped in half by the choice, she had the same feeling she had when she crossed between the two worlds. The sensation that she was neither here nor there—that anything was still possible.

The idea was as sudden and unexpected as lightning and even more terrifying. Before she could lose her nerve, Keira turned to face the Tribunal.

"What?" The middle one asked.

"I'm not going to play. Not unless you agree to spare Walker." She set her chin, pulling on every bit of stubbornness she could summon, and stiffened her spine with the same pride Walker had always teased her about.

The sibilant laughter was icy against her skin. "Then we will simply kill all of you. You for failing to play, Dr. Sendson for failing to prove his success, and Walker for both failing in his mission and also as payment for your insolence. No one refuses our order. No one."

Fury tore through her, but it was replaced almost immediately by powerlessness. There was no way out. The snare had already tightened around her ankle. The noose was looped around her neck.

She turned to Walker. The angle of his body half hid his face from the Tribunal.

"Play," he begged her.

"Walker, no." She shook her head. "If I give them what they want—they won't have any reason to negotiate with me. There has to be some way out."

"It's too late, Keira." Walker's shoulders sank in resignation. He stared at her, his eyes pinning her in place. "I knew this might happen. The only thing that you can do for me is to save yourself. Please. *Please.*"

One of the guards stepped over and pulled her away from Walker, dragging her toward the piano. Keira was so numb with fear that she couldn't even feel her feet as she crossed the floor. She sat on the worn wooden bench, automatically moving herself into position. She glanced over her shoulder at Walker and Pike. They both watched her. Pike bobbed his head in time to a song that played only in his head. The vacant grin was back on his face, and Keira knew he'd lost touch with reality again. She wanted to be angry at him, but he looked so pitiful that she couldn't manage it. He was nothing more than the victim of the holes that too much crossing had eaten into his brain. It wasn't his fault. She felt sorry for Pike, but Walker was the one that broke her heart.

Walker's jaw was set and his shoulders were squared, and he smiled at her with pride. It was exactly how her mother had looked at Keira's first recitals. It was like he couldn't wait to hear her play. Like it was the only thing he wanted.

Keira refocused her attention on the piano keys. A few of them were chipped, and she wondered if the disintegrating piano was even in tune. There was only one way to find out, but her hands curled up like snails at the thought of touching the keys. Everything had taken on a slow, underwater quality, as though the ocean itself had slipped across into Darkside.

Keira shook out her hands.

Behind her, the Tribunal began to stir with impatience.

Keira closed her eyes and put her fingers on the keys, but there was no music in her hands. It was the same way she'd felt in front of her own piano, with her mother waiting for her to remember the Brahms concerto. Only then, she'd just grabbed her sheet music. Now, all she could do was beg her fingers to remember something. Anything.

Deep inside the piano, the hammers struck the strings, as she banged out the first notes of the Beethoven sonata she'd bought the day she met Walker. The piano sounded wrong—not out of tune, exactly, but the noise was *wrong* somehow, the same way the Darkside lights shone strangely. The sound was so foreign that Keira's ear couldn't match the sound to what her hands were doing.

She fumbled the fingering on the fourth measure.

There was a dissatisfied grumble from the Tribunal.

She took a breath and leaned over the keys until all she could see was the piano. She'd never tried to play without *hearing* it. Repositioning her hands, she started again.

She made it as far as the third line by seeing the notes in her mind's eye and matching them up to the keys beneath her fingers, but without the sound of it, without being able to hear what she played, she misstruck two notes in a row.

When the second wrong note sounded, a roar went up from the Tribunal.

"Dr. Sendson!"

Keira whipped around, instinctively leaning against the piano for support.

The middle Reformer pointed at Pike.

"What do you have to say about this? She is not playing. She *cannot* play."

Pike sank to his knees and turned his back to Keira like she was an unanswered prayer; like she was his own personal Judas. He bent low in front of the Tribunal.

"She told me she could," he gasped. "I don't know. Oh, I can hear how it would sound. I remember notes and notes and then we laughed."

The Tribunal members exchanged looks.

"Stand up and stop this raving," one of the Reformers ordered. "We will deal with you later."

Pike struggled back to his feet, next to Walker.

"Please," Keira called. "I know I can do this. If I could try again—the piano sounds strange here and I—"

"Silence!" It was not so much a word as a roar. "You have *failed*," the Tribunal member said. "We have judged it to be so, and our judgment is law."

Keira sank back against the piano, as though she could disappear into the cracks between the keys. Her elbows stuck the keyboard, sending a discordant jangle through the room.

The Tribunal bent their heads together, their whispers scratching through the air. Keira looked at Walker. He stared at her as though he was trying to see every detail of her, one last time. Her hope shrank to a sliver and finally to a pinprick before it died altogether.

A Tribunal member motioned to the nearest guard, who hurried over and then left the room with purpose. Keira watched him go. Fear narrowed her throat as the door slammed shut behind him.

The Tribunal member who sat closest to Walker and Pike stood. "This is our pronouncement. Pike Sendson, as punishment for your failings, you are to witness the end of your experiment. You will live to see the last two Experimentals die, and then you will spend the rest of your lifetime imprisoned in the Darkside penitentiary, contemplating your failures."

Keira cried out as Walker doubled over, his arms wrapped around his stomach.

The smallest Reformer raised her hand. "We are not without mercy," she rasped. "There is an obvious affection between the two Experimentals, which has been the cause of at least some of these transgressions. They will be allowed to say their good-byes." She turned her head toward Walker. "I suggest you get on with it. The extermination room is already being prepared."

If she hadn't already been sitting down, Keira would have fallen. She couldn't see anything except the symphony of starbursts that danced across her vision. But what did it matter if she couldn't see? The verdict had sliced her future off at the neck. There was nothing ahead of her anymore.

Walker knelt in front of her, and her vision cleared as his hands cupped her face.

"Keira." His voice broke when he said her name.

A sob worked its way through her chest. Nothing had ever hurt her like this. It was beyond pain. Beyond imagining.

"Walker," she whispered back, trying to be strong enough to say good-bye.

He smiled at her, but tears slipped down his face. "I'm sorry," he said. "I promised to keep you safe from all this." His head dropped toward his chest.

She reached out and caught his chin. "You're the one who always called me stubborn, right? I made my own decisions. You can't save me from myself." Her voice shook.

The tears glistened on his cheeks. "You're not mad?"

Keira half laughed. "I'm furious. But not with you. You're—" The lump in her throat grew, trapping the words that rose behind it. She swallowed, wiping the tears from her cheeks.

"I love you." Her voice shone with strength as she said it. "That doesn't seem like nearly enough. You gave up everything to try to save me. *Everything.* But—"

"Shhhh." Walker rose from his knees. He wrapped his arms around her and pressed his forehead against hers. She felt his curls tangle in her hair the same way they had that first day, when they'd cracked heads in the music store. The memory had too many sharp edges. Keira shoved it away, unable to carry any more pain.

Walker pulled back enough to look her in the eyes. "Giving up everything *for* you is better than having everything *but* you.

I love you too. I have since the very beginning. Why else would I have done all of this?" He tried to smile and failed.

Keira tightened her grip on him.

"Is there anything I can do?" she whispered.

Walker nodded, slow and sad. "Play," he said. "Play for me, one last time. I want you to do the thing you love most—I want one more memory of you at the piano."

Keira sobbed. She couldn't think of a single piece of music she'd ever studied. Not a single trill, not a solitary chord. The finality of the moment had stripped it all away.

"I'm not sure if I *can*," she said.

"Play something you composed," he said. "Play something that's just for me. Just for us."

She couldn't deny him. Not now. Not this. Keira turned to slide back onto the piano bench. Scooting to the very front of the seat, she pressed herself against the piano, like she was saying good-bye. How could she play, knowing it would be the last time?

In her memory, she saw her own six-year-old hands, struggling to stretch over the keys. She felt her little kid legs, swinging above the ground as she sat on the bench, her feet too short to reach the pedals. The way it felt, when she was just beginning. Only it had always seemed like the beginning, no matter how many times she'd played.

All the hundreds of days that she'd practiced had stacked up into years, and still it had never been enough. The only thing she'd ever wanted was more hours at the piano.

And now this was it. Her time was up.

Poised above the keys, her hands shook like a ship's sails in the wind. She could feel herself faltering. Failing. She looked over her shoulder at Walker.

"Help me. Please. I can't do this by myself."

There was no hesitation. In one motion, he swung his leg over the piano bench, wrapping himself around her. His legs braced hers and he twined his arms around her middle, tucking his chin over her shoulder.

The trembling in her hands slowed. She remembered the day he'd taken her to the shore, the first day she'd ever composed something of her own. She didn't even have to think about the notes—the music was there, in her memory. The strange, dying sound of the notes against the Darkside air didn't even register in her hearing.

She began to play, her eyes falling closed. She didn't need to see the keys. She didn't need to think about the notes. She remembered the day she and Walker had climbed up the point on the coast. The image of the encompassing fog and that first almost-kiss was enough. This music was with her—*in* her—no matter what. She'd still have it when they took away the piano.

It would be with her until they took her breath, too.

As she bent over the keys, Keira felt Walker's mouth brush her ear.

"I love you, Keira Brannon," he whispered. His lips came to rest against the back of her neck.

The moment he kissed her, the air in the room shifted. The music poured from the piano, the notes pealing though the air with the same tone and feeling that they had in her mind. The sound was richer than anything she'd ever heard. It was tangible—she could *feel* it, soft as velvet, against her skin. Behind her, Walker froze, his mouth still pressed against her neck.

An enormous snap reverberated through the room and Keira's eyes flew open.

Something had changed.

Chapter Fifty-Three

THERE WAS A SHOUT from one of the guards and the Tribunal rose in unison.

Keira's fingers slipped from the keys as Walker lifted his head. The silence in the room was the loudest thing she had ever heard. She half turned to Walker.

"It sounded just like . . ." She couldn't even say it. It was too big a thing to wish for.

He nodded.

"It's gone," one of the Reformers cried. A gasp rose from the guards. "The old tear in the corner is gone." He looked over at Keira. "What did you do differently? Why did it work this time? Have you been hiding something from us?" His voice shook, hopeful. Furious. Greedy.

Keira opened her mouth, searching desperately for an answer that she did not have.

Walker's arms tightened around her.

His arms.

Of course.

When she'd closed the rip between Darkside and her living room, Walker had been sitting on the bench with her. She shut her eyes, trying to remember the details exactly.

She'd been playing her own music then, too. And he'd kissed her. That's when it had happened.

Just like now.

She glanced at him and saw the same answer shining in his eyes. "It's us," she whispered. "Us together."

He nodded, barely. "Your music."

"And your kiss," she answered.

The realization was too huge to put her arms around. They could fix the rips, which was everything the Reformers wanted. But it had to be the two of them, together. The musical ability that was supposed to save Keira would be the thing that saved them both.

"Speak up!" the Tribunal commanded. "What do you have to say about this?"

Keira slid off the bench and faced them with Walker by her side. He wrapped his hand around hers and she squeezed it hard.

"I wasn't keeping anything from you." There was too much stubbornness in her voice—too much indignation. She heard it. They heard it. She closed her eyes and breathed in slowly, grateful that she still could. "I wasn't intentionally keeping things from you," she said more calmly.

"I knew that my playing had somehow closed the barrier between the two worlds once before, in my living room, but I didn't know how I'd done it. Right after that, Walker and I found a message from Dr. Sendson scratched into the bottom of my piano. That's why we went to find him. We thought maybe he would know how my musical ability was supposed to work—how it was supposed to help Darkside. Before we could talk, though, the guards came." The anger crept back into her voice.

"Then the guards knocked us all out and brought us here. There was no *time* for me to figure it out, much less try to keep it from you."

Walker squeezed her hand with a quick warning pulse. Stopping her before she antagonized the Tribunal into killing her anyway.

"And now you know?" the female Reformer asked.

"I think so, yes," Keira said. "Both times that the rips in Darkside were mended, I was playing music that I'd composed."

For the first time, the murmur that went through the Tribunal sounded pleased instead of angry.

"But that wasn't all," she pushed on. "It was Walker, too."

Heat washed over her and she knew she was blushing fiercely. She hated having to reveal something that felt so personal—so *intimate*—but she didn't have a choice. "When he kissed me, that's when we fixed Darkside. Both times."

The Tribunal shifted restlessly.

"So, you see," Keira said, her voice ringing with truth, "you can't kill either of us. We can fix the Hall of Records—make it stable again. You'll have all of your information back. But I can't do it alone. It has to be the two of us together. Me and Walker."

Pike sank to the ground. He wrapped his arms around his legs and rocked back and forth, giggling like a madman. But at least he looked happy. Keira hoped he understood what was happening.

The central member of the Tribunal held up a long finger. "Stay where you are. We must return to our chambers to discuss this highly unusual development. Guards?"

The guards stepped forward in unison, tightening the circle around them. The one closest to Pike recoiled slightly as Pike let out a fresh wave of laughter.

The Tribunal swept out of the room.

The moments passed slowly while the Tribunal deliberated. The seconds seemed to hang suspended, clinging to Keira like drops of dew on spring grass. She burrowed into Walker's arms and he tucked the top of her head beneath his chin, his hand tracing the curve of her neck.

She couldn't lose this. She couldn't lose him. Not now.

There was no guarantee that the Tribunal would let them go, but at least there was room for hope now. Keira shifted so that she could see the spot in the far corner, where the rip had been. She let the ocean drift into view around it, staring at the place where the wound had been. The freshly healed bit of Darkside was as tight and shiny as a new scar.

Keira shivered as she looked at it. There was something unsettling about not being able to see through that part of Darkside anymore.

"Cold?" Walker asked, tightening his arms around her.

Keira shook her head against his chest. Part of his shirt flaked away beneath the press of her cheek.

"Oh! I'm sorry." She tried to put a little space between them, but Walker pulled her tight against him.

"Where do you think *you're* going?" he asked. His voice bounced with playfulness, and Keira knew he was hopeful too.

"I didn't want to accidentally undress you in front of a roomful of people," Keira offered.

"Hmmm . . . ," he answered, distracted.

She turned to see what he was looking at.

It was the door to the Tribunal's chambers. Someone had opened it.

"They're coming back in," Walker whispered.

Keira slipped out of his arms and stood next to him, watching the doorway. Everything hinged on the conclusion the Tribunal had reached.

Everything.

Walker reached out and caught her hand. Their fingers twined together like tree roots, keeping both of them from flying apart.

The Tribunal shuffled into the room at an ancient pace. Each step sent a fresh jolt of anticipation through Keira, which built like static electricity. By the time the Reformers had arranged themselves in front of the bench, the air itself crackled with anxiety.

"Stand," the guard closest to the bench commanded.

Keira and Walker were already on their feet. It was only Pike who remained on the floor, huddled up in a ball. His mouth moved aimlessly, like he'd run out of words but had forgotten to stop talking. In spite of the order, Pike made no move to rise. The guard closest to him stepped forward and prodded Pike with the end of the staff he carried.

Pike yelped and shot forward along the floor.

Keira started. She'd assumed the staffs were only used for hitting and smashing. But from Pike's grimace and the jerky way he got to his feet, Keira suspected she'd been wrong in her guess.

Very wrong.

Keira resisted the urge to look behind her, to see exactly how close the other guards—and their staffs—were.

The Tribunal sat down. They folded their hands.

Every inch of Keira dreaded their verdict but at the same time, she was desperate to hear it.

The centermost Tribunal member raised his hand, his palm facing the room, his unnaturally long fingers stretching above it.

"We have decided," he announced, his voice scraping through the room. "That if the Experimentals can repair the Hall of Records, then they will be allowed to live."

The declaration shot through Keira. It swept out her fear, dragged away her tangled thoughts. For a moment, she felt utterly empty. Her terror had left a vacuum that joy had yet to fill.

And then she felt Walker's fingers, squeezing hers. A thousand thoughts and feelings and questions poured into her at once. It was like being buried alive.

"You may live," the Tribunal member amended, "but you will remain in our custody. Do I make myself clear?"

"Yes." Walker sounded like the Reformers might as well have condemned them.

Keira blinked. The Reformers were going to keep them Darkside? Forever?

"No," she said.

The guards stepped forward in unison, their staffs pointed at Keira.

"You do not understand?" the smallest Reformer asked.

"I understand," Keira said, locking her knees to keep them from shaking. "But I can't stay here. I'm not a Darkling."

"This is not a matter in which you have a say, Experimental." The voice of the Reformer ripped through the room.

"I think it is," Keira said firmly. "Because I won't play—I won't fix the Hall of Records—unless you agree to let Walker and me go once it's repaired."

The Tribunal members all reacted at once, their gasps and oaths filling the room with a static so loud Keira could feel it in her fingertips. The guard nearest to her hefted his staff, ready to attack her.

The Reformer in the center raised a hand, stopping the guard. "Our decision is final. Disobeying the Tribunal's decision will result in both of your deaths. We are not *negotiating*."

"I think we are," Keira said quietly. She glanced down at the weapon that quivered in the guard's hand. "You could kill us. But then you'd never get the information that's trapped in the Hall. There's no one else who can repair the damage for you." She looked up at the hooded figures of the Tribunal. "You let us go home, or you lose all those records. Which do you prefer?"

The Tribunal bent their heads together without responding. Keira couldn't tell if it was a good sign or a bad sign that they hadn't bothered to leave the room to discuss their response, but what was done was done.

When they'd settled themselves on the bench again, the center Tribunal member nodded at Keira.

"Though we are not pleased by your impertinence, we concede that the Hall of Records is too valuable to lose. We will allow you to return home—if, and only if, you are able to repair the fabric of Darkside near the Hall."

The Tribunal head turned to Pike. "Dr. Sendson, your life will also be spared, but not your punishment. You will remain here, imprisoned, for the rest of your natural days." He motioned to the guard behind Pike, who seized him.

Pike struggled against the guard's grasp. "No! You can't! They'll need my guidance! I'm the only one who understands it."

The terror in his voice made the air itself quiver. For a moment, Pike seemed completely sane. It was as if the glowing, charismatic man her mother had always described was still in there somewhere. Now he'd be doubly imprisoned, once by the Reformers and once by his own mind. The idea crawled up Keira's spine, raising goose bumps on her skin.

"Wait!" she called out. "You can't take him! Pike—tell them how you can help us!"

But Pike didn't even glance at her. His silence was absolute, as though he'd decided he agreed with the sentence the Tribunal had given him. How could she save him if he wouldn't defend himself?

As they dragged him away, Keira wanted nothing more than to bury her face in Walker's chest. Instead, she squared her shoulders and watched him go. When the heavy door swung shut behind him, she slumped down. She wondered if Smith was somewhere in the Reformers' compound too. If he was, would he be in one of the cells, like Pike, or would he be walking the halls with the guards? She'd saved herself and

Walker, but the feeling that she'd failed Pike and Smith made the moment bittersweet.

The walls pressed in on her, as if the ocean that waited in her world was weighing on them.

She looked up at the Reformers.

"How are we supposed to get to the Hall?" she asked.

The startled jolt that ran through the Tribunal was so uniform that she wondered if anyone had ever dared to ask them for something so directly. She waited.

The Reformers needed her. They needed her badly enough that she could ask them for things in return for her help. She had every intention of reminding them of that. They could make her pay for her life, but they didn't own her.

The centermost Tribunal member answered. "We will transport you back to the Hall of Records. You will repair the damage, restabilizing the Hall. And then you may cross back into your world, no closer than three hundred rescaps to the Hall."

"Rescaps?" Keira asked.

"It's a distance," Walker whispered. "Like meters."

"Oh." She looked back at the Tribunal. "Fine. I accept your offer."

The Tribunal shifted uncomfortably, clearly unaware that they'd still been negotiating. Keira ate the smile that wanted to creep across her face.

"Then you will leave immediately." The Tribunal member hesitated. "Walker Andover? Will you go with her, or do you require separate transport?"

Keira glanced over. Walker's eyes were wide with surprise. He cleared his throat. "I will go with her, your Eminences."

"Fine." The Tribunal member waved them away. "You are dismissed."

As the guards led them from the room, Walker wrapped his arm around Keira's shoulders. For the second time that day, her feet barely seemed to touch the ground. But this time, she felt like she was flying.

"We can do this, right?" he whispered, as the guards ushered them down the hall. "If we fail . . ."

Keira slid her arm around his waist. "We won't fail. We won't." She put as much confidence as she could muster into the words. After all, they'd already fixed parts of Darkside—twice. They could do it again.

They *had* to do it again.

She hadn't come this far just to lose everything in the end.

Chapter Fifty-Four

THE TRIP BACK TO the Hall of Records may have taken an eternity. Keira couldn't tell. She didn't care. The Darklings put them in the windowless belly of a strange contraption that they called a transporter. It was something like a cross between a bulldozer and a stagecoach made of a material that looked like graphite.

But she was alone in the compartment with Walker. There was no one to interrupt them and no risk of accidentally crossing into Darkside. With everything riding on their success at the Hall of Records, there was also no way to tell if this was the first moment they could touch each other without holding back—or if it was the last.

The transporter lurched into motion, clacking rhythmically as it moved across Darkside, and Keira launched herself into Walker's waiting arms.

In the near darkness, their lips met with the tenderness and ferocity of a kiss that was unlike any other they'd shared. They weren't going to crash through into Darkside. They'd already fallen through that barrier. They'd already fallen in love. There was nothing left to keep them apart.

The unexpected scrape of Walker's teeth against her bottom lip was like a match against tinder—it set Keira on fire so fast that her legs buckled.

Walker caught her without breaking their kiss. Gently, he lowered both of them to the floor between the seats. The floor was hard and the space not quite big enough for the two of them, but Keira barely noticed. She just wrapped herself more tightly around Walker, sliding her palms across his skin and gasping when he slipped his own hand beneath her shirt. His fingers traced the shape of her ribs and Keira arched into his touch.

He lifted his mouth from hers, pulling back to look at her. She could barely see his eyes in the darkness.

"Do you remember back in the hotel? When I promised to make up for all that lost time, once it was safe?" Walker asked softly.

"I remember," she whispered.

Walker's fingertips swept across her waist. Every inch of her that wasn't being touched ached to be next.

He propped himself up, his body hovering over hers, the same way he had that morning in the hotel. Keira's breath went ragged.

"Good," he whispered. "Because I love you. And I intend to take back every single minute that I didn't get to touch you"—his lips grazed her neck—"starting now."

The rest of the trip was a blur of warm skin and soft mouths and whispered promises. When the clacking of the transporter stopped suddenly, Keira sat up so fast that she nearly cracked Walker's nose.

"Are we here?" she asked, struggling to pull her slowly disintegrating clothes back into place. Her shirt was tattered, and the fabric at the shoulders was so thin it was nearly transparent.

Walker ducked into what remained of his shirt, and Keira stared regretfully at his clothed chest.

"Probably," he said.

No sooner were the words out of his mouth than the door flew open. Keira had to close her eyes against the Darkside light that flooded the compartment. The intensity of its strange glow hurt her eyes.

"The Hall of Records," the guard said simply.

Keira saw the listing Hall, surrounded by the ring of gnarled trees. Shimmering on the other side of it was her own neighborhood, quiet beneath the night sky.

The night sky—they'd been gone almost a whole day?

Keira stumbled out onto the unsteady ground. It was like

having sea legs on land. At first, Keira thought it was from being in the transporter, or from too many emotions being stuffed into one day. She took a few tentative steps and saw Walker waver next to her, trying to catch his balance.

It wasn't them. It was Darkside itself. It had been so destabilized by all the crossings that she could barely stand. In her own world, she could see her house, not very far from where they stood, but still completely unreachable.

The guard next to her held out a blanket.

Not a blanket. A robe. There was one in his other hand too. Walker grabbed it and flung it around his shoulders, fastening it at his throat. It was just like the hooded robes she'd seen Smith and the other Darklings wear in the Hall of Records. It wasn't as bad as the leathery robes the guards wore, but she still recoiled from it.

"I'll wear my regular clothes, thanks," she said. "It's not that cold."

The guard huffed. "The Reformers insist."

"It's just a robe." Walker's voice was softer. "Underneath it, you'll still have your own clothes. You'll still be yourself. Also—this won't disintegrate over here. Which *I* think is a damn shame, but I'm guessing you don't want to end up naked in front of the guards and the Reformers and whoever else is around?"

She shook her head.

"Come on. I'll help you fasten it. Turn around."

Keira spun in a neat half circle, stopping as she faced the Hall of Records, which tilted like a sinking ship.

Walker draped the robe over her shoulders, and she was surprised to find that it was light and silky-soft against her skin.

"Oh!" she breathed. "It feels nice."

Walker brushed a kiss against the back of her neck as he hooked the clasp at her throat. His fingers lingered by her collarbones and she shivered all over again, though she wasn't in the least bit cold.

"You feel nice too. Come on. Let's go pay our debt," he whispered.

A sudden rush of nerves overwhelmed Keira. She managed a nod, and he put a reassuring hand on her shoulder in response. She could see the piano, right in front of the Hall of Records's entrance. It was a nicer one than she'd played for the Tribunal. The lacquer was still smooth and shiny. They must have brought it into Darkside very recently for it to be in such good condition.

Standing next to the piano was a single robed figure. "You may begin," he murmured. It was one of the Reformers. She'd recognize that voice anywhere.

No hello. No thank you. Just—you may begin.

Fine, then.

Keira slid onto the piano bench. She ran a set of scales to warm up, in spite of the wooden sound of the notes and the impatient shifting of the Reformer next to the piano. It was hard to relax—hard to focus—while she was being watched so intently. She could feel the stares of the guards, who were impossibly curious about what they were about to witness.

Walker settled himself behind her on the bench and tucked his chin over her shoulder. "Ignore them," he whispered. "Ignore all of them."

With Walker wrapped securely around her, Keira felt shielded from the prying gazes. Her fingers moved more fluidly against the keys and she could feel a new piece in her hands, begging to be played. It crowded out the other music she knew, pushing aside Beethoven and Bach and even Keira's own compositions.

"I think I should play something new," she whispered.

"I can't wait to hear it." His lips grazed her ear.

Without preamble, she launched into the music that filled her head. It was sharp-edged and staccato, full of the anxiety of being captured by the Reformers and the terror that they would never be let go. Though the song began with a jittery feel, it built with a steady rhythm, headed toward an explosive arpeggio. She leaned in hard to reach the last notes. As she stretched toward the top of the keyboard, she abandoned herself to that same soaring feeling she'd had when the Reformers had agreed to release them if she fixed the Hall. Walker's mouth found the hollow below her ear as his hand pressed against her thigh, steadying her on the bench.

The notes suddenly sounded the same against her ears as

they did in her head, and she knew what was coming next.

The snap that went through Darkside didn't rattle her. Keira kept playing, determined to reach the end of the piece. The final, aching crescendo slipped from her fingers and hung in the newly strengthened fabric of Darkside itself. Keira lifted her hands from the crumbling keys, but Walker wrapped his arms around her more tightly.

They both looked over at the Reformer who stood with his arms crossed and his head bowed.

It looked as if he were praying.

Eventually, he raised his head and looked from the piano to the front of the Hall and back.

Keira's heart was thumping so loudly that it was hard to hear him when he finally spoke.

From the voluminous folds of his own robe, the Reformer reached out a hand and ran his fingers through the air, as though testing the thickness of the space. "It will be strong enough for us to access the records again. It is acceptable."

Turning away from them, the Reformer called over the nearest guard.

"Disassemble the fence," he ordered. "The Sorters may be allowed back in. The Hall is safe."

Keira felt Walker slump behind her on the bench as the tension drained out of him. Still, her own spine refused to soften. They'd fulfilled the conditions of their release. The Reformer himself had said so, but he hadn't bothered to thank them.

Keira disliked being treated like a . . . well. Like an experiment.

A transport vehicle like the one that had carried Keira and Walker back to the Hall rumbled into view.

"You may go behind the building and cross from there." The Reformer turned to go.

Behind the building? That would put them in Jeremy's yard. It wasn't far from her house, but Keira could think of a lot of places she'd rather reappear in the human world. Before she could protest, the Reformer climbed into the belly of the transporter and he was gone.

Walker slid his hand beneath Keira's robe and hooked his finger into the belt loop of her jeans. The guards were busily taking down the fence, stacking the sections haphazardly against one of the lampposts.

"Let's get out of here," he said. "They don't need us. They don't *want* us. And that's exactly how I like things."

Keira looked at him. The smile on his face was infectious and she found herself smiling back. They had a future spread out in front of them now. It was more than she could have wished for a few hours ago, and she was happier than she could ever remember being.

Keira looked up at the blank facade of the Hall of Records. "I wish we could have crossed next to my house."

"I know. We'll be back there soon enough." Walker ruffled her hair.

They rounded the side of the building, coming to an open stretch where the guards had already finished removing the fence. It felt empty and quiet.

But Darkside still didn't feel like home. Keira glanced around, looking for the best place to slip between the two worlds. A cloaked figure stepped out from behind one of the pillars that supported the facade of the Hall.

Keira froze.

"Oh," Walker whispered.

The Darkling inched closer. Keira wondered what he wanted—if they should go ahead and cross, even though she wasn't sure if they were as far away from the Hall as the Reformers had said they should be. The thought was enough to nearly push her through the glassine membrane between the two worlds.

"Are you guys leaving?"

That voice. She recognized it, though she'd never heard it sound quite that sad before.

"Smith?" The question was out of her mouth before she could think to stop it.

"Yep. They let me keep my name, at least." He pushed back the hood of his cloak. His hair had been shorn off. Without it, the planes of his face looked older. Sharper. "So, is it over? Did they let you go?"

Walker took a step toward Smith. Keira could see misery in the set of his shoulders and guilt in the taut tendons in his neck.

"They said it was 'acceptable,' though I don't know what's acceptable about any of this. I can't believe they shaved your head." His voice was ragged. "Do they still have Aunt Holly?"

"No. They let her go as soon as I told them what I could do for them. As soon as I agreed to give up *everything* for them, basically." He stared at Walker, and a sound slipped through his lips. Keira couldn't quite tell if it was a laugh or a sob. "You should have heard how excited they were, when they realized that I could cross as many times as I wanted without any of the usual side effects."

"What do you have to do for them?"

"Whatever they want. They already took some of my blood for testing. And then they told me to go get your car and bring it back from the shore."

"You drove my car?" Walker looked shocked. "Where is it?"

"On Jonquil Drive." Smith waved vaguely. "What—did you think I was going to pull it around for you? I don't work for you, you know." Smith lowered his head, every plane and angle in his face turning hard and very, very sharp.

Walker shifted warily. "I know you don't. You work for the Reformers now."

"I know. And I know it's my fault. If I'd listened to you and Mom when you told me to stay hidden, maybe it would have gone differently. But I couldn't live like that—suffocated with all those limits and rules." He ran a hand over his raw-looking scalp. "'Course, I'm not sure I can live like this, either." His voice wavered.

Keira stepped toward Smith, her heart cracking in her chest. "I know. I know exactly what that's like."

He stared at her. "How would *you* understand what I'm feeling? You might have Darkling blood, but you're not one of us. You're not *stuck* here."

She ignored the anger that twisted his features. He was like a wounded animal, striking out to protect himself. "No, I'm not one of you. But everyone here has been hell-bent on dragging me out of the life I had planned—a life I was *really fucking excited about*, by the way—so that I could be punished for being an Experimental, something I never asked for to begin with." She jerked her head toward Walker. "He wanted me to run. To hide."

"I was just trying to keep your head attached to your shoulders!" Walker exclaimed. "I happen to think they look really nice together." His voice was heavy with hurt.

Keira ignored Walker, keeping her eyes trained on Smith. "His intentions were good." She thought about the innuendo in Walker's voice. "Maybe not entirely *honorable*, but still. Good. The thing was, I knew I couldn't live like that. Constantly looking behind me. Always making decisions based on what the Darklings were doing, instead of what I wanted. That's why we took the chance on Pike. I knew I couldn't get back the life I'd planned, but I couldn't live with running. So we did what we had to do. The same as you."

Smith's expression softened and he stared at Keira.

She pointed at the landscape around them. "This isn't what

I would have picked either." She stopped with her finger aimed at Walker. "But it's not all bad. You play the hand you're dealt. It's the only thing you can do, really."

Walker smiled the smallest bit at the card-playing reference. "I think everyone's plans have changed," he agreed.

Smith scrubbed at his face with his sleeve. "Speaking of changed plans, if you think the Reformers are going to let me keep seeing Susan, then you're an idiot. I tried to call her but I don't think I was making much sense."

"Susan—" The word leapt from Keira's lips.

The hurt in Smith's eyes lanced straight through her. "I know she wasn't serious about me—not at first. And yeah, mostly I asked her out to piss off Walker and to see what human girls were all about. But you know what? I really like her." He grimaced. "*Liked* her, I should say." The tears that had gathered in his eyes spilled down his cheeks.

Walker stepped forward, his hands out, as though he were offering something. "Smith, I'm sorry. I really am."

"Quit acting like it's your fault!" Smith roared. Instead of bouncing back to them, his voice sank into the outside walls of the Hall of Records, muffled by the stone. Smith crouched down, pulling his hood tight over his head. "Because it's not your fault," he whispered. "Please, leave me alone. I just need to be alone for a while."

In a split-second he was gone, crossing over into the human world.

"Wait!" Walker called, barreling through the barrier after him at a dead run.

Keira slid across after the two of them. It was easier than breathing.

She landed hard on the grass of the Reynoldses' yard, her threadbare clothes offering little protection against the twigs and stones that littered the lawn. Scrambling to her feet, she looked around for Smith and Walker. Smith was nowhere to be seen, but Walker lay against an overgrown lilac bush. He moaned.

Keira turned to go to Walker, but stopped when her gaze got as far as the back door.

Jeremy Reynolds appeared on the other side of the inset window, the light from the kitchen framing him.

Keira froze.

How much had he seen?

Chapter Fifty-Five

JEREMY SLOWLY OPENED THE door and stepped out onto the concrete patio. His feet were bare, and he had on a pair of slippery-looking basketball shorts, which did nothing to hide what he was thinking about.

"You're back," he said, padding over to her like a cat stalking a mouse. "I knew you would be. You felt it too, when we kissed? You like me. Admit it."

Her disgust crushed her relief. Jeremy obviously didn't care how she'd gotten into his yard. All that mattered to him was that she was *there*. He hadn't even noticed Walker, tucked beneath the lilac bush.

"After the rumors you spread? Why would you do that, anyway?" She crossed her arms.

Jeremy shrugged. "I was mad. I know, I know, I shouldn't have done it. But once we're together—*really* together—everyone will shut up about it. Things'll be normal. *Better* than normal." In the light from the door, she could see his pupils, dilated in the darkness and glittering with hope. "C'mere." He held out a hand.

"I don't want you like that, Jeremy. I'm sorry. I'm dating Walker," she said, edging toward the gate.

Walker, who was still lying in a ball under the lilac bush.

"If you don't *want* me," Jeremy insisted, closing the gap between them, "then why are you *here*?"

Frantic, Keira looked at Walker's motionless form and licked her lips.

"If it's Walker you're worried about, don't be. I'll take care of him," Jeremy said, watching her tongue trace her bottom lip. He reached out and caught her wrists.

Keira wrenched her arms against his grip, but he didn't let go.

"Get OFF ME!"

He bent his head, bringing his lips to her neck like he hadn't heard her. The body spray and deodorant smell of him filled her nose and she gagged on the idea of kissing him. She twisted away, lifting her foot to kick him in the groin, but she couldn't get a decent shot at the bulge in his pants. Instead, she kicked his knee as hard as she could. She felt the joint shift sideways beneath her heel and her stomach lurched.

Jeremy screamed and dropped her wrists. All at once, Keira was pulling backward against nothing. She landed hard in the grass with Jeremy looming over her like a storm cloud.

"What the FUCK?!" He raised his arm above his head, flattening his hand like he was going to slap her. Keira barely managed to throw an arm up to shield herself before she realized he hadn't swung.

Another hand was wrapped around Jeremy's wrist.

Walker's hand.

Jeremy yelped and whirled around, howling as Walker maintained his grip, twisting Jeremy's shoulder in its socket.

Walker looked down at him. "Touch her, *ever again*, and I will break you." He twisted harder and Keira could see the unnatural bulge of Jeremy's shoulder joint beneath his shirt.

"You can have her," Jeremy spat between his panting breaths. "She's nothing but a tease any—" His scream cut off his words before he could finish.

Walker let go of him and Jeremy dropped to the ground, moaning and cradling his shoulder.

Keira got unsteadily to her feet. Walker was by her side in an instant.

"Thanks," she said. "I don't love being the damsel in distress, but I wasn't exactly expecting that." Her voice cracked and failed. Keira shook her head.

"It was the least I could do, after disgracing myself by getting knocked out by a shrub."

"You can both go screw yourselves," Jeremy spat, staggering to his feet and lurching toward the house. The door slammed behind him.

Walker whistled. "He's a *shining* example for losers everywhere, isn't he?" Residual anger colored his words.

Keira laughed in spite of her trembling. "Should we look for Smith? Do you know where he might have gone?"

"I think the best thing to do is to let him cool off; get himself together. He needs that sometimes. When he's ready, he'll come back. Chasing him makes it worse. I suppose I should have thought of that before I went tearing off after him and landed in a bush."

"If you're sure . . ." Keira stared into the darkness. She hated to think of Smith out there, hurting and alone.

"Let's go find the car, okay?" Walker wrapped an arm around her and started for the gate. "Where do you want to go?"

She wanted to go home, but she was sitting smack in the middle of a spiderwebbed lie and she had to untangle the deception, first. "I'd better call Susan. I'm supposed to be at her house—maybe she'll let me wait there and I can have my mom come pick me up." Her voice hitched on the last word.

They walked down the sidewalk, heading toward Jonquil and Walker's car. It wasn't until they'd turned the corner and found the Mercedes waiting beneath the yellowed glow of the streetlamp that she trusted her voice enough to speak again.

"That sucked," she said.

"I'm really sorry about Jeremy," Walker said. "Not all guys are like that. Most guys aren't like that. In fact, most guys think guys like that deserve an ass-kicking."

"It's not just Jeremy," she said, climbing into the unlocked car. "And it's not just Smith. But that's all part of it—I mean, I don't want to sound ungrateful. I know I could be dead right now, but what I told your cousin, about not wanting to run from the Reformers because I didn't want to give up the life I had planned . . ." She looked over at Walker. "It was true. And everything's different now. I don't like different. I don't like *uncertain*."

The sad-edged gleam in Walker's eyes was a thousand years old, the look of someone who had seen too much and known too much and had a pretty good idea of what lay ahead. He reached over and cupped her face in his hand, his thumb gently tracing the hollow beneath her eye.

"I'm not going to pretend everything's going to go back to normal," he said. "But we're alive and we're together and your music—it's the center of everything, now. That's a start, right?"

Keira leaned into his palm. "It is. And I know things change—that life doesn't always go exactly the way you think it will. I just never guessed that it would be so . . ." She paused, searching for the right word.

"You didn't think it would be so complicated?" he guessed.

"Something like that," Keira admitted. Her new life—the

one that included Walker, Darkside, and even the Reformers—rose around her like a flood. She battled the sense that it was sweeping her away with it. She wasn't going to think about all the changes at once. She couldn't. It had to be one thing at a time. Apparently, the motto was going to stick. Maybe she should have it tattooed across her wrist. Of course, with the dark matter inside her swirling across her skin like an ever-changing tattoo, she might not need any earthly ink.

Suddenly it occurred to her that she hadn't seen a single dark mark on either her skin or Walker's the entire time they'd been Darkside—and she'd seen an awful lot of their skin there, recently.

She blinked away the sudden rush of heat that came with the thought. "Hey, how come the dark marks only show up on our skin when we're here?"

Walker blinked, surprised. "Oh. Yeah. They don't know, exactly. The scientists who worked with Dr. Sendson thought it was the dark matter trying to get back into Darkside. Kind of the same way that iron's drawn to a magnet. Once you're Darkside, though, it kind of settles down."

Keira chewed on her lower lip, thinking. "So, we'll always have the marks while we're on this side of the barrier? Like—like moving tattoos that no one else can see?"

Walker's mouth curved up into a smile. "Something like that. You'll get used to it. I promise."

Keira sighed. She had a feeling she was going to be hearing

that a lot in the days to come. There was going to be an awful lot for her to get used to; a lot of things to sort out.

Still. She had her music—that was the most important thing. It had always been the most important thing. And now she had Walker, too. As long as those two things were certain, then whatever else happened, she could deal with it.

"What I really want to do is go home, but I'd better call Susan first." She unplugged her phone from the car charger. The screen showed one full battery and thirteen missed calls from Susan. "Would you mind driving around for a minute?"

"Not in the least."

He started the car, steering them out of the streetlamp's halo and into the darkness.

Susan answered halfway through the second ring.

"Keira? Oh, my God. Are you all right? Where are you? Where have you been?" she demanded.

"I'm about five minutes from my house. I'm sorry I didn't call sooner. I got . . . really tied up." She tried to keep her voice light. "Are you okay? I feel bad about the way we left things the other day. Can I come over? Can we talk?"

"Actually," Susan said, stretching out the word until it was hair-thin. "I'm not home. I'm at your house."

Keira sat forward so quickly that her seat belt jerked tight against her chest. Walker looked over at her, his eyes wide with alarm. She shook her head at him.

"What are you doing there?" she choked out.

Walker pulled the car over to the side of the road.

"I came to see your parents. Well, your mom, at least. I'm sorry, Keira. I wasn't trying to betray you or anything, but I was worried. I tried and tried to call you, and you never answered, and I thought, you know, what if Walker'd had a wreck and you were lying in a ditch somewhere and no one knew where you were and—" She stopped abruptly. "I wasn't trying to get you in trouble. I just didn't know what else to do. Are you mad?"

Keira's temples throbbed with a headache. "No. I'm not. I mean, I wish I wasn't about to walk into the worst grounding of my life, but I understand. Are you still mad at *me*?"

Susan was quiet for a moment. It felt like an eternity. "No," she said finally. "I'm not. I'm confused, and I'm still worried, but I'm not mad. I realized that you wouldn't run off with just any guy. Walker must be important—*really* important—and if something or someone means that much to you, then we'll sort it out. But you can't run off like that again, okay? I was half out of my mind when I couldn't get ahold of you."

There was no way Keira could promise Susan that she wouldn't ever disappear again, but she couldn't handle lying right then. Instead, she dodged the question. "Hey, speaking of getting ahold of people, have you heard from Smith?"

"Not really. I sent him those texts and then he texted back and said he was dealing with a bunch of stuff back home and wouldn't be around for a while." Susan sounded disappointed but not heartbroken.

"Are you okay with that?" Keira asked.

"I dunno. We were having fun, but I'm not up for dealing with a bunch of drama, you know? Maybe it's for the best. Anyway. I probably need to go. I was getting ready to leave when you called. I'm sitting in my car outside your house, and your mom is watching me through the window, which is getting a little weird."

Keira closed her eyes. She was in so much trouble with her mom. This was going to be bad. This was going to be worse than bad—it was going to be another tiny apocalypse, another version of her life that was going to end. Only this time, it would be at her mother's hands.

"You might as well come home," Susan said. "I'll see you when you get here."

"I'm on my way," she said.

And then she hung up.

Walker ran his hands around the steering wheel. "Susan told your mom that you weren't staying with her, didn't she?"

Keira stared straight ahead, her arms crossed tight in front of her.

"Yep. She got worried. I want to be pissed, but instead I kind of love her for it, you know? Does that sound strange?"

Walker was silent for a moment as he navigated the three blocks back to her house. Finally, he sighed, pulling the car to a stop in front of her house. He turned to face her. "Things are always strange. That's the way life is."

Beneath the blanket of night, Keira could see every light in her house was on, and Susan's car was in the driveway.

"This is going to be awful," she said simply.

Walker laughed. "After everything else that's happened today? This is going to be no big deal. I'll go in with you," he offered.

"I don't think that's going to help. At all." Keira bit her lip. How was she going to explain her tattered clothes?

"I guess not. We could still take off—get out of Sherwin. Have our own Great American Road Trip." It sounded like a joke, but his voice was tentative. Hesitant.

Keira couldn't stop her smile. This time, Walker didn't have all the answers either.

She took a long breath and leaned her head against the window, staring up at the stars twinkling against the indigo sky.

"It sounds a lot nicer than finding out what's going on in there," she said, waving toward her house. "But it wouldn't be right." She looked at Walker. "I just have to go in. You're right—it can't be any worse than what I've already faced today."

"I really can be right there with you," Walker offered again. "Your mother's wrath doesn't scare me."

Keira shook her head. "Thanks, but I think this is one I need to do on my own." She smiled at him. "If you'd go with me as far as the door, though, I wouldn't complain."

They got out of the car, and fell into step next to each other, the concrete squares of the sidewalk slipping past all too quickly

496   *Christine Johnson*

beneath their feet. At the shadowy end of Keira's driveway, she turned to face him.

Before she could say anything, his mouth was on hers, his arms tight around her waist. It was like kissing lightning. Her skin tingled with it, her heart flailing to find its rhythm amid the electricity. She felt the Darkside wind sweep over them as the kiss sent them across the barrier between the two worlds, and then the cold squeeze as Walker pulled them back to Sherwin again.

Keira pulled away reluctantly. "We really shouldn't do that," she said.

"Not often," he agreed. "But not never, either."

"I love you," she said.

Walker laughed. "I love you too. You don't have to sound quite so sad about it, though."

"My mother's going to try to ground me for life."

Walker leaned in, wrapping his arms around her.

"Doesn't matter," he whispered. "Whatever happens, I'll be waiting for you. I'll wait for you here or I'll wait for you in Darkside. Wherever you end up, I'll be there."

"Waiting," she said.

"That's the idea, yes," he teased.

In the window, over his shoulder, she could see the open top of her piano. It looked like it was waving. Like it was welcoming her home.

Maybe facing the music wouldn't be entirely bad, after all.

AUTHOR'S NOTE

ONE OF MY GREAT regrets in life is that I never took a physics course. I didn't care about calculating the velocity of a falling apple. *Bo-RING*. What I failed to realize was how much there was to learn beyond introductory physics. I didn't understand that, *right now*, physicists are searching for ghostly particles and calculating just how the universe will end.

Dark matter isn't something I made up for the purpose of writing *The Gathering Dark*. It's way cooler than that.

Basically, we know there must be more "stuff" in the universe for it to work the way it does, but we don't know exactly what—or where—that stuff is. Physicists call this dark matter. We know some force beyond the ones we understand must be driving the universe's expansion. Scientists call that dark energy. We can't see dark matter or dark energy—not the way we usually see things, at least. We can't touch them. We just know they must be out there. Somewhere. Somehow.

Both quantum physics and astrophysics are racing to figure out dark matter and dark energy because without understanding them we don't really understand the universe. We don't really understand *anything*.

If you want to know more about this research, you should

read *Einstein's Telescope: The Hunt for Dark Matter and Dark Energy in the Universe* by Evalyn Gates and *The 4 Percent Universe: Dark Matter, Dark Energy, and the Race to Discover the Rest of Reality* by Richard Panek.

And you should take physics classes, because beyond Newton and falling apples lie ideas that are wilder and more amazing than most of the novels on my shelves.

The most fascinating problems have yet to be solved. The coolest imaginable questions are still out there, waiting to be answered. I encourage you to be the one who answers them. There is as much room for dreamers and poets in science as there is in the arts. There is room for *you*.

ACKNOWLEDGMENTS

There are so many people to thank for this book. There always are, but this time even more than ususal. Of course, first and foremost, this book wouldn't be in your hands without the belief and support (not to mention the genius ideas) of my editor, Annette Pollert. Behind Annette stands the entire crew at Simon Pulse, which is unrivaled. I'm so grateful to be part of their team.

Caryn Wiseman, my agent, has as always worked tirelessly on my behalf. Without her I'd be wandering the streets somewhere with a half-finished manuscript clutched in my hand. I can't thank her enough for being in my corner.

The Gathering Dark has been through many drafts and, as you might have noticed, it's a long book. These two things make it necessary to thank the other writers who helped me with even more gusto than usual. My writing family—Lisa Amowitz, Heidi Ayarbe, Pippa Bayliss, Linda Budzinski, Dhonielle Clayton, Trish Eklund, Lindsey Eland, Cathy Giordano, Cyndy Henzel, and Kate Milford—have read drafts, held my hand, Skyped, called, laughed, cried . . . you name it. I love you ladies!

Saundra Mitchell not only read (and shredded) multiple

drafts of this book, she put up with infinite texts, phone calls, e-mails, random-showings-up-at-her-house . . . well, you get the idea. I'm lucky to count such an amazing friend among my authors, and such an amazing author among my friends.

Sonia Gensler and Kay Cassidy also gave me invaluable feedback on drafts. I owe them cupcakes. Lots and lots of cupcakes . . .

Musical suggestions and corrections came from Theodore Harvey and my husband, Erik. Thanks for pointing me toward the right pieces and filling in the theory gaps, guys!

The thing about *The Gathering Dark* is that it's science fiction. *Science* fiction. As in, I couldn't just make up whatever the heck I felt like and call it good. To that end, I need to thank the scientists who helped me. Any mistakes in this book are the result of my stubbornness or error. These guys did their best to steer me straight. Dr. Jerry Curran and Dr. Steve Spicklemeier pointed me toward research materials without looking at me like I was in over my head, which I appreciate.

Without Dr. Matthew Muterspaugh, though, this book would be a wreck. Not only did he point me to source materials, he also answered a blue ton of questions, read drafts, offered explanations, and even suggested solutions when I'd fiction-ed myself right into a physics box. Thank you, thank you, thank you!

I'm also grateful to Eileen Abbott, for her generosity to the local United Methodist Preschool. And without Ashlee Miller, my children would have run wild while I wrote this novel. My mom and dad also provided as much love and support as a girl could ask for—without them, I'd be lost.

And of course, last but never least, my husband, Erik. Thank you for putting up with my odd obsessions and all the physics books. And for not laughing when you catch me staring off into space, making things up. But mostly thanks for loving me. I love you, too, you know.